Jesters' Dance

A novel by

R. Bruce Walker

TELEMACHUS
PRESS

This is a work of fiction. While, as in all fiction, the literary perceptions and insights are based on experience, all names, characters, places, and incidents are either products of the author's imagination or are used fictitiously. No reference to any real person or product is intended or should be inferred.

Jesters' Dance

Cover designed by Telemachus Press, LLC

Cover art
    Copyright © Fotosearch #010741AT Creatas

Edited by R. Bruce Walker

Published by Telemachus Press, LLC
visit our website http://www.telemachuspress.com

ISBN 978-1-935670-80-3 (eBook)
ISBN 978-1-935670-81-0 (paperback)

Version 2011.06.28

Printed in the United States of America
10 9 8 7 6 5 4 3 2 1

For Lynne, always.

"Jesters do oft prove prophets."

William Shakespeare
King Lear, V iii

Jesters' Dance

Before

The door closed and the girl was gone. Almost as quickly as she had appeared she was nearly forgotten and Allan Corbett was alone again in his luxurious hotel suite. He sprawled on the bed exhausted from the sex and the ridiculously early call that had required him on set at five that morning. Waiting for his quickened pulse to steady, the weary businessman now realized just how tired he was and how desperately he wished he could ignore the wake up call that would rouse him again in a few short hours. Already he was regretting how hard he had gone after the rare single malt that they were pouring so generously in the director's room prior to dinner. Then there had been the wine. The second bottle of Petrus that he'd insisted on ordering for the table was now just a bad decision and a credit card receipt that would have to be buried deep in his expense report. Then he remembered, achingly, he'd also scribbled down a two hundred-dollar tip for the same ridiculously overpriced bottle of Bordeaux. Having drank himself sober; his head throbbed from the ill-considered mix of whisky and wine.

Lying motionless, a wave of guilt washed over him, the shame of his infidelity lapping at an already burdened conscience. The warm towel that the obliging young woman had dabbed deliciously about his loins suddenly began to feel cold and damp. He tried to raise himself, but couldn't summon the strength. Instead, he reached for the soggy cloth and tossed it in the general direction of the bathroom. Rolling onto a stiff left shoulder, he silently cursed the girl for not turning off the light that pierced the room through a crack in the partially open door. The harsh brightness from the fixture above the sink cut through the gloom and shone directly into his smarting eyes. He would definitely have to get up now.

Confronted with this prospect, Corbett scanned the night table for his cigarettes. Yet even in his foggy stupor he realized he couldn't light up in the plush non-smoking suite that he had insisted must be booked for him. He also knew he wouldn't dress and descend to the lobby bar where he calculated they might still be pouring last call. Even though it was nearly one, there was too much chance that he would run into someone from the agency and he definitely couldn't bear that now. His craving unsatisfied, he propped himself up on his elbows. Could he pry open a window? Maybe later, he decided, his fatigue hanging on him like a weight.

She hadn't been the one he'd asked for, not the pretty young thing with the flame red hair who had been doing make-up since they'd moved into the sound stage. But the girl who'd shown up had been sweet enough and seemed to understand that it was selfish sex that he was after. He wondered what inducement they had offered her to sleep with him. Another couple of weeks work? Maybe some kind of promotion in the silly pyramid that always seemed to be the way that commercial production companies were organized? He decided to waste no further thought on the matter and reached for the remote control. Releasing the mute button on the late night talk show that had been playing in the background while the girl had climbed on top of him, the sound blared and he knew he'd missed a punch line as the camera panned the smiling faces of the studio audience. Now he stared at the popular host seated at his desk, quietly hopeful that the final guest for the evening might be some attractive young actress appearing to pitch her latest movie. With any luck, she would fold and unfold her bare legs on the compromising couch that was reserved for the show's visitors and coo him gently to sleep.

Again he shifted uncomfortably. Dropping back onto the plump down pillows he stared into the sculpted plaster ceiling of the hotel room. He definitely lived better on the road than he did at home. The luxuriously appointed room on the Gold Floor was handsomely furnished in the timeless Victorian style that seemed to be favored among the better hotel chains these days. Lying still, with his ears wrapped in the ocean sounds of the pillow, he tried to count his pounding heartbeats. It still drummed quickly and he knew it would be a while before sleep would come. He was even out of shape for sex. He hated himself briefly, but got over this, too, with a blink of his stinging eyes.

After another few moments, Corbett turned over again, this time trying to ease a discomfort that was announcing itself from deep within his bowels. He knew he'd put on at least five pounds over the course of this production. A look down, beyond the graying hairs of his chest to his soft belly, confirmed this. Resting on his side atop the rumpled bed covers, his wandering eye took in the valance of heavy curtains that had been drawn tight by the night maid. His glassy stare followed their thick pleats to the floor. Then he traced the intricate pattern of the Esfahan carpet to the pillars of his king-sized bed and the shadowy darkness beneath. He adored the subtle jasmine scent of the freshly laundered linens and the crisp feel of the six hundred count Egyptian cotton sheets that were turned down for him each evening. He was lucky if his wife, Helen, changed the bedding once a month at home. He was glad he'd called her before going out to dinner. He'd call her again in the morning, when his head cleared, he decided.

She definitely had that edge in her voice when he informed her that he was likely to be another day late getting home. Ever since he'd been moved into the role of Senior Advertising Manager with the Pharmaceuticals Division of Carlton & Paxton, he had been spending too much time on the road. His wife was always quick to remind him of this. Fortunately, she had absolutely no idea how unimportant his actual presence was to the filming of this commercial other than what he'd told her. If she'd known, she would have resented him even more. Screw her, Corbett reflected, allowing himself a moment of self-pity. She would just have to be content with the thousands of points he'd earn with this extended trip and the cheap vacation that it would yield later on.

Unfortunately for Allan Corbett, himself, he knew exactly how little the process relied on him at this stage in the game. Sure he was *The Client* and the guy who ultimately approved the finished product. But as far as sitting through the making of this particular television ad, it was little more than babysitting really. Certainly it was something that could have been easily accomplished by any of the junior members of his marketing communications team. Yet, as he always did, he'd betrayed them early on and left them all back at the office. You always had to be there in case something happened he would frequently coach the young product managers. You'd certainly want to be on the set if someone's hair were to catch fire, for example, he would lecture his underlings. This was, of course, an allusion to the ill-fated production many years before when a legendary pop performer's head actually did erupt in flames. Corbett liked to imply that he had been in the studio on that dreadful day and heard a few of the high-pitched screams. But, of course, he hadn't.

In actual practice, Corbett's younger charges rarely got close to a location shoot or a film set. Instead, their boss hoarded these opportunities selfishly. He did this in order to escape the seemingly inexhaustible rounds of meetings and discussions that were required to satisfy his stable of internal clients in marketing and product development and the constant reporting that his senior manager's role now required of him. The good news was that his colleagues back at the office knew even less about commercial production than his wife.

Yet the more shoots he attended, the more Corbett enjoyed the feeling of being part of the work of people much more talented than he was. He relished the chance to mingle in the outwardly glamorous world of making the little movies that his friends and neighbors saw on TV and knew that he was somehow responsible for. Occasionally, his job actually did let him rub elbows with genuine celebrities. But usually these people were performers whose careers were on the wane who were forced to shill products to underwrite their extravagant lifestyles. Mostly he just liked being out of the office and, but for checking in every now and then, largely unreachable. On set, as he had eventually trained everyone on his team back home, it was strictly phones off.

But now there was just a single shooting day left and things were definitely starting to wind down. Though there was still a half dozen tough setups to be accomplished over the next twenty-four hours, everyone who had seen the rushes agreed that there were some absolutely fabulous images— likely enough to make a great spot even if they didn't roll another frame. But all day there had been an unusual number of interruptions for cell chimes and other distractions as the various members of the crew scrambled to arrange their next gigs. Even Stan, the director, had excused himself early from the lunch table that afternoon and it became apparent that he, too, was juggling pre-production for his next job during the breaks. Corbett understood this necessity, but he disliked it nonetheless. It made the entire process seem even more whorish and put on. It also meant that his little getaway would soon be over and, at least until post-production began, he'd be stuck in his office for a solid week or two.

It was in this moment that he remembered the ugly budget reconciliation meeting he was certain would be necessary before the unit disassembled. He cozied another cool pillow around his boiling brain and pinched his eyes shut. He had heard enough of the urgently whispered conversations and seen enough of the frowns to know that the agency was playing hardball. They always did. He knew that Rick, the producer from Lowenstein Holiday, was putting the screws to Best Shot to hold the overages down. But he could also see that Sheila, the no-nonsense line manager from the production house, wasn't giving much ground either. Sooner or later, before things wrapped, he was certain that he was going to get drawn into another tense discussion about money and who was going cover the hundred and fifty thousand dollar problem that Corbett figured the delays had cost them. He would let both sides twist a while longer before he revealed that he still had some fat left in his budget.

After three years in the senior manager's job, he had been around enough shoots to know that the production company's profit on the job had gone down the toilet on the third day, when the weather had socked in. The storm had cost them an afternoon and the following day's location work and there was very little contingency—especially since the weather insurance premium had been waived to save money. It never rains in southern California. On that day Allan Corbett had made his only meaningful contribution to this particular project. Indeed, with a tempest swirling outside, he had been the most listened to voice in the Winnebago. After his intervention, the brooding director and his pretentious Limey cinematographer had been forced to back off from their previously intractable positions for the first time since pre-production as the people in charge of the dollars and cents took over. This was when Corbett truly had shone. Or at least, in his mind, when he had certainly justified his presence on set.

Before then, Allan Corbett had been just another hungry mouth at the craft services table. Ever since signing off on the production estimate and delivering the check that gave the film company their upfront money, he was just someone to be fed ahead of the crew and for whom a standing order for Gerolsteiner sparkling water and sugar powdered Krispy Kremes had to be filled each morning. This had been done even though a PA had to drive into town before dawn each day to fulfill the request. In truth, he hadn't touched a donut since the fourth day and, even though the sweet confections were piling up in the back of the snack girl's van, nobody had dared to countermand the order. Instead, while idling away the interminable fiddling and fussing of filming, Corbett had rediscovered his childhood affection for chocolate Raisinettes and had been regularly emptying the bowl between smokes. A few handfuls of candy were the least they could do for the million bucks he was dropping on this production he rationalized. And, of course, the girl.

Yet with the shoot nearly complete, his hard won influence was clearly on the wane. This was disappointing, as he really had enjoyed things much more after his deft display of budget savvy had caused him to be taken more seriously. Since then, as long as he sat quietly and generally let the director have his way, he was quite a popular fellow on set. Most of the crew had become appropriately deferential and they even spelled his name right on the call sheet afterwards—with two Ts. The legendary director, Stanley Bormann, now fed him inclusive winks and seemed to willingly invite him into technical discussions, even though it was clear that Corbett didn't have a clue what they were talking about. Once inside the studio, the crafty old commercial filmmaker had regularly been enlisting his support in overruling the objections of the agency's creative team. The director had even mentioned a few details about the feature film he had in development, implying that someone with Corbett's obvious financial acumen might be looking to make a smart investment. Corbett had swelled with the flattery even if, in reality, he knew that it was all just so much smoke up his ass. It was such a circus.

Indeed, Allan Corbett was constantly amused by the pathetic self-seriousness with which these marauding bands of misfits seemed to take the formalities of production. It was as if these inconsequential thirty-second movies that they cranked out were somehow on par with *Gone With The Wind*. Worse still, this pitiable parade of caricatures and stereotypes had absolutely no idea that they were such clichés of themselves. The frustrated impresario-cum-director, the pensive producer and the overbearing assistant director were always present. So too was the mediocre *talent* with which they were forced to work—models whose acting and expressive range were so limited you wouldn't dare roll more than eighty or ninety frames in a take. It was pure comedy.

He also enjoyed watching the seething tension between those in charge of the purse strings and the shiftless tradesmen and teamsters that were inevitably dispatched by the union hall. This crew was all IATSE. Other times it could be worse. Regardless of the qualifications of the crew, it seemed to be a rule on set that the heavier the lifting required, the smaller the guys who would be assigned to it. The brawny truckers and seasoned gaffers and grips just leaned on the sides of their panel vans smoking and letting the younger men with less seniority do all the work. Yet despite always managing to decide on the most difficult way to accomplish even the simplest tasks, this ragged press gang had somehow managed to get the shots. For all of its dysfunction, the scenes and images they had captured were about as beautiful as any that found their way to the big screen. It was a bloody miracle.

That was the situation in which they now found themselves. Eight days into a planned five-day shoot, everyone was buzzing about how good the rushes looked. Even Darden Jennings, the Account Manager from the agency who had flown in two nights before to put his seal of approval on the production and kiss Corbett's ass, had already begged off from the final day of shooting. "It's clear that we've got everything under control here," the self-important prig had announced before turning around and taking a late flight back to Chicago. The consensus among the cadre of account representatives from Lowenstein Holiday that had somehow piled onto the docket was that this was indeed the case. It might even snare them an award or two, one of them had quite prematurely predicted. But that had not stopped Corbett from noticing the way the creative team had shaken their heads when Jennings had applied an inclusive pronoun to their efforts. They clearly hated his guts. Lately, he had been feeling the same way himself.

As this production wore on, Corbett had decided that he liked the creative guys far more than his handlers. The young copywriter and art director were at least deadly earnest and paid careful attention to every detail of what was happening in front of the lens—even if they did seem intent on alienating him with their swift dismissal of his contributions. And Toby Meyer wasn't that bad either. The acting CD was an old pro who never really pushed anyone too hard. The longer he was in the role, the more Corbett had come to understand that their insecurity was in direct proportion to their dispensability. They were fragile geniuses and exceptional talents whose abilities the agency's management always trumpeted when things were going well on the business. But just as swiftly they became worthless chattel to be swept aside if there was even the slightest whiff of trouble with the relationship.

The result of this was a palpable tension between the creative people and the suits. Recently, Corbett too, had come to understand that the ones that wore the tailored flannel were, indeed, far more dangerous. While a mistrust of his counterparts from Lowenstein Holiday had been percolating ever since he'd taken the over the lead client role for the Pharma Division, lately his rented friends at the agency had become a regular source of problems. Though Corbett loved the flattering attentions of the pretty young Account Executives with their thigh high skirts and perfect manicures, the Senior Advertising Manager from Carlton & Paxton had eventually figured out that he paid handsomely for their interest. Every bat of the eye or five-minute phone call seemed to add up to an hour against the retainer. So, too, did being taken out for lunch. Their every breath on his company's business was billed out at a blended rate of two and a quarter an hour, plus out-of-pockets, of course.

It was this stuff that was creating real issues for Corbett these days. It was bad enough that Ira Lowenstein was constantly schmoozing above his head, but when Internal Audit started sending back invoices flagged with question marks, he could no longer afford to look the other way. A message he'd picked up late yesterday advised him that Accounts Payable had already requested a meeting immediately upon his return to discuss certain irregularities in last month's billing package. Then there would be this production mess to untangle. Apparently, the agency would receive its due soon enough.

Finally, in the late quiet of the sleeping hotel, Corbett's bleary eyes came to rest on the fat white package that had been waiting with the business floor's cloying concierge.

He'd look at it later, Corbett had vowed to himself before he cracked the mini-bar and poured a double Dewar's ahead of stepping into the shower. Procrastinating further, he had ignored it again in favor of a chase through the channels and a quick nap before going down to Borman's room for more drinks ahead of dinner.

Unfortunately, now it was after midnight and the necessary reckoning with the package's contents couldn't be avoided much longer. He knew what was inside. His assistant Tiffany had called to let him know that it had come down from the senior managers' meeting two days earlier and had couriered it to him overnight. Now it stood against the lamp on the scrolled mahogany desk across the room from the bed, the big purple and orange block letters on the envelope blaring an urgent request for his undivided attention.

But not tonight, he decided willfully. The Endrophat briefing that had been stalled in Research & Development for the past three months would just have to wait until morning. He clicked the remote control and the picture on the flat screen pinched to black. Then he leaned across himself and turned off the small reading lamp beside the bed. Screw the bathroom light -- and the damned agency, too. At this precise moment, at the loneliest hour of the night in an overstayed hotel suite, he decided he would put the most important project of his entire career under review. He'd teach them all a lesson they wouldn't soon forget, he resolved, suddenly furious. He would throw the whole bloody assignment up for grabs and give it an impossibly tight fuse. With a groan and a final restless thrash, he rolled to the side of the bed furthest away from the annoying sliver of light and angrily tried to summon sleep.

Day 1

The registered letter that arrived first thing Tuesday morning from Carlton & Paxton went off like a bomb. Addressed to the agency's president, Ira Lowenstein, it swiftly by-passed normal mailroom channels and was on the desk of his assistant by ten o'clock. Moments later, Account Services Director Chase Hannigan and the day-to-day manager on the C&P business, Darden Jennings, had been summoned to the top executive's office. Now they were perched nervously in the straight-backed chairs opposite his desk paying careful attention to Ira Lowenstein's every word.

Creative Director Steve Holiday slumped on the couch annoyed at the interruption caused by this unscheduled meeting. His hair was still damp from the shower. He'd spilled from a cab barely twenty minutes before following an all night edit session and he was already hopelessly behind schedule. Sinkingly, as the purpose of this hastily called meeting unfolded, he realized his day was already lost. He hated it when Ira flew off the handle like this. But based on the contents of the letter he'd scanned just moments earlier, he knew that his jammed-full day planner, including the rehearsal for the LDI Technologies presentation, would have to wait. Best to sit quietly, at least for now, and let the first of the storm clouds pass.

"How the hell did this happen?" the raging agency head now demanded. "You told me the shoot had gone well and that little pain in the ass Corbett had been well taken care of."

"I don't know," Jennings mumbled to the floor. " When I flew out a week ago Wednesday, they were practically wrapped. He seemed happy enough then. The rushes looked fabulous." The embarrassed account manager barely had the courage to look up. When he finally did, he stared past the angry creases of Ira Lowenstein's brow toward the vibrant-colored acrylic that blazed across the agency president's wall. It was an original Niemanen and it had been used in one of the agency's most famous campaigns. Next to it was an impressive gallery of Clios and Gold Pencils that the celebrated Chicago advertising agency had harvested over the past two decades. " He even fucked the make up girl," Jennings proffered with a hint of a smirk.

"He what?" Now the agency president had up a real head of steam. "He did the make up girl? And you let it happen?" Two weeks after the fact, under the probing scorn of the agency founder, what had been the joke of the set was now obviously a glaring error in judgment. Especially since the young woman they'd sent him was actually a professional escort. But no one was laughing now. "Is there anything else I should know before I call over?"

Chase Hannigan and the embarrassed Account Manager exchanged worried glances. Finally, it was Hannigan who cleared his throat and spoke.

"We sent back a bunch of his credit card receipts last month. About three grand worth. Based on the dates and stuff, he's expensing things that are way out of bounds."

"So you sent them back?"

"Accounting made us."

"But you called him first, right?"

Both men tried their best to duck the searing look that accompanied the inquiry. They had actually enjoyed flipping this little turd back into their client's lap. Ever since Allan Corbett had been promoted to the senior manager's role, he had been getting increasingly sloppy with the quiet little arrangement he had worked out with the agency to bury some of his expenses in their project dockets.

"Well, no … I … I mean we didn't actually speak," Hannigan finally admitted. "Darden came to me and explained and I just thought we needed to send a shot across his bow. We'd have helped him out if he'd called us back."

"Jesus H. Christ," the exasperated senior executive now exhaled. "What about the creative? Is he at least happy with the new spot?" As he said this, he turned his attention from the fidgeting men across his desk to the Creative Director who was still sprawled on the sleek Italian grouping that Ira used for receiving clients.

Steve Holiday knew that it was now his turn to speak up. He and Ira had been together forever and he was certain that his partner was counting on him to deliver some good news. Unfortunately, he had little to offer. He tried to gather himself up from the deep sling of the sofa, but his back still ached from the fourteen hours he'd spent in post-production the night before. "I think so," he said doubtfully, as he attempted to extract himself from the cushions. "At least that's what Toby said."

Now as he finally managed to right himself, he added a disparaging impression of his own. "Personally, I think it's a piece of shit. It's nothing like what we sold through." Holiday now realized that he was being drawn into this mess because he had let his Associate CD Toby Meyer, take the shoot.

"Toby said that Corbett and that old hack he insisted

direct it got together and changed the ending. It doesn't work … and the casting is awful, too." As he said this he knew he would have to choose his next words a little more carefully. He could tell his longtime partner was getting more agitated. Ira was such a micro-manager that he expected Holiday to cover every project in the shop the same way he did—even though they were now an agency that billed over four hundred million and staged fifty or sixty productions a year. In a split second, if he wasn't careful, this could end up being entirely his fault.

There was a time when the two men whose names were on the agency's door could never have dreamed they would be able to pick and choose from among the big money commercial shoots they would bother to attend. Now Holiday was regretting that he'd let the Account guys opposite talk him into skipping this one. But after a week of whining they'd eventually convinced him that the job couldn't bear his travel expenses—let alone his billable time. Holiday charged out at three seventy-five an hour. They were totally comfortable with Toby, they had said. But now that the job had blown up, the pair of weasels was doing their damnedest to somehow make this hang on him.

"I'll tell you what I do know." As he spoke, the rangy Creative Director rose to his full height and stretched. Dressed in jeans and a well-worn pair of Tony Lema's he stood nearly six and a half feet tall. He was a handsome man in a ragged, too quickly put together kind of way. His lean jaw wore the stubble of a beard he hadn't decided he was growing. He had been this way since Clare had gone. "I sat in on the music session and Corbett was so pleased he was practically filling his pants. So I don't know exactly what happened between this week and last." Holiday walked to the window and looked over the precipice to the busy street nearly forty floors below.

"He screened the rough cut at his management meeting,"

Jennings volunteered sheepishly. "He wouldn't let any of us attend."

At this comment both senior partners from the agency shook their heads. Ira Lowenstein took off the headset he wore when returning calls and threw it on his desk in disgust.

"You know better than to let that kinda shit happen," he cursed. But he was past angry and was growing impatient to get on with the unpleasant task of speaking to Allan Corbett himself. He needed to hear from the horse's mouth why they had been put on notice.

It was a hard and fast rule at Lowenstein Holiday that you could never trust what cowardly clients like Corbett would say if things didn't go well when a new spot was screened. Apparently that's what had just happened. Because advertising was something that every CEO and his wife and kids were experts at, there would inevitably be some stupid suggestions and expensive changes requested when they previewed a spot that was still in development. Some of the toughest challenges in Steve Holiday's career had come from trying to manage the expectations of a senior executive who thought he knew better than the professionals how to make a TV commercial.

"He was acting weird before the meeting. Almost like he had something going on even before they started ripping apart the spot," Hannigan now revealed.

Lowenstein looked over his bi-focals with brief interest, but then he realized Hannigan was just speculating. "What's the number?"

"Are you sure you don't want me to talk to him first?" the Head of Account Services asked in vain. He hated it when Ira insisted on inserting himself. "He's at extension 2245," he finally conceded. As Ira punched in the numbers and waited for the line to connect, the other three men had a brief moment to talk.

"Does the letter actually say review?" Steve Holiday inquired. He was a brilliant creative manager, but he had long since quit trying to figure out the subtle client politics that the account guys obsessed about so much. The other men seemed impatient at his naïve question and Ira made a face. Only the most junior of them felt compelled to fill in the blanks.

"It says they're looking at options for the Endrophat launch … that's that diet pill thing they've been working on— very secret. Its finally ready to go. They're calling it a special project, but it may as well be a full blown review," eye-rolled Darden Jennings. "We've heard that they were talking about putting nearly a hundred and fifty million into it over the next three years. If they let someone else in, we may as well kiss the entire business goodbye."

The condescension in his tone caused the Creative Director to bristle. Holiday could never understand where the account guys got their nerve. Just a minute before, the ample shortcomings of Hannigan and Jennings had been laid quite bare. Yet now they were desperately trying to reassert their control. Before he could take a swipe in return, Ira urged them toward the speakerphone that was wired to his desk and gestured them to remain silent.

"Allan? Allan … it's Ira Lowenstein. Yeah, I just got your letter. What's going on?"

As was his habit, Ira Lowenstein had chosen to meet the crisis head on. He despised this weakness in the rest of his team. Even though he paid these guys hundreds of thousands of dollars a year and equipped them with business cards with lofty sounding titles, they could wring their hands for days before confronting an uncomfortable situation like the one that had been taking shape on this key agency account. He, on the other hand, would have none of it. He'd never been willing to let a client of lesser standing dish him any bullshit. The charade of a review that Allan Corbett was organizing most definitely fell into this category. Better to get everything out on the table if they were going to have any chance to pull off a save. Besides, if the call didn't go well, he had already made up his mind to go well above Corbett's head. They had been on the C&P business long enough that he had relationships up and down the organization chart. Upon hearing Corbett's tone, he began searching his mental Rolodex.

Spence Playfair, the Senior Vice President in charge of new business development at Boom, immediately intercepted the package that arrived from Carlton & Paxton. Ever since he'd heard rumor of a potential review by the big pharmaceutical company he'd had his nose to the wind. Last week a phantom call confirming the agency's mailing address had caught his notice. Since then he had been making regular stops by the bustling reception area where couriered packages arrived in a steady stream all day long.

Until today, these trips had yielded little other than a glimpse or two at the fantastically leggy receptionist he was plotting to bed—that and an armload of gimmicky mailings sent by aspiring interns looking for work. But something about the timing of the mysterious call had twigged his sensitive antennae. A subsequent audit of the phone log had managed to get him even more excited.

Now he had the much-anticipated letter in hand and was eager to devour its contents ahead of everyone else. In an hour or so, after he'd had time to manufacture a new mailing label that would be addressed to him personally, he would burst excitedly into Avery Booth's corner office with news of this unprecedented opportunity. A foot in the door with a company like Carlton & Paxton could be worth a fortune. Playfair would also casually make sure that the doctored envelope in which the review invitation arrived remained on the President's desk afterwards, so there could be no doubt as to whom was responsible for this remarkable stroke of good fortune. Playfair was a master of the game.

However, before he could execute this little ruse, the pink-shirted new business impresario first had to negotiate a return to his office. His space was one of the few in the converted warehouse that defied scrutiny by possessing both walls and a door. Unfortunately, to get to it, he would have to wade into the hectic scrum of the busy little warren. It was rare, in the open concept offices of Boom, to travel more than a dozen steps without being buttonholed by someone desperate for the answer to a pressing question on the status of a project. Or, more often, for someone to try and conscript the support of the man who had a direct line to the ear of the President. For this reason Spence Playfair always tried to spend as much time on the phone or out of the office as possible. Stepping lightly across the gleaming plank floors, he stole his way through the labyrinth of cubicles and general morning buzz. It was now after ten and enough caffeine had been poured into the agency that it was waking to the chores of the day.

Playfair was not a particularly handsome man, but an over attention to accessories did cause him to shine brighter than most. Being of average height and quite ordinary build, he was slightly over-coiffed in the way of middle-aged men who have been successful in sales. Today, the starched white cuffs of his monogrammed dress shirt were fastened with gaudy gold cuff links cast in the shape of a pair of Hampshire hogs. One of them caught a ray of sunshine leaking in through the loft's soaring windows and a single white dot danced playfully across the ceiling as he scurried along. To anyone watching closely, Spencer Worthington Playfair moved with the furtive manners of a thief. And indeed, he most certainly was one. The enviably infamous rainmaker at Chicago's hottest agency had pilfered nearly two hundred million dollars worth of business from Boom's competitors over the last few years. Now, with the purloined Carlton & Paxton letter in his possession, his secretive demeanor was even more apparent.

"Spence … hey Spence?" a voice now called out conspiratorially from the direction of the space that belonged to Boom's Creative Director. Playfair paused before returning to the opening of the glass partitioned wall from which the sound had emanated. " Can you do a quick meeting at one? Avery got a peek at the Sloane Rent-A-Car creative and I need you to help me out. He's going to fuck it all up."

The voice belonged to Zig Cartwright and his cockney accent added an especially evil import to this typically profane remark. Playfair glanced at his watch and tried to let his body language say 'no'. While Cartwright seemed to take notice of this impatience, he pressed on with his request nonetheless.

"I really need you there mate," he beseeched.

Playfair hated this assumed allegiance on Cartwright's part. He knew it was as phony as his own outwardly respectful regard for the difficult man opposite. He appeared to think about it for a moment longer and then made a calculated gambit of his own.

"I'll tell you what, Zig. I think we're gonna be getting together sooner and Sloane won't have anything to do with it." As he said this, he held his arm up and waved the white linen envelope playfully above his head. Then he gave the Creative Director a teasing wink. "Something tells me Avery's gonna have his mind on other things very shortly."

The sinister looking man opposite now studied the new business development officer more closely. "What's up?" he whispered conspiratorially.

Why did they always presume to the same dark uniform, Playfair mused? The young Creative Director wore a funereal black suit over top of a t-shirt that blazed with the scarlet flag of the former Soviet Union. He kept his hair long, his beard ragged, and of course, there was the requisite diamond stud sparkling irritatingly from a single pierced ear.

"Let's just say you'll want to make the meeting," Playfair taunted, knowing that he had already reeled in the cagey but infinitely less sophisticated man.

"Anything you can tell me?" Cartwright now asked, eager to be included in the secret.

"Just that it's huge," the man opposite half-whispered. "Huge!" He repeated this while spreading his arms wide like a gull. With a flapping gesture he turned on his heel and danced away in the direction of his own office stranding Cartwright with a puzzled tilt to his head and precious little satisfaction gleaned.

Indeed, a short while later, as Playfair poured over the letter from Carlton & Paxton for a third time, he could barely contain his excitement. Despite the ambiguity of the short missive, the opportunity seemed quite real. It clearly could be the kind of breakthrough that came along once in a career. The chance to pry loose one of the world's largest pharmaceutical accounts would immediately lift Boom out of the ranks of advertising curiosity shops that it currently occupied and into the mainstream in a way that no one would have dared to imagine just a few short years before. Sitting perfectly still, with the letter flat on his desktop, Playfair reached down and wiped his damp palms on the back of his pant legs. Then he slowly and deliberately reread the sparse details on the page in front of him one more time hoping to divine any more clues that might still lay hidden within.

≈

The simple fact was that the Boom to which Spence Playfair presently belonged bore very little resemblance to the unkempt creative boutique it had been when he had arrived almost four years ago to the day. In those early months the rubber-streaked floors of the renovated warehouse had been painted with the markings of a regulation-sized basketball court and shabby secondhand desks and tables had been scattered carelessly around this shrine to the Creative Department's beloved Bulls. For more hours of the day than could be reasonably excused, the bearded bohemians that crafted the agency's creative work would pound the planks of their makeshift arena and toss ill-considered three pointers at a pair of hoops that hung from the loft's sandblasted brick walls. Other times, with little regard for the work to be done, they would line up to shoot meaningless free throws while eagerly concocting game situations as if they were the prep school varsity. All of this nonsense was condoned in the name of staying loose. But loose for what, the new business development candidate had wondered aloud?

That was Playfair's first take when, as part of the interview process, he had been invited to review the upstart agency's lackluster TV reel and a portfolio of even more dubious print. Sure, there were some gems here and there. But mostly there was just an appalling lack of strategic focus. He had offered this frank assessment during his very first visit. It was a dangerously candid observation coming from someone who didn't pretend to be *a creative*. But much to the surprise of everyone else on the senior management team, the agency's founder, Avery Booth, had agreed with him and Playfair had been invited to join the firm.

In the months following the hiring of the opinionated executive there was a bloodbath. Armed with the quiet endorsement of the President, Playfair had identified allies of the status quo and had them rounded up and executed. It began with the public humiliation of one of the firm's founding partners, the popular Creative Director Kurt Manning, and ended on a black Friday during which two thirds of his most loyal followers were fired. On that dark day the names of these unfortunate employees were announced over the office intercom as they were systematically invited into the boardroom and dismissed. Though he would deny his complicity, no one doubted that Playfair was the driving force behind the coup. The man with the Midas touch was intent on turning Boom into a money machine and, apparently, would stop at nothing to achieve it.

During this period the fired red bricks and exposed beams of the calculatedly chique office space had echoed with frequent shouting matches and the clash of strong personalities. Though the lazy imposters masquerading as writers and art directors didn't surrender their playground without landing a few blows, in truth, they never really stood a chance. The remainder of the purge was conducted with a viciousness that resembled the liberation of the Lowlands. Eventually a phalanx of workstations began to advance steadily across the basketball court and, before long, the only thing that passed through the dangling mesh of the hoops above were crumpled balls of discarded roughs and rejected concepts. With his army shattered and any authority thoroughly undermined, Manning capitulated and fled the agency he had helped to start. After, while touring prospective clients through the premises, Playfair would apologize for the stale gymnasium smell that lingered in the air and mock out loud the last remnants of the fading culture.

His victory complete, Playfair then turned to remaking the company in his own image. In the re-born agency *fame* would be the new bottom-line. But it would not be the kind that most agencies promised their clients. Instead, Boom would selfishly define itself by its own notoriety. At Playfair's urging the company adopted a *treat them like shit and they'll love you* approach to servicing their customers. In no time at all, this perverse strategy paid off handsomely, as client after needy client lined up for the chance to be treated badly by the reenergized enterprise.

In the second year of Playfair's contract, a New York hot shot was hired to head up the retooled creative group. Zig Cartwright brought with him the culture of perpetual loathing that now inhabited Boom. Deliver prize-winning stuff and you will be generously rewarded, fail and you will be shot, he had declared upon his arrival. Fear proved to be a magnificent motivator. Soon the hardwood floors of the trendy Wicker Park offices were again stained with unrelenting carnage. Indeed, the name Boom was just about the only thing that survived this tumultuous time.

With each new success the agency enjoyed it became an ever more dangerous jungle. Fearful young creatives and account executives that lacked the guile or stomach for the demonic politics that the ruthlessly ambitious Cartwright cultivated were preyed upon without mercy. So, too, were those with a conscience or brains enough to question the underlying immorality of the place.

In spite of this, or perhaps because of it, Boom became a magnet for the kind of selfish creative talent that was attracted to an agency where only the outcomes mattered. Manufacturing the kind of off-the-wall, outrageous work that earned advertising trophies the world over, in three short years the company had come from nowhere to earn a place on Advertising Age's 'Ten To Watch' list. That was what had probably caught Allan Corbett's attention. Unlike his naive colleagues at Carlton & Paxton, Corbett was aware that creative boutiques like these could not only propel the careers of their own stars forward, but also their clients as well. However, what even he had no concept of, was the price at which this fame was achieved.

The deconstructionists at Boom had long since shed themselves of the over-layered hierarchies that were the way the big Chicago shops and the multi-nationals were organized. Instead, they had replaced it with a more tribal culture that defined itself by constant chaos and the angry edge of anarchy. Zig Cartwright was Ché Guevara in his belief that revolution must be constant and that nothing was to be spared in order to achieve great work. In this peculiar arena, charisma counted and those who were most cool were kings. Everything that was accomplished by the agency was achieved with callous calculation.

The new client services group embraced this ethos with nearly the same zeal as their creative counterparts and expressed it in their severely stylish wardrobes and nearly psychic awareness of the hottest new restaurants and night-clubs. Ambitious ladder-climbers would regularly audit the reports of the hip young trend spotters that the agency employed to infiltrate the urban subculture in search of new campaign ideas. From this reliable intelligence, the suits iden-tified the latest Thai and Moroccan dining spots and other places that were sure to be a hit with their clients. Being in touch in this way allowed the energetic but generally vacuous bag carriers to pretend that they, too, were a vital part of the creative process.

By contrast, the actual creatives preferred much more nuanced demonstrations of style. In their tribe, ridiculously fashionable eyewear and bold statement t-shirts were the cho-sen vehicles by which to communicate hipness and impart the illusion of intellectual depth. Sports nostalgia was always a popular choice in this regard. So too were retro-Escher graph-ics or other signposts of the Sixties. The more inscrutable or singularly iconic the shirt and the message, the greater the stature accorded the wearer. It even helped with the presentation of new ideas and concepts—the group often more attuned and envious of a particularly well-chosen piece of cotton than to the actual work itself.

Even the media group had managed to manufacture a calculatedly inward-looking rotisserie baseball pool that was the envy of other, less imaginative, buyers and planners throughout the city. Only the accounting area of the self-indulgent enterprise managed a blandness that made them entirely interchangeable with their counterparts at other agencies around town.

Spence Playfair's vision for the new Boom was based on the idea that it was time to rethink the bloated agency business and to re-merchandise their angry little enterprise as its future. He sold a big bang theory of marketing reinvention that revitalized the meaning of the agency's name and had done the same for its profits. It was a brilliant branding and self-promotion strategy. Aided by the deployment of a well-considered PR campaign, the company had been successful in positioning itself outside of the agency mainstream as a forward-looking, results-at-any-price alternative to traditional advertising agencies.

And at least it had remained that way for a time. Initially, the creative work of the revitalized agency was outstanding. It was as fresh and edgy as the young titans who now commanded it. The advertising that the shop produced reflected the radical genius of writers, artists and designers who studiously patrolled the fringes of society and popularized the behaviors of its most peripheral participants. They discovered the X-Games when they still belonged to the nihilistic kids who pioneered death-cheating stunts with their street boards and BMX bicycles. Boom used their images to sell energy drinks. They probed the darkest sites of the Internet to detect the language and media habits of its subcultures and sold their findings to clients as the harbingers of the next wave of consumer behavior. Irreverence was prized. Profound cynicism ruled.

Yet in shaking the foundations of the industry for which they espoused contempt, Boom had perhaps, of late, become almost too successful. The head of a famed West Coast advertising agency had once wondered out loud, *'How big can we get before we get bad?'* to remind himself that his agency should never grow so large that its product lost touch with the consumers it served. Boom was on the threshold of becoming about as big and bad as an agency could get. They dominated agency award shows with work that was both irrelevantly brilliant and shocking in its self-manufactured truth. With the guidance of Spence Playfair and Zig Cartwright, Boom had captured the very essence of soullessness and spat it back at an unsuspecting public in an angry full frontal assault. Its fame-at-any-cost mantra produced a kind of cultural screed that drew shameless attention to itself and forced clients into eating their own words about the importance of generating awareness.

Lane McCarthy undid the hook that held her finely tailored skirt tight against her hips and eased the zipper off a few inches before collapsing onto the sofa. With a tired sigh, she hoisted her laptop bag onto the couch beside her, searched out her phone and scanned its contents from habit. There were a handful of messages, but none that couldn't wait until morning. A single lamp and the glow of an adjacent tower were all that illuminated her darkened apartment. A couple of miles out, through the Palladian windows of her luxurious condominium and well beyond the jagged breakwater that shielded the beach below, the lights of an outbound freighter glittered and blinked in the coldest hours of the ink dark night. With one last weary groan she managed to heel off her Prada pumps and lifted her swollen feet onto the coffee table where she tried to wiggle her aching toes awake.

On one hand, she was glad she'd had her driver stop by the office so she could pick up her mail. Burrowing into her briefcase, she retrieved the bulging bundle and began shuffling through it listlessly. On the other hand, she was exhausted from the quick back and forth to New York and now wished, vaguely, that she'd stayed overnight for the Board dinner. She could easily have shuttled back in the morning and still beaten everyone into the agency. Yet after the relentless mauling she'd endured all day, she knew she couldn't have stood another minute in the company of her new colleagues, let alone the three or four hours that such dinner affairs inevitably consumed.

That was the way it had been for nearly a year now, ever since the company had been taken over by Interworld. Urgent trips to New York or to the agency's original head office in Stuttgart for desperate meetings called by the CFO were how she was forced to spend her time. It was a far cry from the days when McCarthy & McCauley had been a fierce independent that had scoffed as the multi-nationals gobbled up the other great brands of American advertising. Reiner Adolph, who now ran the place with the cruelty of his Nazi-sounding sur-name, had assured her that her company would be allowed to maintain its autonomy and that the holding company he captained would be virtually invisible after the merger. It had been anything but.

A global pull back in retail had put pressure on every dol-lar that M&M was earning and seldom a week went by when there wasn't a frantic call for revised projections—improved ones of course. Sometimes Lane wondered to herself if the over-leveraged enterprise would survive, especially given the intense pressures of the Street. Yet somehow the bloated behemoth that had gone on its expansion spree with public money still managed to lurch forward. Currently, it was the South American offices that were surprising everyone with unexpected numbers. Miguel Santore, in the Sao Paulo office, had been working magic with his big airline account and even the packaged goods side of their business was delivering decent revenue. It made the battered balance sheet of M&M Chicago that Lane had been forced to present look particularly dismal by comparison. It also gave the jackals in the executive session all the permission they needed to start circling hungrily. In the end, they'd even come up with a target number and a list of names.

Just two more years, she reminded herself with a weary sigh. That was the way the buyout was structured. Only twenty-three more months of indentured servitude and then she could walk away with all of the millions that had been promised. The first traunch of proceeds from the merger had bought her financial independence. At least that was what her accountant had said—even if it didn't feel much like it these days. The second installment had secured the property in Bimini that was, more and more frequently, the object of her idle thoughts. If she could just keep the company and its roster of clients intact for another couple of years, maybe even lock up another fat contract or two, she would retire as a very wealthy woman. Yet every time another directive arrived from Hitlerland imploring her to scrape a few more dollars toward the bottom line, the task seemed harder and her prospects for escape a little more remote.

She made an aching stretch with her arms wide apart and allowed herself a shuddering yawn. Gawd she felt tired ...

and bloated too. It was the damned lunches and dinners that did it. And, of course, the stress and travel too. She regretted the meal she had pushed in thoughtlessly on the plane and the chocolate dessert that she had indulged in without tasting. The weight hung on her uncomfortably. As well, her eyes smarted from the stew-thick airline coffee and the Sahara-dry climate of the First Class cabin. She reminded herself, wryly, that she had once found such business trips exciting and the entertaining of clients enjoyable. A long time ago, it had even seemed glamorous. Now she resented every request to travel and, even when she sat down to a dinner with clients present, she fussed obsessively over portion sizes, grilled waiters about ingredients and washed down her meal with the bitter bubbles of Perrier and lime instead of the fine wines that she ordered to the table for others. It hadn't always been that way.

During her rapid climb through the ranks of the agency business, Lane McCarthy had always been proud of her appearance. As a promising young account executive she had often suspected that it was her fresh good looks, trim figure and short skirts that had carried her forward, even when she knew she didn't have a clue. A bit of modeling in her early days didn't hurt either. Pandering suppliers would always fuss about her when she showed up to supervise photo shoots. "Are you the talent?" they would flatter. Or "Any chance I can book you for lingerie session?" they would tease. Indeed, more than once, she had been forced to stand in when the professional model that had been hired didn't quite measure up to the beautiful young woman who had sold through the concept. Still later, as a senior manager and even as an Account Director, she would frequently have to fend off advances from clients who seemed to assume that sleeping with her was part of their contract with the agency.

But now, as an accomplished executive just the other side of forty, Lane found herself forced to choose her business wardrobe a little more carefully. While the expensive tailoring she easily afforded gave her a little more breathing room, in the way of a woman who had always been the object of appreciative glances, lately she had found herself avoiding mirrors. On the plus side, there were fewer inappropriate invitations. Most clients' eyes now strayed to the tempting young AEs that she dragged along to meetings for this purpose. But it hurt nonetheless. With so much going for her, and despite all of her recent success, Lane McCarthy wasn't feeling anywhere near as good about herself as she deserved to. She knew what she had to do, but she lacked the resolve to move forward. Right now, all she felt was the weight of her fatigue and the dull throb of a headache that had been all day in the making.

Despite the angry clamor for improved results, by the conclusion of the endless rounds of meetings, Lane had managed to buy herself a little more time—even if it was just another quarter. Otherwise the cost cutting would start. And it wouldn't just be expenses, Adolph had threatened. It would have to be people, too. As she knew from her many years in the business, once rumors of downsizing got started, they were awfully hard to stop. It wouldn't be long before her best talent and then her top clients would be stampeding towards the door. She had lied straight out to the New Business Committee about her current prospect list. Unfortunately, by doing so, she would now have to make business development her primary focus for the next few months.

That's what drew her attention to the fine linen envelope with the Carlton & Paxton logo embossed on it and the address of the company's Oak Park offices printed neatly in the top left corner. When she first extracted it from the pile she had been expecting some sort of corporate announcement, or a routine polling of credentials that the big pharmaceutical company occasionally conducted in the marketplace, before awarding the work to Lowenstein Holiday. She hadn't even bothered to open it in her first pass at the stack. Yet suddenly, here she was with what appeared to be a legitimate review invitation in hand. She stared at the five short paragraphs and read them again, carefully. Yes, it was definitely a pitch request and, by the serious tone of the letter, it was almost certainly a big one. What a coup that would be, she let herself imagine. What an amazing bloody break she thought, while allowing herself a wistful smile.

All that was required was her signature on the standard confidentiality agreement that accompanied the letter authored by Mr. Allan B. Corbett and a detailed briefing package would be forwarded to her the very next day. Still, even with this most unexpected bit of good news, all that Lane could now manage was to pick herself up off the sofa and stagger towards her waiting bed—exhausted. She would make sense of this remarkable development with a few quick calls in the morning.

Day 2

This was the jackpot that Spence Playfair had smelled from the very start. It had gotten him out of bed at dawn and into the office by seven. Sitting in his office, the door tagged with a 'Do Not Disturb' sign cadged from The Ritz, he was busily writing out one of his famous lists of the tasks that would need to be accomplished between now and presentation day. It already covered three pages of the lengthy yellow legal pad he used when mapping out a complex pitch. As usual, each page was divided into a column that identified the item that was to be worked on, a separate tab for the deadline, and a final notation of who would be responsible. Looking at it now, he had unconsciously attached his initials to virtually all of the most important elements. He couldn't help but smile to himself. "Okay, so I'm not much for delegating," he chided himself quietly.

It was both a blessing and curse, but past experience was an inspired teacher. While most of his contemporaries could seldom smell an opportunity beyond what was immediately presented, Playfair had the nose of a truffle hog. He knew, instinctively, how one assignment had a way of leading to another and how three projects later you ended up with the whole account. It was no different in this case, indeed, even more so. What he immediately recognized, and everyone else seemed afraid to acknowledge, was that winning a piece of C&P business could easily open the floodgates to the kind of expansion that no one at Boom would have imagined just a few years earlier. It might even take them international. At the very least, such a victory could vault Playfair personally, to the kind of celebrity status that would earn him a top post with virtually any agency in the world.

It was this aspect of the pitch invitation that had his blood pumping as he worked away at his feverishly scribbled list. He had already decided that he'd put up with very little nonsense if anyone were foolish enough to get in his way. Chances like this only came along once or twice in a career. In this respect, his discussions with Avery Booth yesterday afternoon had gone exceedingly well. Noticing that the invitation to pitch had been personally addressed to his business development officer, the President had granted free reign on the project almost entirely to Playfair.

"Fit me into the loop whatever way you can," had been the top officer's only request. "Maybe I can do some bridging at the top," had been Avery's vague offer of help after assessing the mounding pile of briefing documents that had been couriered over from Carlton & Paxton following return of the confidentiality agreement. "Figure out a role for me off the start of the presentation. Time's going to be precious in there," he'd added sagely. The new business maven wasn't sure whether this was an act of trust or simply laziness. In either case, it wasn't the kind of mistake he would ever make if he found himself in a similar position.

While Playfair didn't dislike his boss, the more successful the agency became, the more resentful he found himself of the way Avery appeared to regard his contributions. Instead of acknowledging his linchpin status, his superior constantly subordinated both he and his team. For such a smart man,

Avery just didn't seem to get it. Though he never showed out-
ward disdain for the street savvy rainmaker whom he had
promoted and to whom he owed so much, the founder of
the company made no secret of his far greater affection for
the agency's creative people. He indulged them paternalisti-
cally, showering them with fawning delight whenever they
accomplished something of note, and regularly ignoring the
substantial contributions of Playfair's people. Lately, Playfair
had decided this was more than just a little annoying.

But in truth, it had always been an unholy marriage. The
reality was the two men couldn't have been more different
in the way they approached the business. Perhaps that was
why Avery Booth had been so marginally successful in managing the agency prior to his arrival, Playfair imagined. His
weak-kneed boss seemed unwilling or unable to make the
tough calls that were necessary to captain a ship as unruly
as an ad agency. He was bright but out of touch, the much
more calculating businessman determined. Writing down the
President's name on his pad, he circled it a half dozen times
and doodled out an oversized question mark. What would
he do about Avery? He would have to devote some careful
thought to this particular dilemma in the coming weeks.

If Playfair were more sensitive, or at least honest with
himself, he would have understood that what Avery Booth
did lend to the company was its largely undeserved air of
respectability. What he brought to the party was an almost
aristocratic manner that played well with a certain old school
type of client—the kind who still preferred a chummy, pick-
up-the-phone relationship with the head of the agency. His
private school education and clubby background allowed
him to move comfortably in society circles that Playfair barely
knew existed. And his cerebral style had always engendered
a grudging respect in the rough and tumble Chicago advertising scene. When invited to talk about the business, Avery

invariably spoke in grand and lofty tones about the importance of strategy and positioning. He believed in building
brands. He read the Harvard Business Review and regularly
cited case studies and leading edge research reports to provide complex rationalizations for the agency's off-the-wall
creative work. The only trouble was, these days his roguish
company was fast out growing his pedantic style.

Too often, lately, the President was becoming a nuisance.
Thoughtful to a fault, his untimely interventions were a hurdle
that many of his people now conspired to avoid. Frequently
advertising that was ready for final presentation or that had
already been sold through to clients would be hidden from
view, lest it be derailed by Avery's meddlesome interference.
Just last week he had ordered Zig Cartwright's team to withdraw a TV campaign that had already gone out for production
bidding. It was a shameful about face that had embarrassed
everyone on the project. But as long as Avery Booth owned
controlling interest, his word remained law. While Playfair
respected this prerogative, it was definitely going to try his
patience as things heated up on this critical pitch. He would
clearly have to invent a distraction.

With this in mind, Playfair picked up a page from the
fat personal portfolio on the Senior Advertising Manager,
Pharmaceuticals Division at C&P USA, that he already had
on file. This was Allan Corbett's formal title—the one that
appeared on his business cards. The business development
officer at Boom kept impeccable records on everyone of note
within the Chicago market, as well as a database on leading
figures everywhere in advertising and sales across the country. His files were a treasure trove of appointment notices,
industry articles and other personal tidbits that he'd accumu-
lated from his tireless networking and careful study of trade
journals over the years. The contents of this file were currently
sprawled across his desktop and he had pinned an oversized

photocopy of Allan Corbett's picture to the wall opposite. Now that he had an open invitation, he would arrange a lavish lunch to introduce himself to his new best friend.

It was the soft warble of the telephone that rescued Lane McCarthy from the anxious dream that had accompanied her fitful sleep. As the sound drew her from the shadow world of an exhausting night, her first impulse was to panic that she might have ignored the alarm that she typically set for five-thirty each morning. Then she remembered the note she had scribbled out during her hasty visit to the office the night before. She had requested a seven-thirty wake up call, just a check-in to be sure that she was up and on her way to the office. Her early arriving assistant had not failed her. She reached for the bedside receiver, fumbled it, and then mumbled a raspy, "Thanks, Bren."

It was the kind of request she could never have imagined herself making of someone who worked for her until she had taken over from Terry McCauley as the President and CEO of the firm that still bore both her name and his. But since that time, nearly a decade earlier, she had given the enterprise nearly all of her waking hours. Even after the merger with Interworld, when her former partner had drifted away from the day-to-day business of the agency, she did the work of both. To any of the clients who still cared, Terry was supposedly available for consultation, but in truth he had spent most of the last fourteen months abroad and out of touch. Though she was quietly pleased to have him out of the way as this left her able to function with near autonomy, lately Lane found herself somewhat resentful of the generous paycheck he still collected and the prime office space that was wasted for his occasional visits.

But that had been the difference between Terry McCauley and herself. While her business partner certainly wasn't lazy, he had made it clear early on that he had priorities in his life beyond work. He traveled, he painted and, even when they were at their busiest, he always seemed to find time to devote to his wife and family. By contrast, Lane had been entirely consumed by the lure of the business. She worked early and late, weekends and holidays, and rarely, if ever, managed to take a vacation. It had cost her a marriage, children, and spoiled every relationship she'd ever been in. "I'm not a bitch," she had once told an industry magazine that was profiling her following her nomination as Chicago's Advertising Executive of the Year, "I'm just busy." Following the merger, when she had every reason in the world to take a little more time for herself, she still gave far too much to the office.

"Lane?" Brenda's voice now chided from the receiver of the phone that was lost in the tumble of bed covers. "Laney?" it persisted quizzically. Brenda Martin was an assistant from the old school and served her boss with ferocious loyalty. She was the kind of helper who never thought twice about requests that blurred the line between secretary and servant. This closeness allowed her to assume a tone of increasing familiarity.

"It's okay. I'm awake," Lane McCarthy now spoke as she lifted herself from the shroud of boiling blankets and let her feet touch the icy cold floor of her marble tiled bedroom. "I need you to organize a meeting … everyone … at eleven. Clear my book, too." She knew that the request would throw the agency into chaos, but then an opportunity like the one she had spent all night churning in her mind was far too important. Instinctively, she already felt like she was late getting started.

"If you can, have Research pull everything they know about weight loss products. Order up some Media Watch and grab a couple of copies of the Enquirer, too. I'd like a dozen or so background packages ready for the meeting, " she commanded as she awakened more fully. "Go on the web and pull down everything you can about Carlton & Paxton, too," she added.

Thinking about the C&P prize had kept her mind whirring for hours into the night. Now she wished she could remember with clarity the thousand ideas that had come rushing to her in her dream sleep and she cursed herself that she hadn't remembered to write a single one of them down. Staggering groggily toward the bathroom, she stepped onto her scales out of habit and frowned when the digits of the LED display spelled out their disappointing conclusion. More awake, she likely would have smiled at the irony.

"Bren … would you also make sure to confirm my appointment with Tahur." Tahur Massad was her personal trainer. He had been dragging Lane through a demanding strength and conditioning program since the New Year. "Make sure you say I'm sorry for skipping last week." With this final request, she turned off the phone and reached for the golden knobs inside her cavernous shower stall.

When Steve Holiday put down the last page of the briefing document he was livid.

"How the hell are we ever gonna get this done?" He asked this question out loud and to no one in particular. He was certain that the rest of the group who had assembled for the hastily scheduled breakfast meeting was in a similar state of shock. The normally unflappable Creative Director had been doing a mental inventory of the projects in the shop that would have to be shuffled to make way for this suddenly critical presentation. He also knew that, as soon as this early morning session broke, he would have to pull together another meeting of his own Group Heads and figure out whom he could free up for the pitch. He already had a pretty good idea who he wanted on the project. But the trouble with trying to sequester your best people for this kind of shootout was that everyone else needed them, too. While he knew it was his prerogative to pull anyone he had to, he detested the unfairness of it all. And worse, the pressure it would place upon his two brightest stars.

"What about money? Did Ira tell anyone how much he was prepared to spend?" asked somebody from the back of the room. It was a very reasonable question. Everyone knew that the honorarium promised by Carlton & Paxton would cover only a fraction of the actual cost of the pitch.

"He said to do whatever it takes," came the nervous reply of Jack Blenheim, the new suit on the business. Holiday eyed him suspiciously, both men knowing that Ira would go ballistic if the hard costs went through the roof. "Within reason, of course," the account manager then hedged.

Still fuming over the incident with Corbett and the hooker, Ira had kicked Darden Jennings off the account. He planned to let him twist in shame for a couple of weeks, then he'd fire him altogether. But in truth, Ira was quietly hoping he could humiliate the foolish manager into resigning and save the company the cost of a settlement. It was the only way he felt he could get the attention of the rest of his sloppy account service team. While Chase Hannigan had initially tried to come to Jennings' defense, it had been a pitiful, self-serving attempt. The Head of Account Services was far too much of a coward to risk his own position by taking full responsibility himself. Ira had relayed all of this to Steve over dinner the previous evening. It would probably be the last decent meal the Creative Director would enjoy for a month. Even after dessert was finished, the two business partners had continued to disagree about the magnitude of the threat. Ira was convinced they were playing for the entire account— almost a third of the agency's billings. He'd half seriously even suggested blackmail. Steve, always more optimistic, had strenuously disagreed.

"I'm gonna go freelance on some of the other stuff," Holiday now announced. As he said this, the account managers in the room let out an audible moan. They knew that meant he would be farming out existing client work. This almost certainly led to screw ups and unforeseen cost overages. But they also knew it was the only way they stood a chance of mounting a credible defense of the account in such a short time. "I don't want to hear any bitching on this," Steve warned sternly. "If you've got any real issues you can see me separately, after."

He could also already hear Toby Meyer screaming bloody murder when he learned that he had been dropped from the C&P business. But he knew that his Associate CD was already expecting the worst since word had shot around the office that the million dollar spot he'd just finished had been shelved and the media money reallocated. Steve decided to load him up with the Ballard campaign, and two other projects that he was already late with, to keep his friend occupied. He knew Toby wasn't truly at fault for this debacle, but just the same, his longtime creative partner would have to take part of the fall. This was the worst part of the business.

"Are Evie and Pete loose?" He knew that it was pointless to even ask. His best writer and art director team of Evelyn Sanchez and Pete Zwicki were almost always full. "I want Evie on this. I know already it's gonna need a woman's voice. I'm also going to need Steve Thorpe and Randall as back ups." The other members of the pitch team that Ira had appointed nodded their agreement. Once Ira had finished working the phones yesterday and was certain there was nothing he could do to head off the review, the President had designated the team leaders for this critical project. The heads of media, production and interactive were all seated at the table. So were representatives of the account services and account planning groups. As was agreed, Holiday would report back to Ira at the end of the day with an action plan.

Not unexpectedly, word of the review had already hit the street. All of the usual rumors about what had caused it, which agencies were participating and who was the front-runner had already made the electronic version of Adweek. More of the gory details would be knit together in a lengthier article promised for the next issue. Steve had already kicked a reporter's call back to the PR group that was running interference for Ira this morning.

By his estimation, the best they could do now was damage control—hoping to keep the hounds at bay with the story that it was just a special project and that the entire account was not up for grabs. It never ceased to amaze him how quickly news of these things leaked. What was even more surprising was how swiftly it had happened in this particular case—especially given the sensitivity of the Endrophat project.

"I'm also going to need some serious input from Research, too." Holiday continued. "What do we know about weight loss and that kind of stuff? Do we still have anything left from that nutritional information campaign we pitched to Arby's?" The experienced CD was a dutiful recycler. He combed his brain for anything else they had done that might be relevant. "Why don't you have them pull that stuff we did for Revlon on body imaging, too," he instructed the eager-to-please young account planner Owen Steele.

"I'll need it before I brief Creative this afternoon. Are there any more questions?" he asked in summary. He didn't wait for anyone to reply and closed his notebook crisply to signal the end of the meeting. For the time being at least, everyone was still taking their cues from the Creative Director.

Avery Booth straightened his splendid silk tie and gave the shoulders of his handsome suit a quick brush before descending the stairs for breakfast. Though the clock in the grand foyer below had just chimed that it was half past the hour, he was in no hurry to get to the office this morning. He hadn't been for quite some time. Around ten would be fine. The drive would be far more pleasant once most of the rush hour traffic had dissipated and, based on their conversation the day before, Playfair seemed to have set everything in motion that he could until the first client meeting took place. Perhaps then Avery would roll up his sleeves and participate more actively. But there was little point in getting too excited just yet. There would be plenty of time for that in the weeks to come. Gathering up his Wall Street Journal from the demilune in the foyer where Muriel placed it each morning, he padded toward the breakfast room and the fresh brewed pot of coffee that would be waiting for him.

For what it was worth, Avery Booth had never been quite sure what to make of the restive little troubleshooter he had hired to shake up his struggling company, either. Despite repeated attempts at polishing away his rough edges, Spence Playfair just never seemed to be able to shake his salesman's roots. He was a born hustler who cared little for the culture of intellectual integrity that Booth had always tried to cultivate within the firm. Part of this was refreshing, but often it was also a cause of considerable strain between the two men.

Even with frequent coaching, Playfair had never been able to grasp the subtleties of style that Avery felt were the requisites of a professional ad man and definite musts for an officer of the company. He also seemed unable to appreciate the agency's quiet disdain for 'retail' as his agency peers sneeringly derided it. Left to his own devices, Playfair would gladly dedicate the agency's precious time to grinding out hurried little campaigns like sausages and thoughtlessly dissipating the company's precious creative resources. Yet his results in the new business arena continued to make him indispensable.

As they had anxiously awaited the arrival of the briefing packet that had been delivered at the close of business yesterday, the President of Boom had wondered out loud why the review project had originated as low in the ranks of C&P as it had. It just didn't make sense, he had ventured. But Playfair had disagreed. Even though Avery's instincts told him that such a monumental decision should have been initiated at the executive or board level and issued under the signature of the VP of Marketing, his new biz guy hadn't seemed at all bothered. Rumors of a 'miracle product' had been filtering into the business pages for the past few months and seldom a week didn't go by when some market analyst or another wasn't encouraging investors to expect a spike in C&P stock. The last thing Avery had expected was a change of advertising agencies on the eve of such an important launch. Especially one that had been initiated so far down the food chain.

But at Playfair's encouragement he had put these doubts aside and committed the entire resources of the agency to the challenge. As the senior team cooled their heels with a late afternoon scotch, he had been forced to confess that he had personally drilled a dry hole while quietly working on some senior C&P people that he'd met out at Medinah a few years back. Even though he owned the company, Avery Booth was still insecure enough to need you to understand that he was connected all over town. He'd also had to admit, somewhat disappointedly, that Allan Corbett was a name with which he was not familiar.

The briefing document that all three agencies received was standard Carlton & Paxton issue. Even though the cover letter explained that the company had decided to go immediately to a short list of potential vendors for this 'special project', a standard resume of each agency's credentials would still be required. So, too, would be their signatures on a binding intellectual property contract to be forwarded immediately to C&P's legal department. In addition, there were a thick bundle of attachments.

While reading the letter out loud to his Creative group a few hours later, Steve Holiday had paused on the word 'vendors'. He snorted derisively. Even after nearly three decades in the business he remained appalled at how cruel the process became once a formal review was announced. Years of trust and loyalty evaporated in few cold-blooded sentences on corporate letterhead. Holiday had dined in the homes of many of his clients and even vacationed with one or two. Over the years most of them appeared to value his friendship.

In fact, one time he calculated that he had spent more time with his clients from Carlton & Paxton than he had with his wife—a remarkable year during which they had executed three new product launches back to back and worked seven days a week for an entire quarter. He had barely noticed that Clare was not well. During this crazy period he had offered his counsel on everything from careers to anniversary gifts. And yet, now that the account was in play, apparently all of this was forgotten. "Its just business," one of Corbett's junior assistants had consoled without apology at a brief, awkward meeting on another project yesterday afternoon. Like hell it was, steamed the Creative Director.

What an asshole Corbett has become, Holiday thought to himself as the group waded deeper into the document. As they read, he couldn't help but remember all of the time that he had invested in the C&P advertising manager and the endless lessons he'd given his client about the production side of the business. Corbett had been a decent study—even if he didn't have a creative bone in his body. Many times over drinks the rising manager from Carlton & Paxton had practically blown him out of gratitude. He recalled the bouquets and champagne that had arrived the morning after they had claimed a Clio and two Gold Pencils for their famous work on PrestoBrite toothpaste. Distracted, Holiday realized he'd paused too long and that the team he'd assembled was already reading ahead. He stepped over to the nearby credenza and topped up his coffee mug, quietly letting them continue. When it was apparent that nearly everyone had finished, Holiday spoke again. "I think it's obvious they're looking for some spec creative. I don't think there's any way to avoid it."

Everybody knew it was coming, but still they despised seeing it in print. There were few things more pointless than speculative advertising produced in the vacuum of a new business pitch—especially for an incumbent agency that knew only too well the briefing procedure that normally would have been followed on a project of this magnitude. It was just a wank and a waste of everybody's time. Still, clients had been using variations of this strategy forever—forcing their potential agencies to give away literally thousands of hours of their precious time while armed with only a fraction of the information necessary to solve the problem at hand. It was like they were interviewing boy scouts. Trying to see who could make fire without paper or a match. The result was invariably work that didn't have the slightest chance of seeing the light of day. It was simply a way to torture the consultants, whose talents they envied, and to reassert their control.

"This is pure bullshit," a senior art director perched on a chair with two legs tilted in the air complained. "Not only is there not enough information here, the time line is absolutely ridiculous." As he said this, most in the room turned hopefully to Holiday somehow praying that their boss could intervene and make the idiotic schedule magically become more reasonable. The Creative Director had done the same himself when Ira shared the full contents of the briefing package that had arrived after his angry exchange with Allan Corbett.

"I'm afraid its already been decreed that we're gonna drop our drawers on this one," Holiday now added, trying to quell the dissent. He nearly choked on the words as he spoke them. "Ira says we're a hundred and ten percent committed, even with the $10,000 insult." He was referring to the pitiable stipend that would be paid for all of their work over the next month. The value of the time they'd invest in the frantic lead up to the showdown would easily be fifty times that amount—at every agency that had been invited to play.

Indeed, buried in the last paragraph of the request for proposals there was mention of a modest honorarium that would entitle the pharmaceutical giant to ownership of any and all ideas that came to light during the review process. Though left unsaid, it clearly implied that mock advertising would be an essential part of the evaluation process. It was the kind of demeaning proposition that most agencies hated, but had little choice other than to accept. Customarily, to land an account this size, you were expected to pull down your pants. This one was obviously no exception.

"I think it's also abundantly clear that they're going to be reluctant to give us anything we really need to do this right," Holiday continued. A senior copywriter near the front of the room shook his head and made a stroking motion at an invisible penis. "I expect all of you who have friends or contacts over there to dig for any intelligence you can pick up," Steve encouraged while ignoring the obscene gesture.

Another writer smirked his disapproval at the irony. Even when conducting a review on a project of such obvious importance, the client always seemed compelled to leave essential details out of the briefing. In this ridiculous cat and mouse chase, they would move the cheese at every opportunity. Thus sleuthing for missing information or drawing knowledge from other sources became a dress rehearsal for the dishonest relationship that the client and agency would eventually enjoy if they were successful in winning the business. It would be laughable, if it weren't so tragically true.

The information released around the new product, Endrophat, was just as circumspect. The name was a 'working one' the briefing document indicated. So too was its 'brand identity and positioning'. This was obviously code for internal disagreement. The naming of pharmaceutical products was notoriously onerous and fraught with the dangers of patent and copyright infringement. Over the years, each of the big drug companies had stockpiled literally thousands of names with their lawyers like warheads, in an attempt to deny them to their competitors.

Compounding the problem for the team from Lowenstein Holiday was the knowledge that most of their allies inside C&P were still mad at them for last year's corporate advertising campaign. Allan Corbett had gotten it into his head that they needed a unified brand umbrella that linked products in the Carlton & Paxton family together. Even though market research had confirmed that the 'When the chemistry is right' corporate campaign the agency had developed was testing off the charts, none of the business units wanted to pay for it. This was typical and Corbett had made himself particularly unpopular by shaving ten percent from every product manager's media budget to fund the TV buy. The line guys hated him for this. Every single one of them believed that his product was the one that drove the success of the rest of the organization and didn't have a dollar to spare. No doubt one of them would be assigned to the Endrophat launch and they would take this out on Lowenstein Holiday.

Beyond the pro forma section of the letter was a single short paragraph suggesting that Carlton & Paxton was 'seeking a partner' to assist in all phases of the introduction of a 'revolutionary new product' that would 'change forever the therapeutic treatment of chronic obesity in women.' In the section of the briefing form set aside for product description there was a glaring red stamp reading, 'CONFIDENTIAL'. Apparently all specific product information would be provided only upon receipt of a project specific non-disclosure agreement. The amazing science of Endrophat would be explained in a joint agency briefing at a mutually agreed date to be determined shortly, the letter further stated.

Among the other contents of the packet was a standard profile on the corporation and its products and a copy of its most recent Annual Report. Both were pieces that had been produced by a rival of Lowenstein Holiday. The Annual was a piece of the puzzle that Holiday had sat up with late last night. Despite Ira's regular urgings, he seldom wasted time on this kind of reading. But the fact that it was beautifully illustrated and printed on an expensive parchment stock had drawn him in. The bulky financial document presented a fascinating portrait of a remarkable pharmaceutical and personal health care products empire that spanned borders, cultures and global distribution channels.

In the parlance of the consumer products industry, C&P was a classic unibrand—one name that stood for quality and trust around the world that was represented by no less than fifty famous household labels. He had always known this, of course, but sometimes working on just the American advertising, the enormity and scope of his client's business was occasionally forgotten. Somewhere buried deep in the numbers there was a single line that indicated annual sales approached nearly fifty billion. By shear size alone, Carlton & Paxton was a nation unto itself.

But it was the last part of the letter that contained the real shocker. Agency presentations would be scheduled exactly twenty-eight days from receipt of this briefing, it had read. The participating agencies would make a single two-hour presentation, the order of which would be determined at Carlton & Paxton's discretion. As part of their submission, the three firms would be expected to develop yet another new product name that could be included with those the company would be supplying to the FDA for final approval; package design ideas, advertising concepts and a media plan for the national launch and rollout of the product over the next three years. All of this work was to be completed in less than a month—a project that normally would take as long as a year. An estimation of the fees to be charged for the execution of the work was also required.

"Are there any more questions?" Steve asked sarcastically. With the meeting breaking up, he searched the faces of his people. Several of them already looked tired. Yet somehow, in just a little more than four weeks, this very same space would be jammed with all of the finished comps and props for the presentation. In his mind's eye, he could see the dozens of mock magazine ad layouts lining the ledges that bordered the room. There was a pretty good chance they may even produce a spec TV commercial. It just depended on how far they wanted to go. Along with all of the advertising, there would also be a strategy deck and media plan the size of an encyclopedia—more thinking in one document than most of his clients could generate in a career. He hated the prospect of all of the work ahead, but at the same time he was feeling a familiar rush of adrenaline. Though he would say it to no one, this was the part of the business he loved the most. Holiday had always gotten off on working with a gun to his head—walking the tight rope between the unlikely and the improbable. They needed a miracle.

"If there's nothing else, lets wrap this thing. I'd like to look at some real preliminary stuff a couple of days after tomorrow's client briefing. I'll send Marsha around with a list of who's going to attend from Creative. For now, assume that all of you are going. We may want to make a show of strength," concluded Holiday.

Ending the second meeting of the day as he had the first, he closed his folio and rose from the table. Pushing his marker stained hand hard through his tousle of graying hair, he exhaled anxiously. Some would say he hyperventilated. Outside the door at least a dozen unfinished projects and deadlines waited, all desperate for the attention and answers only he could provide.

Day 3

I t had been Allan Corbett's idea to hold the agency briefing jointly. Normally, he would have conducted meetings with each of the candidate companies independently, but the aggressive timetable for the process that he had set in motion no longer allowed for it. Besides, it certainly would be interesting to get all of the players together in the same room, he imagined. It had a circus quality to it that would definitely put a scare into Lowenstein Holiday, and it would also send a strong signal to the other participants, that he was conducting this review on a level playing field.

And indeed, the proposed meeting format had immediately gotten the attention of Ira Lowenstein. So much so that they had engaged in their second extremely unpleasant conversation in as many days. After a perfunctory attempt to be cordial, the call from the agency president had ended in a rather heated argument during which several angry expletives were exchanged. Even the normally conciliatory Darden Jennings had been decidedly chilly when he called over to request the briefing document that Ira had neglected to ask for at the height of his rage.

Now the Carlton & Paxton ad manager was genuinely worried if anyone from L&H was actually going to show

up. It would be just like that arrogant son of a bitch to try
and embarrass him in this way, Corbett thought as he busied
himself with preparations for the meeting. The other suitors
had been quick to follow up with confirmation calls and lists
of the key personnel who would be attending, but not the
incumbent agency. The fellow from Boom had been particularly charming and had even offered an invitation to lunch.
But Ira Lowenstein had signed off with what were essentially
threats and a stern reminder that he still had many friends
inside Corbett's organization.

Indeed, within hours of hanging up the phone on
Wednesday, Corbett had fielded the first of a deluge of sympathy calls on behalf of the Agency. Over the ensuing forty-
eight hours, they had come from virtually every corner of the
company. Yet so far, no one above his Hay rank had told him
to stop and, though he'd not yet spoken to his boss, Andrew
Sullivan, the Vice President of Marketing, he felt he was on
pretty solid ground. In fact, Corbett was secretly betting that
several senior executives were quietly applauding his initiative. During C&P 101, all prospective managers were taught
that it could be invaluable to yank the chain of longstanding
suppliers. In the case of Lowenstein Holiday, Allan Corbett
was certain that no one before him had ever had the balls.

The location that he had chosen for this meeting was
deliberately different from the many meeting and breakout
rooms that littered the Oak Park R&D complex. Its theater-
style configuration seemed more suited to lectures than to
commerce. It was housed in the largest of the four pyrami-
dal glass and concrete buildings that surrounded the central courtyard of the suburban industrial campus. He had
intentionally scheduled the briefing away from the corporate
offices off the Mile to avoid the suspicion that such a curious meeting would no doubt generate. He also knew that it
would be important to take away Ira Lowenstein's home field

advantage. The agency president had a way of chatting his way around C&P's downtown offices whenever he came over for a meeting and Corbett couldn't afford for him to run into his old friends just now.

In truth, that likelihood was extremely small since Ira Lowenstein's visits had been less and less frequent over the past few years. While Carlton & Paxton still ranked as his company's largest client, with the success of his own firm, Ira's time always seemed to be stretched too thin. But with the stakes so high, Corbett imagined his nemesis would most certainly be out pressing the flesh on a desperate mission like this one, anxiously trying to revive old loyalties among those who might put a little pressure on Corbett to call off his game. As well, Corbett knew that the agency hated it when they had to cram into a taxi and brave the I-290 to actually get out and see where their clients' products were manufactured. This was part of the arrogance he had decided to punish them for. Yet so far, he hadn't spotted a cab arriving.

From the gray tinted windows of the meeting room he could see beyond the edges of the Carlton & Paxton grounds. Through the winter-bare branches, he could just make out the rooflines of the sprawling complex of the fast food giant who occupied the adjacent property. How ironic, he thought to himself. Here in the labs of the pharmaceutical giant where he was standing right now they had been working for years on a drug to manage the effects of over weight, while just a stone's throw away, there was a company who had made a global mission out of selling the very stuff that made people fat. He shook his head. Only in America, he marveled.

After a quick glance at his watch, he plugged in his company-issued laptop. Before stretching to pull down the projection screen, he removed the jacket of his smart navy suit and paused to admire the monogrammed cuffs of his crisp white shirt. He imagined that all of the people from the advertising companies would be dressed up for this occasion. At least the account service guys would be well polished. Not to be out-done, he had opted for a pair of patterned suspenders and a bold tie that had previously earned him several compli-ments, to make his own first impression. He even dabbed a bit of his wife's make up on the Rosaria that was becoming increasingly noticeable on the sides of his cheeks and nose. Ordinarily, he wouldn't have bothered with such primping, since the company had not long ago decided on a look that was extremely casual. Out here on the research campus, this had certainly been embraced. But today he was hoping to set the tone for the entire review process. It would be decidedly more formal. Besides, there was bound to be a few good look-ing young account executives present, and he was eager to appear his very handsome best.

The room smelled pleasantly of the fresh pot of coffee that had been ordered up from the commissary and that now stood steaming on its hot plate. A basket of pastries and muffins had also been ordered up along with a brimming fruit plate. He was, after all, a most congenial host. Corbett allowed himself a wry smile knowing that such pleasantries would be quickly forgotten as soon as the new agency was selected and it would be they who would have to worry about the catering. But today he would watch closely who helped themselves to the snacks. It had become something of a game. Ever since he had been assigned to the task force that would bring this project to market, he had been studying the eating habits of practically everyone who worked on it. Indeed, it was nearly impossible to sit through the product development discussions and listen to the results of the ongoing clinical testing, without being a little bit self conscious about one's own weight.

Dr. Harold Woodruff, the technical lead on the Endrophat project, would be joining them after Corbett had taken care of the housekeeping questions associated with the review process. Corbett quietly wished that he could take this part of the presentation himself, but the science was just too complicated. Instead, he would have to hope that Woody would manage to keep the explanations simple and the ball rolling. The veteran corporate scientist was English-trained and occasionally he used terms and turns of phrase that complicated things unnecessarily. In anticipation of this, Corbett had culled the project team's standard briefing presentation yesterday night and removed most of the truly proprietary information. He just hoped that Woodruff would not get too lost when he realized that several key slides were missing. Corbett really liked the leader of the R&D team, but he was just so hopelessly obtuse when it came to the way the world of marketing actually worked.

Ten minutes later the floor receptionist buzzed into the meeting room that representatives of the invited companies had arrived. A short while later, they were escorted into the theater by a member of the C&P security team. Each one wore a shiny visitor's tag with photo identification prominently displayed. On their heels, Harry Woodruff chased in late and began making introductions from the back of the queue. In doing so, he disrupted Allan Corbett's carefully arranged receiving line. The friendly scientist immediately recognized a few familiar faces from Lowenstein Holiday and pumped their hands enthusiastically. What an oaf, thought Corbett. Clearly he didn't understand the nature of the competition. But at least several of the clowns from his incumbent agency had deigned to attend. Everyone that mattered was here, along with a few unfamiliar faces and the notable exception of Ira Lowenstein. He averted his eyes when Steve Holiday strode into the room.

❧

"I want to begin by welcoming you all to Carlton & Paxton." Allan Corbett now spoke with appropriate formality. "And by expressing my delight that you have chosen to participate in the challenge of assisting us with the launch of one of the most important personal use pharmaceuticals in the history of our company." The room had been dimmed and the gentle whir of the PowerPoint projector filled the solemn silence that Corbett's serious posturing demanded. "You have been chosen because of your remarkable capabilities and your demonstrated commitment to creating truly wonderful, results-driven communications."

It was a gaudy introduction, but one that allowed the host to swell impressively in front of his audience of nearly thirty agency representatives who had assembled for the briefing. He certainly appeared to be in command of the situation. Even Steve Holiday, who had often regarded Allan Corbett to be little more than an ambitious imposter, swallowed his cynicism and noted the strong presence his client projected in front the large gathering. Mostly, over the years, he had only observed Corbett in his role as a furtive go-between, nervously brokering concerns and approvals on behalf of his internal client groups and the company's executive committee. Holiday wondered whether he should report this back to Ira who was still counting on Corbett to wilt from the pressure he'd steadily been applying.

"I sincerely believe that the successful agency will be integral to the entire launch process. We are seeking a solid partner with whom we can share the bright future of this truly remarkable product," Corbett continued echoing the invitation letter almost convincingly. It might have come off perfectly, except for an untimely cough from one of the copywriters with Steve Holiday's team and to whom Corbett immediately shot a look of angry rebuke.

From where he stood at the side of the room adjacent to his tightly knotted group, Spence Playfair was similarly impressed. The file he was building on Corbett had suggested he was a fairly talented backroom infighter, but it had said nothing about his commanding presence and outwardly charming demeanor. He allowed himself to imagine that he could become quite fond of this prospective client.

For her part, Lane McCarthy did what she did best at such meetings. She managed to arrive a few minutes late and in doing so created its grandest entrance. As she bid a friendly but disruptive farewell to the security guard who had personally escorted her to the meeting, she succeeded in turning every head in the room. The celebrated female executive had made tardiness her trademark and this occasion was no exception. Dressed in stunning spring Dior, her appearance offered nothing inappropriate except the scent of a truly exquisite perfume and a smile that dazzled from a dozen yards. Her charismatic glow pierced Corbett's heart like an arrow as she made what was by far the day's most enduring impression.

"To truly understand the significance of this scientific breakthrough one has to appreciate the magnitude of the obesity problem in America … and indeed, in much of the developed world. It has clearly achieved near epidemic proportions and its health consequences are without doubt every bit as deadly." Allan Corbett let this stark statement settle dramatically over his attentive audience.

"The underlying cause of most premature deaths in this country is no longer the myriad of carcinogens and cancers that plague our society, nor is it the carnage on our highways or our propensity to murder one another with handguns. The single largest cause of death is heart disease, and the number one reason is over weight. Let me repeat that. The number one cause of mortality in this nation is that we eat too much. We are dying because we're too fat."

As he made this declaration, he changed the accompanying slide to reveal a nostalgic illustration of a desperately obese family assembled Rockwell-style around a recently despoiled holiday table. Clad in sweat pants and straining t-shirts, their bellies bulged obscenely from the feast just consumed. A mom with two hams for arms proudly held forth a pair of fruit pies. The father appeared ready to give birth. The comical image allowed the group a small reprieve from the depressing tenor of the presentation. One or two people laughed. Some of the taut-tummied young women in the front row shifted in their seats with obvious disapproval.

"For the past twenty years Carlton & Paxton, along with every major pharmaceutical company in America, has been seeking a solution to this deadly problem. Some of the breakthroughs have been real and some have been lethal." With this statement, the slide show clicked to an aging newspaper article decrying the consequences of the deadly Fenfuramine disaster a couple of decades prior. "Some have been purposely and dangerously perpetrated on a trusting public by opportunistic charlatans. While others have simply been poor science ... misapplied."

It was a sobering sermon, but everyone in the room knew that the next slide or one that followed would soon reveal the ultimate purpose of this meeting and a much more cheerful conclusion. And indeed, after a dramatic pause, Corbett clicked the remote and the single word 'Endrophat' appeared.

"And that is why we at C&P are so excited about the prospects for our latest breakthrough. With the discovery of Endrophat, we believe we have a solution to obesity that taps into the body's own healing chemistry."

At this juncture, the PowerPoint slide dissolved into

the kind of awkward animation that was so typical of client-developed presentations. The color choice for the slide was garish and the image contained an overused stock illustration of the human body. A sequence of flowing arrows traveled between stomach and brain tracing a path up the spine and returning to the hypothalamus. While Corbett beamed at his ingenuity with the Power Point software, the art directors and designers in the room squirmed uncomfortably with the crudeness of the animation and its supporting graphics.

"So how does it work?" the proud advertising manager continued. "Imagine introducing a synthetic substance that enables the brain to bypass the instinctive demands of the body for food and replaces them with the pleasurable sensations of satiation. We're not talking simply about appetite suppression here, but an actual substitution for the need to eat … with nutritional supplementation, of course. And it really works!"

With this climactic statement Corbett thrust his arm in the air like a cheerleader or an over enthusiastic television pitchman. The similarities were not lost on the observant audience and they couldn't help but laugh. Corbett, too, realized how animated he must have appeared and with charming self-deprecation he forgave them. "You can tell I've gotten with the program," he mocked himself dryly. But then just as quickly he struck a more serious tone. "I just really want you folks to understand how important this new product will be." And with that introduction, he called upon his more expert colleague.

Harry Woodruff actually enjoyed fielding the questions from the people who belonged to the advertising agencies. They clearly lived in a world far removed from the one that he inhabited. Even though their inquiries were obviously devoid of any proper scientific training, they were at least insightful about the human effects and impact of the product in ways that he had seldom thought about before.

It was also quite clear that some of them were very bright. This was in contrast to some of the others, who appeared to be there simply because they were pretty. As he'd waited for Allan Corbett to change folders on the computer's desktop and set the stage for his segment of the presentation, Woodruff had cheated a few peeks at the long-legged young women in short skirts who had taken seats in the front rows of the theater. From what he could deduce, they were from competing companies. Yet they all possessed an appearance of perfection that was similarly manufactured. The Robert Palmer girls, he dubbed them nerdishly, remembering the popular music video that featured a cast in similar wardrobe. Dressed nearly identically in their seductively tailored black suits, they were like shiny chess pieces to be pawned ahead of the obviously much more important individuals seated further back.

Woodruff had spoken uninterrupted for nearly half an hour. When he eventually yielded the floor to questions, initially there had been none. Clearly, the dueling agencies were being careful not to reveal any of their thinking out loud. But eventually their curiosity had gotten the better of them. From the rows further up, that were inhabited by roguishly dressed young men with shaggy hair and women with less make up, questions filtered down in whispers that were repeated more enthusiastically by the more appropriate seeming men and women in suits and ties. After voicing these queries aloud, the ones who asked the questions would preen and beam vacantly, but then never actually listen to his answers. Instead, responsibility for recording the scientist's responses seemed to belong to the young beauties up front. They penned out each word with robotic efficiency using the kind of curly queued long hand that he imagined would have annoyed the hell out of their college professors.

For a moment, in the midst of the explanations and discussion, he'd even allowed himself to wax philosophic on the ethical implications of Endrophat. It was an issue that was rarely contemplated out loud by the scientists and marketers who propelled the success of the big pharmaceutical company. To them it was all strictly business. In fact, in the succession of internal briefings that had already been made to the sales and marketing representatives, virtually all of the post presentation discussions had centered for the most part on input costs, margins and distribution schedules. Definitely nothing about its human consequences. After seeing some of the initial performance data and some of the before-and-after photos, the over eager sales reps nearly had to be iced down, so excited were they about getting Endrophat to the street. None of them had dared to speak about the potentially extraordinary societal impact of this new drug.

"Ladies and gentlemen, I think what you have to appreciate most is the staggering implications of this product. I mean, if we are successful here, I believe we have the potential not only to address an issue of incredible medical and scientific significance, but to reshape our entire view of ourselves and the human aesthetic. We are talking about not a single woman, I repeat not one, ever having to suffer the health consequences or emotional trauma of being over weight." As he said this, he scanned the fresh faces of the attractive young women who were scribbling so diligently for a reaction. But none looked up. Instead, the first response came from the handsome woman who had arrived so disruptively as the meeting was just getting underway.

"If I understand you correctly then Doctor, what you're saying is, that with access to Endrophat, every one of us can be slim and beautiful," simplified Lane McCarthy. "I mean, you're telling us that with a single pill every woman on the planet would finally have the chance to eat like a man and never pay the price with her figure." The highly ironic observation earned snorts and smiles from every corner of the room.

"You're exactly right … Ms …?" the awkward scientist attempted to connect.

"Ms. Lane McCarthy," Allan Corbett inserted. "Ms. McCarthy is President of one of the most brilliant creative shops in the Mid-West," the host of the review fawned. After saying it, he held the attractive woman's eye for an uncomfortable moment too long. She made no attempt to break it off. Even as she flirted so outrageously with the prospective client in front of a room full of competitors, her business brain was reeling.

The implications of what this scruffy scientist had just declared were staggering. In her mind she was quickly assessing the potential effect on her own roster of clients. In a second, she had calculated the impact for Stud Fast, her agency's fashion jeans client. And, of course, there was Big Burger and Conglamara Foods, two accounts who the agency handled nationwide whose businesses would skyrocket if this thing was for real. She wracked her memory to recall the precise wording of the confidentiality agreement. Despite the temptation, she knew she would have to withhold this scorching piece of information from her broker and her New York counterpart, Jeremy Whithers. With a little judicious investing, she could probably make a small fortune if this thing were ever actually able to make it to market and do what they said it would.

"You must be getting an incredible amount of pressure to get this product into the channels," she cooed sympathetically to the two gentlemen making the presentation. They bit shamelessly at her encouragement and tripped over each other to respond. Both were clearly smitten.

"You don't know the half of it," the scientist spluttered. Corbett nodded his vigorous agreement and smiled beamingly at Lane as she magically commandeered control of the meeting. As this was being so smoothly accomplished, the senior people of the other agencies exchanged worried glances. Somebody had to step in.

"What about your IR guys?" Spence Playfair now interrupted. It was a left field question that had the same effect as splashing cold water onto two dogs in heat. At the asking, both presenters had to shift their focus to the unwelcome intrusion. Allan Corbett chose to handle the question, though he fielded it with a hint of irritation.

"Great question," he lied solicitously. "As I'm sure all of you can imagine, the process of even getting this product this far has already been hugely expensive … nearly a quarter billion in development money to date. Isn't that about right, Woody?"

Woodruff blinked his eyes dumbly, still entranced by the attention paid to him by the beautiful and vivacious Lane McCarthy. "Uh, yes. I guess. More or less." His stumbling response immediately annoyed Corbett. Very unprofessional, he eye-rolled. He instantly resolved to teach the attractive woman who had now disrupted his meeting twice a quick lesson about who was going to be in charge. He'd also let her know that he would play much harder to get than he'd just let on.

"Thanks very much for bringing this key issue to the table, Mr. Playfair." It was a subtle rebuke, but one that was not lost on the keen observers of the room's fast evolving dynamics. Agency people were notorious for desperately glomming onto such non-verbal cues and nuances within the meeting. It would give them the grist they needed for the endless rounds of debriefing that would occur upon each competitor's return from the meeting.

Being mentioned by name immediately elevated the status of the new business maven from Boom among all who were assembled. Several people leaned into one another and exchanged whispers while looking in his direction. The uninformed nodded and others shot disapproving looks. Everyone, it seemed, had an opinion about Spence Playfair. He soaked up the attention unashamedly.

"As you have suggested, sir, one of the key issues affecting the profitability of this entire program will be our ability to build awareness and claim solid market share before the copycats can analyze the product and get an imitator to market. And, of course, we've always got to keep an eye on when our patents expire. We've already lost nearly a year and a half of our NDA to further testing and refinement."

"NDA?" someone from the pack at the back of the room called out.

"New Drug Approval ... it's what we get from the FDA ... the Food & Drug Administration ... to introduce a new product." Corbett beamed at his alliterative wit, but only the suits in the audience indulged him with a laugh. "The simple fact is, the longer we use up our NDA in testing, the less time we've got to make money off the original patent," he added.

The point Corbett was making was a continual raw spot within Carlton & Paxton's executive suite where everyone was especially eager to get Endrophat to market. At the company's highest levels, it was widely assumed that R&D was costing them a fortune by dragging their heels. A couple of guys from Investor Relations were already starting to soften up the analysts for the announcement of the amazing breakthrough. While the leaks had been deliberate and, for the most part were confined to a favored list of loyal C&P stock watchers, the company's share price had been inching up quietly for the past few months in anticipation of final regulatory approval. This was why Woodruff's R&D team was feeling so much pressure. They had already accelerated the NDA by several months and cut the clinical evaluation to the bone.

This decision to fast-track Endrophat had already led, in Dr. Harold Woodruff's professional opinion, to some very sloppy science. But that was the difference between saving mankind for altruistic reasons and doing it for dollars. The veteran clinician had long ago reconciled this mildly troublesome dilemma in his own mind. He had put teams to work around the clock for the past six months and had personally overseen the authoring of the final application that the FDA had received a couple of weeks prior. Now he was being pressured to deliver a production schedule and a firm release date.

"I think, as far as this group is concerned, we can assume the product is virtually approved," the scientist now interceded. He shot Corbett a look that suggested betrayal and seemed genuinely uncomfortable with sharing this kind of information with outsiders. He scanned the audience for more questions. He fielded one from the back, where a few familiar faces from Lowenstein Holiday were seated.

"Woody … Dr. Woodruff …" an intermediate account guy from the incumbent agency began, allowing his familiarity with the researcher to show, "Are there any problems you foresee with the introduction of this kind of product. I mean, you know, as far as uptake is concerned?"

Now it was Woodruff's turn to compliment the questioner.

"Richard, that too, is a very good line of inquiry." The normally forgetful scientist seemed delighted to remember a name. "As I know all of you are aware, people have been looking for a miracle solution to this problem for years and too many times consumers have been rewarded with false promises. I think one of the biggest issues you're going to have to help us overcome is good old fashioned skepticism."

Again many heads nodded. A few of the creative types even swiveled in their seats to seek affirmation from their counterparts in account management. Certainly, this issue was ringing a few bells with the crusty cynics that inhabited most agencies and had already been kicked around in the bullpens.

Woodruff then continued with an insight that had been gathered during the early clinical work. He paused before sharing it, but then carried on. "I'll tell you one more thing that we came across when we were doing our Phase I and Phase II work. Please don't take offense ladies … but as soon as most of our subjects achieved their desired weight goal most of the women who were reliant on Endrophat simply stopped taking their medications."

"But why?" someone again called out.

"Fear … laziness … I'm not exactly sure, Woodruff pondered. "Most likely cost would be a big motivator once they imagined they had control of the problem—especially since they would have to begin purchasing the medication instead of getting it free as they did during the trial." The scientist scratched his head as he weighed the value of his own answer. "I guess it shouldn't be too surprising that once you've reached your goal weight and can get more pills if you ever put the weight back on … you just stop, " Woodruff explained. "Let me ask you," the doctor continued, addressing the group as a whole, "How many of you have a few pills from a prescription lying around or a few tablespoons of medicine that you've never finished?" The question was greeted with an ocean of hands.

"My point exactly. It is the same with Endrophat. Or at least that was the case until …" Before Woodruff could finish the point he was making, Allan Corbett interrupted. He gave the scientist a look that was clearly intended to silence further exploration of this particular issue.

"Actually, Woody," he said tapping his watch, "I think we're just about out of time for questions and I'm sure we've just about covered off everything these folks are going to need to proceed with their work."

Initially, Woodruff seemed annoyed, but then a look at his own watch appeared to startle him. "Oh my, you're right Allan," he apologized. It was obvious to all that the scientist had forgotten another appointment. "I just want to thank you all for your kind attention. I look forward to meeting with you again. Don't hesitate to ring if you've got any more questions," he added as he flustered together his notes and hurried toward the door.

Woodruff's hasty exit earned a patronizing smile from Allan Corbett who now quelled the others who had actually begun to pack up. "As you can see, Dr. Woodruff is a man in demand." He shook his head at the lack of professionalism his colleague had just displayed and resumed control of the forum.

"Actually ..." he inserted, "Please don't call Dr. Woodruff with your questions. Direct them through me. Though I'm sure I don't have to remind you, as per the terms of the review process that you've all agreed to, anything I give to you individually will be shared with the entire group." This comment was immediately met with some eye rolls—especially by the team from Lowenstein Holiday. It was another of those standing pain-in-the-ass procedural things that reduced an agency review to little more than a purchasing exercise.

"Otherwise, please help yourself to the literature packets I've left by the door. They capture the bulk of the Power Point, as well as a few other housekeeping details. Thank you for coming out today. I would also like to remind you of the terms of the confidentiality agreement that you all have signed. Let me assure you that any breach of this contract will result in the most strenuous means of prosecution at our disposal. I will be contacting you individually to arrange for my agency visit and to introduce the rest of the review panel. Thank you."

On the last two words, the room erupted like a classroom at the bell. "Good luck to you all." Corbett concluded.

Day 4

The debriefing session had been going on for nearly two hours and Lane knew she needed to check her messages. But one of her young copywriters, a kid too junior to attend the initial client meeting, had just asked a very good question and she was listening closely to hear if anyone could answer it intelligently. Indeed, it was the kind of issue that went right to the heart of the entire campaign that they would ultimately have to create and she was amazed that no one else had thought to ask it when they were at the agency briefing the day before.

"What do you think Bryan?" Lane now inquired of the senior account manager, Bryan Raider, she was planning to assign to the business if they were somehow successful in winning the pitch. "Is it a consumer product or is it a prescription drug? Did either of them say anything yesterday that would suggest which way they were going on distribution?"

"It's got to be prescription, Lane. I don't think either of them said so specifically, but I don't believe you could deliver that kind of chemistry over the counter could you?" The uncertainty in his voice betrayed the same doubts that everyone else in the meeting was having. "I could call Allan

Corbett and check. You know we need a reason to follow up,"
he added trying to be helpful.

"I'm not so sure just yet," Lane hesitated. "I may want to
make that call myself," she countered.

That was the trouble with the entire weight loss product category she thought as she assessed Raider's opinion.
Everywhere you looked there were television commercials
and expensive print advertisements promising incredible
results, while at the same time there was a nearly unassailable
wall of dissenting medical opinion. Was Endrophat simply
another diet pill or was it the real deal? If it was the former
she knew that the advertising could be creative and interesting—if not entirely factual. But if it were the latter, it would
end up burdened with page after page of legal qualifications
and disclaimers and the inevitable consumer skepticism that
followed as a result.

"I definitely don't want to ask something so obvious that
it's going to embarrass us. I mean, I think it makes it pretty
plain that we don't have any direct pharma experience if we
were supposed to know this kind of stuff and didn't," she
continued. "When is that consultant friend of yours available
to help us out?"

In that moment Lane McCarthy made a decision she
was usually reluctant to pursue. They would hire the guy
that Bryan Raider knew who had worked for a competitive
pharmaceutical company. Rarely in her experience did it ever
make sense to bring in a hired gun to help the agency get up
to speed on a product category, but she was ready to make an
exception in this case. More times than not such outsiders created more confusion than they were worth as they tried to justify their fat consulting fees by coming up with ad campaigns
and ideas of their own. But this time the stakes here were just
too high. She'd have to get him to swear up and down on the

confidentiality agreement and hope that no one at Carlton & Paxton found out.

On top of that, Lane had not yet alerted Reiner Adolph to the fact that they had a C&P invitation in hand. At one point she had seriously thought about the idea of going it entirely alone, but that was just a fantasy. The publicity this review was sure to generate would definitely blow her cover. Indeed, that was the difficulty of the circumstance she now found herself in. On one hand the beauty of now belonging to a global agency network was that she could draw upon its resources and experience with clients all over the world. But at the same time Lane knew that to do so would likely come at far too high a price. The minute she made the phone call to Stuttgart, they would be all over it. If victory came, it would no longer belong to her office and her people. It would be immediately claimed and harvested by the brain trust in New York or wherever and her people's contribution would be forgotten. She reminded herself that her agency needed a victory in the worst way.

A cough brought her back to attention and she suddenly remembered that the group was waiting for a definitive answer on whether or not to call Corbett. She waved it off. "Bryan, lets get your guy in. If he can't answer that question, then we'll figure out who we should talk to over there, okay," she instructed Raider.

This was typical of the chess of pursuing new business and no one doubted her mastery. "In the meantime, I want you to break this thing down and figure out how we're going to get it done," she added.

For the time being Lane decided that she would hold off calling the mother ship for another day or two—even if the tight timeline was already beginning to squeeze them. She had already turned a creative team loose on the assignment and she was hopeful that maybe they would hit on something quickly. Lane McCarthy had always lived by her instincts and her gut was telling her that bringing in outsiders was the last thing that Allan Corbett wanted. Judging by his performance yesterday, she had already figured out that he was extremely needy and was really looking for a hand holder. He would not be easily impressed by a couple of fly-by-nighters brought in for the pitch from Interworld's New York or London offices.

"Were there any more reactions to yesterday's briefing?" she now asked protracting the discussion. "Did anyone else get the sense that the scientist … Woody… was holding something back?" Her playfulness around the good doctor's nickname caused a few of the group who had been in attendance to snicker.

"He was definitely holding something back alright. He's lucky he didn't sprout one at the front of the room," a guy from the Creative Department chimed in, picking up on the obvious joke. "Did you see the way he was undressing those little foxes from Boom? I mean, with all due respect Madam President, why can't we ever hire any women that hot?" A pretty young female account executive seated next to the copywriter gave him a playful shot to the ribs.

"Because I'd be dealing with their lawyers within a week thanks to you bad little boys in the Creative Department," Lane shot back, allowing everyone the opportunity to smile. "Besides, I hire all the bimbos around here, and frankly, the kinds of toys I'm interested in don't wear skirts." This caused the entire group to laugh out loud—especially the women.

Lane enjoyed the easy banter that flowed among her team and was pleased that everyone, at least on the surface, appeared to be loose. The unbearable tension of the demanding project would arrive soon enough. Besides, part of the fun of being a woman in charge of an agency was that she could set the bounds of appropriate discussion and behavior more easily than at the shops of her male counterparts. In this regard, the Chicago scene was notoriously Neanderthal and harassment suits were all too common. In her duties as local chapter president she had been forced to invite in a guest speaker from the National Ad Council to speak to her peers about the problem.

"Seriously. Did anyone pick up the vibe that Dr. Woodruff had something more to say?" Searching the faces of those who had been attendance, it appeared no one else had shared her impression. "Okay. Maybe it was just my imagination then." Letting the issue drop she brought the meeting to a close. "Be brilliant," she reminded the group aloud as everyone crowded out of the room.

Spence Playfair had been delighted with how quickly Allan Corbett had responded to his luncheon invitation. In fact when the C&P advertising manager had buttonholed him following the briefing session and told him he was available at noon the next day, Playfair barely had time to secure a decent table and make the necessary preparations for such an important first date. But then that was why the new business impresario was delighted to belong to the Midtown Club. Perched in the lofty floors of the Chase building, the private dining room offered a commanding view of the skyline and the driest martini in the city. It had been the scene of some of his most successful first encounters and he was certain it would make an impression on an obviously ambitious climber like Corbett—especially on such a glorious early spring day.

Now he sat with a watchful eye on the entrance to the dining room and the clock above it that had barely reached a quarter of twelve. He tapped his foot impatiently in anticipation of the meeting, but didn't have to wait long.

The elevator chimed in the foyer and, moments later, Allan Corbett appeared looking like he'd spent the entire morning preening for the appointment. As had been arranged, Curtis the maitre d' swept him to their magnificent window-side table where the view was absolutely breathtaking.

"Allan, I'm so delighted you could make it. I certainly knew you wouldn't have any trouble finding the place. I thought I might have seen you in here last week, before we'd met," Playfair now offered ingratiatingly. This last remark allowed his guest to pretend that he was familiar with the aerie that was home to some of Chicago's most prominent men of commerce. But his wonderment was difficult to conceal.

"Say, that's a fantastic looking suit ... almost as nice as the one you wore the other day," Playfair now piled on.

As expected, Corbett bloomed visibly with the compliment. With a deft wave of his hand the luncheon host flagged their waiter and within seconds a crisp black linen napkin was folded into the lap of each of the businessmen. Mere moments later, oversized leather-bound menus were presented with a flourish and drink requests were taken. Playfair certainly knew how to choreograph this most important of American business rituals. He was a master of the power lunch. Now he focused all of the beaming sunlight of his attentions upon his guest.

Too eagerly, Corbett had requested a Chopin on the rocks from a surprised server who was clearly more used to offering a selection of mineral waters at this time of the day. The veteran waiter assented with quiet disapproval and looked in askance of the member. "Excellent call, Allan," Playfair mirrored. "I think I'll have one of those myself." In that moment, the host decided he would allow himself a drink. He'd been consuming ice water with olives so long he'd almost forgotten what a real martini tasted like. He indicated this desire with a prearranged signal to Ralph at the bar. Now he began to warm to his prospect in earnest.

"Allan," he continued, "You've just got to tell me everything about how you came to occupy such a key role at C&P? I mean, especially so quickly." Coming from anyone else the question would have been too unctuous to bear, but Playfair flattered and lied so naturally he was able to sell it with nearly believable sincerity.

Corbett bit with poorly concealed vanity. Before their lunch order arrived he had recounted virtually his entire twenty-three year career with the pharmaceutical company including the substance of his last three annual performance reviews. In less than thirty minutes Spence Playfair had undressed the man of his family's first names and birth dates, his college alma mater and the details of a first unhappy marriage. With the second martini he had pried loose a confession that Corbett was also deeply unhappy with his current marital circumstance. Corbett was on his third cocktail now.

In return Playfair had traded little more than the usual well-known facts about Boom. He told the story of his arrival at the shop, understated the tumult that he had caused, and dropped all of the names that he calculated they might have in common. All the while he shone his winning smile at Corbett. Playfair had long ago perfected the art of "*I like you, you like me.*" He projected this onto his quarry the way most men would ply a beautiful woman.

Strangely this lunch wasn't unfolding as he had imagined. Typically first lunches were a game of poker with his guests holding all the cards. He had thought that was the way it would be with Corbett. Certainly he was expecting him to be far more circumspect. That was definitely the book on most Carlton & Paxton executives. Virtually all of them had been sent to the same corporate finishing school—one that demanded the three D's—diligence, decisiveness and, above all, discretion.

Instead, he found the senior advertising manager to be almost embarrassingly forthright on far too many sensitive issues. Initially, he wasn't sure whether he could trust this outpouring of candor. However, after two quick martinis and a hastily ordered third, when his guest had insisted on looking at the wine list, he realized that Corbett was very likely alcoholic. Like every executive in the advertising business, Playfair was extremely adept at managing the exploitable aspects of dependency. Maybe this would be easier than he thought. With the completion of their main course—his guest had selected a native caught Arctic Char with truffle butter that was easily the most expensive item on the menu—Playfair finally managed to point the conversation in the direction he had always intended quite easily.

"I have to tell you, I was truly surprised when the review was announced," the new business officer from Boom ventured cautiously. Though both men knew this was the real reason they were here, Playfair still chose to approach the subject sideways.

"Even at our agency we've always been impressed with the outstanding work that's been done on your behalf by L&H," he feigned. He emphasized the inclusive pronoun *our* to suggest that a certain bon homme was shared amongst competitors. The truth was Zig Cartwright and his pack had ripped apart the reel of Carlton & Paxton spots that had been immediately ordered from the media watch service. It had been screened at the agency that very morning to catcalls and vocal disdain. "You must have personally had a hand in some of the best of it I imagine," he continued to praise.

Corbett received this compliment as he had all the others, smiling dumbly through the pleasantness of his emerging buzz. He drained the last drops of expensive Chablis from the beautifully ballooned stemware and set the glass down with an unspoken suggestion that another glass would be very much appreciated—even though an empty bottle bobbed upside down in the perspiring metal ice bucket. Playfair responded to this implied request with a quick nod in the direction of the server and within moments a full glass appeared on the table. Its golden contents spread a prismic rainbow that danced playfully on the white linen tablecloth of their sun-soaked table.

"We've got a spot in post right now that's in big trouble. Pissed away a million bucks," Corbett now lamented.

As he revealed this, his whisper thickened with a tiny slur that suggested all of the drinks he'd consumed were finally having some effect.

"Absolutely gorgeous pictures … just somehow they lost sight of the concept. Damned agency put their number two guy, Toby Meyer, on the shoot. He let the director walk all over him," he recounted conveniently ignoring any sense of complicity. "Pathetic. Got me in big shit upstairs." Playfair's ears perked at the coarseness that had quietly crept into Corbett's language. More truth wouldn't be far behind.

"I can assure you that would never happen at our place," Playfair responded with more honesty than had accompanied any remark he'd offered all day. Unfortunately, he alone appreciated the irony. The truth was commercial production at Boom was a truly hateful process in which virtually everyone's opinions were overridden by the Ayatollah-like pronouncements of Zig Cartwright. Indeed, on a recent shoot, the Creative Director had actually gone so far as to banish a junior client from the set. Only the intercession of Avery Booth had saved the agency from being fired in the angry aftermath. Another time, late last fall, there had actually been a physical scuffle between the CD and the Director from the production

company after the latter had ordered the crew to move on
before seeking Cartwright's permission. But Playfair wasn't
about to share any of this.

"Production is just too damned expensive these days to
let egos get in the way," he lied commiseratively.

"Don't get me wrong. I really admire Steve Holiday,"
Corbett now continued as if seeking to rationalize his decision. "But the guy is just stretched too thin. Our contract says
he's one hundred percent dedicated to C&P business, but we
all know that's bullshit." It was the chorus of every client in
the business. Everybody wanted the best and brightest and
wanted them exclusively. But they also conveniently forgot
this during their annual contract negotiations when they
would balk at the outrageous hourly rates charged for the
agency's most talented personnel.

"Do you want to know the real reason L&H is under
review," the client now volunteered indiscreetly. Sensing
that he had captured Playfair's full and undivided attention,
Corbett decided he had best make his expectations understood. "Let's just say, I've had enough of Ira Lowenstein's
little games. The account guys and I, we had certain understandings. But that prick Lowenstein ... well ... lets just say
he's forgotten to pay the piper." Corbett let the words sink in
for a moment. "Am I making myself clear?" he then asked
with sobering clarity.

"Indeed, Allan. Quite clear," was Playfair's carefully measured response. He made a point of looking directly into his
would-be client's eyes as he said this. Now they were playing
a game with which he was very familiar. He had seen virtually every variation of it during the course of his sales career.

Most commonly, good clients used their company's
money to command added value from the agency and to
leverage more favorable terms on their hourly rates and
media rebates. Playfair had worked with straight arrows for

which even the slightest whiff of impropriety was grounds for the agency's dismissal. But he'd also been down unsavory paths such as the one that Corbett had apparently just revealed himself to be interested in.

It was a sad reality how often senior guys in big organizations—the ones with multi-million dollar budgets to spend—used the power of their positions for their own personal gain. Sure, some just liked bowing obeisance and invisible perks. However, other less scrupulous executives often wanted a cut or kickback of some sort on every dollar they spent with the agency. His guess, as far as Allan Corbett was concerned, was that this guy was somewhere in the middle—but falling fast. The drinking and indiscreet behavior he'd already demonstrated over lunch made that much quite obvious.

Playfair continued to nod his understanding, but this time his response was more deliberately oblique. "Certainly we've come to some understandings with our clients once the contract is awarded. While I can't guarantee this on behalf of Avery Booth, as far as I'm concerned, it's all part of the negotiation." At least for now, Corbett appeared satisfied with this answer. Hoping to avoid further discussion of such an unseemly issue this early in the relationship, Playfair now offered a dodge he was sure would please his guest.

"You know Allan, they have the most exquisite collection of Ports here. Ivan the sommelier has tucked away a couple of dusty old vintages that truly are quite extraordinary." The ploy had its desired effect and the conversation shifted to matters of much less weighty consequence.

Later, on the way down in the elevator, Corbett asked something that on reflection shouldn't have surprised his host. It came shortly after his luncheon date had slobbered out an effusive thank you and he had squeezed Playfair's shoulder gratefully like a long lost friend.

"Do you really have to go back to your office?" the senior

manager from Carlton & Paxton had asked as the heavy golden doors of the lift opened into the cavernous lobby of the Chase. The familiar way he said it suggested that playing hooky on a mid-week afternoon was something that he did routinely.

As tempted as he was to accompany Corbett on whatever expedition his new *friend* seemed to have in mind, Playfair decided that it all seemed just a little too reckless. After the lengthy lunch and all of the alcohol that had been consumed, he desperately wanted to get back to the office where he could make notes on everything that had been discussed. He might even steal a well-deserved nap. Begging off the implied invitation as they strolled across the vacant vestibule of the prestigious bank building, the two men shook hands in the street. It was nearly two-thirty. The bright sunshine of the noon hour had given way to a charcoal colored sky and a chilling breeze now swirled through the canyons of steel and glass. On their parting, Corbett turned up his collar and bent into a chilling March wind that had sprung from the lake and headed east toward Michigan Avenue. It was the opposite direction from his office. As curious as Playfair was to follow the man, he instead climbed into the warmth of a waiting cab. There was clearly a side to Allan Corbett that didn't match the profile he had been constructing in his mind—and it was a much darker one at that.

Steve Holiday relished this time of day. As the late afternoon light gave way to shadows of the early evening, the anonymous office towers that hoarded his view on all sides became a checkerboard of black and white. Some glowed with the apparent tirelessness of their occupants, while others had been dimmed with the day's proper end. As the Creative

Director imagined it, the relative success of these companies was probably expressed in the random matrix of illuminated windows that filled the crowded corridors of commerce south of the canal where L&H was headquartered. The bright ones were hives of restless energy -- stockbrokers and commodities traders he always thought -- able to make money at any hour of the day or night. After six o'clock, the men in the corner offices of these buildings shed their jackets, loosened their ties and spread themselves more expansively than they did at other times of day. With feet up on desks and hands folded behind their heads, they basked in the brilliance of their own bullshit and hatched the schemes that would decide the fates of the lesser men that surrounded them.

Though they were far away and small, even at a distance Holiday imagined he could hear their conversations. He and Ira had shared so many just like them as they plotted to win the pitches, grow the business, and somehow get most things right as Lowenstein Holiday rose to the top of the local industry. Every now and then the Creative Director had entertained the idea of waving to his neighbors or holding up a sign expressing commiseration with their long days and deep devotion to the soulless mistress called work. Once in a while he would spot one of them on a busy street corner or at the little coffee shop run by the Greek where you could get a sandwich late, but there was no recognition they shared anything more than loneliness and too much time spent at the office.

Tonight, as the darkness settled, a few late arriving snowflakes darted past the onyx panels of his wide windows. Reflecting back the interior of his office, he carefully studied the illusion of himself seated at his desk. It was suspended magically in the cold emptiness of space and reminded him that the business as he knew it was literally shifting beneath his feet. The day that earlier had carried with it the first few hints of spring, was now giving in to the last desperate clutches of a long winter's grip. Forty floors up, in his lonely office, the wind moaned and a brittle metal window frame snapped aloud as the building flexed with the strengthening storm.

Inside the labyrinth of offices occupied by Lowenstein Holiday things were finally beginning to quiet. While there were still a few juniors stalking the halls hoping to impress someone with their devotion, most of the agency's senior staff had migrated toward home. There would be plenty of late nights in the weeks to come and most members of the Creative Department would be trying to negotiate forgiveness in advance. Or, at the very least, attempting to make a substantial deposit in the bank of domestic goodwill. Steve knew the routine all too well. It had mattered so much more to come home when Clare was there waiting.

But now the only sound that disturbed the hush—more apparent since the building's billowing ventilation system had finally been turned down—was a lonely jazz horn leaking from the paste-up studio down the hall. Recently, the agency had added a second shift in the Art Department. They worked all night in order to make proofs available for review first thing the next day. The Creative Director smiled to himself at the irony. This was the great benefit that placing a computer on the desk of every person in the agency had been rewarded with—the chance to work nearly round the clock without interruption.

But Holiday was in no hurry to call it quits this evening. He scrolled the seemingly endless list of e-mails that waited on the crowded screen of his book-thin laptop. Even though he'd been reading and responding to these notes for nearly an hour, the anxious little icon in the corner indicated that there were still twenty-seven more messages that needed to be answered. Five of the items carried the urgent red flag that

Ira was currently fond of attaching to all of his memoranda. Holiday grouped these ones together, knowing that the replies he issued to his partner would have to be more carefully crafted than those he could dash off to his group heads and staff. Certainly they deserved more thought than the curt replies he issued back to account managers and underlings trying to cover their butts by copying him on their every move. It was this drudge that made him truly weary.

Taking a break from the screen, he tilted back in his chair. He closed his eyes and allowed himself a stretch that hurt in a dozen joints and reminded him that he hadn't made it to the gym in a week. Rolling his aching neck from side to side across his shoulders, the tension reminded him that he had also not yet invested more than a few moments thinking about the actual problem that the Endrophat launch presented. Sooner or later he knew he would have to begin to focus. That was the way the creative process worked. Idea stew was the way he was most fond of describing it. "You stuff everything into a pot and throw it on a back burner for a couple of hours or a couple of days. Before you know it, you've got something delicious," he would patiently recount when called upon to explain how he managed to come up with his ideas. The trick, these days, was to find the time to even get things into the kettle.

So far the overwhelming logistics of the pitch had not allowed him to take in even the most basic ingredients of this particular creative challenge. He would need to find some time soon to absorb the many pieces that had been provided. Only then would he have a chance to distill them into a single strategy or the one great ad that would be the template for the campaign that followed. All that he'd been doing up until now was just messing around, hoping that someone else would deliver an answer he could build upon.

After nearly thirty years in the business, he was finding

the blind search at the outset of a new project ever harder to deal with. Worse, he was also wrestling with finding the energy to get excited even after a solution had been found. While he still loved a well-crafted headline or a deft play on words, and he would still light up eagerly when he reviewed an idea that contained a crystal clear grain of human truth, increasingly he found himself becoming quite cynical of the entire process. Lamentably, somewhere along the line, the complex act of consumer persuasion had become confused with entertainment. And while he had made more than his share of clever commercials, including a couple that had been the buzz of the Super Bowl and earned the agency a boatload of awards, the adult in him knew that such things had little do with effective communication—let alone selling.

Often he found himself arguing on the side of his more rational clients in rejecting the trite ideas advanced by his junior staff and apparently favored by advertising industry award juries these days. When did making you laugh ever become the basis of a meaningful contract between a customer and a brand? When did five musical notes that you could whistle in the shower ever cause you to want to buy a new kind of breakfast cereal? But that was the voodoo his industry had always sold—miracles. Sure they wrapped these conclusions in bundles of pseudoscientific market research, and the rising sales graphs couldn't be ignored, but somehow Steve Holiday, the grown up, suspected that the marketing solutions that his own company now manufactured were, for the most part, pure hokum. This made him a dangerous man to be around and he knew it. Maybe this time … this campaign … would be his last.

Emerging from his melancholy repose, he opened his eyes and reached for one of the yellow pads he always tried to keep an arm's length away. He scribbled down another headline that joined the jumble of words and scribbles that had been accumulating on the page. This was the way it happened more often these days. Where once the muse had visited him freely, now he had to beg it out of hiding, hoping to trick it into dispensing the magic words or the playful pictures that had once floated into his mind from the world beyond much more easily. He looked carefully at the letters of the words he had just written quietly hopeful that there was something there that had prompted his ghost hand to move. Instead, what appeared was a simple two-word expression of the benefit of Endrophat. "Slender Hope" was what he had written. He scoffed at himself and the delicious irony of the phrase. "If that's the best you can come up with, your days are numbered Holiday," he chastised himself. He scratched out the words crankily and yawned again.

When his gaze returned to the computer screen, the bold type announcing that another new message had arrived immediately caught his eye. Initially, he expected to see another of Ira's urgent missives—they came at all hours ever since his partner had acquired his new iPhone. But instead, what quickly got his attention was the address that appeared on the e-mail menu. It originated from McCarthy & McCauley, a name that had taken on an especially evil import around his shop ever since the C&P review list had been announced. He pointed the curser at the message bar and clicked it, even though he didn't recognize the sender's name.

After tapping the send icon that launched her final e-mail of the day, Brenda Martin leaned forward and turned off her monitor, exhausted. Except for the glow of the green-shaded accountant's lamp that washed her desk with a single lonely pool of light, the executive floor of McCarthy & McCauley was dark and quiet. The agency was currently engaged in the

phony war as Lane's loyal executive assistant had likened it—
the quiet period of denial that would eventually give way to a
desperate struggle as the company mobilized for the big push
toward presentation day. The best the dutiful assistant could
do now was try and clear all decks in anticipation of the chaos
that would ensue in the coming weeks.

She didn't wait for confirmations of receipt for the message that she had dispatched to the half dozen invitees on the
list her boss had provided. There would be plenty of time for
that in the morning. The reminder to the participants on the
Ad Council panel that Lane was responsible for hosting in
less than a week at the Board of Trade was the last item on her
day's lengthy to-do-list. She would begin follow up calls the
next morning, urging her secretarial counterparts at agencies
across the city to get their bosses' slides and disks together for
the joint presentation that they would be making on behalf of
the industry. It was the kind of nuisance show that agency's
were frequently called upon to deliver at the networking lun-
cheons of sales organizations and second tier clients and for
which there was, typically, very little reward.

This year, the task of organizing the onerous program
had fallen to Lane McCarthy. The topic requested was the
always popular, *'Humor in Advertising: Effective or Not?'* and
while most of the panel participants could deliver this kind
of material in their sleep, it nonetheless required a certain
amount of coordination if it were to be properly presented by
a group. Lane had split her reluctant conscripts into two teams
to argue the pros and cons of the topic. The trick now was to
dial up expectations and avoid having to deal with any eleventh hour bailouts or getting duplicate presentation materials
at the very last minute. In that respect, Brenda Martin knew
that her own boss would be difficult enough to manage and
she wasn't looking forward to it. Since its arrival, the Carlton
& Paxton pitch had the agency caught up in an increasingly

desperate swirl, Lane McCarthy included. She pulled on her coat, gathered her purse and switched off the lamp. It would have to wait until tomorrow.

Day 5

"Come on baby. You know you want it." As Zig Cartwright moaned these words he pressed his hands against the smoky glass window and lewdly pushed his pelvis forward in a series of urgent thrusts. "You want it real bad, don't you?" he grunted hungrily as she approached slowly from across the room. When the heavy girl with the dripping chin was only inches from his face, he pushed his lips hard against the mirror and gave it a heavy slather with his swirling tongue. "Eat me! Come on and eat me," he panted with an exaggerated groan.

As the Creative Director begged out this last command most of the assembled group could no longer control themselves. Some, whose shoulders had been shuddering with tightly bottled restraint, finally let their laughter escape in loud guffaws. Elsewhere in the murky darkness there were various snorts and giggles. Spence Playfair had to shush them all with a hiss. It had been his idea to organize these focus groups and he had called in a favor with one of his most reliable suppliers to pull the sessions off so quickly. Unfortunately there were no clients present, so the creatives were giving reign to the full range of their sophomoric wit. As they watched intently, the chubby girl who had been the object of Zig Cartwright's attentions guiltily lifted a sticky Danish from the caterer's silver platter at the side of the room, pausing ever so briefly to contemplate the thick slabs of brownie that were her other option. After a moment's hesitation, she slid one of these delicious confections onto to her plate as well.

"I told you she was a pastry girl," whispered Cartwright with a self-satisfied grin. His point made, he returned to the group and settled back into the chair at the writing ledge that served as a desk for those seated closest to the two-way mirror. He was absolutely oblivious to the insensitivity of his remarks. "A dozen donuts a day … whether her lardy arse needs them or not." This comment drew no reaction. To his right the studious monitor from the research house was sitting stiff-backed in her chair pretending to be all business. Perhaps this uptight Yank didn't know what an arse was, he surmised.

"Note that subject number seventeen went directly to the tray of desserts," she commented quietly into her Dictaphone. "Also note that six of the subjects from Group Two drew samples from the sandwich plate and only one went to the vegetable platter first."

While there was absolutely nothing scientific about the experiment, the researchers went busily about their work making careful observations and pseudo-clinical assessments of the subjects. A man in the corner of the viewing room quietly worked a video camera, panning from face to bloated face as the ladies began to seat themselves around the big boardroom table. Occasionally, he would tilt down to show a particularly meaty haunch or pan back and forth to capture an over-sized bottom. In the first big 'aha' of the research exercise the entire group had started noting the snacking preferences of the research participants and tried to draw a correlation to their size. But in this, the second two-hour group in as many nights, guessing their food choices had grown old. Few of the observers were more bored than the hyper-kinetic CD from Boom. His childish performance and the response of his colleagues' moments before were certainly evidence of that.

"I'll tell you what we should have done," Cartwright interrupted again. "We should have laced those little beauties with laxatives. Then we sure would have elicited some more interesting reactions," he continued. The leader of the creatives leaned back on the legs of his chair and laced his hands behind his head, closing his eyes in pretend sleep.

It wasn't like they were going to be testing any actual concept work tonight. That was the only time the Creative Director actually paid attention during these things. It was when these spuriously recruited amateurs were actually commenting on storyboards or layouts that they could really be dangerous. More times than he cared to count Cartwright had sat through nights during which visionless assholes just like these ladies had demolished some of what he imagined to be his finest creative work. It was an experience he didn't wish to repeat on his own company's dime. Once he had actually come across a focus group participant in a coffee shop following a particularly damaging session. He had been so enraged at the earlier outcome that he had accidentally brushed her arm and caused her to spill a scalding latte into her lap. Even tonight, with little at stake and no nervous clients present, he could not conceal his contempt for this aspect of the marketing research process.

"Gawd, look at the jowls on that one," Ziggy called out to the dark room as another of the focus group participants drew attention to herself by slurping the straw in an empty diet soda can. "Don't imagine we'll see her in Elle anytime soon," he gloated cruelly. "Unless, of course, she can get a gig this Easter as a Hormel Ham," he mocked.

Restless with the appearance of this new group, Zig Cartwright surveyed the list of names, ages and weights of the women just beyond the looking glass. They were the precise demographic all right. But then he had predicted they'd have very little difficulty recruiting twenty overweight women between the ages of 25 and 49 who were considered the prime target for Endrophat. After all, these were same women who assembled themselves for every focus group he'd ever attended. However, he still was amazed that some people apparently had so little going on in their lives that for seventy-five dollars, car fare and a bite to eat, they would forsake their evening for the chance to look at half baked creative concepts and make comment on things of which they had little knowledge or understanding. Whether it was cars, cosmetics or breakfast cereals, it was this same group of bored and lonely losers who provided the litmus test of what would pass for great advertising in the American marketplace. He was appalled with this reality and didn't bother to hide his contempt.

"Are we doing anything different with these ones?" he questioned out loud. No one in the gloom had the courage to respond. Instead, most busily made notes and diagrams of the people now settling into their chairs in the meeting room. Each of the research subjects wore a sticky tag that bore their name and an identification number. A couple of the ladies, who had obviously been chatting in the waiting room, resumed their conversation. Cartwright thought he recognized one of them from a group held a month or two before. He shook his head with disdain and dashed off a quick note that was spirited away by a research assistant. A few moments later the door opened in the boardroom opposite and the woman was excused from the room. "That'll fix the bitch," the CD exclaimed delightedly. By having her removed from the group early he had shorted her honorarium by twenty-five dollars. "I thought I recognized her from the PlayPort stuff," alluding to a testing session for a TV campaign for their toy store client that hadn't gone particularly well. "I owed her one." He could feel Playfair bristle.

Now the moderator, who had entered the room on the heels of the guinea pigs, began to speak. She was seated with her back to the mirrored wall behind which a dozen representatives of the agency's many disciplines listened and began to pace her way through a set of well-rehearsed remarks.

"Welcome," she said mock-cheerfully as she drew the hen house to order. "Thank you all for coming." She waited for the room to settle and then continued. "Tonight we're going to have a discussion in which there are no right or wrong answers and no bad ideas ... as long as I agree with what you say, of course." The moderator then allowed the few polite giggles that usually accompanied her little joke to pass before pressing on. "Specifically, we'll be talking about eating habits and weight control products." As she said this, she noticed several of the ladies in the room shifting in their seats and looking down at themselves to avoid direct eye contact. The meaning of their body language was unmistakable. A few of the women tugged at their clothing, suddenly uncomfortable. "So how many of you have ever been on a diet?" she continued. All of the women groaned and every one of them raised a hand. "Can you leave them up so I can do a quick count," the moderator encouraged.

As she said this, Zig Cartwright immediately noted the fat dimpled wrists and gelatinous upper arms that jiggled as they were raised. "My gawd," he moaned aloud, shaking his head so that his cheeks flapped and his voice wavered in synch with the quivering flesh of the research subjects. "Look at them ham hocks." A pretty account executive seated behind him had noticed the same thing. She whispered it to a nodding cadre of observant junior account managers who dutifully noted it on their clipboards. He wouldn't mind fucking her, thought Cartwright to himself. He pivoted in his chair and gave the young woman an approving smile though he doubted she could see it. He cheated the blackness of the room and gave her bare knee a squeeze. He could feel her blush even in the dark, but when she didn't pull back, he left his hand there. He loved being the Creative Director, he thought to himself, as the group discussion shifted its focus to the causes of obesity in America.

Now a woman, the same one who had picked up the doily-wrapped Danish at the outset of the session, was speaking. "I think sometimes the ones to blame are the advertisers," she observed. "They're the ones who make all the food look so good. Sometimes when I'm watching TV, even when I'm not hungry, I find myself getting up and going right to the fridge." A few of the women in the seam-straining sisterhood nodded agreement.

"Oh you dreadful cow. Pull...ease," Cartwright felt himself pleading out loud. As soon as he made this remark he felt the young woman's leg retreat from where his hand had been resting. "It's always someone else's fault, isn't it?" With both hands now free, he wove his fingers together into a basket and delivered a loud, wince-inducing crack of his knuckles. The observers in the gloom all moaned.

Back in the conference room, the lady seated next to the one who had just spoken whispered something into her ear and, together, they both waved at the mirror. Cartwright hated the focus group professionals who knew that they were performing for an audience. "Lets be serious now ladies," the facilitator admonished. "Anyone else?"

"I think she's right," volunteered a voice from the corner of the table furthest from view. A few people behind the glass craned to try and see who was speaking. It belonged to heavy young woman who many had been speculating was pregnant. "I mean, aren't the same ones who make the commercials for McDonald's the same as the ones who sell us Weight Monitors and things?"

"I don't know, what do you think?" the researcher probed the question with another question.

"Well, aren't they?" the pudgy faced participant continued. "I bet there's some skinny people behind that mirror right now who take no responsibility whatsoever for what they do. They just see us as ... I don't know ... they just take advantage of us all the time." She welled with tears as she said this.

Ten sets of eyes now swiveled in the direction of the moderator, but in reality they were focused on the mirror beyond instead. One particularly unattractive participant actually stuck out her tongue. This set more pens scribbling among the beautiful people from Boom. But certainly, nowhere in the dark, was there a reaction that would have passed for remorse or any sense of complicity for these poor peoples' plight.

"My sister once told me that some of the fast food restaurants put things into their fries that make them addictive," volunteered a simple looking woman wearing a particularly unattractive pair of stretch pants. The telling of this popular urban myth got some more heads nodding.

"Do you really think that's true?" The moderator stood up as she asked this question and moved to the other end of the room, diverting attention from the two-way mirror. "Do you really think that food manufacturers conspire to feed us more than we really need?

"Uh huh," the woman who had made the comment about the fries responded affirmatively, while several more participants wobbled their chins in agreement. Indeed, it was quite clear that they all felt they were victims of their eating habits and they took very little responsibility for it themselves.

"Well, I think I've seen enough," the Creative Director

said standing up. "I'm not sticking around if that herd is going to stampede," he joked as he rose to his feet.

Cartwright knew there would be a detailed report published in the next couple of days. It would be the bible upon which the account planners would try and build their case for their recommended advertising strategy. Depending on how it fit with their ideas, the creatives would then either dismiss it out of hand or warp it to suit their favorite concepts. He had already instructed his producer that he wanted a ten-minute cut down from the eight hours of tape these sessions would yield on his desk by tomorrow afternoon. It would be a good presentation prop. The tape of the ladies talking about how they felt about diet products would be a powerful exhibit to support the campaign that was only just beginning to take shape in his mind.

Now as he fitted himself into his heavily zippered motorcycle jacket, he deliberately brushed his leg against the arm of the young account executive he'd been attempting to woo. She was too petrified to move and no one else was brave enough to leave with him either. Gathering his scattered notes up noisily, he bid good night to the group and quickly fled the room. As the light of the opening door swept across the faces of the team still trapped in the darkness, he couldn't help but notice a look of immense displeasure smeared across the face of Spence Playfair. "Oh, screw him," thought Cartwright to himself. "I've never seen a focus group that could write an ad or an account guy who ever had an idea that didn't come from one," he reminded himself. A glance at his watch as he escaped into the elevator revealed that he still might have time for drinks and a decent dinner. He dug out his phone to try and find a date. He hadn't been having much success lately.

ॐ

Steve Holiday searched out the light switch with his free hand
and tossed his keys on the cold granite counter of the dark and
hollow house. Peeling off his jacket he extracted his phone
and wallet from the inside pocket and dropped them next to
an unopened pile of mail. On the top of the elastic bound bundle he had retrieved on his way in tonight he couldn't help
but take in a rather urgent Final Notice on a serious looking
brown envelope. It must be getting near month-end he imagined vaguely, making note to gather everything up to leave
with the personal financial manager he had retained to help
him stay on top of things. Yet chances were he'd forget again
in the morning. The details of living alone invariably seemed
to get in the way of the unrelenting demands for his time and
he would likely have to dispatch his assistant to drop by and
do it for him—again.

It had been so much simpler when Clare was still alive.
During the time that they were together she had made everything easier. But she had been gone for nearly three years now.
Without her, even the most routine domestic chores escaped
him. It wasn't that he was absent-minded or eccentric in the
way that many people imagined creative people to be. He just
genuinely couldn't muster the energy to perform the tasks
that most adults knew were essential to managing their lives.
And it was getting worse.

It was no different at the office. Every week he was chased
ceaselessly for incomplete time sheets and billing records by
the harpies from Accounting. Just as often his expense reports
were filed months late and practically needed a forensics
expert to decipher. His wallet was regularly an uncomfortable
lump in his jeans jammed as it was with accumulating credit
card receipts. To the tormented Administration Manager who
was responsible for ensuring that this tedious accounting was
completed in a timely fashion, his apparent unwillingness to

cooperate was viewed as a sign of disrespect. She returned this perceived injustice with abiding contempt. Even though he was a principal in the firm, she had called him out a thousand times—usually with the encouragement of Ira. He had cut his friend some slack for a while, but eventually Ira decided some tough love was just what his partner needed. But the simple truth was, by the time Steve had done the meetings, worked and reworked the ads, wrangled with his department heads and reported it all back to the executive committee, he was quite thoroughly spent.

The only woman he had ever met who seemed to understand this was his wife. At least she saw how little was left of him at the end of each day. But even Clare had occasionally resented the omnipresent mistress that was his work. Once she had left him and fled back to LA, returning to work at the talent agency where he'd first met her. Leaving him had underscored the sad reality that Steve Holiday, the husband, was a disappointment. Forgotten occasions, spoiled vacations, and a million interruptions with too little left over for the two of them was not the proper foundation on which to build a successful marriage. It had taken him nearly three months to woo her home.

When she had gotten sick he had tried to be better, but there wasn't enough time left. She was gone before he could ever properly show her that she was all that really mattered in his life. Thankfully, there hadn't been children. Or at least that was how he felt until the emptiness of his current existence closed in around him. Now he shared the big townhouse they had so lovingly restored together with these regrets and Sox, their aging, overweight golden retriever. Recently, he had started paying a pretty college girl, whose name he consistently forgot, a $100 each week to walk her for him. He must remember to leave a check out for her. She'd left him a note on Tuesday … or was that last week?

Lane McCarthy pushed the last few bites of her meal listlessly around her dinner plate. Like so much that she had sampled lately, while the sole meuniere was deliciously prepared, she had immediately regretted ordering it. The remains of the decadent butter sauce that gave the mild fish its heavenly rich flavor were smeared across the handsome gold-rimmed dish and she felt a flash of remorse. For a moment the host of the business dinner feared that a stray fleck of parsley might have lodged itself in her smile. She lifted her stiff linen napkin from her lap to her mouth and gave her front tooth a discreet wipe. If only the gentleman opposite, who had barely stopped talking to breathe for the last half hour, could be disposed of so easily, she thought to herself.

She had disliked the pharmaceutical expert that Bryan Raider had introduced from the moment she shook his hand. Their working supper tonight had only confirmed her initial, unfavorable impression. Not only was he a dreadfully long-winded bore, but his patronizing manner—he was Johns Hopkins he had informed them early on—left little doubt as to his assumed intellectual superiority. There is nothing worse than a consultant who has forgotten who is paying his invoice, Lane had already reminded herself more than once. If this weren't bad enough, it appeared that Ron Pleasance, their self-proclaimed authority on 'drug pushing' as he lamely joked, had already started angling for a bonus beyond the generous hourly compensation that he was receiving should they be successful in the pitch. Steeling herself for the final dreadful stretch of the dinner meeting, Lane rejoined the conversation with a question that had been on her mind since the briefing session.

"So Ron, help me with a notion that's been troubling me for a little while now. I mean, is this chemical that Carlton & Paxton has invented a preventative or a cure?" It was a nuanced line of questioning that Lane was pursuing, but she intuitively sensed the answer was important. "Certainly, from a pure marketing perspective, I suspect it is not necessarily in their best interest to simply eradicate the problem of obesity, now is it?" she queried innocently.

As she finished the question and before Pleasance could answer, their conversation was interrupted by the rather portly waiter who had been tending to them all night. He carried with him a gorgeous platter of dessert samples and presented it temptingly even if the chore of crossing the floor had left him slightly winded. When all three of the otherwise preoccupied business people refused, he could barely hide his irritation, dismissing them with an audible huff. It was the only truly comical moment in what had, otherwise, been a very dull evening.

"I guess that all depends on your definition of a cure, now doesn't it Lane?" Pleasance continued. He had immediately taken to referring to the agency president in a far too familiar tone and she now bristled each time he spoke. "My guess is that from what you've told me so far, what they've got is some sort of impulse blocker. I suspect it only works for as long as you use the pill. They didn't say anything about it actually contributing to the dissolution of fat cells, did they?"

"Not that we heard," interjected Bryan Raider, who had been brokering the conversation and who now seemed to be sensing his boss's emerging impatience. "Why don't you tell Lane what you told me about the product you were working on before you left Brighton Labs?"

"Well, it was a few years ago now," Pleasance responded without pausing to allow Lane to evaluate whether this particular anecdote would be germane to her previous question. "But the weight control products we were attempting to design could only accomplish one objective or the other. Maybe what they've figured out at C&P is something that will do both … though that's extremely hard to imagine."

As much as she hated to, Lane now had to ask why.

"Well, think about it," Pleasance gathered breath for another gale. "Most weight control products simply work to either speed up the metabolism … fat burning. Or to suppress the appetite. In the latter case, it's actually the person who is not eating who is doing all the work. They're the ones that are starving themselves into oblivion. The trick has always been to offset the health risks that emerge from denying the body the essential nutrients it requires to function in a healthy fashion. I mean, if you want to call not eating a cure, then I guess I can agree. Otherwise its just malnutrition by another name."

"So when Corbett suggested suppression he wasn't being entirely honest?" Lane followed. "Or at least, not complete."

"Precisely. You can only fool the body into not eating for so long. But that denial cannot sustain itself in perpetuity. Somewhere along the line, there has to be a reason for the dieter to want to continue to use the product. People don't fail at diets because they don't like the results. They fail because, inevitably, the sense of deprivation overwhelms them. Surely you've been down that road at some point, haven't you Lane?'

The question was so direct and clear in its meaning that it stung. Lane shifted in her seat self-consciously and nearly let the comment pass before inquiring, "Whatever do you mean, Ronald?"

"I mean the diet thing. You know … trying to lose a few pounds?" he continued insensitively.

A few moments later Lane excused herself from the table

and for the night. She would ask Bryan Raider to fire their consultant in the morning, just as soon as she got off the phone with Reiner Adolph.

It was nearly seven when the meeting broke up and Allan Corbett was liberated from the lengthy planning session. He had wanted a drink since five o'clock and needed it badly for the better part of the last hour. He had the dull headache that usually signaled this requirement on his part and he imagined his stinging eyes were probably a little red and glassy. But each of the team leaders had been required to present a project status report. His announcement that he was conducting a review of advertising agencies for the Endrophat launch had garnered considerably more interest than he had anticipated. He'd almost taken as much flak as Harry Woodruff received when the scientist suggested he was still experimenting with the carrier compound and dosages for final release. Gathering up his notes and papers hastily at the meeting's conclusion and stopping by his office only long enough to grab his overcoat, he had quick-stepped his way to the lounge at the big hotel up the street without even bothering to call and let Helen know he'd be late getting home. Fortunately, there was nobody here that he recognized and he slid into a discreet table in the dimmest corner of the bar room alone.

The rationale for the review that he had eventually settled on had played quite well with the group of senior managers. As he explained it, for a product as important as Endrophat, they would need an agency with broad international resources. While previously Lowenstein & Holiday had represented that they had affiliations with several other agencies around the globe, in practical experience this loose network had proved to be of little real value. He had further impressed his boss, Andy Sullivan, when he told the group how he intended to bicycle the creative work and media plans that were developed for the U.S. launch to other countries as the product was introduced around the world. He even went so far as to suggest that he had already been investigating such things as talent releases and rebroadcast rights, but in truth he had been talking through his hat. This review, he explained patiently, was not personal. It was all about creating efficiency. The meeting had ended with a favorable nod from the VP of Marketing to continue working this strategy. Indeed, Sullivan had indicated that he would begin paving the way with several of his international counterparts though in reality, most of the subsidiary organizations would simply follow the American lead without question.

Now, as he mulled his performance with a deliciously icy vodka martini in hand, Corbett began to assess the impact of what had been accomplished. Clearly, it had installed M&M Interworld as the early favorite. Their agency network was almost as large as C&P itself and it had well-established capabilities in creative adaptation, translation and media buying. He also imagined that Lane McCarthy would play extremely well with his executive team once they got a good look at her. Certainly he, himself, would enjoy the prospect of a year or two of traveling the globe with the attractive agency president as his constant companion. But just as importantly, he had slid a potentially lethal torpedo into the hull of the incumbent agency. It had taken a lot of reassurance and handholding, but eventually the group had come around. He was certain that some of his colleagues were quietly doing the bidding of Ira Lowenstein and they would, no doubt, be reporting the outcome of this meeting back to him.

About the only question that still remained was what to do with Boom? He had really quite enjoyed his afternoon with Spence Playfair and the generous fellow had already followed up with an invitation to a Blackhawk's playoff game. While he wasn't much of a hockey fan, there would most certainly be pleasant cocktails beforehand and a delightful dinner to follow. Maybe there was a way he could split the assignment? It wasn't unprecedented for one agency to handle the development of creative and another to place the media. After all, Boom was the odds on favorite to develop the most exciting creative work. Perhaps he would be able to harvest the best of all worlds. It would be a tough sell internally, but then again he had been expecting a much harder buy-in this afternoon. He raised the frosted glass to his lips and allowed himself a self-satisfied smile. So far, so good.

Day 6

"Every one's just looking for a magic pill. That's the simple truth of it." Zig Cartwright made this point with his usual angry insistence. "The bloody researchers can say anything they want about ... what did those assholes say? ... the target audiences' need for esteem building and reassurance. But every fat pig I've ever seen just wants to keep stuffing her pie hole and not change her eating habits one bit." The choice of this particular piece of southern slang drew sniggers from a couple of the creatives who had been watching the heated exchange between their boss and the side led by Spence Playfair.

"For once, could someone on your team just read the goddamned research and get it," the new business officer responded icily. He pushed his hands through his hair and huffed another exasperated epithet under his breath. The junior members of the creative group searched the floor with fear and embarrassment. The argument had been going back and forth like this for nearly half an hour—ever since their boss had barged into the room uninvited.

"Jesus, Spence, I don't know why you can't control your emotions better," the Creative Director now taunted. "I mean show a little professionalism," he dug. He said it in a tone that was sure to provoke further reaction and Playfair didn't disappoint.

"Oh, fuck your hat!" Spence Playfair spat out. With this final remark he gathered his notes and pushed back from the boardroom table. "Let me know how this pointless little circle jerk turns out would you please Leslie," he instructed before storming from the meeting room.

"Don't you want to see the rest of the stuff?" Cartwright called after him sarcastically. "I certainly know I'm curious." As he said this he offered a wink to the prettiest of his young art directors causing her to redden. Then he childishly thumbed his nose in the direction of the departing executive.

Up until this point, the more experienced veterans of the process had been enjoying the spectacle of their top creative going toe-to-toe with the head suit in the animated pissing contest that had just played out before them. Some were anxious for revenge for the hastily called 'sneak peek' meeting. They had waited with considerable anticipation for the fireworks they knew would occur if Cartwright returned from lunch and found a meeting underway without him. Their boss, Ziggy, could spar with the best of them. But they also knew their delight with the show would be short lived. Most understood that the tense session was just a brief reprieve from the lashing they would receive as soon as the remainder of the account managers had been bullied from the room. Cartwright would definitely be all over them for being cowed into a premature internal presentation—especially since he had not yet reviewed all of the work himself.

That was the way the process worked at Boom. As soon as the initial executive team meeting broke, Cartwright had immediately mobilized his people on the project. They'd have a gang bang, as he liked to call it. A dozen of the best creative teams in the shop had been tossed the brief as soon as it was completed and they had been gnawing on it ever since. As was typical at Boom, a project like this came with a bounty on it. If you delivered the best idea, or at least the one that became the centerpiece of the pitch, you were suddenly the agency's hottest star. There was also usually a cash bonus or some other highly desirable perk that made it worth your while to work night and day to slit the throats of your colleagues. Indeed, shining capitalism was alive and well within the creative ranks of Chicago's hottest boutique agency.

But the internal competition on the C&P pitch was already becoming particularly brutal -- even by Boom's grim standards. Though everyone who was asked to participate went into these things with their eyes wide open, in particularly demonic fashion, Cartwright had fed each of the writer and art director pairings a slightly different version of the project brief. That was what made the process so hateful. Not only would they have to labor away at the assignment as if their very lives depended on it, but they were being conned from the very beginning. After blowing their brains out for whatever unreasonable amount of time was allowed, they then had to wait for the god-like verdicts passed by Zig Cartwright, Spence Playfair and Avery Booth. While everyone understood that you eventually had to come to Jesus with the Creative Director and get him onside with your ideas, who knew how the political winds were really blowing on this one? Remarkably, this was only day six and everyone knew that things would definitely get worse as time grew more scarce.

"Well, I'm not sure there's much point in carrying on now is there?" Cartwright mused aloud in order to break the awkward silence that had befallen the group. "You knew it was too soon for a meeting didn't you Leslie?" He asked this question without looking up from the table where he stood with his head bowed and his arms leaning hard into the cold stainless steel surface.

All eyes in the room now shifted to the next most senior representative of the Account Services group. Her name was Leslie Stride and she was Playfair's most trusted lieutenant. Earlier that day she had been dispatched to check on the progress of the pitch creative even though the summary from the focus groups had just come down. Knowing that such a review was grossly premature, Stride had timed this investigation to coincide with a lavish luncheon that was being put on by one of the big television production companies. She had been fairly confident that their Creative Director would be late returning or, if drinks were being poured, that he may not come back to the office at all. But he had surprised everyone by returning early and sober.

Though she was barely thirty years old, Leslie Stride was very much a player. She had risen like a rocket through the upstart agency since arriving as a Yale-educated intern. A strikingly attractive young woman with jet-black hair and piercing blue eyes, her sleek good looks and sharp mind were a particularly lethal combination at Boom. Among the boy men of the Creative Department who coveted her ass but who lacked the courage to pursue her, it was widely surmised that she had the mating instincts of a praying mantis—savagely biting off the heads of her lovers at the very height of her climax. To others she was known simply as The Black Widow, a nickname that had been earned by her wardrobe of dark tailored suits, skirts and dangerously spiked footwear. With little effort, Leslie Stride composed herself and responded to Zig Cartwright's challenge.

"I think what Spence is asking for is an approach that has a little more heart ... something a little more genuine." At Boom they talked about emotion like it was an ingredient that could be incorporated into an ad the way you added salt to a recipe. "I think what he heard the client say at his lunch the other day was that weight control is a very sensitive issue. I think the research report certainly confirms that as well."

"You know what I think about the research," Cartwright sneered back derisively. "Or did you forget that I was there?"

"I don't think you're being fair," Stride countered.

"When was fair ever part of it?" he responded petulantly.

"Oh, come on Zig," she sighed impatiently. "You know we were just hoping for something a little safer on this one. Not everything we do has to have an edge." She smeared the 'edge' word deliberately. She knew it was the mantra of Cartwright's creatives and she was making it clear she wasn't prepared to back down from the briefing document she had prepared. Besides, she and Spence Playfair had choreographed this precise exchange only a few hours before against this exact eventuality. Now she slipped more easily into that pre-rehearsed role knowing that sooner or later Cartwright would come around. "This is only the pitch. You heard Spence say he'd be happy to push harder once we get the business."

That was the other reality of the way new business pitches were done at Boom. Promise them anything was the easiest first step in the mating dance. Yet it was amazing how many agencies threw themselves on the sword of imagined integrity by standing resolutely by the creative work they had developed on spec. Playfair was notorious for pitching campaigns that would win the day and then switching concepts after the winner of the review had been announced in the trades. The same was true of personnel committed to new accounts and promises to stay within budget. In the honeymoon of new agency client relationships, Spence Playfair almost always ended up on top.

"Do you agree with him, Les?" Cartwright now interrogated. He seemed to be hoping that she would jump sides with Playfair out of the room, but she was far too shrewd to fall into such an obvious trap. "Do you really think we should play it safe with this one?" the CD pressed. As he spoke, his eyes narrowed to two catlike slits.

"It's not as simple as that and you know it," replied Leslie Stride. She tried it first nicely, but everyone in the room knew that the CD was testing her patience. "If you'd just pay attention to the research," she implored, returning to the document she had in front of her, and holding rank with her boss. "I think the insights are all right here."

Her pink tongue darted out quickly as she moistened a sharp-nailed index finger and quickly flipped to the middle of the bulky research report that no one but she had yet attempted to penetrate. Reading slowly for the benefit of the creatives who she doubted had even gotten past the executive summary, she delivered the statement that she and Playfair had decided must be the focus of their efforts and had highlighted with yellow marker.

"In most instances, the chronically obese feel they have little control of their eating impulses. In this respect they are little different from the alcoholic or the compulsive gambler. Therefore, any successful communications approach must be both sympathetic and engaging. It must present the solution to the user as one would offer advice to a family member or a friend."

She looked up from the large volume unblinking and braced for the challenge she was sure would come. Zig Cartwright didn't disappoint.

"What a crock of shit," the angry CD waved dismissively. "Of course we can take a look at a couple of concepts that try and take that approach, but I just don't think they're right." His posture was defiant, but something in his tone had softened. No one else in the room noticed it, but Leslie Stride allowed herself a carefully hidden smile. He would give in. He was already giving in. He just needed to show off for his people and save a little face. Ever since they had slept together, there had been a lot less fight in the previously intractable CD. Perhaps she'd have to do him again before this pitch was delivered. But for now she allowed herself to be content with this quiet victory. She gathered up her papers and signaled to the two other nervous young account executives watching anxiously that it was time to go.

"So we'll look at some more stuff in a couple of days?" she said as she reached the door. Sensing that terminating the meeting might be overstepping her bounds, she now added with a sweetness that fooled no one, "You can schedule the meeting through me and I'll try and make sure Spence is there." With that she slipped from the room, her stylish heels clapping noisily on the hardwood as she disappeared down the narrow corridor outside the meeting room.

Steve Holiday couldn't help but smile. He always did when he sat down with Evelyn and Pete to share concepts. Already there were two or three solid directions that he could take into his meeting later this afternoon and he could recommend any of them for further development without reservations. Also, Dirk Forchette their house geek, had already come up with an innovative web application that would allow users to track their weight loss on-line with a simple feedback loop that even the morons at Carlton & Paxton could get their heads around managing. It was just the kind of stuff he relied on from his top creative people. It was also the kind of work that could win a pitch if it weren't for the fact that Holiday knew they didn't really stand a chance. The incumbent almost never did in these things. Ever since Ira had gone on his rampage through the ranks of C&P, the Creative Director was even more doubtful.

He chose not to let these reservations show in his enthusiasm for the outstanding work of his favorite duo. What was the point, he thought to himself? In a little more than three weeks there would be yet another remarkable demonstration of the impressive creative firepower of Lowenstein & Holiday. Based on their knowledge of the client and the company's culture, their work would be head and shoulders above their competitors. Yet despite the quality of their efforts, Allan Corbett would poison the review panel and the agency would be fired anyways. Ignoring this ugly fact of life, he now listened to the carefully crafted ideas of the much younger writer and art director team. They had aced the problem and didn't even know it yet.

To the experienced CD such displays of talent were a source of endless delight. Even though their workload was overwhelming and the pressure to produce was intense, his best team managed to focus almost entirely on the problem at hand. It showed in the fresh thinking they had already brought to the table. He shouldn't have been surprised.

Steve Holiday had built an entire department that could face this kind of challenge unblinkingly. They would work day and night if he asked them, indeed many of them already had. Just yesterday he had looked at some truly first rate PowerPoint templates completed by the Art Department and the young kid who was apprenticing in Broadcast had done an amazing job on a rip cut that demonstrated the competitive landscape. It was an inspired piece of editing that put together nearly a thousand images of current diet advertising and the faces of the people who lived with the problem of over weight. It was cut to a powerful, upbeat piece of rock and roll that had been stuck in his head since the screening he had sat through first thing this morning. He'd been so impressed that he sent the bleary-eyed young man home to get some sleep, but he had already spied the kid back at his machine and it wasn't yet lunch. He marveled at the apparently endless energy of his youthful charges.

This was the part of the pitching process that he loved. Even though he generally hated the burlesque of new business presentations, he was always astounded by the resourcefulness of the people who inhabited the Creative Department of the agency. His agency. Though he no longer had the time to interview each of them individually, having delegated this task to his group heads, he couldn't help but smile at the similarities of his people. They were all tireless workers who were smart and resilient. And Pete and Evelyn were the best among them. He envied their ability to delve into the task and not worry about the politics swirling around them. It had been a long time since Steve Holiday had enjoyed that luxury. It had been years since it was his job simply to pull a clever headline out of the air or nail the copy in time for a ridiculously tight deadline. It made stolen minutes like the ones they were now sharing behind the closed door of his office truly special.

That was one of the enduring ironies of the business. The better you were at creating advertising, the fewer chances you actually got to do it. Instead you were swiftly promoted into the ranks of agency management. In this regard, Holiday's rise through the fool's pyramid had been nothing short of remarkable. Yet with each promotion and each new appointment, there were fewer and fewer opportunities to craft anything other than an occasional ad that would help solidify the direction for a campaign or give the young guns something to shoot at. These days his main contribution consisted mostly of being able to spot glimmers in the rough diamonds that his younger charges brought to him with apparently limitless abundance or taking bold risks staked on his hard earned reputation to ensure that the right work was sold through in client presentations. He constantly had to remind himself that this was just as valuable as the work itself. But it certainly hadn't always been this way.

When Steve Holiday had first broken into the business it was all about the work. At twenty-two years of age and just out of school he'd been identified early on as a rising star. Maybe it was just that he was naturally in tune with the yearning appetite of the American consumer, or perhaps he had simply been left alone too long in front of a television growing up, but the young copywriter found his feet in the limited-attention-span-world of advertising with very little difficulty. In five short years he had climbed from being a disposable young grunt that had begged his way into a media estimator's job to one of the Chicago scene's brightest and most promising young creative talents. Before he was thirty he had a business card with the title of Creative Director on it and had been courted by no less three of the city's largest multi-nationals. He had also turned down two invitations to come to New York in favor of his South Side roots.

Steve Holiday just couldn't imagine the coddled college interns that joined his agency today acquiring the skills of the business the way he had. Two decades before he had been schooled in the craft of this most dubious profession from a tired old hack who had mastered the art of persuasion in the catalogue department of Sears. Though a bit of a prick when he was drinking, and even worse when he was sober, his first boss Blair Creighton, remained one of the most skillful writers that Holiday had ever worked with. Usually stumbling drunk from two o'clock on, Creighton had *mentored* the unpolished but promising young Holiday through a demanding apprenticeship.

It was then, at Dunston & Kerr, that Steve had learned the discipline to focus his ideas and make every single word of his copy count. For twenty-seven interminable months the sharp red pencil of his unrelenting taskmaster had mercilessly bloodied his work. Words and phrases that he would work late into the night to compose would be hacked to ribbons by lunchtime the following day. Sometimes his copy sheets would simply be crumpled up and flung at him. Other times his writing coach would patiently deconstruct Holiday's over-elaborate concepts and pare them into concise fifty word arguments that were airtight in their purpose and intent. "Make your point and make the sale," Creighton would emphasize sounding like copy for a matchbook miracle product. "Close the goddamned deal," he would implore, entirely unselfconscious of his old school approach.

Always, it seemed, the most valuable lessons were accomplished within a razor's breadth of the insanely tight deadlines that drove the business back then. There was no Internet full of fonts or images. Layouts were rendered in marker. Type for concept roughs was hand drawn or rubbed down onto the page. The words always had to come first. Many times, with just hours or minutes remaining before materials had to go to the client's or to press, Holiday would find the work of an entire week reduced to tatters. Ten minutes later his loose ideas would magically reappear from Creighton's office tighter and more precise than the junior copywriter imagined possible. Somewhere during the endless writing and rewriting, this gift was eventually passed on to young Holiday. He promptly rewarded his patient employers by jumping at the first offer that was dangled in front of him and he had never looked back.

What a time it had been. He could still remember racing from the office to the typesetter's with last minute changes that today were easily bounced between agency and printers in seconds. More than once he had hailed a taxi while propping up a boss too drunk to stand up, but who'd somehow managed to retrieve an account-saving concept from the unfathomable depths of his whiskey-besotted brain. Along the way he had been exposed to all of the magnificent excesses and legendary characters of the Chicago ad scene—the crazy manic geniuses for which the business was a magnet back then. Steve Holiday had lived all the marvelous clichés of the wild and wonderful world of advertising in the time before the bankers gobbled up the business during the market mad nineties and ruined it. He had watched the highly skilled and disciplined European typesetters sculpt his words into documents of imperial power and majesty. He had paced anxiously while gifted illustrators and artists freehanded marker comps that were worthy of a gallery wall. It was not that he didn't appreciate the incredible speed and functionality of the desktop-dominated world that he now inhabited; it was just that it wasn't fun any more. It was as if the entire industry had traded away its soul.

Try as he might, Steve could not shed the belief that somewhere in the favoring of electrons over human contact and the trading of paper and markers for computer-generated comps, some of the magic had disappeared. With each campaign and year that passed, he could not escape the haunting notion that the ideas were just not as fresh or the turns of phrase as clever. Maybe there truly were a finite number of ideas out there and that total had been reached. Certainly nine-tenths of everything he saw these days had been done before. His encyclopedic memory of award-winning ads and art direction annuals reminded him of that. Even though he was only in his late forties, it made him feel terribly, terribly old.

At this moment Pete Zwicki was humming out the base strains of Aretha Franklin's *Natural Woman*. With each 'harrumm' that he delivered in his deep untrained baritone, the Creative Director beamed at the pair who was perched forward on the cushions of the sloppy sofa that filled a corner of his office. In her best imitation of the queen of soul, all ninety-five pounds of Evelyn Sanchez leaned into the aching lyrics. *"Oh, baby what you've done to me, you make me feel so good inside."* Holiday didn't have to pretend to be waiting on the lyrics the way his creative team had when they'd unearthed the song on iTunes. He knew all the words by heart and understood instinctively why they'd chosen it. *You make me feel so alive, you make me feel, you make me feel like a natural woman,"* Evie belted out. As she approached the song's conclusion, the pretty art director with the even prettier voice, let the final phrase fade then returned to reading her copy sheet.

"Feel good inside … Endrophat … or whatever it is we end up calling it," she quickly qualified. Before Holiday could offer a reaction, her partner Pete chimed in over top of her nervous reservation.

"What we think the song does is speak to empowerment. It says when you're in control of your weight you feel better about everything … that you're attractive." He was about to press on making his point, but the Creative Director waved him to a stop.

"I get it. I get it," he pleaded. "Is it a campaign idea or is it just a one off? As he asked the question, the young pair searched each other for an answer. Both were hastily trying to conjure the response they thought their boss was looking for. What made the two creatives so attractive was they still didn't really know just how good they were. It was part of what made working with them such a treat. Finally, it was Evie who spoke up.

"Right now I think it's just TV, but you can see where if we were able to tie up the music rights we could easily take it across to radio."

"And we could even work it into some kind of Web offer or cross-promo with I-Tunes," Pete continued to sell. "I asked Rick if he could do a preliminary costing with the music publishing guy out in LA. He said he could probably at least get us a working number by the end of the week. It's so ancient I can't imagine it will cost that much."

Again Holiday admired the thoroughness of his top team's thinking—he didn't have to waste time explaining how things worked anymore on the business side of the business. Yet in this precise moment he also knew that they would be stolen from him within the year—maybe the winner of this ridiculous charade of a pitch would even pick them off. He'd had so many of his brightest stars recruited by competing agencies over the years offering salaries and perks that were far out of line with what their emerging talents were actually worth. In some ways the outlandish offers that the poachers made flattered him as a teacher. But then would come the numbing realization that they would have to be replaced and the same groaning cycle of training fresh young creatives would have to be repeated. The thought of Pete and Evie's inevitable departure saddened him deeply.

"So have you got anything else?" he now queried. The coffee table and floor of his office were littered with quickly markered squibs and sketches. The wall above the sofa was also covered. It took the writer and art director a moment, but eventually they realized that their boss was joking and their worried looks turned quickly back to smiles.

"Honestly guys," Holiday now continued, "I'm blown away with the stuff. I think those print concepts over there are right on the mark." As he said this he gestured to a handful of roughly sketched half page sequential reveals. "And I think that work that you've done that parses the problem by age and ethnic groups is outside the box. I've also got a lot of heart for Natural Woman. By the way, it's as campaignable as anything I've seen yet, " he complimented. "Just find a cleaner link to the weight loss benefit. And we might want to check on the legal implications of saying *natural*." The pair beamed like proud children with the praise.

"I'll take all of it into my meeting with Ira this afternoon. I may even call you if you want to come in and pitch it yourselves." He knew that the team would sit on pins and needles all day at the prospect of being invited into the President's office to talk about their work. Before he could offer more feedback there was a sharp rap at the door and Marsha, his assistant, stuck her head in. "Okay kids, party's over, Mr. Holiday has to get back to work." They all smiled adoringly at the middle-aged woman who was the gatekeeper to the CD's office and trusted that she wouldn't have disturbed them if there weren't something requiring the creative head's urgent attention. Holiday knew this, too, and reluctantly declared the meeting adjourned.

They still needed a hook. That was the thought that had kept Lane McCarthy up all night and that was the impression that was with her now as she slipped quietly into the war room that had been set aside for the Carlton & Paxton pitch. As soon as they had received the briefing document she had assigned a senior creative team to the project in the vain hope that they might hit pay dirt early—nailing a strong idea before everyone got bogged down in the complex details of the presentation. Now, as she settled into a chair at the back of the room, she realized that this approach had been doomed from the start. It was increasingly becoming a problem with M&M's new business efforts. The strategy development process that had arrived with Interworld was big on research and up front thinking, but it left little room for the intuition that had been her agency's trademark prior to the merger. Too often these days her people seemed to hide behind the strategy document and appeared afraid to put something truly daring into play.

Looking at the pile of research and marketing data that

littered the table it was clear that the left-brains had won the early battle. In the week that the creative team had the brief, they had gotten no further than a few rough scribbles. From what Lane gathered in with a quick glance, their first attempts looked like every other weight loss product ad she'd ever seen. Now she had to begin the tedious process of weaning them off their initial efforts and drilling deeper into the problem. That was always the trickiest part—shooting down ideas while trying to keep everyone engaged. Best to get this debate out of the way early she resolved, though she waited a moment longer before interrupting.

Gordon Turnbull, her long time Creative Director and one of her favorite people at the agency, had the floor and was pitching a somewhat interesting twist on a before-and-after campaign. But it wasn't right. Lane knew in her bones that there was something truly different about this product—that the *before* might no longer matter. Certainly the investment C&P was planning to make suggested they knew this was more than just another diet pill. She would have to kill this approach quickly. Unfortunately, Gordon had a stubbornness that made him particularly hard to deal with if he got it in his head that this was the route to go. His doggedness, once he got behind an idea, was invaluable in bullying existing clients into sticking with an ongoing campaign. But at this stage in a pitch it was anathema.

That was one of the ironies of the ad business that Lane had always marveled at. *"There are a million solutions to any marketing problem,"* she was fond of saying ahead of presenting creative. *"Today we're going to show you three of them."* It was a line she had used with great success with their more sophisticated clients, especially the ones who understood the hopelessly subjective nature of advertising. But within the Creative Department, among those who hung their hats on distilled thinking, the thought that there might be more than one perfect solution to a task was almost incomprehensible. After banging their heads at a problem for whatever time was allowed, their final idea had a way of becoming the only conclusion possible. It was a conceit she had always found difficult to swallow, especially when dealing with the amazingly talented inhabitants of the most important department of her agency. Despite their reaching imaginations and innate creativity, sometimes they could be so frustratingly narrow-minded.

"Gordon," she finally interjected. She caught him in mid-explanation of how they could use a cool new computer-generated morphing technique to not just show the before and after effects of Endrophat, but also every stage in between. "Gordon, don't you think people are sick to death of this sort of stuff? You know, the miracle pill approach," she assessed bluntly. "I mean … doesn't your bullshit needle redline the minute you hear anything that sounds like it might have come out of the pages of the Enquirer." It was a deliberately tough jab.

"I don't really think that's what's happening here Lane," he countered defensively. "I think the idea behind this approach is that the effects of Endrophat are truly transformational. If we wrapped it in some pseudoscience and delivered it with a sisterly female voiceover, I'm sure it would cut the clutter with its visual impact alone."

Lane studied him carefully as he spoke these words and knew he really didn't believe them. She figured he'd just as likely fallen in love with the demo reel from the animation house or its pretty sales rep and was hoping to be among the first to bring their newest technique to market. If you got on the bandwagon soon enough, execution could sometimes pass for an idea.

"Come on Gordon," Lane prodded, "I just don't think that's going to be what turns on Mrs. Overweight America. And it sure isn't sexy enough to win us the business."

It was early on in the process and Lane knew she could still shame her Creative Director into searching further. He was just being lazy. It was an accusation that was being leveled at him all too often these days. She also knew that Gordon was desperately trying to protect a week's vacation at his retreat in Aspen. Sadly, he was unaware that his name was at the top of the list of changes that had been suggested during her meeting in New York. Unfortunately, if he were bounced he would land hard. Nobody wanted intelligent, well-considered fifty-something creatives anymore. He'd be in trouble even if he were ten years younger. These days all of M&M's clients seemed to want someone twenty years old, arrogant and edgy. It was everything that Gordon Turnbull wasn't. So far she had not had the courage to share this news with her friend.

"It was just a first attempt," Gordon now relented. "I think there might still be some other great stuff on the wall," he said drawing her attention to the pile of straw dogs that had been tacked up on the corkboard as a prelude to the idea he was currently pushing. Lane let him save his dignity with a passive retreat. Both of them knew that what had already been reviewed and rejected was crap.

"Why don't you go back at it for another day or two? We'll regroup on Friday … ahead of the weekend … and then we'll see where we're at." From the way she said it Lane made it clear that she was expecting everyone to be in on Saturday and Sunday to work on the pitch. The mention of it caused Gordon's shoulders to sag. There were only three weeks to go until presentation day, but that time would disappear in the hectic din of trying to cobble together finished comps and mock TV spots. Plus there was the media plan and the obligatory strategic deck to prepare. His vacation was lost. As always, he had briefly hoped that they would land on a creative direction early, but it seldom worked out that way. In the elephant hunt of searching for big advertising ideas, the first one to come along was seldom still alive on presentation day.

"Thank you ... all of you," Lane added inclusively as she extricated herself from the stuffy room that reeked of Sharpie markers and Benfang tissue. She knew that as soon as she closed the door there would be some bitching and complaining. But she also knew she was right to put a fork in that concept early on. You could sell that kind of shit to existing clients, but you couldn't get away with it in new business. Besides, the team from New York would be arriving soon enough. It would be nice to have something decent on the table to show them.

She had pretty much decided she couldn't put off contacting Reiner Adolph any longer. She had also confirmed that Lowenstein Holiday was still in the hunt. A rumor had been making the rounds that they were poised to pull out. Part of her had been secretly hopeful that they would withdraw from the review and that M & M would have at least a coin toss of a chance. She had smelled some tension during the briefing session and the trade mags had also been full of speculation. But who could afford to walk away from a hundred and fifty million dollar contract these days? They would be there until the bitter end. And of course, Boom struck terror into everyone—New York included. She checked her watch and bustled after her next appointment. It was somewhere between the defeated meeting room and the elevator that an extraordinary notion crossed her mind.

Day 7

Nervously extracting the wisp of cotton that blocked its narrow neck, Lane McCarthy rattled a single pill from the amber-tinted prescription bottle into her palm. The tablet was smaller than what she had imagined it would be. The magic powder in which Carlton & Paxton had invested so enormously had been compressed into a small diamond shaped prill, its edges beveled for easy ingestion. A minute 20 mg symbol had been embossed in the chalky pink surface, as had a logo, along with a thin line girdling its circumference that suggested the pill could be divided into two equal sized portions. The briefing document had suggested that the final manufactured product would be individually packaged in a blister of foil to protect the drug from oxygen degradation. This was the assumption that her design team had been working with to develop the loose renderings that stood on the ledge opposite her desk. But the artists had also obviously imagined that the individual tablets would be somewhat larger and this would have to be addressed if they were going to take any of these packaging ideas into the final presentation.

She'd had quite a difficult time coaxing this bottle of samples from their prospective client. In fact, Lane wasn't entirely certain that the pills that she now held in her hand weren't in reality just some kind of placebo that had been dispensed in the hope of quieting their persistent requests. There really was no reason to expect that the actual product would be supplied to M&M at this stage in the process. When her dogged assistant had finally given up after a futile afternoon's pursuit, it was Lane who had figured out what might get them what they were after. Waiting until after hours, she had dialed directly into Harry Woodruff's office voicemail and left a breathy message explaining that they desperately needed precise samples in order to manufacture meaningful packaging prototypes and that she would most certainly take the intervention of such an important and busy man as a personal favor. This morning a couriered package with an unsigned covering note had mysteriously appeared. Now Lane had in her possession what she hoped were some of the very few samples of the new wonder drug ever to have escaped the tight security that had surrounded every phase of the project at Carlton & Paxton. She was also pretty sure that the same opportunity hadn't been extended to any of her competitors.

Holding the small pill between the thumb and index finger of her impeccably manicured hand, she held it at half an arm's length to study it more carefully. After staring at it for a long minute, she passed the tiny tablet slowly back and forth beneath her nose and tried to take in its scent. All this revealed was the antiseptic odor of the laboratory in which the drug had been developed and the pleasant smell of her very expensive moisturizing lotion. While Allan Corbett had indicated that the active ingredient was derived from a natural process, the pill that she was now studying so intently had clearly been through a refining process that married it together with additional carriers that would aid with the drug's efficient absorption into the bloodstream. She knew this from experience the agency once had with the manufacturer of a pain reliever. Lane was also fairly certain that the chemical itself had now been successfully synthesized in a way that would enable it to be mass-produced. One of the witty young copywriters had teased that the secret ingredient was likely extracted from the balls of a bat or some other ungodly source and had worked up a mock storyboard of its discovery in a remote cave deep in jungles of Peru. But the sterile substance she now contemplated gave no clues of such an origin.

Having satisfied herself that the pill was not going to be difficult to swallow, she now tested its taste with the tip of her tongue. Nothing. A dose of Endrophat would have none of the barnyard-like taste of so many of the nutritional supplements and all-natural vitamins that many dieters were required to ingest. She mentally chided herself to purge the word *diet* from her vocabulary. As Dr. Woodruff had suggested at the briefing," This is not a diet pill." He had made the point strenuously. "It is a psychotropic drug that manages the interface between the brain and the body's physiologically driven impulses to eat." To let the word diet slip out in the final presentation meeting would be death if the C&P scientist were part of the review team, as Lane suspected he would be.

It was this eventuality that Lane was betting on as she stared at the tiny wonder drug. How would the review team from Carlton & Paxton react if she admitted to trying Endrophat herself? Would they be shocked at her recklessness or impressed with the courage such a bold gesture required? Certainly her confidence might earn favor with the scientist. That was the idea that had occurred to her the other day. Wouldn't it be fantastic, she had decided, if she were to make a guinea pig of herself and be able to comment first hand on the effects and performance of the drug.

Actually, it hadn't been that big of a leap. After all, didn't they do this all the time on other new business pitches? When they were chasing a major hotel chain, she'd had everyone on her pitch team check-in for a week and sample the services. When they were in pursuit of National Discount Airlines they had flown the low-cost carrier from one end of the country to the other. Routinely, whenever the agency needed to gather quick customer insights, they would distribute samples to friends and family and ask for their candid feedback. How was this any more unusual, she had debated with herself. It was the same, only different, she had concluded once her mind was made up.

To reinforce her decision she'd read and re-read the comments of respondents in the report from the Alpha and Beta clinicals that Carlton & Paxton had included with the brief. Most of the reactions were overwhelmingly positive. Many women even seemed to enjoy the experience based on their diary comments. Plus the Client had been emphatic that the drug had passed through Phase I testing without evidence of any noticeable side effects even if final Phase II results were still pending. In this respect she was practically certain that the product was entirely safe. This was no Jekyll and Hyde act she was contemplating. This was just smart business, she'd finally convinced herself. And, hell, what if it really did work? She had already allowed herself to imagine that she would look fabulous if she were able to shed ten or fifteen pounds by presentation day and had already picked out a prospective new suit. She scolded herself for this vanity and focused on steeling her resolve to sample the still experimental drug.

"It is now or never," she whispered aloud. With a final moment's hesitation and a nervous swallow she at last drew the pill to her lips. Tamping the tiny tablet onto her suddenly parchment-dry tongue, she flushed it down with a gulp of water that allowed no room for second-guessing. In that moment, for the first time, Lane allowed herself to believe that Endrophat might actually be the miracle its inventors promised it would be. It must be, she rationalized. After all, the giant pharmaceutical conglomerate was preparing to invest millions of dollars in its production and promotion. Indeed, they already had. And yet, like so many women before her, she struggled to ignore the demons of past diet failures and disappointments. She remembered the lonely battles she'd fought with her own mirror and the feelings of betrayal that had accompanied the inevitable defeats.

But what if this really was the solution? What if this was finally the answer that would allow all of womankind to never again have to battle the natural, healthy impulse to eat? It could be as liberating as birth control, maybe even more so. She allowed herself a moment of schoolgirl hope and then tried to visualize the pill arriving in the dark unimaginable regions of her stomach. She waited for some sort of reaction— a confirmation of its arrival. There was nothing but a gentle murmur easily attributable to the breakfast she had skipped that morning and a vague awareness of the hard dry pellet deep within. Apparently, she would have to be more patient for the appearance of a sign.

The single file line of visitors snaked its way through the maze of cubicles that crowded the Creative Department's portion of Boom's stylish office space looking terribly out of place in their Dockers and buttoned down Oxford shirts. Carlton & Paxton's attempt at workplace casual was so obviously out of place here that it caused the younger members on Allan Corbett's team to feel acutely self-conscious. The bohemian inhabitants of the agency's most stylish quarter, with their studied avant-garde apparel, did little to alleviate this discomfort. If it was 'fit' that the members of the review team were looking for, there was little chance of finding it here. If the visitors had been hopeful of getting a feel for who might actually work on their account, any such illusions had been quickly dashed. In the simplistic view of the busy young people from the agency with urgent work to complete, the visitors from the billion-dollar-a-year advertiser were just another unwelcome interruption. In the absence of any interaction between the two factions, the tour progressed quickly and quietly.

At the head of the procession Spence Playfair held the elbow of his most honored guest, ushering Allan Corbett gently forward while pointing broadly at the colorful posters and award certificates that lined the walls. At the back of the queue Leslie Stride performed a rear guard action ensuring that none of their guests from the pharmaceutical company were exposed to the rude salutes and childish expressions that the petulant adolescents from the agency offered behind their backs. She accomplished this with an array of steely stares and whispered threats quietly hissed in their directions. Even with the obvious importance of the opportunity, it was an uneasy peace.

The unruly crew from Boom was particularly resentful of the clean-up order that had been circulated by e-mail the day before. Such memos invariably upset the intense young artists who thought little of burying themselves in the residue of their work. Even though crumpled papers had littered the hallways and food scraps and unwashed dishes were piled up on every ledge and flat surface, they took little notice of their mess. During especially busy periods, like the one in which the agency now found itself, the workstations and meeting rooms belonging to the Creative Department often resembled the untidy bedrooms of teenagers which of course, so many of them, had just recently been.

Leslie Stride had demanded that order be restored and it had been an extremely unpopular request. However, as if to prove her point, during the grudging clean up at the end of the previous day, a multitude of horrors had been unearthed. At one point a dehydrated dog turd had even been swept from beneath a desk. Apparently Churchill, the print production manager's aging bulldog that occasionally accompanied his master to the office on weekends, had deposited a pile there. Its discovery and subsequent disposal had resulted in much childish squealing and other foolishness among the cleanup detail.

As had been arranged earlier, Zig Cartwright and a small team of his most presentable personnel waited in the Creative Director's office—a staged meeting having been hastily choreographed for benefit of the client tour. But until the visitors actually arrived, the shaggy assemblage fiddled anxiously. Seated on their boss's pillowy couch, two of them playfully poked at each other and a third scoured the cracks in the cushions for loose change. Just as calculatedly, a big sheaf of concept squibs had been scattered casually across Zig's desk and allowed to spill onto the floor. On display was a set of fairly ancient roughs from one of Boom's most famous campaigns. They had long ago been mothballed in the agency's archives, but Spence Playfair had ordered them resurrected for this special occasion. It was always useful to remind prospective clients of the brilliant work that the agency had manufactured on behalf of others. The group had been charged with demonstrating a mock brainstorming session—ostensibly to develop the next ad in the popular, long running series. But in reality it was just a hoax and a chance to show off some more of the agency's award-winning work.

Just as Playfair had promised, at eleven-thirty sharp the group arrived on the Creative Director's threshold. A group of spies down the hallway had signaled the tour group's pending arrival moments before and now the faux work session was in full swing. Most of the players mugged hopelessly and overacted self-consciously. But enough of the group was managing to put on a believable front. Playfair rapped on the stainless steel frame of the glass block wall that surrounded Zig Cartwright's workspace and bent his head inside.

"I hope I'm not disturbing anything too important," he boomed in an overfriendly way that suggested a much healthier rapport with the Creative Director and his people than had ever existed. Ordinarily, the surly creatives would have ignored this kind of intrusion or rebuffed it with the variety of rudely dismissive tactics that they reserved especially for the Account Services group. "… but I've got some people I really would like you to meet." He said this with near breathless excitement while making a sweeping gesture toward the curious assemblage who now crowded over his shoulder.

On cue Zig Cartwright swung his feet off his desk—a calculatedly relaxed pose he had struck to make this important first impression. With his eyes lit by a merry twinkle, he smiled engagingly at Allan Corbett and the other onlookers who had crowded into the opening to catch a peek of the place where the famous creative company worked its magic then sprang to his feet to extend a hand. By prearrangement Playfair had his arm draped over the senior client's shoulder to make him easy to identify. Though he hated to admit it, even by the new business development officer's high standards, Zig was a damned convincing bullshit artist.

"You must be Allan Corbett," the Creative Director beamed. "Spence and Leslie have told me so much about you," he fawned. "It's nice to finally get a chance to make your acquaintance." Before the senior client could respond, he poured on another dripping unction. "I must say, I thought your briefing the other day was just brilliant."

On that afternoon at C&P, Cartwright had elected to skulk in with the rest of his team and thereby avoid the crowded, inauspicious introduction that Corbett's session seemed to afford him. His vanity precluded him being mentioned in the same breath as the cadre of junior account execs who had also been present and introduced that day.

"I only hope the work we develop for you will be just as worthy," he added with feigned humility.

Corbett acknowledged this bow of obeisance with an indifferent nod. He had certainly been around long enough to smell its insincerity and he reminded himself that he would have to get used to many more such supercilious compliments as the review process unfolded. Good manners and the newness of the acquaintance prohibited him from offering back the sarcastic response that had immediately crossed his mind. Instead, he answered with his own unblinking rejoinder.

"I'm certain that you will. In fact, I'm counting on it," was all he said. The directness of the response, delivered without even a trace of a smile, caught Cartwright a little off balance. All he could manage was a polite chuckle in return. When Corbett's gaze wandered to the other people who were sprawled about the Creative Director's office, Zig shot an angry look toward Playfair.

"Guys," he now directed toward his people. "I'm afraid I'm going to have to excuse myself from our little session. I've been looking forward to meeting these folks all morning," he gushed. In truth, Zig Cartwright had never excused himself for anything since he'd arrived at Boom. "Do we have that show reel we put together for these nice people?" he asked of a young art director perched on the arm of his couch. Without having to search too hard, he located the disk beneath the tissued rough of a famous One Show award winner and tucked it under his arm along with a notebook.

With Corbett's team still peering curiously around the corner, the group inside Cartwright's comfortable enclosure rejoined their animated discussion of a rough layout that was spread out on the coffee table in front of them. Sensing the eagerness of the C&P people to engage, they looked up and flashed their most winning smiles. But then just as quickly, they returned to the faux dialogue of their imaginary meeting. They had hit their intended marks like expert performers in a well-rehearsed play. The little show was just as tightly blocked as the thirty second television commercials they scripted and they projected it with a nearly perfect blend of personality and professionalism. Even Leslie Stride, who had staged these pseudo-spontaneous encounters a hundred times, had to concede it almost felt like there was a flicker of connection. She would be sure to pass along plenty of bon mots later.

"I have to apologize for my people. As you can see, we're chasing a bit of a deadline here. We'll never have that challenge working with you guys, now will we?" Zig kidded. As he made this last presumptive remark, he playfully squeezed the shoulder of one of Allan Corbett's more junior people. In practice, this was the kind of young client that Cartwright savagely bullied and then squashed like an insect. "Why don't we all go down the hall and have a peek at some work that I think you will enjoy, eh?"

No sooner was the word 'enjoy' out of Zig's mouth than a delicious gust of garlic-scented smoke arrived in the corridor. Further down the hall there was the sudden, unmistakable hiss of meat being tossed onto a fiery hot grill. It immediately seized the lunch-ready entourage's attention and set their stomachs rumbling. Proceeding down the long hallway toward the office's main boardroom, they were treated to a glimpse of Boom's stylish corporate kitchen where luncheon preparations were busily under way. In anticipation of the tour, the agency's talented in-house chef was preparing an exquisite Mediterranean-inspired spread of lamb chops and lentils. It was one of the more decadent perks that the agency used to ply longer hours from its employees and to win favor with prospective clients. The tantalizing smells emanating from this unlikely source regularly drove everyone in the office wild and today's feast promised to be even more delicious than usual. The hungry visitors from Carlton & Paxton, who routinely arrived at their offices by eight each morning, were fairly salivating with anticipation. They easily surrendered any flicker of jealousy they might have possessed to the promise of the fantastic repast ahead. The deal was sealed completely when they heard the unmistakable clink of a couple of bottles of white burgundy that were being loaded into a dewy, ice-crowned chiller that stood waiting to be wheeled into the boardroom.

"Maybe we can all share a bite of lunch after the presentation," Playfair now interceded. While he couldn't quite put his finger on it, he had been a little disappointed with the initial chemistry between Cartwright and Corbett. Maybe it was nothing. Perhaps it could be worked out over lunch or drinks later, if their prospective client was willing? He resumed his place at the head of the column and urged everyone forward in the direction of their intended destination. "I believe our President, Avery Booth, is going to join us a little later on, too."

It had been nearly a week since Ira Lowenstein had treated himself to a cigar. It was an indulgence he typically reserved for victory parties, the arrival of babies, and other special occasions around the office. It was why he'd had his office equipped, at great expense, with an air exchanger that vented all the way to the very top of the building—still another ten stories above. This was a concession he had negotiated from his landlord with renewal of their lease and the subletting of yet another floor and a half during an expansion just last year. L&H now occupied eight full stories of the soaring downtown skyscraper. Sometimes the scale of this commitment frightened him. After all, beyond his people and the accounts they managed, the company really had very few tangible assets.

This afternoon, with his door closed and the day winding down, the agency president found himself feeling the pull of the fresh box of fat Cubans that he had deposited into his humidor prior to all of this Carlton & Paxton nonsense. He might even pour himself a stiff brandy to go along with it, he allowed himself, after he'd made up his mind to indulge in a smoke. He knew he had a delicious old cognac locked up in the bar that was discreetly hidden from view in a hand-painted Tansu chest over which hung a handsomely engraved Samurai sword purchased from the props of a once popular TV show. The way things had been going lately, he had absolutely no reservations about drinking alone. With very little provocation he could probably also be encouraged to use the razor sharp saber that adorned the wall on a client or two. He peeled off his headset and stood up and covered the distance from his desk to his private reserve in three quick steps.

For the most part, while he had nearly come to terms with the fact that the Endrophat review would proceed, Ira had by no means conceded defeat. Accepting this reality had left him in a particularly foul mood and with very little patience to suffer some of the fools that still surrounded him. Indeed, it was this irritation that had caused him to reverse course and have Darden Jennings forcibly removed from the office this very same morning. It had been accomplished with great ignominy. At nine-thirty, shortly after everyone had arrived, the disgraced account manager had been escorted to the elevators by a professional de-hiring consultant and a uniformed security guard. It wasn't that Ira feared violence or any other untoward behavior on Jennings' part. Instead, it was simply the keen desire on his part to make a powerful statement that he would tolerate no further ineptitude. Making a scapegoat of Jennings was merely the last necessary gesture to ensure that his company would rebound from its current situation. It was the final ugly act of a week in which, even he would concede, he had behaved atrociously. He poured two fingers of the chestnut brown liquor into the wide mouthed crystal snifter and then topped it with another heavy splash.

In this regard, the President of Lowenstein & Holiday was strictly old school. Ira took the business of losing business very personally. The thought of giving up millions of dollars in revenue, with the corresponding loss of people and projects, kindled an angry fire deep within him. Who was going to pay for the layoff packages if C&P were to walk? How would they cover the rent on the surplus space they had taken until replacement business could be found? And that wasn't taking into account the damage that this undeserved review had already done to his agency's otherwise spotless reputation. The last thing he needed now was a run on the bank, which was always the risk when a large account departed. That they should suddenly find themselves so threatened by an annoying little worm, such as he regarded Allan Corbett to be, was doubly galling. So for the past seven days, with this dark cloud over his head, Ira had been cruelly torturing everyone attached to the Carlton & Paxton debacle. And anyone else who dared cross his path with anything other than good news.

This was the inherent contradiction of the man. On some levels Ira Lowenstein was as gracious a gentleman as had ever inhabited the advertising business. Not only did he captain one of the city's most accomplished and respected agencies, but he had also founded the local chapter of the industry benevolent society. Indeed, the countless stories of troubled former employees and struggling colleagues he had rescued from the brink were legendary. Just as laudatory were the generous gifts that he donated to at least a dozen worthy causes.

He raised money for underprivileged kids, he sold out the opera and, every year, he ensured that his people gave just as freely of their time and talent. A local charity group had recently nominated him as their Man of the Year for his pro bono work on their behalf. He returned to his desk and put his feet up. With a free hand he leaned over and extracted a heavy crystal ashtray from a lower drawer. Then he struck a single wooden match to the side of the hollow sounding box and puffed his fat brown turd of tobacco to life.

But there was another side to Ira Lowenstein—one that was decidedly darker. As he had once laughingly commented to a nodding audience of industry peers at a national agency conference, you could not become the head of a half-billion dollar enterprise that lived by its wits alone without occasionally being the meanest son of a bitch in the valley, too. And so he was from time to time. When he was cornered he was a vicious street fighter—prepared to do whatever was necessary to outmaneuver his opponents. When at times in the past the agency had encountered adversity, it was he who reached deepest and fought hardest to ensure they ended up back on top—Steve Holiday included. Sometimes this determination bred anger and resentment, but more than once he had literally raised the company from the dead by the sheer force of his own relentless fear of failure. Other times he had rescued it by inspiring a near-messianic sense of devotion.

It was this quixotic combination of strength and charisma that enabled Ira to hold the many strong personalities and egos that came with the business in check. When called upon, he could be a masterful conciliator able to broker the most unlikely relationships. In other situations, he was as divisive a force as had ever headed an agency. Right now, he knew that all of these skills would be required if his agency was going to pull off a save against the daunting odds that Allan Corbett had stacked against them. He took a full swallow of the ancient amber contents from the voluminous crystal balloon and then swirled it again contemplatively.

After a few days of considering their current situation, Ira was nearly certain that his tormentor had made the mistake of underestimating both the agency and his standing within his own organization. For a man as vulnerable as Allan Corbett, these could be fatal mistakes. While the rest of L&H was now preoccupying itself with the mad scurry of the review assignment, Ira was quietly formulating a plan of his own. Heretofore, the avaricious ad manager had only been exposed the generosity and bonhomie that Ira typically showered on his most valued clients. But the miscalculating fool from Carlton & Paxton would soon see a side of the agency president that he had not encountered before—and it would be an experience he would not likely soon forget.

What Allan Corbett had misjudged was both the rancor and reach of his adversary. How could he possibly think that the great Ira Lowenstein would stand by and allow someone to plunder his kingdom? He was a powerful man with influential friends and a bankroll of favors that could be called upon from every corner of the industry. For nearly thirty years he had shrewdly cultivated a network of friends and allies that could be pulled in for precisely the purpose he had in mind. You definitely didn't want to mess with Ira Lowenstein. After a futile week of trying to contact Corbett's boss, Andy Sullivan, he now had little choice but to reach even higher into the C&P organization. With as many phone calls he had arranged to meet with two of Carlton & Paxton's most influential independent Board members. If necessary, he could probably conscript even more help over the next few weeks.

But until then, Ira would have to be content with allowing the pitch to move forward and letting Max Weller get down to work. While he hadn't heard anything yet, he had a get together scheduled with the private investigator early next week. He already had his own suspicions about Allan Corbett, but you just never knew what else a slimy sleuth like Weller might unearth. When his intercom buzzed, his first inclination was to ignore it. But then he remembered the request that Steve had made of him earlier. He drained the remainder of the brandy in a single swallow and set the glass down hard on his paper-strewn desk.

"I'll be down in a minute," he answered huskily as the smoky liquor burnt its way down his throat. Whatever happened, he reminded himself, there were always a few more cards to be played. He knocked the glowing ember from the tip of his cigar into the waiting ashtray. This thing was a long way from over just yet.

"I hate it. Do you want to know why?"

The bluntness of the comment startled the group who, until Ira had joined them in their late afternoon meeting, had been enthusing excitedly about the concept that Steve Holiday had just shared.

"I don't know Ira … do we really want to?" Holiday now asked back. He was the only one in the room with the courage to question Ira's rude assertion. With a challenge issued to explain his criticism, every head in the room now turned in the direction of the agency President.

"It's simple, really. Advertising alone isn't going to sell Endrophat." He was being deliberately inscrutable and he paused on the group's collective puzzlement before continuing.

"Do you not understand that this could well be one of the

most startling inventions in the history of the world? Think about it," he commanded. "Why on earth would you use the tried and true to sell something so remarkable and new?"

Steve Holiday had been about to wade in with a defense of the idea that Evie and Steve had come up with, but as usual, his partner's coldly delivered insight had pierced the soul of the argument he intended to make and he was immediately taken aback. "I'm sorry?" he asked for clarification.

"It's got to be more different ... the whole goddamned campaign. It can't be just ads," Ira declared in case there was any doubt as to his meaning.

It was the kind of blunt criticism that his partner seldom ventured, but when he did, it needed to be acknowledged. While he and Ira had long ago agreed that he would make the ads and Ira would run the business, his associate of nearly twenty years was rarely off the mark on matters of strategy. And this was a fundamental strategic issue.

What Ira had just so brilliantly proposed had eluded virtually everyone as they rallied eagerly around the first set of executions that his best team had developed. Even though he had initially been encouraging, Steve's inner voice had already told him that something wasn't right—that the work, however fresh and original, was off the mark. He was immediately grateful that he had left his two young charges out of this executive session. Though he hated to admit it, it meant that everything that they had worked on for the past week was going to be flushed. Somewhat strangely, he felt relieved—even if it meant starting over again from scratch.

"So let me get this straight, Ira. What you are suggesting is that we need an advertising campaign that isn't advertising?" While many in the room were still uncomprehending, Steve had gotten it immediately.

"Precisely. Other than that, I don't know what the fuck I mean. All I know is that the minute whatever we say about

Endrophat starts to sound like another miracle product from the fine folks at Carlton & Paxton, any chance we've got to spike sales of this shit through the roof are diminished by half. Don't you see that guys?" he implored toward the blank stares of the others.

"So you're thinking PR then?" questioned the Media Director. The most accomplished senior woman in the company, Julia Hemmings had an amazing ability to crunch numbers and was a ruthless negotiator. Even after the consolidation of most media into bulk buying conglomerates, many Lowenstein & Holiday clients preferred her tough-minded, strategic approach to media planning. "But come on Ira ... I mean it's a hundred and fifty million?" she reminded.

"That's not what I'm saying Julie. I'm just saying that, however we plan to launch this product, we can't get hung up in the same tried and true formulas we've used in the past. Maybe we could get the goddamned President and the FDA to hold a joint fucking press conference. I don't know. That's what I pay all you geniuses for, isn't it?"

As usual, it was now Steve Holiday who had to make the peace. As much as he hated to consign all of the work that had been done to date to the scrap heap, he let it go in a single remark.

"I think Ira's right," he capitulated. As he said this, he tried his best to ignore eye rolls of the team from account services and the barely concealed exasperation of Toby Meyer and the other two creative group heads present. They clearly resented him for what they imagined was bending over for Ira. But the truth was, they just didn't get it. All they could think of was the deadline, the budget and their own selfish requirements. It was far too early in the game to concede that 'good enough was good enough'.

As inevitably happened with the most difficult assignments, somehow the weight of the entire effort had now slid squarely back onto Steve Holiday's tired shoulders. Hiding somewhere out there was a solution they hadn't yet thought of. Goddamn the muse can be elusive, he thought to himself.

"Let's try again people," he instructed the group as yet another meeting ground to its unsatisfying conclusion. "Let's plan to get together ... same time tomorrow."

Day 8

The teleconference with Reiner Adolph was every bit as unpleasant as Lane imagined it would be. Having misjudged the time difference between Chicago and Stuttgart, she had managed to catch the Chairman of Interworld PLC as he was hurtling along the autobahn at the end of a particularly difficult day for the overleveraged investor. Had she seen what the markets had done to them that day, he had inquired agitatedly. "They slammed us on the Footsie and that downward momentum spiraled all the way to New York. We lost nearly a hundred million," he announced before she could speak. Adolph expected all of his global executives to track the price of Interworld stock as closely as he did, even though it had nothing do with the business of advertising. He was especially hard on his most recent acquisitions, somehow holding them responsible for the enormous debt that made the pain of market gyrations particularly acute. Despite his professed fondness for her, Lane now definitely fell into this category.

"I'm afraid I haven't seen a report all morning," she was forced to confess. She wasn't sure whether the pause that followed was a bi-product of their transatlantic connection or some other judgment her boss was making. "But I do have some very good news," she found herself yelling as she imagined the inattentive executive weaving through traffic at high speed while ignoring the hands free feature of his overpowered Benz. One of the most harrowing drives she had ever experienced was with Reiner Adolph behind the wheel during the early days of their corporate courtship. That was when he had been trying to be on his absolute best behavior. She could only imagine his driving on a day when the misfortune merchants had battered his company.

"What good news?" he questioned, his clipped German-accent made him sound even more remote and intimidating than usual.

"We're short-listed on Carlton & Paxton ... a hundred and fifty million special project." Lane telegraphed this as if she, too, were hurtling along the lawless concrete super highway. "Just two other shops and us."

"What kind of product?" The international advertising agency's CEO's first question betrayed a worry as to whether there would be conflicts with any of the company's other clients. In the age of globalization, such conflicts were becoming increasingly commonplace and just as difficult to manage.

"Pharma ... weight control," was Lane's short reply. "I did a quick scan of the international roster last week and it looks like we're clean." As soon as she said it, she bit her lip and hoped Adolph wouldn't pick up on the glaring mistake she had just made. Unfortunately, he was much too smart—even while driving at two hundred kilometers per hour.

"What do you mean 'last week', Lane darling? You haven't been sitting on this for that long have you?" The way he asked this question suggested that he was already aware—that he was past any anger and was just toying with her. She could tell he was measuring his tone, uncertain whether he should congratulate her or issue the stern rebuke that she knew she deserved. "You know how I hate it when I'm the last to know? Something like this could have really helped us today," he chided. He was quite right. The market in advertising company stocks traded on rumors like this and the mention of C&P might have provided a nice lift.

"I'm sorry. It only just became clear that we're actually in," she lied. "I didn't want to bother you until I was certain. But we've taken the briefing and it's for real," she tried to explain. "The trouble is it's on a ridiculously tight fuse."

"How long?"

"Three weeks … a little less actually," she confessed.

Again there was an uncomfortable pause as her bondholder weighed whether or not to torture her some more.

"I expect you're going to need some help. New York or London?" Adolph offered the two choices like dueling pistols or her preference for a means of execution.

Now it was Lane's turn to weigh her options. The team from New York was difficult and arrogant. She'd done a DM project early last year with the Brits that had been quite successful, but their ad guys were famous company-wide for being awful. It was the devil she knew versus the devil she didn't. At least the New York boys would save her some travel expenses.

"If it's okay, I'd like to go American on this. The guy who's running the pitch over here is a bit of a loose canon. I think I can handle the relationship stuff but I'm going to need help … "

"With creative?" Adolph anticipated before she could finish her sentence. Lane swallowed hard knowing that an answer in the affirmative was effectively the end of her loyal friend Gordon Turnbull.

"Maybe just a team or two … some fresh thinking. We've got the legs here on the ground to do most of the heavy lifting." She certainly made no mention of her own reckless plan.

She still hadn't figured out exactly how it fit into the presentation. But then she probably wouldn't know that until the very day she revealed what she had been up to.

"I'll talk with Jeremy tonight," Adolph volunteered. Jeremy Whithers was the head of the New York office and he was definitely on ass-kissing terms with his CEO. He would be salivating at the chance to swoop in and save the day and then funnel the work and fees into his office at the first opportunity. "Give me a couple of hours. Then perhaps you can follow up with him before the end of your day. Anything else?"

Lane knew exactly what was dangling with the question, but she couldn't bring herself to accede. Reiner Adolph was waiting for her to invite him to participate. Pride and her certainty of the circus this would create caused her to go quiet. There was not a chance in hell she could afford to reveal this evil avatar of international advertising to the fine mid-western folks of Carlton & Paxton.

"I don't think so, Reiner. Thank you so much." She performed this homage as sweetly as she could in the hope that he would choose to ignore the obvious slight. "I'll keep you posted." As she finished her final bow, the phone went silent making it clear that he had already signed off.

"Okay, what do we really know about the overweight in America?" Steve Holiday asked the group again. "I mean can we separate the facts from the myths. It seems to me if we're going to crack this thing we have to understand the difference between just being, say overweight, and being truly obese. Has anyone done any research?"

It was typical of how the Creative Director of Lowenstein & Holiday liked to tackle a problem. After letting everyone on the team regroup overnight, he was anxious to see if anyone had managed to come up with another insight or was holding back on an idea they thought was too foolish to share earlier. Sometimes the spark for an entire campaign could come from the most outlandish or ridiculous notion. He had already apologized to the group at the outset of this meeting for yesterday's capitulation. After some initial moaning and griping, he was hopeful that the group would move on—even if everyone seemed a little annoyed. Nobody liked going back to square one.

He had also admitted that he was personally having trouble separating the basic question of whether Endrophat was intended as a drug that would treat chronic morbid obesity—that was the term he had come across in his own web research—or was it simply a weight control product that would deliver results for dieters and women looking for cosmetic improvements. The answer to this question would be absolutely critical to the positioning strategy the agency would present and, ultimately, their creative recommendations. It was one of the nuances of the challenge that Ira had chosen to ignore, though his suggestion of the importance of the product pointed to the latter. Pete Zwicki was the first to wade in—albeit with a bit of a sneer. Who could blame him?

"According to a source I read, there are more than thirty two million frickin' overweight women in America right now," he stated. "At any given time between thirty-five and forty percent of them are actively trying to control the problem," he added with wounded nonchalance.

"Let me get this right," Steve Holiday cheer led. "So you're saying that at any given time there are nearly fifteen million women on a diet. No wonder I can't get a date for dinner, " he mocked himself. The group rewarded the joke with stony silence. Holiday's dating exploits had been a source of amusement for a long time, but no one was giving him any quarter today. Now Evie Sanchez volunteered a comment.

"It's based on body mass index ... weight divided by height. I read a piece that said, 'Minority women are disproportionately affected. Approximately fifty percent of African American and Latino women in this country are overweight.' She read this from an article she had printed off from the Internet. She smiled a little embarrassed at the last part of what she'd said. Evie barely weighed a hundred pounds.

"Terrific. That's very useful," Steve enthused. "We'll want to make sure in everything we do that blacks and Hispanics are well represented. I think we should also consider the value of an ethnic based media schedule." As he said this he spoke directly to Mel Cousins, the buyer from the Media Department that had been assigned to the working team. "We should be thinking about possibilities in segmented print and TV," he added referring to the strata of advertising that targeted minority groups in their own languages that had become a staple of the contemporary periodicals scene over the past few years. "I'm not sure these will form the core of the recommendation, but they're certainly worth addressing."

This was what Steve Holiday did so much better than most other creatives. After twenty-five years of solving all kinds of advertising problems he was able to frame positioning and media strategies better than most people who specialized in these disciplines. As an accomplished generalist, his instincts were invariably borne out after the numbers had been crunched or the research summaries came in. Most of the team had learned to take his hunches seriously. No one from Account Planning or Media balked at this latest assertion. It just made sense.

"So, does anybody want to venture a guess then?" he challenged the group. "I mean to the hundred and fifty million dollar question. Are we selling a cure for all humanity or are we just selling a diet pill?" It was the question everyone on the team had been wrestling with since the very first discussion of the brief and that Ira had brought into sharp focus.

"Why does it matter so damn much?" Jack Blenheim the account guy asked with an exasperated sigh. "I mean haven't we been around this block a hundred times already. Why can't it be both?" he challenged again. Expedience invariably seemed to be the hallmark of all account managers. Steve Holiday didn't have to answer. Evie Sanchez jumped in ahead—channeling her frustration at the easiest target.

"You know exactly why, Jack. Because if it's a medical breakthrough we're not going to wrap it in all of the bullshit usually associated with weight loss products. If this stuff really works, it's a whole lot more important than Slimshakes and whole grains and holding a goddamned measuring tape around your waist. It would be the most fantastic scientific breakthrough in generations. Come on, Jack," she goaded. "Don't be so lazy."

The rest of the creative team nodded their heads in unison. Before Holiday could balance the attack, Evie's partner Pete ventured another criticism of his own. They always liked to feed aggressively on a defenseless account guy.

"You know how the briefing form works, Jack. Just because it's a new business thing doesn't mean we don't need a tight strategy." It was an unfair shot and the young writer delivered it petulantly. Such flagrant antagonism wouldn't be tolerated in any other type of business—especially since Jack Blenheim was easily twenty years the young copywriter's senior—but somehow he felt he could get away with it. The emphasis Steve Holiday had been placing on strategy since the agency's last retreat had empowered the creatives to be bold in their challenges.

"I'm just saying that for presentation sake we should think about two approaches," the account manager countered a little too predictably. His somewhat patronizing tone caused nearly everyone else in the room to clench. With it he reignited the conflict that simmered constantly between the two strong tribes of the agency. It was what always made these kinds of projects difficult. Invariably the intellectually lazy guys in the suits always refused to commit to a single selling proposition or tried to hedge their bets with an approach they imagined the prospect might like—whether it was on strategy or not. Unfortunately, the result of this was an unavoidable duplication of effort and more work for the Creative Department. The exact opposite was true of the writers and art directors. Instead of conducting a ranging exploration of potential solutions, they always seemed to be pressing for a simple answer that seldom respected the true complexity of the problem. They worshipped single-mindedness to a fault. The head creative now had to step in and referee.

"Evie, you make a great point about the potential impact of Endrophat, but what about the business case? Jack, are there any clues about which approach would be most profitable for Carlton & Paxton?" The experienced Creative Director had learned long ago that sometimes the best way to understand a client's true motivations was to follow the money. The beleaguered account manager looked relieved, appreciating that Steve Holiday had thrown him a rope to haul himself out of this messy debate. While Holiday could be every bit as ill-tempered as his charges if he felt the group was being misled, he was also smart enough to ask grown up questions. His confidence restored, Blenheim answered the question obligingly.

"Certainly, Steve. What we know from at least a half dozen other C&P products is that they will make a fortune if they can get this crap distributed over the counter. Sure it trims their margins, but it liberates them from limiting the distribution via doctors and prescriptions, as well as a mountain of FDA and other bureaucratic bullshit. If the docs don't have to write the scrip, anyone can ask for it. It's like a license to print money"

"But shouldn't a drug like this be closely monitored?" Steve puzzled aloud.

"Maybe ... maybe not. There are three billion women on this planet. They're all going to want it at some time or another—some for the long haul and some just to drop a few pounds for a wedding or the prom. That's what makes this thing so amazing. If they can successfully plant a flag on the category, they will control market share for a decade."

"Let me see if I follow you, then ..." the Creative Director now asked seeming deliberately obtuse. "You're saying that by going mass with this stuff to start off with, they can out-flank the generics and the imitators." He asked the leading question for the benefit of the less patient people in his own department who would otherwise miss the point.

"Precisely," Blenheim concurred. "I'm guessing, based on the kind of numbers Pete and Evie were talking about, they'll wrack up a billion in sales annually for three or four years before anyone can possibly catch up. And that's just the U.S. market. I don't even want to hazard a guess as to what it would do to their bottom line globally. I mean, we may be the fattest goddamned country in the world, but I'm guessing this stuff is going to be a smash hit worldwide."

"But that's exactly my point," Evie Sanchez jumped in passionately. "If Endrophat is what they say it is, they should be celebrating it like the cure for smallpox or the invention of insulin! That's why I think we should be going hard after the news angle. If this is the scientific breakthrough they say it is, we should be nominating old Woody Woodruff for the fuck-ing Nobel prize."

It was a point that no one had considered or understood until this juncture and it took the passionate argument of the young art director to communicate it. As she spoke, lights seemed to be going on around the room. Steve was thrilled. This was what he meant when he pushed the group to dig for gold. Now he'd have to reconcile it toward the middle that had been agreed yesterday in his executive session.

"Okay, Evie, let's pretend for a moment that we all agree with you," Holiday inserted himself again. "Where do we go with this? If I get your gist, you're saying we should tilt this entire thing towards PR." At the mention of public relations, Jack Blenheim began shaking his head in strenuous opposition. If they went that route, the agency's fat media commissions would be strongly compromised and they would descend into the frustrating netherworld of soft impressions that made the calculations of PR's impact on marketing nearly impossible to measure. Worse still, they all knew they would have to engage their fatuous, incredibly uncooperative Public Relations Group President, Dick Eberhardt. By the pained expression on his face, the thought of it made Blenheim want to take a razor to his wrists—especially with so little time to spare. He looked beseechingly toward the Creative Director.

The reality was, a debate like the one they were having now, could go on for days. Steve Holiday now had to lend his weight to one side or the other and rein it in. Unfortunately, in this instance, he would have to come down on the side of being the responsible businessman.

"Evie, didn't they tell us at C&P that they had nearly a quarter billion dollars tied up in research and development on Endrophat? Do you really think they're going to trust the introduction to voluntary media uptake—especially when all of their competitors will be doing their damnedest to discredit everything that's written about it?"

Hearing the doubt in his tone, the young art director began to deflate. For a moment she had almost seized control of the entire strategy, but now she knew a compromise was coming. Holiday did his best to make the betrayal as gentle as possible, but it was his second in as many days.

"I think what we should do is proceed with the development of a branding strategy that assumes over the counter distribution. That still means advertising, a far better name, some interesting packaging concepts and an extraordinary point of sale hook. We might even want to look at some defensive stuff too, that will counter competitor misinformation. Look at the brief again. They've told us what they want."

It had been a difficult hour, but at least he had managed to get things pointing in the direction that he and Ira had agreed the day before. It was exhausting work keeping everyone in the boat, but he knew from experience that to allow anyone to become disengaged would be deadly to their chances for success. Sooner or later someone is going to crack this thing, he allowed himself to hope. He just had to stop them from rebelling so much that they lost sight of the task completely.

"Less than three weeks to go people," he now reminded. "I need to see some genius soon."

The basic chemistry that Harry Woodruff had been working with on Endrophat had been knocking around the Carlton & Paxton research lab for years. And it was here that he found himself this evening following yet another brutal round of presentations to the senior leadership team. It was also where he would very likely have to spend the night. Alone again in the sterile laboratory, all that could be heard were the quiet whir of the air exchanger, the hum of the fluorescent tubes that bleached the room, and the steady grind of his overworked hard drive as the computer that he now sat in front of churned yet another series of complex calculations. The beleaguered scientist had not been home for dinner in a month and the prospect of accomplishing this simple goal anytime soon was nowhere in sight. He bowed his head, squeezed his eyes shut, and massaged his temples gently while waiting for the machine to spit out the results he was searching for.

The request from the VP of Production had seemed straight forward enough: tell him exactly how much active ingredient for the Endrophat launch needed to be manufactured and what was the anticipated timetable for delivery. In essence, it was the same question that had been asked for the past twenty-four months, ever since the first successful trial of the company's new weight control product had been completed. Unfortunately for Harry Woodruff, the precise answer had remained elusive for almost all of that time. Between setbacks in formulation and regulatory approvals he was still having trouble committing to a firm schedule, a cross that increasingly had become his alone to bear. All the rest of the senior project team was simply interested in tumbling numbers and figuring out how much of their bonuses for the year ahead would be tied to the successful introduction of the miracle pill. They desperately wanted it in the field by the end of the second quarter and they were getting increasingly impatient. He understood their greedy impulses, but he also wished they could appreciate that his ambiguity was only about ensuring that the product they were racing to the street had been properly tested and could be safely introduced.

The hi-tech facility that he was in charge of encompassed nearly three acres of the vast suburban corporate campus that C&P occupied. As Endrophat prepared to go to market, the most advanced of the company's manufacturing facilities were being completely retooled for its production. That was where the pressure was now coming from. Did they have a final NDA? How much line time would be required? When can we promise we'll have it in the pipeline? With two false starts on the approval of the drug to his credit already, the harried doctor had very little wiggle room left should any further problems with the product be identified. Even as all of these plans were being made, he still didn't have the precious final regulatory blessing in hand. That was the issue that was keeping him up tonight and had left him sleepless for nearly a week. He sighed wearily as another disappointing screen of data appeared before him.

It seemed such a long time ago when word of the amazing product he had invented had first filtered through the company. At that time Harry Woodruff had been the toast of the organization. In fact, there were many who were quietly speculating that Endrophat could, indeed, earn the group Nobel consideration. More importantly, the ardent stock watchers who tracked such things speculated that it could eventually double the massive pharmaceutical company's market valuation. It was that big. When the weight control initiative was green flagged ahead of virtually every other major research and manufacturing project in the organization, Woodruff's star had rocketed toward the heavens. Instead of being just another of C&P's brilliant but obscure corporate scientists, he had been immediately elevated to the role he now occupied. With it came responsibility for delivering the most important new product introduction in a decade. But it was becoming clear that management was not his strength. After years of hiding in the anonymity of his quietly productive research niche, the scientist now found himself front line to all of these quite unreasonable expectations. Worse still, he had known all along that his acclaim and promotion had been somewhat undeserved.

The truth was that while he had been the senior section manager, it was only when a clever young neuroscientist, recently graduated from Carnegie Mellon, had joined his group that things had really taken off. Using a computer-assisted scanning tool they had finally been able to isolate the

endorphin-releasing neuron that was at the heart of the new
weight control product's performance. That was the key, he
had explained many times to his fellow scientists and to the
FDA monitors who had been carefully studying the product
as it made its way through the clinical trial process. To achieve
the effects of satiation that were essential to curbing appetite
and the subsequent reduction in the desire to eat, he had to be
able to precisely target and stimulate a minute region of the
hypothalamus. The solution had been found in a *brain tickler*
as Woodruff had become fond of calling it. What it was in reality was a small quantity of the naturally produced hormone,
dopamine—a hybrid version of which the company had been
manufacturing for several years. They had developed it as
part of their ongoing research into a fertility drug they jokingly referred to around the lab as *the love potion*. While this
particular product had gone nowhere, its effects as a sexual
stimulant were well documented. In effect, all that Woodruff
had done with the development of Endrophat was recycle
and redeploy.

Once this initial breakthrough had been accomplished,
the task was to refine the compounds that would mitigate the
typical side effects of the hormone manipulation which was,
in fact, what was really going on inside the body. This was
where things typically got tricky and Endrophat had certainly
been no exception. The first wave of testing had revealed
symptoms of irritability and depression, hair loss, insomnia
and, at least in most male test subjects, an almost debilitating
case of erectile dysfunction. It had been this latter effect that
had caused Woodruff's team to abandon the development of
the drug for use by men and to focus their entire effort on
providing the product exclusively to women. More recently,
as the mixed results of the second clinical trial filtered in, the
bedeviling question of dosage had also come to the fore.

As he had tried to explain to his management peers at the

meeting from which he had just escaped this afternoon, it was this aspect of the Endrophat formulation that was vexing him now. Because of the tremendous variations in the weight of the individuals who would be taking the drug coupled with their declining weight once they began using it, it was extremely difficult to ascertain the correct amount of the active ingredient to include with each tablet. Clearly it would require more of the brain- tickling ingredient to affect the body chemistry of a three hundred pound subject than it would to address the needs of someone half that size. Surely that was obvious. But the senior team had been adamant and unrelenting. One pill, they had insisted. Design it to be cut in half if it had to be, they had insisted again. Believing that they could no longer ignore the pressure of the analysts to get Endrophat to market, they had agreed that they would deal with the matter of misdosage after the fact. In doing so, they had overruled the misgivings that Harold Woodruff had expressed and done their best to saddle him with responsibility for any adverse consequences.

That was the problem that plagued the scientist this evening. While he had a pretty good idea what the outcome of an overdose might be, even after pouring over the anecdotal diaries compiled by the clinical test subjects, he had nothing truly quantifiable on which to base his theory. Perhaps that was what had compelled him to furnish a sample of the drug to someone he could observe personally. The handsome lady from Allan Corbett's advertising agency search had practically begged him for it. Though she had said she needed it for some packaging treatments, he was fairly certain she would succumb to the temptation to try it. He had seen the same behavior in many of his test subjects after their initial trial—calling back looking for more. He would contact her in a few days and probe. If his calculations were correct, she might have experienced some fairly dramatic side effects— especially since a woman her size probably needed only a half-dose of the active ingredient. If he could just gather a few more discreet examples to validate his concerns, perhaps he could be successful in winning himself a little more time.

Day 9

Until she became a featured performer, the exotic entertainer Stella Starr was simply Ellen Starnowski a pretty but big-boned girl from Stanton, Indiana. An aspiring actress and part-time model, since arriving in the city she had picked up a couple of extra dollars by dancing in the rash of titty bars and strip joints that dotted the edges of the Cook County line. But that was before the remarkable transformation that had taken place over the past couple of months. After successfully shedding twenty-five pounds of unwelcome weight that had clung to her since college, Stella was now the hottest dancer in the most popular of the cleaned up clubs that still struggled along in the old North End. Suddenly slender and toned, she was even getting legitimate callbacks for catalogue work. Young, fresh and beautiful she was everything the gentlemen who frequented Wriggly Field's All-Girl Cabaret desired. And, unlike the other girls who worked the joint who were all fake tits and poorly concealed resentment, there was something unnaturally real about her. The club buzzed wildly every time she was introduced and hushed reverentially whenever her clothes hit the floor.

But on an afternoon like this, during the last few chilly weeks ahead of baseball season, Stella wasn't sure what to expect as she emerged from the dressing room when the DJ bellowed out her name. Some days, usually summer Fridays when the Cubbies were in town, the place would be jumping before noon. Boisterous baseball fans in caps and numbered jerseys and businessmen eager to play hooky for an afternoon would crowd the luncheon buffet before heading to the park. This pre-game matinee was a time honored Windy City tradition and one that was celebrated with great enthusiasm by the opportunistic young ladies who took their clothes off at Wriggly's.

But today was an off day. With the team still down south, there were only a few regulars scattered around the gloomy cabaret. Two of the three stages where the girls performed their gyrations were dark, their footlights dimmed until later when, hopefully, the place might come to life with an after work crowd. But on this particular Wednesday at one-thirty in the afternoon only a handful of tired patrons lurked in the swivel chairs that bordered the single working dance floor. As Stella made her way up the steps wearing a sophisticated black cocktail dress, overdone with satin gloves up to her elbows and a choker of glittering rhinestones, a single whoop was all that greeted her arrival. She acknowledged it with a saucy wink in its general direction and started a lazy stroll across the stage.

Following a first listless number, during which all she shed was the slender straps of her gown, Stella retreated to the shadowy folds of the tired velvet valance that served as her backdrop. Sensing her boredom, the irrepressible emcee made another appeal to the quiet house. Finally, with the colored stage lights pulsing to the opening bars of another song that the DJ had cranked up even louder than usual, she felt her muscles begin to respond and a chilling sweat break out upon her back. As the raunchy rock and roll tune increased in tempo she shimmied her dress to her ankles and heeled it toward the curtain-hoarded passageway leading to the dressing rooms. Grasping the tall silver pole that connected the stage floor to the ceiling, she leapt half its length and treated the muted observers to a lingering view of her nearly perfect ass. Letting go with one hand and tossing back a mane of perfume-scented curls, she allowed herself to slide seductively toward the base of the sweat streaked metal. Upon reaching the floor, she leaned backward and with a quick swipe gathered up the faux fur blanket she had deposited on the steps of the stage. She then began a slow, knee-aching crawl toward the patrons seated at the apron of the parquet-covered platform. As she drew closer, the men silhouetted by the glare of the klieg lights began to come into focus. She studied them carefully, as she always did, keeping an eye out for the ones who would grab at her or make some other inappropriate gesture in exchange for the grimy dollars they dangled for her attentions. Turning her head slowly from left to the right, she sought out the familiar faces of the regulars whose behavior she could trust and whose admiration was nearly innocent.

Looking beyond the eager face of the overweight construction worker who begged her forward with two grimy bills, she spotted a form in the darkness that she immediately recognized. She flashed him an eye-crinkling grin and a wink that was intercepted by the other hungry patron. Emboldened, he thrust his cash forward expectantly. Keeping her eyes fixed on the man in the shadows, Stella pressed her breasts into the face of the excited man in front of her and pulled the money he held away with her cleavage. As she pulled back, she gave him a playful kiss on his balding forehead and then lit up the room with her best hoochie girl smile. Her audience responded with a few yelps and whistles. In the nethering gloom, at a table a few rows back, a dark suited gentleman raised his glass in quiet appreciation. He knew she would be coming to him soon.

Max Weller made note of all of this for the report that he would deliver to his client at the end of the week. Sitting alone in the plush banquet that bordered the velvet brocaded walls of the bar room, he palmed a stale glass of beer and discreetly recorded his findings in a small coiled notepad. Though he wasn't quite sure yet of exactly what it meant in this case, the usual pieces of the puzzle were beginning to fall into place. The plot lines were nearly always the same, he decided as he mulled the profile that was taking shape after just a couple of days of discreet, but not particularly difficult, inquiry. There was the miserable wife and the secret relationship with the dancer. There were the afternoon liaisons and too many expensive gifts. Already he had knit together a sloppy money trail that suggested his subject, Allan Corbett, was just another expense account cheater and petty corporate embezzler. The private sleuth had done so many of these kinds of investigations over the years that he often wondered whether there was actually a single honest man left in the world of business. Certainly it didn't appear that there were many in the circles that his clients like Ira Lowenstein moved in.

Having noticed the presence of her business-suited paramour, Stella idled through the motions of the last number in her set with disinterest. Stripped to a flimsy thong that crept deep into her backside, as soon as the song ended she swept up her blanket, her scattered clothes and a fist full of crumpled dollars. In doing so she signaled that she intended to ignore the pleas and howls for an encore. Narrowing her eyes in the direction of the DJ booth, even the loudmouthed emcee thought the better of begging her for more. This was one of the few privileges she enjoyed as a featured performer—the right to call off the hard sell that usually accompanied her finale. This was typically when the house funny man would implore the patrons to seek her or any of the other girls working the room out for a private dance. Stella confirmed this decision with a look toward Mario, the floor manager, and he consented with a nod. The burly bouncer was making a bundle off her and she was trusted to spot her best mark from the stage. It was his job to make sure the house got its cut from the girls' earnings, but this was never a problem with his most popular performer. Most shifts she was covering 'expenses' and kicking back thousands of dollars more.

Clutching the bundled blanket close to her chest, she slipped hurriedly toward the dimly lit corridor where the girls disappeared immediately following their appearance on stage. As she fled the room she ignored the men who reached after her. A few minutes later she was back on the floor dressed in the same black cocktail dress she had worn on stage, but with her hair pulled back sternly. She smiled nicely as compliments were whistled her way, though she deftly fended off the propositions that accompanied them as she slid among the empty chairs of the half-deserted club. As she moved, her eyes never left the man in the shadows.

"I didn't think you'd be coming today," she whispered into the ear of Allan Corbett as she slid into the vacant chair next to him. She pulled the seat closer and deliberately let her soft bosom brush his arm.

"How could I resist," the businessman responded playfully drawing in the delicious scent of her perfumed hair. He slid an arm around her bare shoulder familiarly and felt the warm dampness of the perspiration with which she glowed. His cold hand caused a shiver and his eyes dropped instinctively to her breasts, where he noticed the nipples beneath her tight dress stiffening in response to the chill. "My lunch meeting went a little long so I decided to check out for the afternoon."

"That's wonderful," she whispered seductively. Stella studied him in the timeless half-light of the club being careful not to betray her concern that this meant he was hoping to be with her for the rest of the day. Mario had already noticed that she had settled in with Corbett and had given her an impatient look that she was pretending to ignore. "Maybe we should slip into my office then?" she flirted. As she said this she coaxed him up by the hand and steered him gently toward the dark shadows that housed the club's private dance booths. Placing his hand on her gently rounded hip, she winked at her burly boss going by. He tapped his watch lightly as a reminder not to linger too long.

This was the game Stella Starr and Allan Corbett often played. To the envious men who watched them make their way across the room, the well dressed middle-aged businessman was just another customer, though obviously he must be a high roller to afford the undivided attentions of the club's most beautiful and popular girl. To the other dancers, Stella's regular was cool and remote—almost a creep. When he came by and she was with another man, he resisted all offers and waited impatiently. To the ever-watchful Mario, he was just another sucker who paid too much for the attentions of a girl who likely cared little for him, if she cared at all.

Most times Allan Corbett would appear unannounced, just as he had today. When he did, Stella would slip comfortably into the role of his secret mistress the way she always had. It was a routine she often used with the desperate gentlemen who sought her out after she'd finished up on stage. But both of them knew that their relationship had gone far beyond this. In the months since they had first met, when he had picked her out of a dozen or so girls who were working a grubby little joint off East Pershing, she had learned a lot about Allan Corbett. She knew he was married, how many kids he had and where they went to school. She had also discovered where he worked and what he did, though despite his lengthy explanations, she still had no understanding of what actually was involved. She had acquired all of this knowledge while dancing naked in front of him in the afternoon, and at least initially, coaxing twenty dollars from his wallet with each song and hanging on his every word in the uncomfortable time they spent together afterwards. That was the irony of their curious relationship. While they were frequently intimate, it certainly wasn't an affair. She was not his girl friend or his lover. She was his private dancer. After all the time they spent together inside the club they had never once met outside—even after all that he'd done for her.

From his seat outside its entrance, Weller could make out the shadowy movements of the dancer and her mark in the murky depths of the so-called VIP room. At Wriggly's this place was aptly named The Bullpen—a not too subtle wink to the randy men who entered it. Occasionally, a flash of violet white lace or a pair of phosphorescent lips would emerge from its dim lit depths. So, too, would a quiet murmur of pleasure from the only patron that occupied one of the deep leather tub chairs that lined the walls of this discreet section of the club. After a half an hour, most of which was spent with the dancer hovering between his legs, the subject of the private investigator's interest appeared to break things off. In the gloom, Weller could make out the man attempting to straighten his tie, the bib of his white dress shirt appearing purple in the club's black-lit glow. Rising, he tucked in a tail of his shirt that had sloppily escaped from the front of his pants and tried to comb back his disheveled hair with his hand. While Weller couldn't say for sure with the darkness, he would be willing to bet that Corbett was sporting an erection or another embarrassing outcome that the writhing lap dance might likely have caused. Stella Star's private performance had been amazing. Even watching from across the bar room, Weller had found himself becoming aroused.

Yet it wasn't the extraordinary dance that the attractive young woman had just performed that caught his attention at this point. That was something he might try and investigate personally a little later on. Instead, what he now took note of, was an unusual occurrence that a less attentive observer wouldn't likely have spotted. It happened as Corbett was preparing to leave. As the gentleman leaned in to say good-bye to the popular entertainer who had once again been summoned to the stage, the private investigator made his most important discovery of the day. At precisely the point when most men reached for their wallets to settle up for the pleasure they had just purchased, no cash was exchanged between Corbett and the girl. Instead, what appeared to pass between them in the half light, was a small bottle of pills. The dancer had been excited to receive them and expressed her delight by grabbing her paramour's tie and pulling the businessman's face deep into her full breasts. Then, just as quickly, she had stashed the drugs into her tiny, glitter-studded clutch and headed toward the dance floor. Now we're onto something, Weller imagined.

Spence Playfair checked his watch before stepping into the crowded downtown barroom. Though it was barely half past five he knew his appointment would have been cooling his heels for at least twenty minutes. People he was attempting to poach invariably made a habit of arriving a few minutes late for their scheduled rendezvous expecting that this somehow suggested indifference to the clandestine meeting to which they'd been invited. Playfair had long since mastered the reversal of this particular ploy by arriving later still and being equally unapologetic. It was always a power game and his unsuspecting quarry had no idea just how artfully he played his every move. Spotting his mark seated at the table near the back of the popular cocktail spot, he had to wade sideways through the crowd that crushed the bar in the noisy din of the happy hour.

"Gordon?" he asked from a short distance, shaping the name with his mouth more than speaking it aloud. As he closed the last few steps between them, he turned on his beaming smile and extended his hand. "Gordon ... it's so nice to finally meet you. I'm Spence Playfair," he added though he needed no introduction as he climbed onto the adjacent bar stool.

Playfair enjoyed the obvious irony of his surname, even if no one else in the Chicago ad scene did. Despite his remarkable success, most people in the local industry had no idea just how far the ambitious new business hawk from Boom was prepared to go in pursuit of a prize. If he had, it was doubtful that Gordon Turnbull would have returned the call that had been placed from an unknown cell number yesterday afternoon. But curiosity and the seasoned Creative Director's recently bruised vanity had given him more than enough reason to respond to the mysterious entreaty.

"Hi," Turnbull mumbled with a hint of irritation and not truly meeting Playfair's shining eyes and encouraging grin. "I'm afraid I haven't got much time. If we can, lets make this quick," he responded getting swiftly to the point.

"If you don't mind, I'm going to order a drink," Playfair countered, flagging a pretty waitress who was working nearby. He knew that Turnbull's ass was glued to that chair for as long as he wanted it to be and he would take all the time he needed to slowly reel in his mark. "Can I get you another?" he obliged noting his tablemate's empty wine glass. Maybe he's gay he allowed himself to speculate as he sized up the man opposite along with his choice of after work beverage. "A Chardonnay?" he half teased using the popular pick-up code. Turnbull didn't seem either interested or amused.

"No thanks. Seriously, I'd appreciate it if you would get to the point, Mr. Playfair."

"Spence ..." Playfair corrected. "There's no need for us to be so formal," he pressed again. "Actually, there are two things I was hoping we could cover ... one that we both know we're not allowed to talk about and the other ... well, that would make talking about the first issue a whole lot easier," he added in cryptic reference to the C&P pitch. "Why don't we talk about the second opportunity first?" he said with a wink.

There had often been speculation about the uncanny coincidences that inevitably arose in the pitches in which Playfair's company was involved. Sometimes there would be untimely publishing of potential internal conflicts or speculation about unpaid bills that would quickly torpedo a front-runner's chances. Other times it would be an eleventh hour revelation that a key member of a competitor's organization had decided to defect to Boom. Occasionally, there were even rumors of bribery and other acts malfeasance. While none of these were ever directly attributable to Spence Playfair, the regular occurrence of such incidents was too frequent too ignore. Gordon Turnbull was justifiably wary of all three possibilities.

"The simple fact is, we are seriously thinking about some changes in personnel if we are successful in this little adventure that we're all presently involved with," said Playfair casting out his bait. "You probably understand as well as I do that our current guy isn't likely a good fit with ... you know ... our friends over there." His head turn pointed in the general direction of the Carlton & Paxton building several blocks away. "He's just a little too rough around the edges... volatile ... unlike a talented gentleman like yourself."

It was an obvious stroke of Turnbull's not insubstantial ego. Try as he might, it was difficult to resist. It had been months since anyone in the new M&M Interworld organization had suggested anything other than that his performance was substandard. Even Lane had been pushing that button lately. "Go on, I'm listening," the creative guy now encouraged dropping his guard just an inch.

"Well, from what we hear, you've maybe got an inside track on this thing and the way I figure it, you just might be the key to the whole deal. What I was hoping was that maybe we could come to some sort of understanding."

"In what way?" Turnbull now questioned. He was an experienced ad executive in his own right and wouldn't allow himself to be so easily gulled. "Are we talking about a job or a switch … or what? What are you saying, Playfair."

"I'm thinking that maybe if we get the chance, we can make it clear to our mutual friend that we could maybe deliver the best of both worlds if they ditch L&H." He paused and let this sink in. "Of course, I know we probably can't compete with the haul you made in the Interworld transaction, but I bet we could come up with some form of compensation that would make it worth your while." Creatives who fancied themselves to be extremely talented always had the same mercenary streak, thought Playfair. Perhaps it was because they were paid so poorly when they were just starting out. In any event, it was very easily exploited.

"What are we thinking about, if you don't mind my asking?" Turnbull now queried. The mention of money had immediately piqued his interest. While he was reasonably confident that only he knew how badly he had fared in the market lately, it was pretty much inevitable that someone would eventually find out that he had managed to blow his takeover windfall.

"If we win this thing, the sky's the limit for Boom. You know it will likely take us international overnight. At minimum I'm guessing there would be a round of start up options and, for a guy with your seniority and experience, a pretty good bet that you could head up an office," Playfair dangled. The idea of running an entire office was another conceit that many Creative Directors shared. "And, of course, I'm sure we could probably beat whatever they're paying you now by fifty or so."

There was no need for him to exercise any restraint as he speculated about this trumped up offer. Playfair had already accomplished his goal of fucking up Gordon Turnbull. The only challenge he had now was how to extricate himself from this meeting and let the imagination of his eager dupe run wild. Greed plus vanity was a powerful tonic.

"I'd have to think about it," Turnbull now countered in a weak attempt to commence negotiations. But in truth he had practically come out of his skin as Playfair pushed all of his hot buttons. There was no hiding his obvious excitement.

"I don't blame you," Playfair now weighed his quarry skillfully. "I would too, if I were you. If you're at all interested, why don't we try and get together in the next week or so?"

With this last ambiguous commitment, he slid off his tall wooden chair and shook Gordon Turnbull's sweat moistened hand. He was pretty much certain that the Creative Director of their closest rival wouldn't have another good idea for a month. Sometimes it was all just too easy.

Lane McCarthy's first noticeable reaction to the pills she had taken twice in the past forty-eight hours came completely out of the blue. Or more precisely, it came out of the red. That was the color she was certain her face was glowing as Tahur Massad pushed her through a second demanding set of stomach crunches while forcing her to hold a weighty medicine ball tight to her abdomen. She had been enjoying the workout immensely, feeling more energetic during her routine than she had in months. But nothing prepared her for the unexpected wave of pleasure that passed through her as she completed her final few sit-ups. With her spandex shorts riding high and the gentle agitation of the seamed leather sphere pressing against her parted thighs, she became aware of a vague but pleasant sensation that accompanied each completed rep. And then it happened. The contraction that erupted deep within her was sudden, intense and most definitely enjoyable. It was unmistakably an orgasm and it caused her to cry out in a way that turned more than a couple of heads in the tidy corporate gym in the direction of the attractive female executive and her personal trainer. As the tremor of delight passed, she collapsed backward onto her floor mat, dazed at this remarkable occurrence.

Tahur, who had been supervising her drill with only half interest—he was much more intent on studying the shapely young woman driving hard on the elliptical machine across the room—came back to attention immediately. Peering down at her from directly overhead, the handsome featured East Indian trainer looked frightened, anxious somehow that his negligence had caused his client injury. Straddling Lane's prone body, he gently lifted the medicine ball from her tummy and rolled it aside. As he did so, he caught a whiff of some pleasant but unaccustomed odor in the sweat-scented workout room. His nostrils twitched in puzzlement.

"Are you all right, Missus McCarthy?" he asked in an accent that mingled his Punjabi roots with an extended stay in America. "Have you strained something very much?" he queried with concern, misplacing the modifier, as he typically did, with his inquiry. He never has figured out what to call me, Lane smiled to herself through the daze and exhilaration of the sensations that were now, finally, beginning to subside.

"No … nothing like that Tahur," she responded amused

and embarrassed at the same time. "But I have to say, I certainly have been enjoying today's exercises more than I have in ages. Is there any chance we're working something different?" she questioned, half hoping that which had been unlocked could be more logically explained.

"I don't know Missus McCarthy. If I could venture a guess, I sensed that you had some sort of contraction of the muscles, a spasm perhaps. Did you feel pain?" he asked quizzically, crouching down beside her.

With his elastic hamstrings he could squat in this position for hours. He was so earnest and intense, she thought of the smoldering-eyed attendant who was now gently touching her mid-section probing for pain. For a fleeting moment she contemplated inviting him to give her a massage as she knew he sometimes did for his other clients. Lane had never before taken advantage of this service being far too self-conscious to indulge herself in this way. Even though Tahur had placed his hands on her many times in her most intimate regions during their exercise routines, his touch was entirely professional. Though muscular and fit and possessing a dazzling white smile that he dished around the gym flirtatiously, her physical response to him had never been anything other than neutral.

"Oh no, quite the contrary," she confessed trying to keep herself from laughing. "That was quite possibly the most satisfying drill I've ever enjoyed. Are you sure we didn't do anything different?" she asked again.

As she waited for his reply, she did a mental inventory of all that they had worked on for the previous half hour. Certainly she had been pushing herself, trying to leave the office and the pressures of the pitch far behind, but specific thoughts of sex hadn't even entered her mind.

"Maybe it's just your body telling you what it needs. Have you been taking your vitamins?" he chided, playfully turning the situation to his advantage. Tahur was a great believer in nutritional supplements. In fact, he sold many of these products on the side while pretending to be a swami-like authority on the subject. "Sometimes when we work hard or we are feeling stress, we release chemicals that do the most amazing things."

Lane recalled reading somewhere that this was possible—that athletic women occasionally exerted themselves to points of pleasure. The context with which she was familiar usually pertained itself to distance runners and other extreme instances where these individuals had pressed themselves well past the normal limits of performance. Once, when she was much younger and had been in training for a marathon, she had pushed herself to the point of involuntary urination. But this was nothing like that. Today her body's delicious response had been entirely different. It had been deeply and intensely pleasurable in a way that she had seldom experienced before.

"Maybe you're right, Tahur." She concluded choosing not to tell him of the specific symptom she had experienced. Instead she decided to attach it to the incredible pressure she'd been under. She never imagined it might have anything to do with the new medication she was experimenting with. It couldn't possibly, she resolved.

"Why don't we call it a day, missus?" the trainer concluded. "Maybe you'll feel good with a shower and some rest."

"Right," Lane laughed at the irony. "Though to be truthful, I can't imagine feeling any better than I do right now." With that she offered up her hand and allowed Tahur to pull her to her feet. "I'll see you at the start of next week. Brenda will call."

Day 10

"Do you really think this is good enough?" As he bellowed this assessment, Zig Cartwright snatched the last remaining marker comp from the wall and shredded it with a half dozen angry pulls before tossing the pieces onto the table with the rest of the rejected work. "What part of me wasn't being clear when I said I needed something right fucking now?"

The assembled group of nearly a dozen creatives lowered their heads in fear of what might come next. They didn't have to wait long. In a final violent outburst, Zig flung himself at the mounding pile of rubbish in front of him and swept it to the floor. Along with it went an ashtray, a coffee cup and a scattering of felt pens and notebooks.

"Instead, everything I've looked at is complete garbage. You've had this bloody brief for nearly a week and this is the best you could come up with? I'm so pissed I could fire someone right here and now!"

It was a typical motivational speech from the angry young Creative Director, but with Zig's hair trigger temper, the group knew better than to dare imagine he was anything other than sincere in this threat. Especially fearful were the senior team leaders. At Boom they were reluctant to call these people Group Heads, but in reality that was what they were—more experienced writers and designers who provided intellectual muscle and guidance to the undisciplined youngsters who filled out the rest of the creative ranks. They were also the one's who took home six figure salaries.

"If for a moment I thought this was a difficult assignment, I might be more reasonable. But come fucking on, it's a pill that makes fat women thin. What could be less complicated? It should be fun ... and sexy!"

"But Zig, you said yourself at the last meeting that we would look at some safer stuff." The complaint belonged to Trent Byrum, a clever guy who'd come over from Burnett last year promising that he could shed the creative straight jacket he'd worn over there if he were given half a chance. Zig had been doubtful, but hired him anyway.

"Really, Trent? Is that what you think I said?" Cartwright pounced angrily. "Has that ever been the way we do things around here?"

"Well no, or at least, well, I thought what you said to Leslie was we'd look at a few different approaches that were more consistent with the brief," he stammered and stumbled realizing he had put himself directly in the crosshairs.

"This isn't bloody Burnett, my friend. Did you really think I was going to like an animated little fat cell singing like fucking Pavarotti?" Cartwright challenged.

The concept that had set Zig off on this morning's tirade had been a comical character modeled after the Baker's Doughboy. Such playful icons were the hallmark of Byrum's previous agency. Cartwright despised it immediately. Now he was channeling some of that hatred toward its creator.

"I just thought it might be, I don't know, kind of fun." Byrum had not produced anything thing in a month that Zig had bought into. He was on a list to be whacked and most of the others in the room knew it. Frankly, Byrum knew it too.

But he and his wife had just had their first child, so he was in strenuous denial of this inevitability.

"Did anyone else think Trent's idea was *fun?*" Zig taunted. "Did you, Rick?" he asked of one of his more trusted lieutenants. The shaggy punk he was addressing shook his head. "How about you, Karrie?" Before the hip young art director could respond, she was interrupted.

"Come on Zig, I don't think you're being fair," an agitated Byrum interrupted. "It was just one bad idea."

"You're right. It is a bad idea. It's just like all the other bad fucking ideas you've had since you've come here."

"Please … Zig," begged the embarrassed copywriter. But his plea was pointless. Everyone knew exactly where this was going.

"Trent, why don't you just get your things and clear out," Zig now said coldly.

"You bastard," Byrum countered as he fought back a wave of fast forming tears.

"Better that than a hack," Cartwright responded without the slightest bit of remorse. As the broken man fled the room, he turned to the rest of his charges. "Is there anyone else who isn't clear about what I'm after?"

"**P**erhaps I misunderstood. Honestly, we were expecting a larger group," responded Lane McCarthy briefly doubting her notes that at least six people from Carlton & Paxton would be touring the office the day after tomorrow. As she said this, she smoothed the hem of her skirt behind her trim legs and settled into the furthest chair of an exquisite grouping that occupied the windowed side of her expansive office.

The gilded coffee table that separated her from her lone visitor was the centerpiece of an elegant suite of 18th Century

French antiques. The highlight of the collection was a spectacularly restored plum wood trimmed chaise that was more decorative than practical. It sat in a pool of gleaming hardwood perched on a vast Persian carpet of similar age and quality. Invariably, this eclectic choice of office furnishings was the topic of many first conversations and it allowed the President of McCarthy & McCauley to do what she did better than nearly everyone else in the business, which was to put her guests at ease.

"Actually, it was probably me who created the confusion," Allan Corbett apologized. "Sometimes if I forget to check my planner, I get a little lost." He had already made himself quite at home. The surprise guest was draped into the corner of a richly upholstered Recamier. Its gentle slope caused him to lean back awkwardly and he was forced to grasp its handsomely carved shoulder to remain upright. In this pose, his shirt cuff and a couple of inches of white sleeve stretched out from beneath his suit causing Lane to notice that the top button of his shirt was also undone beneath his tie. While she couldn't say for certain, she thought she had picked up a whiff of alcohol when she had greeted him in reception.

"Of course, its not a problem, Allan," Lane continued cheerfully. "I'm sure your people are as busy as mine these days." Part of her was actually delighted that she finally had some one on one time with this important prospective client. Before sitting down she buzzed Brenda to advise Bryan Raider to have the troops stand by, though based on his unscheduled arrival she would be surprised if Allan Corbett cared to see any more of M&M's facilities than what he had noticed on the short stroll to her office. "Are there any limitations on your time?" she now inquired considerately.

"I guess I've got as much time as we need," he said a little solicitously. "If I have fouled up the appointment, I guess it's your time we have to worry about." As he offered this response he righted himself on the settee and leaned forward for the fine china coffee cup that had been placed on the table before him. After taking a tentative sip, he jiggled it back onto its waiting saucer, his unsteady tremor difficult to conceal. Fortunately, he now turned the conversation toward the business at hand.

"I guess what I'd really like to understand most about your organization is how much global reach you've actually got. I mean, compared to the others, is it for real?" It was a soft question and Lane fielded it easily. She had answered it a hundred times since the merger.

"Real is probably the absolute best way to describe it, Allan," she complimented him. "I have to confess that prior to hooking up with Interworld we would pretend that we could access resources in foreign markets, but the honest truth was we were bullshitting."

Lane tried to let the odd bit of profanity slip out when she worked in close and most businessmen seemed to enjoy it since it established the ground rules for poor behavior later. Corbett clearly liked the roughness she betrayed. He broke into a smile as soon as she said it. "That's all changed since we aligned ourselves with the Interworld network." Lane was always careful to avoid the words *purchased* or *bought.* She knew that for most prospective clients it signaled that she had likely scored a large amount of cash from the sale.

"Creative and media?" he queried trying to telegraph his knowledge of agency speak.

"Actually, strategy first, " Lane corrected before slipping back into the standard script. "But then, yes of course, creative execution and media buying."

These were, in fact, the most compelling reasons most clients had for assigning their business to a large multinational advertising firm. As more and more companies expanded their global reach, almost all of them were looking for transcendent marketing and advertising approaches as well as favorable economies of scale that allowed them to move more easily across cultural and linguistic boundaries. For most of them it worked, so long as everyone else in the world bought into American aspirational views and values. "As I noted from your annual report, we've got nearly perfect alignment," Lane sold a little harder. "One hundred and twenty-eight offices in ninety-four countries ... and with strong emerging presence in southeast Asia and the Eastern Block."

"Have you worked with your colleagues overseas?" It was a very good question and Lane knew she had to measure her answer appropriately. Clients like Allan Corbett, from organizations like Carlton & Paxton, often had mixed views of their international counterparts. Many of them often had enjoyed expat postings or had extensive experience in foreign countries as part of their own resumes. To provide an overly optimistic portrayal of universal cooperation amongst affiliated offices would suggest a naivety about the company she had bought into.

"I've worked with a few. We did a joint launch with London for Abraxus last year," she explained alluding to a very famous software launch. "We handled positioning and global strategy. The Brits handled creative execution and we farmed most of the web work to our office in Mumbai. I don't think I need to tell you that it was a smashing success." Indeed, the program had not only won awards all over the world, but Lane had recently provided details to a marketing professor preparing an article for the Harvard Business Review. The focal point of the piece would be global branding. "And we did that only two months after the merger."

"Outstanding. I remember seeing it at Heathrow last year and was blown away by the graphics. So that was yours?" Though he congratulated her generously, he seemed somewhat disinterested in the actual substance of her answer. He certainly wasn't a note taker, either. Corbett had presented himself without either a briefcase or even a smartphone with which to diarize the outcomes of their meeting. She also observed the slackness in his posture and concluded that he had, indeed, been drinking over lunch.

"Do you have any questions for me?" As he made this inquiry, the visiting client stood up. "Or about Endrophat … or whatever we end up calling it?" By the time he had completed his question, he had somehow managed to span the distance between himself and Lane and quickly settled into the seat next to her—their knees almost touching. It was an uncomfortable invasion of her personal space, but not something with which she was entirely unfamiliar. Reiner Adolph and a half dozen other men the agency worked for had the same annoying habit.

Now it was Lane's turn to stand up. She rose deftly and stepped toward the elegant service on the cart across from them and offered up a refill knowing full well that Corbett had barely sipped from his first. The evasive maneuver sent an unspoken but fairly obvious signal. Corbett returned a look that seemed to suggest that it had at least been worth a try.

"I'll tell you what we have been dying to ask Allan," Lane now continued. "Have your people done any work on pricing strategy?" In their previous discussions with the distasteful consultant that Bryan Raider had brought in, this had been a hotly contested subject. It hit the mark with Corbett, too.

"Great question, Lane," he rewarded her. He hadn't given up entirely and allowed his gaze to linger in the region of her breasts. "We have. But to be absolutely truthful we haven't arrived at a final answer just yet. As I'm sure you can imagine, we know fairly precisely what our development and manufacturing costs are. What our people are wrestling with now is how quickly we want to recapture our upfront costs and what kind of long term dividend we want to reap."

It was a fairly reasonable answer, but Lane felt she had to press. The team had concluded that the only practical way for the drug to be distributed was by prescription, and with this they had entered into considerations of the murky world of health insurance and drug plans and such. The answer would affect many of their final recommendations.

"But are we talking five or ten dollars a pill or what? A hundred?" Lane insisted. Her tone suggested that in her opinion, it should be the former.

"What price would you charge for a miracle," Corbett countered. "Lane, what you have to understand with this product is we could charge just about any price we wanted … and someone would pay."

It was an angle that neither Lane nor any of her group had considered before and the implications were profound. From the very beginning, the agency had automatically assumed a mass distribution strategy that would make the treatment available to all who wanted it—not just those who could afford it.

"Surely you're kidding, Allan." It was the first time in a long time that Lane had been given reason to doubt the good intentions of a prospective client. Contrary to the public's perception, most well-regarded agencies had a conscience and were fairly principled when it came to matters of business ethics. Corbett's answer just didn't sit right.

The only other occasion in her career that she had experienced a similar reaction was when she had been approached by a somewhat spurious mail order company who explained that their business model was based on charging a shipping and handling fee that actually exceeded the real value of the merchandise they were selling. It felt fundamentally dishonest and she had said no to nearly twenty million dollars a year in annual media billings. Surely Carlton & Paxton had much more honorable intentions.

"What I'm saying Ms. McCarthy, is that we have the enviable opportunity of allowing the market to establish the price for this product. And my guess is that this will result in a fairly substantial premium. I mean who would have thought you could charge a man so handsomely for every erection."

Lane smiled at the allusion to the wave of popular ED treatments, although her embarrassment was more a result of the inappropriateness of its mention in the context of their rather intimate meeting. Corbett's expression darkened a little when it became clear that Lane had chosen to take this dim view of his little joke.

"But don't you owe it to the world to bring this product to market in a way that would make it accessible to everyone?"

"That's certainly an idealistic view, Lane. But I guess I'm just not as certain of that as you," he answered.

It was a basic philosophical question that all drug companies invariably dealt with. For all of the trumpeting of the need for competitive pricing in the area of pharmaceuticals, the government agencies that were so intensely involved in the administration of the business actually leant very little material support to the enormous cost of research and development. Deregulation and the limiting of patents also squeezed margins severely.

"But think of all the people you could help. From what we've been reading, obesity is an illness of the poor and less educated. I mean, don't we owe it to them to help?" Lane pleaded.

"Fine." Corbett countered. "But think of all the regulatory hoops that we are forced to go through. And all of the barriers that the FDA and every other branch of the government puts in our way," he explained with growing impatience. "There will be room for those people once the initial patents expire and the generics come along. Until then, we will very likely charge what the market will bear. You're a businessperson. Surely you understand that?" His last comment on the matter was deliberately patronizing and was intended to silence the discussion.

"But Allan ..." Lane began and then censored herself. There was no use pursuing this unsatisfying line of questioning for either party. While the exchange was by no means fatal, she now understood that Corbett was the kind of client who did not like to engage in debate. She decided, for the better, to let the matter drop.

Self-conscious for the first time that he had arrived unexpectedly and that his first direct conversation with Lane McCarthy had not gone as well as he had hoped it would, Allan Corbett, too, began to think about taking his leave.

"You make some very interesting points, Lane. But I'm afraid we're not going to solve them here today. I'll tell you what I will do. Let me ask around a bit and I will forward all of you an e-mail with some preliminary pricing. It may not be one hundred percent accurate, but at least all of you will be playing on equal footing." With that he checked his watch and stood up. "You really do have a magnificent office here. I'll be sure to let everyone know they should try and see it if they can."

This final comment was as chilly as the entire visit had been odd. The last thing Lane had wanted to do was get off on the wrong foot with this important prospect, and now it appeared that this brief visit was going to have to pass for their agency tour. It was a tactical blunder and she kicked herself for it. A moment later, Allan Corbett excused himself curtly and was gone.

❧

He had passed the sign a hundred times on the avenue that housed his neighborhood package store, but until now Steve Holiday had barely noticed the name *Suite Sixteen*. Nor had he ever truly taken heed of the collection of oversized mannequins that occupied the front windows. In truth, he would most likely have failed to make the connection again this evening had the large glass panels of the storefront not been adorned with a colorful banner loudly announcing that new spring arrivals were now in stock and catching sight of a well-dressed, but severely overweight woman entering at that exact moment.

Instead of buckling his shoulder belt and reversing out of the parking space that he occupied adjacent to the entrance to the small shop, he watched with curiosity as the big woman engaged a similarly large salesperson once inside. The object of their interest was the soft velour warm up suit that adorned one of the figurines in the playfully arranged window display. Peering around the steering wheel of his low-slung sports car, Holiday ducked his head and looked up at the words that appeared beneath the boutique's stylishly scripted logo. In a line of smaller type that was knocked out of the glowing pink fascia sign, it read:

'Good Looking Clothes For The Good Sized Girl.'

He smiled wryly. It wasn't that Steve Holiday didn't know that these kinds of stores existed. In fact, as part of a past assignment for a large national retail chain, they had once been invited to come up with names for a new department being developed that catered to the store's oversized clientele. Perhaps because of this, the cleverness of the name registered with him for the first time. It was clearly an allusion to the availability of fashions for women size sixteen and above. He recalled reading an article on retail trends that reported with the average American woman wearing a size fourteen, they were one of the fastest growing categories in the country. The author of the piece, without an apparent sense of irony, had suggested that they were on the rise because of fat margins that could be charged for such specialty apparel and the ballooning demand for clothes of this style. The copy editor in Steve Holiday had blanched at the repeated clumsy puns.

But the fact was, ever since he had received the Endrophat briefing, Holiday was becoming increasingly conscious of the language and code words that were used to speak to the overweight market. What had struck him almost immediately was the fine non-judgmental line that such appeals carefully treaded. The other day he had stopped into a popular fast food joint, which he still did from time to time, and while waiting his turn in line he had watched two teenaged boys, both heavy, order the *value meal*. It was only then that it registered that what they had requested had nothing to do with money at all. It was, instead, thoughtfully orchestrated permission that had been introduced into the consumer's lexicon to allow them to request a meal that was twice as large as was necessary to satisfy.

At the same time he had noticed a wall poster offering 'nutritional information' about the other products on the tempting menu boards. It was illustrated with a magnificent, fresh-looking salad—clearly a young art director's simple conception of healthy—and it offered details about nutritional and caloric content. The actual numbers were enormous, but the type was small. So, too, were the suggested portion sizes. He had little doubt that the company's legal department had encouraged the distribution of these materials. Best to transfer onus and liability to the customer, he imagined. Sometimes what he did for a living made him quietly ashamed.

Perhaps it was his simple, professional curiosity. Or maybe it was the fact that he couldn't stand the thought of arriving home to his empty house again so early. His only companions for the evening were his big dog and the bottle of scotch that lay on its side in a plain brown bag on the seat beside him. Whatever the reason, Holiday now decided he would continue his stakeout of this newly discovered source of market research for a little while longer. He shut off the idling engine of his sleek little import. With this, the two bright halogen headlights that had come on automatically in the twilight and that were reflecting back at him with a blinding glare, extinguished themselves. As they went dark he was able to see more clearly what was going on in the brightly illuminated clothing store.

It was a friendly and animated exchange. The large woman who had been attracted into the shop by the display had been encouraged to try on a canary colored version of the two-piece outfit. To accomplish this, she had shed the jacket of her bulging business suit and in so doing, revealed she was a perfect sample of the store's target market. As Steve watched, the two ladies smiled and laughed at the challenge that fitting into it now presented.

In her first attempt, the would-be buyer's hand stalled as she tried to stretch the garment past her swollen upper arm. Reaching up, her fingertips wiggled through the puckered sleeve, but only her brightly painted nails of her three longest fingers made it through the narrow tunnel of fabric. No bother. Another larger version was hastily found and exchanged with the other garment. When it slid on more easily, both women crowded closer to the three-sided mirror mounted by the entrance to the fitting room to take a look. Though the next step was obvious, neither of the ladies seemed too eager to meet the challenge presented by the pants. From their body language, Steve sensed that the impulse that had drawn the large lady into the store was losing momentum and that the potential sale was all but lost. In a last, valiant attempt for the save, a softer pink version of the outfit was hurriedly presented. But this, too, was dismissed with a wave nearly as quickly as the saleswoman had managed to position it beneath her customer's ample chin.

At this point Steve Holiday had expected to witness some signs of embarrassment. But there were none. Instead, the unsuccessful fitting was dismissed with a laugh and, from what he could tell, what seemed like a friendly apology. But what had they said to each other? What had been the gentle exchange that allowed both parties to walk away from the failed transaction without either the resentment or hostility that he had been expecting? Clearly these women didn't seem to attach any judgment to their size the way Clare always had. Or the way that the wardrobe and fitting people on his commercial productions always did as they pinned the waif thin talent into their wardrobe on set. He remembered the protracted discussions he'd had with his wife and his clients about size and weight and how the camera always made them appear ten pounds heavier. But in the exercise he had just witnessed, there was no such apology or apparent humiliation. Instead, they were just two large people interacting on very natural terms.

As he watched the big woman pull her jacket back on and gather up her purse, Steve sensed that he had learned something fairly important. When she exited the store and looked in the direction of his parked vehicle, the voyeur in him was immediately embarrassed. What he realized now was that maybe her body image was his problem, not hers. Maybe it was he and everyone like him who projected judgments onto people who they decided were overweight. Sure there were serious medical issues arising from the condition of obesity, but maybe the biggest problem most heavy people encountered was the insensitivity of the slim. Steve thought about his own eating impulses. He was lucky, he knew. He had always been able to eat everything he ever wanted while barely gaining a pound. He didn't understand why and he seldom gave a thought to his weight. For the first time since he had read the review briefing, he felt like he finally understood the unfairness of obesity and the very personal nature of the challenge. Whatever messages they created and recommended would have to reflect this newly realized truth.

Day 11

"How many of you watched this year's Super Bowl?" Steve Holiday inquired of the people seated in the crowded ballroom. As he spoke, he tried his best to ignore the clatter of the dinner plates being collected and pretended that he had the undivided attention of his audience. But as the service door adjacent to the stage swung open, the noise of the bustling hotel kitchen threatened to drown him out entirely. For the naturally reticent Creative Director, his first instinct was to vault from the dais and flee the boisterous din of the disorderly room. He waited again and smiled wanly, pleading sympathy for his plight with another lengthy pause. Instead of quiet, he was rewarded with a crash of breaking glass behind the valance of pipe and curtain that had been erected behind him. Doing his best to ignore it, he pressed on valiantly, if a little reluctantly.

"Did you watch the game or the commercials?" he asked again of the crowd. In an attempt to substantiate the hypothesis he was advancing, he went one step further, "Can anyone tell me the score of the game?" Those who were listening, though none of them were correct, called out various numbers from the floor. "Obviously our Bears weren't there," he teased, earning a few chuckles down front, but not yet gaining control of the majority of the audience.

"Now, can anyone tell me about some of the ads you saw?" In response to this question, a much healthier show of hands went up. "Precisely my point. And I'm gonna guess that the ad you all remember most was that brilliant send-up by Burger Barn with all of those chimpanzees, right?" As he mentioned the famously humorous commercial that had stolen the show that January, dozens more were raised among the sea of tables. A little more engaged, they smiled and laughed and nodded their agreement.

"The reason I remember that one so well, is that it kicked the ass of all three spots that my agency ran in the big game this year." As he said this, he bowed his head in shame, and shook it slowly from side to side. After a moment, he returned to the microphone with a sheepish smile. "We haven't got any L&H clients out there do we?" The audience laughed heartily at this self-deprecating remark and began to warm to him more than the gelatinous parfait desserts that had been placed in front of them. Only the occasional clink of a spoon on a saucer disturbed Steve now. He allowed himself to cheat a glance in the direction of Lane McCarthy who was seated up front, close to the podium, and she smiled back her encouragement. Seven preening businessmen surrounded her at the big round table.

What the Chairwoman for the event didn't know was how close Holiday had come to pulling the plug on this badly-timed speaking engagement. With the creative direction for the pitch not yet resolved, Ira had feigned ignorance of Steve's Ad Council obligation and pronounced that a luncheon meeting would be held to look at the work that been developed since their last review session. It was typical Ira—especially since it was the agency President who had volunteered his Creative Director for this particular opportunity in the first place. As much as he hated to do it, Steve had designated one of his group heads to take the team through the latest round of concepts in his absence. With any luck, the meeting would be over when he returned, or better still, it would have been aborted altogether. Despite the unfortunate timing, as he watched Lane McCarthy light up the group around her, he was glad he had decided not to cross their beautiful hostess.

"So I think it's fair to say that, contrary to what my colleague from Owen & Marshall attempted to prove with all of his charts and graphs, I believe it is quite undeniable that humorous advertising works. The trick is just to be really, really funny. And not everyone can do that."

He waited for the words to register with the audience. The speaker from the competitive agency, who had gone to such great lengths to justify his agency's theory that repeating a client's name three times and showing five seconds of logo was just as effective as an entertaining advertisement, scowled his disagreement. However, as if to prove Steve's point about likeability, the audience was now beginning to pay far more attention to the charismatic Holiday than they had ever conceded to the long-winded speaker who'd preceded him. In fact, no one who had spoken thus far at the annual Ad Council Luncheon, except for Lane McCarthy who kicked things off, had received as favorable a reception. The vivacious hostess of the luncheon had looked absolutely dazzling in the spotlight in her smartly tailored ivory suit accented with a playful string of Simon Sebbag stones. Telling a slightly off color warm up joke that few women would have dared to attempt, she had nearly brought the house down. With her unspoken approval, Holiday now continued on more confidently.

"The philosophy of my agency is that its not just about generating awareness numbers—it's about earning a share of the consumer's psyche. It's about winning hearts and minds. Mrs. American Shopper may recognize you on the shelf, but she won't reward you with her hard earned dollars unless she really likes you." As he warmed to his lecture, the engaging Creative Director settled into the easy conversational style that had long been his trademark. Now he was equal parts showman and favorite dinner guest. After working so hard to finally win their attention, he decided to press this brief advantage.

"I'm going to play a reel of ten of my all time favorite humorous ads. I apologize if you have seen some of them before—many are Cannes Gold Lion winners," he said referring to the famous international advertising festival where great television commercials were celebrated as if they were marvels of the cinema. It was one of the most truly obscene wanks of the industry, though he had attended it regularly with clients who seemed to value this kind of attention. With this, the lights in the hotel ballroom dimmed again and all eyes focused on the large screen above where the panel was seated and on the various monitors that had been stationed around the room. With each completed commercial and its requisite related product plug, the room erupted with swells of laughter.

After the first few spots had run, Holiday was struck by the irony of his words. Despite his growing frustration with the fatuousness of the business in which he toiled, and more often than not, the singular absence of a genuine selling idea in most of the work that he had reviewed lately, clearly earning a laugh was worth something—likely far more than he was willing to concede. The smiles and head nodding of this audience of business professionals would certainly seem to be evidence of this. He suspected that there was likely some sales data that bore this out as well.

The trouble was that, to some extent, the advertising industry was now a victim of its own cleverness. This was Steve Holiday's present theory. He could lament the nation's withered intellect and apparent lack of an attention span all he wanted. He'd read recently that more than fifty percent of the nation no longer ever bothered to pick up a book. Yet at this precise moment, with the people in front of him absolutely rapt by the little movies he was running, he was struck by his own complicity for this deplorable condition. How could he expect to hold anyone's interest for more than a fleeting second when they were fed provocative pictures and images like penny candy—each one more colorful and exciting than the last? Each one with catchy pop music and extraordinary computer generated graphics and special effects that often defied imagination? Over the past year, every commercial he had produced had cost nearly a million dollars or more. At thirty-five thousand dollars per second, each one of these densely loaded visual vignettes packed more production values than a Hollywood feature.

Having reviewed the reel several times in rehearsal, Holiday knew where and when the laughs would come. Satisfied that he had a few more minutes before the lights went up, he looked away from the screen and quietly turned his attention to Lane McCarthy who was busily working the table at the illuminated edge of the room. There was an older man seated next to her. He was obviously an existing client and this familiarity showed. After a particularly funny Japanese soap commercial finished, she jokingly jabbed his arm and nodded to the others as if they had been taking bets on its outcome or someone had successfully anticipated the punch line. On closer inspection it was clear that the other men at the table were M&M account executives and lesser members of the senior man's entourage. Steve admired the ease with which she engaged these adoring males, obviously enjoying their attentions, but just as successfully putting up an invisible barrier that none of them dared to cross.

In a few moments Lane was scheduled to relieve him at

the podium and offer concluding remarks. He noticed that she had a tiny set of cue cards by her water goblet, no doubt to remind her of everyone who needed to be thanked. They were curled at the corners from constant fiddling. It was damned cute. Anticipating the conclusion of the reel, he smoothed the lapels of his dark cashmere sport coat and leaned into the microphone in anticipation of regaining control of the audience. The last spot was a hilarious British spoof that brought howls of laughter and approval from the crowd. "And with that, ladies and gentlemen, I rest my case." Holiday concluded as the lights came up. It had been, despite the annoying obstacles, a remarkably engaging and successful presentation. This was expressed in a handshake that unfolded into a warm hug from Lane, who had rejoined him on stage, and sincere applause from the group that was now beginning to disassemble.

What neither Steve Holiday or Lane McCarthy had any way of knowing was that their performance at this industry function had managed to take on far greater importance than either had imagined. At the back of the room, close to the exit, a table had discreetly been assigned to the marketing team from Carlton & Paxton. At the encouragement of Allan Corbett and with the promise that they could observe the proceedings with relative anonymity, even the VP of Marketing, Andy Sullivan, had elected to attend. By accepting the invitation he had signaled his approval of the review process that had been initiated by Corbett. By actually attending, he had finally had a chance to catch up on the process that had been initiated by his senior manager. As the executive responsible for management of the brand around the globe, this was a significant breakthrough. Sullivan's endorsement would be critical if there was to be any change of agency.

Now he sat quietly observing from the shadows, leaning into the ear of his Senior Advertising Manager and asking questions each time Lane appeared on stage to introduce another speaker. Hoping to avoid being recognized by anyone from L&H who might be in attendance, he excused himself before Steve Holiday's reel ended and the house lights came back up. He had been traveling for much of the past two weeks and had avoided the persistent calls from Ira Lowenstein, but he wouldn't have to do so for much longer. Andrew Sullivan had an agenda of his own taking shape and it didn't necessarily bode well for Carlton & Paxton's longstanding partner.

Spence Playfair flipped through the pages of the brochure that was filled with beautiful handmade leather items. There was nothing that would work here either, he thought to himself. The luggage was attractive but somehow too personal. It also seemed to offer the promise of a trip. Moments earlier he had considered and rejected a handsome billfold for the same reason. The trouble with giving a wallet was that he didn't want to set up the expectation that there might be cash or a check inside. Stymied, he tossed the glossy catalogue onto a tilting stack that already included the spring Neiman Marcus book and at least a dozen other similar publications. No, the gift he wanted to send along to Allan Corbett as a thank you for visiting the office last week and to provide a taste of what might be following, had to be absolutely one of a kind. To make the desired impression, it would have to be something that was totally unexpected and sure to inspire delight.

His first idea had been a case of vintage burgundy.

Exquisite wine always made a splash with his more sophisticated clients and he had already sourced twelve rare bottles of 1989 Chateau de Pommard on the Internet. But part of him was reluctant to waste a wine of such superior quality on a volume consumer such as he now appreciated Allan Corbett to be. Besides, fine wine or expensive champagne was something that was more typically sent in celebration of victory and he didn't want to jinx himself or the agency with something that might be viewed as presumptuous.

What was it Zig had said when Spence had asked the busy Creative Director for ideas? He had quite rightly suggested that he try and make it something that would resonate with the Boom brand or, at the very least, might somehow be relevant to the pitch. This had led him down the path of gourmet foods, which had taken him to Loebel's meats, which turned into Artisanal cheeses and another dead end. How could you send someone a cache of calorie laden specialty treats when the product they were pitching for was specifically designed to address the problems that arose from over indulgence in such things? He hadn't gotten anywhere yet with the Boom thing, either.

There was definitely nothing appropriate in the standard corporate tickle trunk. He had already sent the rest of Corbett's group home in matching Boom team jackets. The handsome Melton and leather coats had been a huge hit when they had been presented following the agency tour and Leslie had fielded requests for three more from people who were not in attendance last week. Corbett had smiled broadly when he received his, but the collegiate style bombers had been cut in quite a youthful style and Playfair was fairly certain that the one Corbett had been given would have been passed along immediately to a junior staffer or to his teenaged daughter.

Based on the conversation they'd had at their very first luncheon, he was fairly certain a fish this size couldn't be landed with the usual swag and cotton.

Doubtful of success, Spence reluctantly returned to the last remaining catalogue in the folder that had been provided to him by their production manager. And suddenly, there it was. The perfect gift was staring right back at him from the magazine-style brochure's glossy front cover. It belonged to a corporate travel incentive company and the photo that adorned the front was a spectacular image of a duck blind in a marsh at dawn's first light. Under the headline 'Hunting Up Business', a middle-aged executive type, clad head-to-toe in Orvis hunting gear, stood silhouetted against a blazing sky. But it wasn't the private hunting lodge being advertised that had caught Spence's attention. Nor was it the high-end sportswear that the cover copy promised was available inside. Instead, Spence's eye was immediately drawn to the enormous twelve-gauge shotgun that the cover's model had raised expertly to his cheek and was pointing skyward. Now that was a gift that said, Boom!

A few clicks through Google and a short while later, Spence Playfair found himself on the phone with an exclusive gun dealer in St. Louis, Missouri. After half an hour on the line he was turning over the personal information necessary to secure the permit to purchase a limited edition, Italian-made Perazzi SCO Easy Loader with an engraved sterling silver inlay reading: "For the Big Shot, from your friends at Boom." He knew that Avery would go ballistic when he saw the invoice for the twenty-one thousand and change that this magnificent weapon would set him back. Thinking about it, he smiled at his own clever pun and the delighted reaction he was positive his gift would elicit from Allan Corbett. Such was the price of hunting big game. He would make certain the President didn't see the final price tag until Carlton & Paxton was safely in the bag.

Was it wrong to expect more from your people? That was Lane's reaction as she reviewed the sloppy first pass at the strategy document that her account group had provided. After finally getting back from the Ad Council presentation that had tied her up for much of the past day and a half, she was tired and irritable and hopelessly behind. Someone had dropped the draft on her desk at the end of the day clearly hopeful she wouldn't have a chance to read it. Everyone else involved appeared to have fled. Even Brenda must have gotten a whiff of how awful it was. Her normally attentive assistant had disappeared without waiting for Lane to return, no doubt certain that her boss would be on the warpath once she'd had a look. Brenda heard the drums that beat through the halls better than nearly everyone else in the tribe and it was clearly no accident that she was nowhere to be found.

After scanning the executive summary, Lane's first impulse had been tears. Whether it was the drug or the stress, for whatever reason, her emotions had been on the surface all day. If she hadn't had her period last week, she would have concluded that her weepy response was likely premenstrual. As it was, there was no such simple physiological explanation and her eyes welled with frustration. Unfortunately, the best effort of her so-called 'thinkers' was just plain shit. At six-thirty in the evening, perhaps the best way to deal with it was just to let it pass and pick it up in the morning. But Lane had never been one to let things like this linger overnight. Instead, she picked up the office wide intercom and paged everyone involved with the Carlton & Paxton pitch that was still in the building to report immediately to the main boardroom.

That was where she stood now—at the front of the office's largest meeting space with a ragtag team of junior account executives, a handful of creatives and two unfortunate slobs from the media department who had been left behind to crunch numbers on a proposed radio buy. Bryan Raider, her designated project leader, was nowhere in sight. Someone said they thought he had mentioned something about one of his kids having an Easter pageant. His designate, Cindy McMahon, had ducked out for dinner after promising the two nervous young AEs that she would be back by six. That was nearly half an hour ago. When one of them tried to raise her on her cell, all that they heard was the chaotic buzz of a bustling happy hour somewhere.

"Since Bryan and Cindy aren't here, I'll make my comments brief," Lane began. She was secretly hoping that one of the senior team members would magically appear so that she wouldn't be forced to deliver this angry tirade again in the morning. But with none of them in sight and the troops summoned, she was forced to press ahead anyway. "Ladies and gentlemen, we are barely two weeks away from the most important presentation in the history of this advertising agency. For the past nine days, since we received the brief, I have been trying my absolute level best to protect you all from the horrific pressure that is accompanying this project. Whether we like it or not …whether you know it or not …life as we currently enjoy it here at McCarthy & McCauley will no longer be the same if we are unsuccessful." She paused for effect, only to be disappointed by the apparent lack of comprehension from this most unworthy audience. A couple of them were, at least, trying to take notes. "But our first attempt at addressing the formidable challenge we are facing with this product is absolutely inadequate. In fact, it is just pure crap." With this comment, she tossed the skimpy document onto the table in disdain.

There was a reason most of these people were still here at this time of day. Most of them were just not very good. They used the hours at the end of the day to catch up and otherwise compensate for the shortcomings that they brought to their assigned tasks through the normal working hours of the day. Looking at their vacant expressions, Lane was so frustrated she almost fired them all on the spot. But it was not really their problem. They would just be the messengers. Still, she pounded them with an ultimatum that she was certain even the most dense among them would understand. Maybe their fear and anxiety would at least infect the minor contributions that these individuals would make.

"There are three things we are trying to accomplish with this pitch," she declared. "One ... we must create nearly instantaneous awareness among the largest portion of American women possible. Two ... we must somehow encourage them to overcome their intuitive skepticism of such a product. And three ... we need to accomplish this by spending approximately fifty million dollars each year for three years—less agency fees, of course." Her last line was an attempt at wry humor, but nobody got it.

The working document that Lane had received from her project team had come nowhere near to achieving this simple enumeration of communication priorities. Rather than pursue those tactics that would ensure swift media uptake, the poorly conceived document had managed to get preoccupied with the necessity for building a *dialogue* between physicians and the end user. It was a pointless strategy and nothing like what they had been discussing. It would be suicidal to suggest that the launch of Endrophat could be handled almost exclusively via referral channels, as the document had chosen to describe the role of doctors. 'Ask your doctor,' was a cop out, pure and simple. It significantly diminished the brute power of advertising to stimulate demand. This was the well that Lane wanted primed. She wanted every woman in America beating down the door to their doctor's office with a copy of one of their advertisements in their hand.

Lane suspected that the champion for the flawed approach was her Vice President in charge of Relationship Marketing, Angelina Gomez. Their one-on-one marketing guru had an exclusionary bias towards narrowcasting, as she liked to call it. For her, every communications problem could be solved with a personalized letter or e-mail. Trained at one of the ubiquitous letter shops that had pioneered personalized marketing back in the early nineties, she was a strong personality who could easily bully Gordon or Bryan Raider into thinking that such an approach, without mass marketing, could turn the trick. What she always forgot was the absolute importance of *brand*. As Lane had pointed out to her many times, people may let you into their homes because you address them by name, but they won't let you into their hearts if they don't know who you are. Gomez's proposal earmarked nearly two thirds of the total budget for outbound mail, electronic and traditional, and a comprehensive literature distribution strategy emanating from physician's offices. It was nowhere near sexy enough to win a pitch.

Compounding Lane's agitation was the first woeful attempt at creative that would drive this approach. Looking at it, she could barely conceal her anger at Gordon. In what appeared to be total abdication of his responsibility as Creative Director, he had allowed his counterparts in the Relationship Marketing group to art direct the messaging. Unfortunately, much less talented graphic designers and writers staffed this department and it showed in their ham-fisted efforts. Instead of a sophisticated and subtle representation of the product and its benefits, they had overloaded the messaging with a 'Free Trial Offer' that screamed from a particularly offensive looking mailer. Thank God this was only a draft and they had two more weeks to get things right. Lane was now glad she had conscripted some creative help from New York.

Studying the sea of vacant expressions in front of her, Lane reassessed her approach. "Ladies and gentlemen, you know what, why don't you all just go home." She wasn't angry or emotional any longer, just very very weary. "Clear up your desks, pack up your things, and take the rest of the evening off." In case there was any doubt about her sincerity, she turned on her heel and left the room but not before gathering up and heaving the useless proposal into a trash can that stood sentry by the door. "I'll be out of the office tomorrow morning until around nine. Would somebody make sure Bryan comes to see me immediately after I get in."

Day 12

T he two of them barely made it to the car before they burst into uncontrollable fits of laughter. "Just shut up and drive," Lane howled at Gordon Turnbull, wiping tears from her eyes as she struggled to fasten the seat belt in her partner's sleek black Jaguar XLS. "I think they may be coming after us," she joked as she turned to look over her shoulder.

"I'm pretty sure nobody in there is going to catch us," Gordon quipped with a wide smile as the storefront of the Weight Monitors studio with the swarm of mini-vans parked out front disappeared in his rear view mirror. "My oh my, wasn't that something else?"

"It most certainly was my friend," Lane agreed. "Unbelievable."

The two of them had crashed a meeting of the popular diet organization to do some ad hoc research. After regaining control of her temper yesterday evening, Lane had invited Gordon to tag along in the hope of getting her Creative Director kick started. While she was becoming increasingly doubtful that he was going to rise to the task, she felt he might benefit from seeing first-hand the challenges that many women faced when trying to lose weight and the tools that they used to help them cope. Neither of them had been prepared for what they had witnessed this morning at the support group that she herself had occasionally turned to for assistance.

"How long ago did you say you were last there? Gordon asked.

"It was a year and a half ago. You remember ... when we were in the preliminary negotiations with Interworld. I was so stressed out, I had gained a ton."

"Oh, yes. I remember." As he said this, Gordon Turnbull winced at the recollection. "Like a small elephant I would have said." Sometimes he could be such a bitch. Lane pounded him in the shoulder with her fist and they laughed again.

Unfortunately, Gordon hadn't been far off the mark. The truth was that this period had been a personal low point for the accomplished President of McCarthy & McCauley. Throughout the period surrounding the transaction that had made her a wealthy woman Lane had eaten compulsively, piling on nearly twenty pounds in the process. In desperation, she had reached out to the resource that so many other women seemed to turn to.

"Honestly, I don't ever remember a meeting like the one we saw today." What they'd watched and what had eventually caused them to be asked to leave was their snickering reaction to the messianic zeal of the session leader. Instead of generously sharing everyone's results and the usual weight loss sermon, she had infused the early morning get together with the wild-eyed fervor of a revival meeting.

"I nearly expected that woman in the track suit to start speaking in tongues," Gordon kidded. "Was she more excited about her five pound sticker or the availability of that new fudge dessert?"

"Stop it, Gordon," Lane cautioned. "It wasn't that bad." Her tone became a little less playful than before. It was clear that she was feeling remorse for their immature behavior and some residual frustration with her friend's half-hearted efforts to date. "But I think you get the idea of what I was trying to explain to you on the phone last night."

"How is that?" He stared straight ahead through the windshield as he negotiated the gathering rush hour traffic. His sporty Jaguar was too much car for him and, even after a year of driving it, he accelerated and braked unevenly.

"Don't you remember how I was saying that the trouble most overweight women have is a feeling of exploitation. Think of what we just saw. On one level, that organization exists ostensibly to help them, but on another, they've built a food processing empire off of their problem."

"Yeah, but doesn't the end justify the means? I mean some of the women seem to get what they're after—they lose weight. This is still America, isn't it?"

"You mean, free to profit from the misfortune of others?" Lane was surprised at the apparent anger of her own response and she worked to shape her next thought a little more carefully. "I guess part of me is grateful these kinds of companies exist. It certainly works for some people. But to me, I guess its like they're running AA for a profit," she now concluded, comparing them perhaps a bit unfairly to the voluntary alcoholism support network.

"So you're saying obesity is like an addiction?" Gordon pushed back.

"I think you have to look at it that way sometimes. I mean, you can't tell me that anyone in that room this morning was truly enjoying themselves ... or could really enjoy the shit that woman was hawking." Lane had been particularly offended by the length of time devoted to the promotion of a new line of processed meals. "Sure, when the music came on and a couple of them stood up and started dancing ... they were having fun. But they were making the best of a tough situation."

"It still didn't stop it from being hilarious," Gordon

reminded her. They had sat respectfully through the weigh-in and clapped enthusiastically for the people who had achieved milestones. But they had lost it completely when a particularly large black woman had come out of her seat and bellowed, "Praise the Lord," during the testimony section. It left the pair of them giggling uncontrollably and had caused them to be expelled.

"No, seriously," Lane continued. "I mean, was it just me, or has food somehow become an enemy? That session leader spoke about transfats like they were a terrorist conspiracy. I know that there are things out there that are unhealthy, but these people have declared war on the very thing that sustains us."

"That's a pretty complicated argument, Lane," her Creative Director cautioned her just a hint too patronizingly. "Next you'll be saying we're going to war with Nutri-Meals."

"But that's my point, Gordon," she countered. "Now that you mention it, they do all compete. The same gal that's paying ten bucks to attend a meeting is the same one who's dropping a hundred a week on approved meals." As she said this she made a set of quotation marks with her fingers around her final adjective, though all that Gordon noticed as he glanced sideways was the chip in her glossy red nail polish. Lane caught his disapproving look and it only served to heightened her exasperation with the man who seemed unwillingly, or perhaps was unable, to grasp her subtle reasoning.

"I'm just saying that taking on Weight Monitors may not be the way to go," he tossed back glibly, seemingly unaware of Lane's rising irritation.

"You don't think for a minute that some of toughest resistance to Endrophat isn't going to come from the people who profit from America's weight problems?" The experienced tactician in Lane knew all about how to blunt a market threat. So did Gordon. Discrediting a competitor was a strategy they occasionally had to recommend to their clients. "I'll bet that between the diet food manufacturers, publishing industry and the health care professionals and cosmetic surgeons, this is a hundred billion dollar category. Do you think they're just going to open their arms and welcome a drug that puts them out of business?"

"It's just a damned diet pill, Lane," he countered, finally realizing that his boss was quite serious.

"But maybe it's the solution," she tried one more time. A peek at her own scales this morning had given her more reason to believe. "Gordon, I sometimes get the sense that you aren't taking this pitch nearly seriously enough," she offered as a final rebuke.

Fortunately the entrance to their parking garage was in sight. Lane pulled out her phone and put Brenda on notice that they would be in the office in a few minutes. She quickly checked her make up in the small mirror that folded down from the sun flap and went silent until they pulled into Gordon's space next to the elevator. The New York people were scheduled to arrive that afternoon.

"**F**inally, something to friggin' work with," Zig Cartwright exclaimed. It was the first time he had flashed excitement at any of the proposed pitch creative in nearly two weeks. "It's bloody friggin' genius!" he added with emphasis, waiting for the others in the room to catch up to his enthusiasm. He had been purposely working on managing his profanity, a stupid request that had emerged on one of Spence Playfair's eternal pitch memos. "Friggin'" was his current favorite substitute and it now saturated his speech as tensions mounted with the Endrophat presentation exactly two weeks away. "Don't you friggin' see it?" he exclaimed.

The object of his attention was a single sheet of yellow legal paper turned sideways that had been tacked onto the section of corkboard allocated to potential slogans, or taglines, as they preferred to call them at Boom. There, in the crude hand of its writer and as yet undecorated with even the slightest hint of art direction, were the five words that Cartwright had immediately decided would be the basis of the agency's campaign recommendation. Placed beneath the product name, the way they might appear at the end of a TV spot or magazine advertisement, two solid weeks of thinking by nearly forty people had yielded the following simple phrase:

Endrophat
Use It. Lose It.

Cartwright knew it was the winner as soon as he laid eyes on it. Now he had to begin the arduous process of catching the rest of the group up to the revelation that was unfolding in his mind. He seized the sheet from the wall and kissed it. A moment later he drilled it, with a push pin, into the place of honor at the front of the room that everyone knew had been reserved for the idea that would trump all others.

"Seriously, I'm asking you …" he begged of the small pod of creatives seated immediately in front of him. "Don't you get it?" he exclaimed forcefully.

"I guess it's not a bad line … a little cute," conceded Rick Sedgwick who was sitting nearest to him. It was clear that he was hedging since the slogan hadn't originated from anyone on his team and he knew that this would have consequences later. "I'm not sure, but I think I might have seen it somewhere before," trying to toss the nearly always fatal dart of unoriginality.

"I don't think so," the Creative Director countered belligerently. "Even if you have, it's still bloody brilliant. Don't you see how it opens up the whole damn thing? What about you Les?" he now asked of Leslie Stride.

Up until then the young Account Exec had been busily working on revisions to the PowerPoint slides of the strategy deck that she and Playfair were responsible for finishing. They were well ahead of schedule and getting impatient to incorporate a rationale for the proposed creative solution. Realizing that she had only been half paying attention, she peered over the top of the pair of fake reading glasses that she wore low on her nose while proofing documents and rendered her opinion.

"It could work," she agreed, though noncommittally. Everyone in the room knew that she would remain neutral until she ran it by her boss later. The trick at this point was to temper the Creative Director's ardor for a concept that at this moment only he could envision. "What are you thinking? I mean where would we go with this, Zig?" she encouraged him to explain.

"Don't you see … whatever the bloody writer … who did this? … he gave us two pieces to play with. *Use it* is the kind of bullshit line that the client is going to want us to say. You know, an active verb and a clear call to action and all that other crap that everyone over there is bound to be pushing. 'Make sure you ask for the sale,' eh, what?" He offered this first part of his explanation derisively, intentionally parodying the language that the pantheons of classic advertising had somehow managed to preach into lore.

Now he leaned into the attentive group conspiratorially. "But it's the other part … *Lose it* … that well … that's just fuckin' genius," he shouted excitedly and forgetting his foul language vow. "Don't you get it? The pun … the play on words? Not only do women want to lose the weight," he explained slowly. "They want to l-o-s-e ... lose it," he spelled out for anyone still in doubt of his meaning. " "They want to lose control rationally ... emotionally ... sexually ... whatever. They want to lose weight so they can get laid," he celebrated. "Finally, we've got a line that taps into that. Now that's a big frickin' campaign idea!"

The uptight representatives of the other disciplines in the meeting room were still uncomprehending. Most were hung up on Zig Cartwright's use of such graphic profanity. Sensing the fact that he hadn't yet caused any lights to come on, he grabbed a thick black marker and went to the big white board that covered the wall on the opposite side of the meeting room table. Cartwright had been a fine arts graduate a long time ago and had come up in the business when the ability to draw freehand was still a requisite part of the job. With his back turned to the group as he spoke, he began to sketch out the opening scene for a storyboard.

"Okay, imagine a spot that opens in one of those tropical beach bars. You know somewhere in the Caribbean where every thing is bamboo, palm trees, coconuts and shit." As he spoke Cartwright quickly scribbled the scene to life. "In the middle of the set ... a thatch roofed tiki hut ... is a woman ... she's got a great figure ... though at first we see her only from behind. As the camera dollies in we notice that she is drinking and flirting outrageously with two or three men at once. Clearly, she's like a real mid-western schoolteacher on her first tropical holiday... innocent but real bad at the same time ... Mary Anne from Gilligan's Island-like." The agency always used seminal cultural reference points like old TV shows or bits from pop culture to rapidly communicate their ideas. "Eventually, after we show a couple of really choice T & A shots ... tight abs, tight ass, glorious rack and some more back and forth with the guys ... our girl gives out not one, but two room keys. We then go to a long shot of her holding hands on the beach as all three of them head for the hotel room. Motion freeze. Finally, a really sexy voiceover says something super sly and inside like, *"She asked the bartender for Sex on the Beach. Little did she know. Endrophat. Use it. Lose it.* It's simple, but it says it all." He paused again, as if waiting for applause. The room was stone still.

"What? You still don't get it?" he questioned unbelievingly. "She's gonna be the meat in the bloody sandwich," he said slowly for emphasis. "Thanks to the miracle product from our friends at Carlton & Paxton, her new acquaintances are going to have her sideways and standing up," he grinned like the devil.

The first reaction on the face of the head of the media group was shock. It was followed quickly by headshaking and a moan of disgust. The reaction was similar among the small knot of eggheads representing the account planning function. They had taken to heart Spence Playfair's directive that the approach for this particular pitch had to be safe and had contrived a brief that would hopefully lead to some fairly predictable campaign directions. But across the table where the creatives sat, slowly one by one, the shaggy art directors and copywriters began to catch on and to nod their approval. Zig was right. The line really did open up a whole new direction for their work. Suddenly the group head, who just moments before was being bullied by his boss, lit up and offered another potential commercial scenario.

"I've got one," he declared as he rose from his chair and began to pace around the room as he channeled the idea that was unfolding in his mind's eye. "Open on a scene at a shopping mall. A mom and her daughter are shopping for prom dresses. You know … a real bonding moment. We cut to a changing room and strip the kid down to her underwear to reveal that she's packing a few pudding pounds or whatever.

The kid is upset and the mother is frustrated, so they give up. On the way home they pass a billboard for Endrophat or some other visual cue we design in. Flash forward a couple of weeks and a boy arrives to pick up the girl for the big night. She looks fantastic. Slim, tight ... no underwear under the gown. Sitting in the back of the big pimpy limo, he's got his hand on her thigh—the money moment. *"She always wanted a ride in the backseat. Endrophat. Use it. Lose it."*

Zig Cartwright's eyes flashed. "I love it ... its simple, exciting and ... oh so sexy. I might even want to do the casting myself," he leered. As he says this, it is clear he has largely forgotten the account executives and planners in the room who are exchanging worried glances. As the creatives begin to break off into huddles and separate conversations, the others in the room look to the face of Leslie Stride for confirmation that the proposed executions are way too over the top. But instead of the disapproval they expect, the attractive businesswoman is smiling and somewhat bemused.

"Its awfully risky," she finally pronounces. "I mean it's certainly not what we originally asked for," she hesitated.

"But it would make us bloody famous," Cartwright now urged, sensing the first signs of buy in from one of the grown ups. "You know we would end up dripping with awards if we could pull it off," he enthused. He now coaxed his unexpected ally on the idea delicately forward, trying his best to charm and cajole. "Come on, what do you say, Les?" His mortal enemy of the last two frustrating weeks could now become a very valuable ally.

"Well, it's certainly more interesting than anything we've looked at so far. I bet we could twist the psychographic stuff from the research to point more towards the ... what did you call it Zig ... the true motivation angle? I'll tell you what ... why don't you have your guys bang out a few more executions and I'll give it a little more thought from my side."

"Ahhh ... you're the best lass," the Creative Director cooed. "I knew I could count on ye," he said with a thickening of his accent that magnified his sense of genuine excitement. "Now take it down the hall to old Spencer and see if ye can sell it. We've got some work to do."

The meetings now were nearly impossible to attend and everyone in the room felt the same way. Steve and the team from Lowenstein Holiday occupied the chairs on one side of the room and the adversarial product manager from Carlton & Paxton and two of Allan Corbett's young marketing communications staffers were seated opposite. It had been a long afternoon and he longed to escape the airless room.

"So what do you think?" Steve asked finally. He had been tap dancing hard before this stoic audience for nearly twenty minutes with very little encouragement. "Personally, I think there might be two or three perfectly appropriate next ads for the campaign here," he said waving at the selection of concepts that was spread out on the table.

The break out room that had been selected for this presentation was an exceptionally bleak little space with foul air and no natural light. The strobe-like flicker from a neon tube in need of replacement threatened to elevate his already throbbing headache to migraine status and cast an unflattering shadow on the series of concepts he had just presented. Propped on a credenza not designed for the purpose, one of the magazine layouts they were discussing had already tipped to the floor and been returned to the table. A wrinkled dog-ear now marred the upper right corner of the carefully crafted exhibit. It was just one more insult in a session that seemed to have been designed expressly for this purpose.

"Not only do I think it is off strategy, but it seems vaguely imitative of something I saw years ago," said Michael Pearlman, the product manager responsible for Zettamin, Carlton & Paxton's popular seasonal allergy medication. "This is even more unoriginal than the stuff we looked at last week."

As the insolent young client made this biting remark, he turned to his peers who were responsible for managing the relationship with the agency and gave a dismissive shrug. Steve Holiday was nearly certain he saw two of them exchange a conspiratorial wink and it took every ounce of restraint he possessed not to grab a layout and try to jam it down the throat of the ungrateful little jerk that had just issued this baseless criticism.

"Interesting that you should say that. I was sure that you knew we received a One Show pencil for last year's campaign," Steve countered. He hated bringing advertising awards to bear in the defense of a concept, yet in this case the insult was just too unfounded to tolerate. "But that's right, you were still responsible for Dextaphin then."

The Creative Director's measured dig referred to an ill-considered sport supplement that had crashed and burned in test market last year. Pearlman had foolishly insisted the product did not need advertising support, but instead would grow by word of mouth among athletes. He had thrown all his money at a celebrity endorsement contract that ended badly when the player was suspended following a strip club brawl. In some ways, it was remarkable that Pearlman was still around.

"Regardless, I can't buy any of this shit," the designated asshole now asserted with a wave of his hand and invoking the final judging prerogative he enjoyed as *The Client*. "Unless you've got something else to show us, I don't see that there's much need to carry on this afternoon."

It was Steve's third terrible C&P meeting since the review

had been announced and there was very little he could do about it. He looked over at Jack Blenheim who was just getting his feet wet on the business, but his weak account guy lacked the backbone to step up and the opportunity to challenge the ignorant young man passed.

"You're right, Michael," Steve now said, signaling to his people that the meeting was just about over. "There is nothing further to discuss. Why don't you just hang onto this work until the review is complete, then we'll talk about it again?"

"I'd like to be able to, Mr. Holiday," the calculating young bastard countered petulantly before delivering the kicker that he had been specifically empowered to employ. "But unfortunately, we can't afford to sit on this. I've got some media booked and I don't intend to waste it."

"Surely, you can delay it another month?" pleaded Jack Blenheim. It was not unusual to buy time by running existing materials until a new execution could be worked into rotation. The award-winning ad they were discussing was nowhere near worn out and that was how this kind of impasse would be solved under normal circumstances. Unfortunately, as everyone in the room knew, these times were anything but.

"I'm afraid not, Jack. Can't wait," the little weasel now taunted. "I know you guys are swamped with the pitch and all so Allan has said it would be okay if I looked elsewhere for help." He waited a moment before tossing the grenade he'd been holding onto all day. "I've already asked Boom for some alternatives."

"You've got to be fucking kidding," Steve exploded. "You presumptuous little prick." Before he could say anything more, Jack Blenheim grabbed his sleeve and practically dragged him from the room. There was nothing they could do but take word of this latest development back to Ira.

Allan Corbett's betrayal was now complete.

Day 13

"Goddammit Laney, I'm telling you once and for all. It's either they go or I'm out of here." Though she had nearly stopped listening, Lane decided to let her senior partner rage a while longer before responding. Gordon Turnbull had been in her office venting without interruption for nearly ten minutes, yet he was still too angry to listen to reason.

"I'm about ready to gather up their stuff and have it thrown into the street. I want you to call Reiner Adolph and tell him 'No thanks, asshole' if these people are the best he can come up with," he fumed.

As he circled back to his original complaint, Lane tried to hide her annoyance. She could just imagine the reaction of the steely businessman from Stuttgart who now controlled their fates if he were to hear her ungrateful Creative Director's unrelenting rant. Even her patience was beginning to wear thin. Adolph would have squashed him like a bug and not have given it another moment's thought. He had been even pricklier than usual since their phone conversation and her reluctance to invite him to the final presentation. While he hadn't come out and declared he would be joining them, there were strong hints from the New York contingent that they should leave room in the presentation agenda for him. It was also becoming increasingly clear that Adolph had installed a mole within her office and that, in truth, he'd probably known about the C&P invitation within hours of its arrival.

The team that had shown up from Interworld's largest office had turned things upside down from the moment they appeared on the scene the day before. Despite her boss's assurances that they would be respectful, they had been anything but. He had dispatched five of them in total and each one of them was nearly as bad as the other. The three creatives were arrogant and immediately dismissive; the account guy was a preening poseur; and the remaining fellow, a media planner, was little more than a New York-trained junior estimator. His shallow grasp of the complexity of the problem was apparent quite quickly and, in less than half a day, the group had succeeded in pissing off nearly the entire agency.

Their first transgression had been to commandeer Gordon Turnbull's immaculately maintained office as their own. Lane had deposited them there after taking them to lunch, anticipating that her Creative Director would find a suitable place to quarter them for the duration of their stay. Instead, without bothering to ask, they had stripped his walls of artwork, pushed his comfortable seating arrangement into a sloppy circle and gone straight to work. By the time Turnbull returned from his own luncheon engagement, the tidy space of the fastidious creative head was littered with scraps of ideas and tissues—his orderly little world in total chaos.

The most vocal among these unwelcome visitors was Barry Rabinowitz, a brash Jersey-born copywriter who had the most remarkable capacity to alienate people from the moment he met them. He accomplished this with a combination of sandpaper-like abrasiveness and poor personal hygiene. Coming from the epicenter of the industry, even as the youngest among them, he judged quickly and unselfconsciously. Within a handshake he had succeeded in discrediting the entire Mid-West ad scene and, along with it, the best efforts that the entire M&M Creative Department had developed to date.

"We ditched the stuff we saw on your desk," he had said to his host when Turnbull inquired of the work that his people had manufactured and that he intended to use as the starting point for a status review. "It was shit," Rabinowitz summarized insensitively. "I can see why you called us."

But worse than the swiftness of this judgment, Rabinowitz had offered his appraisal without a hint of apology nor any questions about the context of the work he had so quickly dismissed. In fact, he had followed the statement with a snicker and a smirk at his colleagues from New York. Obviously, they had been instructed by head office to usurp Turnbull's authority the moment they arrived. Knowing what she did, Lane was certain this cruel permission had been granted prior to departure. All she could do was counsel patience. That was where she found herself now as her longtime colleague carried on.

"Lane, you're going to have to do something. They're bloody barbarians," he whined shamelessly. "I mean the criticism of the work is one thing, but the total disrespect is another matter entirely." As he spoke, he was visibly crimson. Clearly, it was his humiliation in front of his people that had unnerved her Creative Director most. Plus the fact that these punks were barely half his age.

"I'm afraid you're going to have to find a way to make this work, Gordon," Lane coached in answer. "You know the grief we're getting to deliver the numbers. Don't give them the excuse their looking for to come in here and make changes."

"Is that what this is about Lane? I told you this would happen," he reprimanded. Gordon could get quite nasty when he argued, especially when he was right, and she couldn't disagree with him on this issue. Even though he was a minority partner and he had profited handsomely from the sale to Interworld, he had predicted early on that the good faith of the courtship would soon give way to the unrealistic pressures they now faced.

"You knew it, too, Gordon. But I didn't see you refusing the check." Lane responded somewhat coldly. "Maybe when this thing is over you can take a little holiday to that place of yours out west?" The allusion to his vacation property was a not too subtle jab at his lackluster performance to date.

As fond as she was of her Creative Director, she had found herself growing increasingly impatient with his truculent attitude towards the pitch and the affairs of the agency in general, lately. Unlike some creative people who found personal wealth liberating, Gordon had become increasingly complacent since receiving the windfall from the sale of his ten percent. He had immediately piled it into an expensive fractional ownership club and a series of risky investments that she was certain he didn't fully understand. It was no secret around the office that he had become a compulsive stock watcher and that tracking the NASDAQ had become an enormous distraction for him.

As much as Lane had admired Gordon's efforts in the past, his productivity had declined steadily since the acquisition. The concepts he was presenting lately were dull and safe, and too often he appeared to be reaching into the same tired bag of tricks. While no one wanted to say *burned out,* consensus was that he had most definitely grown lazy. He must have sensed it, too. Recently he had tried to blame the staleness on the excessive structure and strategic approach that the acquisitors had imposed upon the creative process. But it really wasn't about process. It was just time to go.

"It's two weeks Gordon," Lane now stated assertively. "I know it's going to be hard and I sympathize with you. But we weren't going to win this thing with what I saw from our

people. And if we don't at least come close, there will be hell
to pay." She hated to have to put her foot down so hard, but
he had crossed the line.

"But Lane," he attempted one more time. Before he could
finish, she cut him off.

"Make it work," she commanded. "We've wasted too
much time already."

As he sat waiting for his client to react to the initial report,
Max Weller fidgeted absently. While Ira Lowenstein slowly
read through the written material and casually inspected the
accompanying photographs, the private investigator exam-
ined his fingernails and gnawed hungrily at his badly dam-
aged cuticles. When Ira caught him, he dropped his hands
quickly to his sides. But after another few idle moments, he
resumed a game of attempting to pick up the scattered sugar
granules that had missed his coffee cup with the back of a
dampened spoon. Seated in the back booth of the coffee shop
around the corner from the L&H offices, where their clandestine meeting was now taking place, Weller had little choice
but to wait patiently until his client got to the good parts.

So far the investigation had been more or less routine—
with one very notable exception. As per his instructions he
had followed the subject, Allan Corbett, on three occasions
the previous week from his home to his office and everywhere
in between. This had been accomplished unnoticed and was
documented extensively with a sequence of photos. The day
before yesterday he had also been successful in intercepting a
residential mail delivery. Though dangerously illegal, he had
managed to borrow and make copies of the Corbett's most
recent bank, phone and credit card statements, all without
detection. The remainder of the surveillance had been done

via computer. As was more and more common these days, Weller and his geeky sidekick had conducted a fairly exhaustive search of the Internet—Googling Corbett up and down and drilling deep into the sex-for-hire blogs and chat rooms where guys like him typically hung out. While he noted that this part of the report was still very preliminary, he had already found some fairly incriminating stuff. He was currently working on hacking his way onto Corbett's hard drive and he felt fairly positive that, with the reckless surfing habits this subject had already exhibited, he would soon be able to phish his way in.

"He's a bit of a predator as you can see … and very sloppy," Weller editorialized.

"Clearly," Ira agreed. He said it in a hushed tone that invited Weller to be similarly discreet. Though only half way through the report, the results had obviously been worth the effort. With most of his worst impressions of Corbett confirmed, Ira now felt a twinge of regret at the entire unseemly process.

As the documentation succinctly captured, all of the usual signs of a middle-aged man in distress were present. The drinking problem had, unfortunately, been easy to verify. He was stopping into a variety of package stores daily and masking the rest under the guise of business lunches and corporate entertaining. This came as no surprise to Ira who had observed the behavior on several occasions. A peek at Corbett's purloined credit card statement had yielded confirmation of another long held impression. There was a significant monthly overhang, steep interest payments, and a substantial overdraft balance. Not unexpectedly, the Corbetts were having severe financial difficulties.

The electronic surveillance was another matter entirely. While his cell phone records appeared reasonably clean, even Weller's cursory web search had yielded tracks through several particularly dank porn sites and frequent visits to live video chat rooms. Also highlighted, were regular attempts by Corbett to make connections for extramarital liaisons via online hookup sites. While nobody appeared to have responded to his solicitations, his profile appeared with three different services. The only good news, the private investigator had noted, was that these postings were currently stale dated and had not been visited for quite some time. More likely, though, he had given up on the Internet and found some other way to stalk women.

As Ira Lowenstein flipped to the last page of the report, Weller leaned forward in anticipation of his client's reaction to his most important discovery. He had deliberately saved the very best part of this lurid summary for last and he wanted to be certain its significance wasn't lost. When he was sure that his client had read through to the middle of the page, he interrupted.

"He's involved with a stripper … a real beauty. She's a regular at Wriggly Field's and, from what I can tell, he's paying her off with drugs of some kind."

As he telegraphed these essential details, Weller beamed proudly. He had rightly anticipated that this was the kind of information that would get the agency president excited. While he figured that his client didn't actually engage in blackmail, the kind of compromising information he had uncovered typically warranted further investigation and a few more weeks of work. If it led where he was fairly sure it would, there might even be a handsome bonus.

"You've got to be kidding me," Ira smiled broadly. He leaned back into the booth and shook his head in disbelief. "Sometimes its just frickin' hard to believe." Yet as he measured the contents of the report against the inappropriate behavior that had been described by his account guys, none of it really came as a shock. "Does his wife have any idea?"

"Not so far as I can tell," the PI responded quickly. "But if you don't mind me saying so ... and I haven't paid too much attention to her ... she appears to be a piece of work in her own right."

"In what way?" Ira asked, briefly curious.

"Drinking mostly. Looks pretty loose, too. Spends money like it's water. Do you want me to check her out?" Weller asked eagerly.

"Nah ... stick to him," Ira requested. "It looks like you're onto something that'll suit our purposes anyways."

"Should I press on with the electronic stuff or just focus on the girl?" Weller practically panted. "As far as I'm concerned, I think its pretty clear we've got a real computer creep here. But if I was a betting man, I'd say the stripper thing is gonna be a lot more interesting. I mean, he's in the drug business, right?"

"You followed him to the office," Lowenstein reminded. "Something tells me he's doing more than giving away free samples," he added with a wry smile.

"I think that's what she might be giving him. If you know what I mean," Weller winked.

"So you're pretty sure they're having a thing, right?"

"I'm not exactly sure. Right now it appears that he's just getting done in the VIP room. I mean, I only found this out late last week, so I haven't got much on what she's doing *away from the office* so to speak," the detective apologized.

"But he's definitely giving her dope?" he asked.

"Saw it myself, Mr. Lowenstein. He dishes her after she's danced for him and she seems pretty grateful for it."

"Any idea what?"

"Not for certain, boss. My guess is its likely prescription stuff—antidepressants and perk or whatever. You know most of these girls are popping all kinds of pills and snorting their brains out. I'm guessing he'd have access to all kinds of shit."

It was a logical enough conclusion to draw, thought Ira. Every now and then rumors leaked out of Carlton & Paxton of someone who had gone native, as they liked to say. The more he thought about the contents of the report, the more it disappointed him. Instead of dealing with a respectable senior manager working for one of the country's most admired corporations, his longtime client appeared to have enough serious issues that he should probably be checked into a mental hospital. Or worse, prison.

"Thank you, Max. I don't have to remind you that all of this is highly confidential." Ira was suddenly quite embarrassed with the whole sordid situation in which they now found themselves. "Why don't you keep an eye on the stripper for another week or so? Something tells me that our friend, Mr. Corbett, is capable of a few more surprises." Concluding their meeting, the troubled executive tucked the file folder into his tidy leather valise and slid gingerly out of the booth.

"Oh, by the way, does she have a name ... the girl?" As Ira made this inquiry he stood up and inspected his expensive suit for any residue from the grimy bench.

"Stella ... Stella Star is what she goes by. I haven't been able to get the real one yet, but I'll find that out soon enough."

With that Ira Lowenstein dropped a few bills on the unpaid check and departed the restaurant swiftly. The only thing he had to do now was figure out what to do with all of this incredible information. But he would have to wait until he got back to the office before he could give the matter serious consideration. He had a pressing client meeting and, after that, an important luncheon. For the first time in a couple of weeks there was a spring to his step. And why not?

Even with what had been discovered thus far, one option was to confront Corbett directly with what he now knew. But the review had already gathered too much momentum to be called off, and besides, who could guess how Corbett might react. He certainly appeared to be quite unstable. Part of Ira wished he could share this new found knowledge with his partner, but Steve Holiday would be appalled that his associate had sunk so low as to seek out this kind of material. He was just too much of a gentleman.

Instead, what Ira had to do now was find a way to share this information with his Board connections. But he would have to do it in a fashion that didn't compromise his own integrity. This kind of stuff was dynamite and Ira knew, intuitively, that it could just as easily blow up in his face. He would mull his plan a while longer. Yet for the first time since this whole damned process had been set in motion, he felt a calm returning. It wasn't the way he'd hoped they'd accomplish it, but maybe they could to save this thing after all.

"Have they got a talent recommendation yet?" He didn't ask the question impatiently, but Leslie Stride thought she could detect a hint of irritation in his voice. Barely five minutes before Spence Playfair had been panting and thrashing around on top of her. Now they were resting -- or at least she was -- while it was clear that her lover had already returned to the office. It was just like him to want to get back to work so soon after they were finished, even if it was just in his mind. Something in his tone caused her to wonder, fleetingly, whether his disappointment wasn't now with her.

"Not that Zig is sharing." As she said this she shifted from beneath the weight of his soft upper arm. Turning her head on the pillow to face him, she studied his features in the dim light that filtered through the drawn curtains of the hotel room they had taken after lunch. Catching him unaware—he was now staring unblinkingly at the ceiling and beyond—she was forced to wonder, herself, exactly what she was doing here in the afternoon with this vain and selfish middle-aged man.

He wasn't a particularly good lover. His attentions to her were entirely mechanical as he had labored over her and once, briefly, down below. Half way through the act, she had decided that her pleasure was just one more thing that needed to be accomplished before it could be stroked from the list she was certain that he kept in his head throughout. Come to think of it, he hadn't been too good a boss lately, either.

"Any idea when?" he followed up. The voice seemed oddly detached from his cadaver-still body.

"He said something about a meeting first thing tomorrow morning at the production house. You know Zig. It's all pretty loosey-goosey."

"Fine," Spence added with surprising calm. "Les, when he does bring us into the loop, I want you to do me a favor?"

"And what might that be, darling?" His unusual tone perked the naked young woman's attention. Leslie Stride was truly spectacular without clothes on. She shivered and sprouted goose flesh at the suggestion of some intrigue.

"I want you to like whoever and whatever they present?"

"What do you mean, *like?*" she asked, suspiciously.

"You know, really like it," he said again with emphasis. "Get all excited about it, like it came from Albert … frickin' … Einstein, or Lee Chow for that matter." His allusion to the legendary Chiat Day Creative Director surprised her, even if he did manage to mangle the name.

"That's taking a pretty big chance, isn't it?" As she spoke, she began to survey the room, discreetly seeking out the likely location of her underwear and the balance of her clothing. Earlier, Spence had insisted on tossing things about as he playfully peeled them from her. With it becoming apparent that they would be returning to the office soon, it was essential that she begin to take this inventory. "I mean, what if we actually hate it?" she asked, spying one of her sheer stockings snared on the handle of the bedside table.

"Well Leslie, that depends ..." Playfair now counseled patiently. There was always a chance to teach his young protégé another lesson. "... on what it is that we want the creative to accomplish."

"That's obvious, isn't it?"

"Maybe ... maybe not," Playfair patronized. "Haven't I taught you anything at all young lady?"

"So you think the creative doesn't matter?"

"Perhaps," he said, being deliberately inscrutable. "Though I suspect we could probably shit on the boardroom table and still walk away with this thing."

"You're kidding, aren't you?" Even with her own dark instincts, Leslie was still young enough in the business to imagine that the work always mattered. She waited for him to explain. Now it was Playfair who turned in her direction.

"Well, for one, it's already clear that Lowenstein & Holiday is out. This whole thing couldn't have gotten this far without there being some serious problems with that relationship." As he began to enumerate his reasons, he gently counted her ribs with his fingertip and stroked her soft, pale skin. "Two ... I think M&M is going to have some unforeseen problems in their Creative Department. Don't ask me how I know this, but I think there is some serious angst over there. And three ... this stuff is going to be a hit whatever happens."

"What? Endrophat?"

"Can't miss. Unless they manage to kill somebody, it can't possibly be anything other than the greatest drug introduction in the history of the whole goddamned world."

"But if the creative sucks ..."

"Who cares? Don't you see, Les?" he admonished. "If the

work doesn't cut it, that's all Zig's fault. But the stuff will fly off of the shelves regardless. Besides, I've already told you that I've got Corbett right where I want him."

"So it really doesn't matter?"

"If we can win this thing in spite of Zig ... and I'm pretty certain we can. Well then, I think we'd have all the permission we need to dispose of that particular problem at the same time."

"You mean Zig?"

"Precisely. I've been wanting to nail that ungrateful little prick since the day after he arrived."

"But what about Avery?"

"He'll have no choice. I'll say that Corbett insists."

With his plan revealed, Playfair now rolled away from the girl and righted himself on the bed. With his back to her, he spoke again. "I really need you to sell it, kid. Ziggy can't doubt for a moment that we're anything other than one hundred percent behind him."

Climbing onto her knees, Leslie Stride crawled over to the opposite side of the bed. Placing her soft hands on Playfair's doughy shoulders, she began to knead them gently. "You're the boss," she whispered seductively into his ear as she pressed herself against his back. The last thing the cunning young Account Executive wanted to do at three in the afternoon was head back to work. With a little bit of extra effort on her part, maybe she could even wiggle her way aboard the actual pitch team.

Day 14

The first few rays of the morning sun bent around the charcoal colored corner of the Sears and shot a glint of fiery orange light into his shadow cloaked office. The brilliant beam cut sideways across the wide window and painted a ragged skyline of silhouettes from the menagerie of trophies and awards assembled on the ledge. Looking up from his desk, Steve Holiday tipped a swallow from his oversized coffee mug, but its contents were cold and unsatisfying. To the west, an ash colored quarter moon still hung in the cloudless sky and the stars that remained from the evening before were extinguishing themselves one by one. It was barely seven a.m. and he had already been at work for a couple of hours. Still, he had been rewarded handsomely for the ungodly hour of his arrival. For the first time in two weeks he had a fresh idea and, at least until someone told him otherwise, a name and a line that could easily become a campaign.

As always, Holiday wasn't exactly sure where the magical phrase had come from. Perhaps it was a combination of things. For nearly a week now, the work he had done with Evie and Pete had been percolating in the back of his mind. They had come so very close to nailing it. Unfortunately, a clever slogan had continued to elude them and their initially promising ideas had subsequently withered and died. Also, there was little doubt that Ira's idiosyncratic observation about the profound importance of the product had set him in pursuit of a new direction. As recently as a few days ago, the Creative Director had been tilting towards a fairly literal translation of Endrophat's primary benefit. Though he hadn't come out and said as much, "Lose 15 Pounds in 15 Days" the way many diet ads promised was still the most compelling proposition he had encountered—especially if the product could actually deliver. But it definitely wasn't a pitch winner, and it most certainly wasn't inspirational, in the way that he knew the campaign for this product had to be.

No, what had inspired this morning's success had come to him yesterday night in the twilight time between sleep and dreams as he replayed the haunting image of the big woman in the clothing store over again in his head. It was then, in the most honest hour of the day, that for the first time he had sensed some of the crushing sadness that must inhabit her life. Subsequently, it had occurred to him that he was, in many ways, responsible for her pain.

He thought of the award-winning work he had created for at least a half dozen products over the years. Meals in Minutes, Urban Gourmet, the absolutely drop dead gorgeous food shoot he had arranged for one of Chicago's most iconic chef's new cookbooks. He thought of the days and nights he had spent in studio encouraging the immensely talented photographers and stylists he hired to capture image after enticing image of a thousand gastronomic delights. Food is fabulous, every picture had to scream. But don't you dare gain a pound was the unspoken admonition that accompanied each of them. Savor every sumptuous bite of this deliciously sinful chocolate dessert, but be sure you can still slip into a size six when you're done. Ah, the exquisite whip of temptation and denial. Shame on you if you gave in, or worse, gave up. Such was the cruel contradiction with food and eating that he had helped to perpetrate.

Ordinarily, Steve wasted little time on this kind of introspection. A conscience is a luxury few copywriters can afford. Besides, he was still unclear about how he actually felt about an overweight individual's responsibility to take ownership of their problem—to exercise some restraint and practice a little self-control. But he also knew in his heart, that he was as powerless as anyone to resist the endless temptations his best work inspired. After all, didn't he wear exactly the same designer boots and jeans that his models wore in the commercials he shot? Didn't he drink the same scotch for which he had produced an award-winning magazine campaign? As much as he tried to pretend that he was the master of his own buying impulses, he could no more ignore them himself than he could choose not to draw breath. Such was the frightening power he wielded. Contrary to popular opinion and most people's strenuous denial, the shit he produced really worked, and he knew it.

What did this have to do with his campaign for Endrophat? It was shortly after coming to this conclusion that it dawned on him that what that big woman really needed was hope. In fact, maybe this was precisely what he and Carlton & Paxton owed her. This was the debt to be settled with the vulnerable and easily exploited before they could win the trust that parting with hundreds or thousands of dollars for a cycle of drug therapy would require. The more he thought about it, the more he realized this might also be the key to solving the problem that they were now faced with.

What the advertising that Lowenstein Holiday developed had to do was give this unfortunate woman a reason to fully commit herself to the transformation that the miracle drug would make possible. Somewhere the prospect for this product had to awaken to the idea that, just like a butterfly emerging from a chrysalis, there was a whole new world of possibility waiting on the other side. What she most definitely didn't need was another of the false promises that had always been the hallmark of the weight loss industry. At three o'clock this morning, while most sane people slept, all of these random thoughts had somehow pushed themselves back into his consciousness. The result was the four short words that he had scribbled out on the pad that he kept on his nightstand for this purpose.

As had become his custom when he thought he'd found a solution lately, he pecked the words into his laptop and selected his favorite, neutral font—a clean and non-committal cut of Helvetica. Then he paired it with the name that had been his favorite from the lengthy list that everyone had been contributing to. Now he waited for the sandwiched together thoughts to emerge from the laser printer that had hummed to life just moments before. After a protracted pause, during which it seemed like even the soulless machine was passing judgment, a single sheet of plain white paper was disgorged onto which the following words had been electronically scribed:

ACHIEVA®
Your Life is Waiting

To his relief, the written expression of his idea looked just as good on paper as it had in his mind's eye. This was the first important litmus test the experienced professional always put his ideas through. Holiday always liked to picture the campaign tag as it might appear at the bottom of a magazine or newspaper advertisement. He was still a print guy at heart and always would be. More importantly, he was sure he had lit upon a solution that he could sell.

It was always like a jigsaw puzzle. Finally, all of the pieces of the brief, the research and the endless rounds of discussion had fallen into place. At last he had a line that he thought he could build a campaign around and maybe even a new name that complimented it, as well. Certainly, he had a strong core idea for which he could build a compelling rationale. He knew from past experience that with a highly analytical client like Carlton & Paxton, sometimes the logic of the recommended positioning was just as important as its expression. The early morning muse had indeed been kind.

All he could do now was wait for someone to share it with. The rest of the agency wouldn't be in for another two hours—definitely no one from creative, anyway. While killing time he would Google the name and hope that he could get the necessary trademark registrations that he prayed might still be available. Thank god it was Friday. Maybe there would even be some time to breathe today. The tsunami of work that was washing through the shop had finally shown some signs of abating. Maybe, finally, they would be able to focus on one campaign idea and begin to move forward.

"Show me the head sheets again," Zig demanded.

The antique pine table in the handsomely furnished pre-production office of Tight Rope was littered with photos of dozens of attractive young ladies. Most of them had glossy black and white pictures of their beautiful faces on one side and images of them in high fashion apparel, sportswear and swimsuits on the other, along with the names of the agency's that represented them. All of the girls were gorgeous and the flattering statistics that described their heights, weights and measurements erased any doubt. This was the data that Zig Cartwright was most interested in right now.

"Whoever plays the lead has to be absolutely flawless,"

he continued. "But remember, this is more about body type than face. And it has to be absolutely believable that she was once heavy. I'm not sure what that looks like exactly, but we'll know it when we see it.

"Maybe its just a little hint of baby fat? You know, just a hint of softness under the chin." This suggestion came from Melanie Cameron, the helpful talent coordinator from the commercial film company that had consented to help out Boom with this hastily assembled production. "Something that makes her, I don't know, cute rather than just beautiful."

"Maybe, she's just got big tits." This dubious contribution came from Gunnar Helstrom, a promising young art director from Boom, whom Zig had decided had a fairly good eye for selecting on-camera talent. He had chosen to reward the young man for his early work on the pitch by allowing him to participate in the cattle call that would likely be staged this afternoon, as soon as a short list of candidates for the leading lady's role had been culled from the pile of images they were currently sorting through.

A fairly attractive young woman herself, Melanie shot him a disapproving look and turned to Zig for confirmation that the comment had been inappropriate. The production people had to be very careful since, while they were essentially doing tomorrow's shoot as a favor, with a false step they could easily be blackballed from the lucrative future assignments that winning the pitch might yield from Boom.

"Try and keep your python in your pants," Zig admonished the young artist with a sly wink. He was barely more professional than Helstrom himself. "And remember, there is a lady present."

Sometimes Zig's boys could be terribly sexist. And television production brought out the very worst in them. Around Boom there was even more than the usual clamor to attend the filming of their commercials since, invariably, Zig had a way of pushing every idea to the very edge. In fact, he was already legendary for bringing with him his peculiarly English sense of prurience to the formerly staid Chicago production scene. Given the sexually charged concept that they would be executing tomorrow, excitement was running high and Helstrom had been the envy of his peers when he'd been selected to accompany the master to the pre-pro meeting.

This session, like the entire production, was being pulled together on the fly. The idea was to create a simulation of a finished television commercial at a fraction of the cost. Zig had agreed to do it for Leslie and Spence who were convinced that this kind of over-the-top investment in spec work would show exceptional initiative and an added degree of commitment on the part of the agency. It might also help the dull-witted literalists, as Cartwright assumed the unimaginative people on the review committee would be, to better understand what he was talking about as he walked them through the myriad of concepts he would be describing on presentation day.

To execute it, Zig had called in the favor from Tight Rope. Together with a skeleton crew of professionals and a cast made up of employees from Boom along with their families and friends, they would do in a single day what might take them three or four if they were working with the expensive talent, tools and props of an actual film production. Thanks to people like Melanie, they might even be able to pull off something pretty cool.

"What about this girl, Zig?" The pretty talent coordinator handed the Creative Director a sheet from a binder they hadn't looked through yet. "We just got this one in a couple of weeks ago. I've never worked with her and it looks like she's inexperienced, but she's definitely got the goods." As she made this remark, she tipped a nod to young Helstrom that suggested the candidate might even possess enough of a rack to satisfy the horny young man's adolescent requirements.

"Oh, I like her," Zig said gleefully as soon as he saw her attractive head and shoulders shot. "Oh my," he practically gasped when he flipped the page and saw her fantastic figure squeezed into a microscopic string bikini along with a couple of other particularly tempting poses.

Hearing his boss's approving reaction Gunnar Helstrom crowded over his shoulder. He, too, was most definitely impressed. "That's quite a package," he observed admiringly.

"It says she's a dancer, too, doesn't it?" asked Melanie. Watching their drooling reaction, the ever-practical production talent coordinator was anxious to place a call and make the booking. With less than twenty-four hours before tape was scheduled to roll, they would be lucky if she was available. Or anyone else, for that matter.

"Dancer, part-time aerobics instructor, done some catalogue work," Zig read from the brief resume that accompanied the pictures. "Doesn't say anything about television, but bloody hell, I might be willing to make an exception in her case. Can we find out anything more?"

Melanie picked up her cell and punched in the number of the girl's representative using the business card that was stapled to the sheet. "Hey, Karen. Yeah, I'm trying to pull something together super quick … like tomorrow … can you tell me anything about one of your new girls … Ellen Starnowski?"

As the woman in the corner of the room chatted with her counterpart at the talent agency, Zig Cartwright slipped his hand over the shoulder of the Art Director who now realized that his fantasy of presiding over a bathing suit audition was fast going out the window. "Too bad Gun," Zig teased the young AD who could barely conceal his disappointment.

Speaking loud enough for both men to hear, Melanie looked in the direction of her clients. "So she's available …

uh huh ... for eight hours tomorrow." She raised her chin and asked Zig with her eyes if this would be adequate.

"Fine ... book her," he conceded practically. "She's definitely the one."

With this critical decision made he could now turn his attention to the other urgent preproduction issues. And there were a million of them.

"Sorry, kid," Zig smiled at the younger AD. "But I think I just fell in love."

Until recently, Lane used to relish Friday afternoons in her little kingdom. It was the one and only day of the week when sanity had a chance of prevailing. Once the wild weekend fire drills were all extinguished and the usual desperate last-minute requests had been put to bed, a near calm occasionally descended on the place. As long as no one was foolish enough to pick up a phone after four o'clock, or worse still, answer the nightline once it had been switched over at five, there was even a chance that the agency might be mistaken for a normal place of business—crazy times like these excepted, of course. It was then that discreetly stashed scotch and wine bottles would find their way out of secret hiding places and the people who had not already fled for the weekend would try to remind themselves that they were all still playing for the same team. It was on Friday afternoons like this when bonds were renewed and friendships were revived after the grinding turmoil and demands of the preceding week. Someone would put on some music; someone else would chase down a few snacks; and before you knew it, a little party would often break out.

Sitting here now, alone at her desk with her door ajar, Lane could hear one of these informal little get-togethers gathering steam. She didn't want to squelch it, but she didn't want to join it either. Instead, she hunted out the bottle of Johnny Walker Blue Label that she kept around for impressing clients and rewarding the people who had done something exceptional in the course of the week and who were bold enough to dare to take a drink with their boss. She poured herself two fingers, neat.

The reports she was receiving from her spies in the Creative Department were no more encouraging today than what Gordon had delivered yesterday. Not only had the New Yorkers managed to alienate most members of the creative and production groups, but they had also succeeded in pissing off the account planning team as well. Apparently, they'd gotten hold of the earlier draft of the strategy document and were nearly as disgusted with that outline as she had been. In the ensuing argument, Angel Gomez had literally been told, to her face, that she was an idiot and everyone else in the room had been thrashed roundly, as well. At least in this case, they weren't all that far off the mark.

Maybe, she prayed, this weekend's efforts would yield something worthwhile. It virtually had to.

And then there was the matter of her little experiment. Sipping at the deliciously mellow whiskey, she savored the warmth that it ignited deep within her. After more than a week of surreptitiously ingesting the little pills that Harold Woodruff had so generously provided, there was no denying that something else was going on down below. Not only was she sensing that some of her unwanted weight was quietly melting away, but there was also another, much more subtle sensation blossoming within. She smiled to herself. In a Victorian romance novel it would be politely described as *a restlessness*. In a detective thriller, it would be called an itch that needed scratching. Whatever way she imagined describing it, she couldn't deny that she was suddenly, if irregularly, experiencing waves of sexual desire that she hadn't felt in a very long time. What remained unanswered, of course, was what exactly she was going to do about it.

He was definitely glad that they had sent the enormous package to his home instead of to his office. And now that it was clear what was inside, he was doubly sure. The security team that guarded the corporate offices of Carlton & Paxton would have had a field day with the spectacular weapon that he now had resting across his legs. The floor at his ankles was strewn with the handsome gold paper and tissue that the amazing gift had been wrapped in. Amongst the mess was an assortment of additional accessories including a shell pouch, a pair of protective glasses, and something that looked very much like the headset he used to wear while listening to music late at night when his young children had gone to bed.

"I don't know what the hell you think you're going to do with it all," ragged Helen jealously. She had signed for the package when it had arrived via courier and had demonstrated uncharacteristic restraint by not opening it until Allan had gotten home from work. Now she was both disappointed and disturbed by the contents within. "And you most certainly are not going to be caught dead in that jacket."

Corbett had to confess he was just as amused as his wife by the bulky Barbour field coat that had accompanied the beautiful shotgun. Patched at the shoulders and elbows with swatches of fluorescent orange fabric, the obviously expensive jacket might make quite a style statement in a hunting camp, but it looked decidedly silly in the living room of a man who wouldn't know the butt end of a rifle from the bead.

Nonetheless, it was quite a fantastic gift. Corbett was immediately impressed with the beauty of the carefully sculpted walnut gunstock. He raised the smooth varnished wood to his cheek and sighted down the cold steel barrel of the weapon naively unaware that he could have easily picked off any target in the room without the barest attempt at taking aim. The big gun's generous scatter could blow a hole through the carpet, or the cheap veneered coffee table at which he was presently pointing that would be at least three feet wide. Bringing the gun down from his instinctively cocked eye, he now ran his thumb across the beautiful silver plate onto which some handsome scroll work and custom engraving had been applied. Say what you will about the appropriateness of such a gesture, but clearly no expense had been spared by Spence Playfair to make such a distinctive impression.

He picked up the handsome card that had accompanied the parcels and read it again.

Dear Allan,

On behalf of everyone at Boom, we greatly appreciated your kind attention and encouragement when you visited last week. Thank you for giving us a shot at such an amazing opportunity. We hope you will be blown away by our efforts.

Sincerely,
Spence Playfair

He smiled at the playful puns that had been woven into the short note. More enjoyably, at this moment, he was relishing the bewildered expression that now dressed the face of his selfish and miserable wife. While it was clear that she despised him and had recently begun to hold him responsible for their fast-deteriorating marriage, even she was forced to acknowledge that he must be respected somewhere. That he was an important man worthy of such consideration could not be doubted based on the impressive gift that he had just received.

Allan Corbett didn't have the faintest notion of what he would do with the gun or where he would put it. But he was definitely most delighted by its implicit promise and the not insignificant impression that it had made on Helen. He would definitely have to find an appropriate way to express his gratitude to his good friend at Boom. But he wouldn't have to think too long and hard. The answer, he knew, was quite obvious.

Day 15

L ane McCarthy buried her chin in the lose-knit scarf that was knotted around her turned up collar. Already hating the scent that would linger in the coarse woolen fibers, she allowed the tobacco smoke to escape in thin wisps that mingled with her clouding breath. Huddled in a waist length jacket, a shiver trembled through her and she cursed herself for the ridiculous concessions this unpopular vice now demanded. It was a habit left over from her modeling days that had somehow managed to reappear in the past few weeks. Even on the alley side of the deserted downtown coffee shop it was impossible to escape the chilling wind that now swirled around her. It was barely seven o'clock and only a few lonely souls had ventured out so early this Saturday morning. She was grateful for this. Pacing a few steps in either direction to keep her feet from freezing, she kept her head bowed, begging to go unnoticed.

As she moved, she alternated sips from her tall white coffee cup and drew in the stinging mint flavored smoke. The noxious mix fought its way down her throat and she could taste her own stale breath. Her sleek calf skin Jimmy Choo's offered no warmth on this unseasonably cold morning, nor did the clinging jeans she had shimmied herself into an hour or so earlier. Dressing in the shadows, she had been quietly delighted when the zipper slid up so easily and even her calves had seemed more receptive when she'd tugged on her tall leather boots. But now she wished she'd put on something warmer. A peek at the scales the night before had revealed nearly nine pounds missing in little more than a week. At first Lane had wanted to attribute this change to the near fast she had been on since the Carlton & Paxton pitch had been announced, but to have this kind of weight melting from her when it had proved so stubborn in the past, left little doubt that the magic pills she had been taking were having their intended effect.

With her teeth chattering, she took one last drag on her cigarette and imagined, wistfully, what her life would be like if she had one. She tried to picture herself cheating an extra hour's sleep or lingering over a second steaming cup of coffee in the morning. Instead, she had awoken from a restless night and set out on foot for the office at the time of day when even the cab drivers try to steal a nap. Rather than idling over the weekend's bulging newspaper, Lane had managed only a quick scan of someone else's discarded Trib at the coffee shop counter. She had been anxious to see if the double spread they'd shipped late on behalf of Titan Developments had made it into the real estate supplement. There would be hell to pay on Monday if it wasn't there. Lost in these thoughts, she didn't notice the rangy man huddled into the heavy sheepskin coat approaching until he touched his hand to her shoulder.

"Lane... is that you?" The tall stranger asked the question with confidence even though her most recognizable features were well hidden in the scarf. Before she could respond, the playful twinkle in Steve Holiday's bright blue eyes gave him away. "You know, those things'll kill you," he admonished.

"Damned silly habit," she responded dropping the

cigarette to the pavement and toeing it out. "Don't you just hate pitching?" she added with a smile and a wink.

Funny things sometimes happen when business competitors meet—especially away from the office. An hour later, Lane McCarthy and Steve Holiday found themselves unwrapped inside the still quiet coffee boutique sharing stories like forever friends. The awkwardness of what made them rivals easily gave way to the thousands of things they shared in common. Dancing around the fact that both had been compelled out of bed by their work at an indecent hour on a weekend morning, it quickly became clear that they were more alike than either would have dared to admit. Though both were professionally discreet in the way that their roles and situation forced them to be, they were also both obviously delighted at finding someone who understood the precise horror of their current predicament—two lost souls working slavishly at a task which neither relished.

"At least you can write your way out of this mess," Lane had taunted. "I mean you've certainly got the talent."

Steve Holiday was immediately taken with the artful way she teased his conceit. She offered this compliment sincerely, making it obvious she wasn't seriously attempting to poach any intelligence, but at the same time both knew that the statement dripped irony.

"I practically have to sleep with my Creative Director to get anything worth pitching," she flirted playfully. At face value the statement was a surprisingly honest betrayal of a lifelong career lament.

"Yeah, but I don't imagine you'd be threatening your client's children as a way to endear yourself two weeks ahead of the presentation," Holiday countered jokingly.

He hadn't bothered to conceal his frustration with Ira's bullying of Allan Corbett. His partner's intimidation tactics were the first ones that any self-respecting ad man would employ with his back to the wall and he didn't hide it from her. Lane had snorted out her approval and nearly spilled her coffee with laughter.

"What's so funny?" he deadpanned. "I'm serious."

"Been there, done that," she confessed. "Tell Ira I know a couple of guys from Stuttgart who know how to play hardball if he needs any help. You know that Interworld has no corporate history between '37 and '45. Just a reputation for great propaganda," Lane added irreverently. She knew that her trials at the hands of her Teutonic tormentors were regular grist for the industry rumor mill.

As they talked, they walked an invisible line of professional discretion that both treaded carefully. Yet each of them was offering every bit as much as the other was taking away and it made the pursuit delightful. Often this kind of chat could be a wonderfully helpful way of filling the vacuum that the review process created. Sometimes it was better to swap half-truths with a competitor than to be misled by the false encouragement of a prospective client. Both of them were well aware of this. But there was clearly more chemistry in their exchange than either would like to admit and anyone who had chanced into the coffee shop would have recognized it immediately.

"Do you think it actually works?" Holiday now asked entirely unexpectedly. It was a naive and ingenious question to ask. It certainly crossed all bounds of appropriateness.

"What? You mean the product?" Lane dropped her voice to a whisper incredulous that Steve Holiday would broach an issue of such critical importance so baldly.

"Yeah," Holiday pressed on. "I mean, do you really think they've found the magic bullet?

"Steve, I really don't think we should go there," she cautioned. "I mean what if somebody overheard?"

"It really would be something, wouldn't it?" he continued.

He disarmed her protest with a look of genuine wonderment. His soft blue eyes still had a bit of boy in them. "It'd be the most important thing that we'll ever touch in our careers."

"It would be pretty goddamned amazing," Lane replied with a tone and punctuation to her voice that tried to suggest their conversation had to move on. Yet even as she spoke she felt herself blush slightly. Ever since she had sat down with Steve Holiday, the pleasant but unfamiliar sensations she had been experiencing since she began taking the pills had been stirring within her. "You know we can't have this conversation," she now cautioned.

Lane had hung her legs over the arm of the small sofa that flanked the little gas lit fireplace that warmed their spot in the window of the coffee house. It was the latest comforting feature of the ubiquitous other place. She looked great in her jeans and Steve had inched his velour-covered easy chair toward her, closing the distance between them. While this closeness might suggest a sense of clandestine purpose, in truth he was simply being selfish with the beautiful woman's attentions and indulging his desire to have them all to himself. He had immediately adored her rough and indelicate sense of humor. He loved her laugh. But most importantly, he knew that she knew exactly what he was thinking before the words found their way from his mouth. He understood this because he could anticipate her thoughts in exactly the same way. He was already a half hour late but he couldn't pull himself away. Ira would be furious, but he didn't care.

For her part, Lane hadn't chatted with a more interesting man in ages and she was genuinely puzzled at how they hadn't crossed paths more often. But other than a few local award shows when she had observed him from afar and their Ad Council session last week, he had been just a name and an occasional picture in the trades. Sitting beside him now, she definitely found him handsome in the unkempt way that creative types always felt they had to be. He was also charming. Or at least as charming as someone that you had met before breakfast had to be—when pauses and moments without sound could occasionally pass for conversation. She felt immediately at ease with him, sensing a relaxed self-confidence that wasn't common in the insecure men who typically owned his role. In fact, this Steve Holiday was not the least bit like she had imagined him to be based on the press she'd read nor the first impression he had registered at the conference earlier. She definitely liked this version much better.

Lane had always heard that the CD of the agency she'd quietly tried to emulate was a gifted people person. She had usually dismissed this, however, imagining that it was a compliment that young creatives accorded someone who was more willing to pay them the outrageous salaries that they demanded. He had picked off a half dozen of her most promising juniors over the years. Yet all of them had said they just wanted to work for Holiday. After talking with him for just a few minutes in this informal situation, she certainly couldn't deny the appeal of the man. She adored the delicious absence of ego that seemed to inhabit his impressions about himself and his company and the ease with which he expressed his passion for his people and his work. Indeed, it made him fantastically attractive.

"Have you got the slaves in all weekend?" he now asked.

"Ten until ten … both days. No deaths in the family allowed," she replied without missing a beat.

"It really is an appalling process, isn't it?"

"The worst. You should ask Ira to withdraw."

"Yeah, sure. Same for the boys from Brazil?"

"I can't imagine they'd have any trouble walking away from a hundred and fifty million. Besides, Boom will probably do better work for them anyways."

Both laughed. It was as close as either Lane McCarthy

or Steve Holiday dared dance toward the flame. It was also the first time all morning that each seemed to sense that the coffee shop was starting to busy around them. Lane lifted her legs from the arm of the sofa and began to gather herself up. Holiday took a last long tilt at his coffee cup then wiped his soft Saturday stubble with the back of his hand. Neither wanted to break the spell that held them here, but both were now being tugged by what awaited them outside the warmth of this chance meeting place. When it was apparent that neither of them could no longer ignore the pull, it was Steve Holiday who spoke first.

"Is there any way we could do this again?"

"What … a coffee or a smoke?" Lane shot back being just a little too glib.

She hadn't anticipated the troubled frown she received in response. It was the only awkward moment between them all morning and she wondered what she had said that had wounded him so.

The jib arm that held the camera aloft swung smoothly from the crowded dance floor. Climbing toward the lofty rafters of the studio, the wide angled lens rotated automatically, holding steady focus on the bacchanalian scene below. The young man in charge of the remote control looked up from the joystick toward the director awaiting instructions on when to stop its spiraling ascent.

Watching the flickering monitor closely, Zig Cartwright began counting out loud, "Okay… slowly now … lock it up … one … two … three … four … and cut!" he bellowed over top of the throbbing music. As soon as the green light on the bulky camera pack switched to red, the audio was abruptly stopped and the dancers came to a standstill. "Thanks people, that looked really good," he called out to the fifty or sixty people now standing motionless in the dimly lit set that was dressed to resemble a trendy night club. "We're going to look at this one, but lets be ready to go again in five minutes." With this final instruction he peeled off his headset and turned to confer with the knot of people who had been watching over his shoulder.

"I'm not sure I can make that move any better," he explained to Leslie Stride and the others as they crowded around a small video monitor to review the playback. "At least not with this piece of shit," he continued. He was referring to the small industrial crane that had been rigged up to allow the circling pan of the scene they had just recorded. "If we were doing this for real, the arm would telescope and we could synch up the motion through the computer. Either that or we could get one of those flying rigs like they use at the football games. But for what we're doing, I think the client will be able to understand the effect. Besides, bloody hell, I'm not sure how much longer I can keep everybody with the program. I'm losing them fast."

The taping of the mock TV ad they were attempting to produce had been going since seven o'clock that morning and it was now nearly five in the afternoon. Even though it was a Saturday and most of the volunteer cast had arrived after lunch, the pretty model who had been selected yesterday for the principal role had only agreed to give them eight hours at cost and had mentioned that she was going to have to call her agent if the shooting went on much later. That was the trouble with these kinds of exercises, Cartwright knew. It was always dangerous to try and take a concept to this level of completion and do it on the cheap –even if it was such a powerful presentation prop. If it were a regular shoot he'd just go into overtime—and let the client worry about the cost overrun.

Budget issues notwithstanding, he was definitely

enjoying playing the role of director. Even more than in his usual position, it gave him room to exercise his megalomania and the chance to demonstrate another of his indispensable talents. Normally a top-flight director or DOP could command twenty or thirty thousand dollars a day when they were shooting for real. The fact that Zig Cartwright had the ability to orchestrate such an elaborate production without the aid of a more experienced professional shooter, only further impressed his value upon the group. Unfortunately, he also brought with him just about as much baggage as the coddled dilettantes who made their living behind the lens full time.

Even though he had been the one who established the parameters of what could be accomplished in this low rent production, he had already charged off the set in the morning, throwing his hands up in disgust at the limitations of the equipment. Only the levelheaded Leslie Stride had been able to coax him back onto set, and even then she had to compromise herself severely to do so. Not surprisingly, Zig had attempted to negotiate sex in exchange for his cooperation. While she had not given in entirely, she had at least been willing to keep this dangerous marker in play. That had gotten the camera rolling again and since then things actually hadn't been going too badly.

In fact, a lot of things had been going Cartwright's way lately—ever since Spence Playfair had so surprisingly, and enthusiastically, endorsed the 'Use it. Lose it." approach. With the account team's support, the campaign had since come together brilliantly. After their initial meeting, Zig had made his team pull an all-nighter and they'd lined the walls with nearly a hundred concept roughs and squibs by the following morning. Subsequently, the exhausted creatives had enjoyed a wonderfully productive review session with the pitch team. In an unexpected gesture of solidarity, even the normally more reserved Avery Booth had given his first pass at the recommended solution an encouraging two thumbs up. Three days and a million phone calls to Tight Rope later, they had pulled together today's production. Maybe they were serious about doing some good work for this client after all, the cynical Creative Director allowed himself to imagine. So far his good fortune was continuing.

After the tantrum, everyone had buckled down and taken the work more seriously. Considering the fact that most of the talent was amateurs, he was delighted with how good they looked. If he kept the takes short and the camera moving, they easily passed for the much more costly paid extras that would be used if they were to ever to actually take this concept to final production. But Zig was especially thrilled at the performance by the relatively inexperienced model they had selected so hurriedly. She was absolutely gorgeous and the camera loved her. Plus she asked very few questions and simply followed his directions, which of course was helpful, since the secrecy of the project precluded any explanation of what was really going on. Despite Zig's certainty that she'd never had to worry about losing a pound in her life, she seemed to play the part with intuitive sympathy. On several occasions he was so mesmerized by her seductive dance moves that he had let the camera roll on several lengthy takes that there obviously wouldn't be time for in the final cut. Yet he couldn't resist.

The execution they were shooting was a lot like the one in the beach bar that he had created on the spot in the meeting room a few days earlier. However, in this version, the Endrophat user was *losing it* during a girls' night out. It was 'Cinderella at the Ball," he had explained to the group when selling it through, "It's the same idea, really, only she's going to ask the bartender for an Orgasm," he had teased, almost as delighted with his second clever cocktail pun. They had chosen to produce this concept because it had been much easier to pull together in the short time they had available than the others. Certainly, the agency personnel that were being featured as extras were right in their element. Most of them would likely be found later in bars and dance clubs very much like the one they had created on set as soon as this production wrapped.

"Guys ... guys," Zig now called out to the group. "If you can just keep it together for one more take I think I can let you all go home. We'll do the close up work when you're gone. You're all looking fabulous ... just fabulous," he encouraged.

After ten hours of shooting, the self-appointed production impresario was feeling fairly confident he had enough shots to make an interesting spot. Even working in HD video instead of film, the pictures looked good. He also knew that what he hadn't captured on camera he could likely manufacture in the editing suite using some stock cutaways that Denzel had sourced. Working on a Mac in the studio's Ready Room, his house producer had already pieced together two thirds of a working edit. It was quite amazing what they could accomplish these days with a laptop and some pretty basic software. He knew it would only get better when they had a chance to play with it in post.

They were cutting the commercial to a hip-hop version of disco queen Donna Summer's *Love To Love You Baby* and the updated retro track had been thumping loudly all afternoon. The sensuousness of the music had infected nearly everyone on set and, as far as Zig was concerned, the more aroused everyone had gotten the more believable the action appeared on tape. He'd even had the crew point a couple of warm air blowers towards the stage of the drafty studio and the sweat that now glistened on several of the more energetic dancers was quite real.

Though he had not explained his plan to anyone out loud, he was deliberately overplaying the hints of tension that simmered between the commercial's heroine and her girl friends. Was it jealousy or was it lust? Why not a little gender twist, he had calculated once the cast was assembled and it was obvious that the women on set were so much better looking than the men. He'd always found girls dancing with girls somewhat erotic and he imagined, on some level, everyone watching the spot might, too. In one version of the final climactic scene he had chosen to show them dancing orgiastically with one another oblivious to the guys in their midst. Now, in this last set up, he had to cover the much more expected girl-meets-boy conclusion using the handsome guy who was the scripted love interest. He would make his final selection of which way the spot would tilt in the editing suite when the account group wasn't around. In his mind, the much sexier all girl version could be an award winner. Or, at the very least, it might be something he could include on his personal reel. With a little coaxing over lunch break, he had also managed to secure the pretty model's phone number. All in all, it had not been a bad day's work.

"Okay people … we're ready to go again," he shouted. "Ellen, darling, you're looking absolutely wonderful," he whispered to the stunningly pretty girl in front of the camera as he dollied into his start position. Without lifting up from the eyepiece he continued with his coaxing. "Now in this take, I want you to pay a little more attention to Jeff over there. Got it, gorgeous? And don't forget to make love to the camera my pretty," he implored in his worldly English accent. Though he would admit it to no one, he was thoroughly smitten.

The dinner was as delightful as the invitation had been unexpected. When Lane had rung through on the nightline to ask him out on this unanticipated date, Steve Holiday had barely been able to blurt out his acceptance fast enough. He had been packing up to leave when someone shouted that there was *a girl* on the phone for him—news that had been greeted with hoots and whistles up and down the halls. Their boss had already begged off from the usual charity offers that had been extended with the claim that he was planning to spend Saturday night at home trying to scratch out a few more concepts. Yet after she had casually suggested meeting for drinks at the Drake around six and a 'nothing serious' bite at Bertolucci's to follow, the normally unflappable executive had barely been able to contain the silly sense of excitement he was still feeling right now.

The truth was he had thought of little else than the beautiful head of the rival agency since their chance encounter earlier in the day. Even as his people walked him through the latest round of ideas and treatments, his mind had wandered to the enjoyable hours they had spent together and the amazing way that they had hit it off. The tricky issue of this pitch notwithstanding, the time that followed this evening had been every bit as pleasant. Better than that. As the waiter cleared away the last of their dishes and the shortness of their time together was becoming more apparent, he wracked his brain for an excuse to linger a while longer.

It had been practically perfect from the beginning. He had found her seated comfortably on a barstool in the Coq d'Or sipping unselfconsciously from a tall-stemmed martini glass. He was also a fan of the bar's famous four-ounce 'Executive' and he had been anticipating his all the way there. To find her already having one was enervating. The place was uncharacteristically empty—too early for the dinner crowd and missing the out-of-town businessmen absent until Monday. When he arrived Lane was enjoying a playful exchange with the lone barkeep on duty. As Steve approached, their gentle laughter was the only sound in the hollow quiet of the rich, wood-paneled lounge. Spotting his approach in the room's enormous mirror, she had greeted him with an eye-crinkling smile and a willing cheek that allowed him to drink in her exquisite perfume. Like himself, Lane had clearly raced home and changed for the evening. The molded jeans and bulky sweater of the earlier trip to the office had been traded for a stylish slip-on sheath and a doe soft cashmere wrap. The look was casual but elegant and Steve was delighted he had thought to pull on a sports jacket himself. For an hour or so afterward she had regaled him with tales of her own unproductive day. Having sworn him to an oath of secrecy, she had delighted him in recounting the idiotic interactions of Gordon Turnbull and the visiting creatives from Interworld.

"You wouldn't believe it, " she had rollicked. ""After Gordon spent nearly two hours last night flushing them out of his office, they had recaptured his space by lunchtime. He practically needed a fumigator to rid himself of the smell of B.O. and tobacco that these guys from New York guys travel with," she snorted nearly losing a sip of her frosty cocktail through her nose in the process. It was the second time he had seen her convulsed with laughter that day. It was fantastically endearing.

Steve had countered with his own confession of the petulant sparring that continued between his creative people and the awkward oaf, Jack Blenheim. In an apparent attempt to make himself appear more human, the unpopular account guy had shown up with his chubby little nine year old daughter in tow. He had set her up with some markers and a drawing pad and the promise that they would only be there for an hour or so. Instead, after huddling secretly for a quick strategy session, everyone that was in for the day from the Creative Department had conspired to meet with him without interruption.

"If the kid hadn't ratted him out to his wife, he would

have been there until midnight. When Security let her in at three o'clock, she practically dragged him out by the ear. And that was before the screaming started in the elevator," Holiday laughed.

It was an innocent story, but so typical. Everyone who worked in the business understood the fragile domestic accords that were struck and the uneasy peace that too often passed for getting along in many unhappy households. 'Either Saturday or Sunday, but not both,' was among the most common of spousal refrains. Or 'You take the kids and you better not take them anywhere near that place.' That was the unwritten law that Blenheim had violated. As Lane reminded Steve lightly, it was easier to have an affair than it was to try and sneak in extra time at the office. With the best agency people easily spending fifty or sixty hours a week at work and usually traveling or dragging stuff home, the business was toxic to relationships. Certainly the two of them knew this from hard experience.

By the time they had made their way to the cozy little Italian restaurant other truths and confessions were flowing. But instead of talking about work, Lane had moved on to affectionate stories of her childhood, family, and finally, her dreams of escape. She had made her retreat in Bimini seem dreamlike, which of course wasn't hard, following what had been an interminable Chicago winter. But Steve had drunk it in like the second delicious bottle of red wine that had disappeared along with their dinner and the precious time they had left. He had chosen a rich Brunello that was his favorite seduction wine and he was delighted that his date appeared to enjoy it as much as he did.

Through it all, Lane McCarthy had eaten ravenously and he'd loved her for it. There was bread and salad followed by a tiny portion of pasta and a perfectly grilled veal chop that she attacked with gusto. She ate judiciously, but with obvious relish. There were few things more boring to him than a woman who picked at meals, counted calories and worried incessantly about her weight. Clare had been like that—obsessing constantly about a pound here and a pound there—all the while seeming unaware of the tediousness such vanity suggested in a woman who maintained a model's figure. She'd continued this habit even as the cancer ravaged her and she swelled with the chemo treatments.

As he watched her eat, Steve couldn't help but smile. He was attracted to Lane's trim but soft figure—even though he was having trouble looking past her brilliant, lively eyes. All evening long, wherever they went, she radiated something that drew men to her. When he had excused himself to the restroom moments earlier, he had returned to find their ancient waiter ardently engaging her in a lengthy tale of his boyhood in Salerno. She had flirted back playfully and won them a glass of a treasured moscato. It had been the same with the bartender and the doorman at the Drake. Not only was she beautiful, Lane McCarthy was magnetic. He would have to find a way to go home with her.

"I think we can give this to our good friend Spencer," bellowed Zig Cartwright when the check for the lavish dinner was finally presented. "We'll call it a little investment in new business development," he roared from the head of the table. His hoarse voice could barely be heard over the din of the boisterous Saturday night crowd that had jammed into the popular steakhouse. A 'Hawks game had just let out and, even though it was nearly eleven, the place was still jumping with the noisy after hockey crowd.

The gang of young people that were gathered around the inebriated Creative Director greeted this announcement with enthusiastic approval. Their put together table was a crowded landscape of empty beer and wine bottles and the untidy aftermath of an extravagant meal that no one was looking forward to paying for. Even after their guests from Tight Rope had begged off earlier, there was still at least a dozen of them present—hoping to sponge a last drink or two off their boss before heading out into the night and praying anxiously that he was going to pick up the bill. Fortunately, he didn't disappoint.

"Are we sure everybody's had enough?" Zig slurred out before sliding his platinum American Express card into the logo embossed leather valise without bothering to inspect its contents. He waved it above his head unsteadily in an attempt to flag the attention of the harried waiter who had served them so heroically over the past few hours. As he did this, many in the group took this as their cue to depart. Pulling on bulky sweaters and coats and pushing back chairs without care, they extracted themselves from the restaurant as noisily as they had arrived. After a scattering of gratuitous *thank-yous* and hasty *good nights*, Zig Cartwright found himself suddenly and unexpectedly alone. He wracked his booze-addled brain, but he couldn't quite recall what time it was when Leslie Stride had slipped away. But now there was no evidence of her to be found anywhere—nor any of the other beautiful young staffers who had seemed to be in such abundant supply just a few moments before.

It had been a raucous celebration. Exhausted by the long day in the studio and the spontaneous 'wrap party' that had ensued, he now paused to enjoy the pleasantness of the buzz that had arrived courtesy of a brimming whisky glass and the abundant red wines that had flowed so freely. Zig Cartwright was a single malt man and he had enjoyed sharing this hard acquired knowledge with the less sophisticated drinkers in his entourage. Now he was clearly feeling the effects of his extensive hands-on instruction. The group that had gone to dinner had been comprised of the lucky ones who had stuck around to clean up and steal a peek at the quickly assembled rough cut that had been screened shortly after the conclusion of the shoot. Everyone had agreed the spot was very cool. He struggled through his liquor-fogged memory to recall where he had left the disk that had been burned for him to share with Avery in the morning. He was due there around eleven for a screening along with Spence Playfair. Little did he know that Leslie had already beaten him to the punch having sent a downloadable version to Spence prior to joining the group for dinner. She was, as always, two steps ahead and the ambush was already set.

A short while later, Cartwright stepped unsteadily into the empty street. Searching in vain for the taxi he had asked the hostess to summon, he cursed its absence and the coldness of the night. I'm definitely not taking the El, he thought to himself, ignoring the stairs to the platform across the street. Instead, he set out on foot with the evening chill settling into his skinny, designer jean clad legs. On the deserted avenue a humming streetlight cast a blinking amber reflection on the melt slickened asphalt and the shadow of the imposing structure nearby seemed to darken his prospects of finding suitable transportation even further. To his right, on Addison, there was nothing in sight. It was the same to his left, though he thought he saw a flash of yellow whipping by the next distant intersection. Maybe he would get lucky further down Clark, he allowed himself hopefully. A half a block and a left turn later he stumbled into the garish pink glow of the neon tubes that illuminated the marquee of Wriggly Field's All-Girl Cabaret. Frozen, drunk and lonely, Zig Cartwright couldn't believe his good fortune. Without hesitation he fumbled out the ten-dollar cover charge and shuffled past the hulking bouncer toward the throbbing music that escaped from the steamy darkness of the club, drawn there by a cloud of sweet smelling perfume and his own drink-fueled desires.

Day 16

The last place Steve Holiday expected to find himself at nine o'clock on this Sunday morning was wrapped in the disheveled covers of a beautiful woman's bed. Yet that was exactly the delightful predicament in which he now found himself. The luxurious boudoir was bathed in the soft light of a perfect spring morning. Sprawled across the bed with his head buried beneath a cool down pillow, he could sense that the sliding door opposite was cracked to the terrace beyond. A whisper of wind billowed the gossamer curtains and, as they lifted, he could see Lane standing before the sweeping waterfront view. The warm yellow sun haloed her handsome profile as she leaned into the balcony's railing. Without the least bit of effort she managed to look absolutely stunning. One delicate foot was raised to the lower course of the balustrade and her robe parted to reveal her toned calf and the curving ascent to her thigh beyond. She raised a slender white cigarette to her lips and took a lingering drag. When she exhaled, the not unpleasant smell of the tobacco smoke rose with the gentle current of the morning breeze and found its way to him through the open door. He gave a languorous yawn and stretched until his own ugly foot poked its way from beneath the sheet that had come loose from the bottom of the bed. His muscles ached in the very best way and the sting from a rake of scratches across his sinewy shoulder reminded him of their energetic efforts the night before. The sex had been remarkable and the lovemaking that followed, sublime.

He could tell from her stiffened posture that Lane was immersed in thought. No doubt she was thinking about all that had transpired in the past twenty-four hours and the endless complications that their unanticipated liaison might now cause. Both of them knew it would be difficult. They had talked about it quietly in the safe darkness of the night. But now it would all have to be revisited by the judging light of the waiting day. He thought about the review. He thought about Ira. Oh, shit. He imagined the sense of betrayal that sleeping with their competitor might cause his partner and some of his more self-righteous colleagues—the ones who still foolishly believed that somehow she was actually the enemy. He scanned his watch from habit though he already knew that he was indifferent to its report. His previous plan for the day had disappeared along with any sense of obligation he felt toward the work that might, for today at least, keep them apart. He had already calculated that a lie and a phone call might buy them an entire blissful day.

Now, more fully awake, he began to take in his surroundings. She certainly lived fantastically. Drunk with excitement and anticipation, last night they had giggled their way past the security station that guarded the condominium's opulent lobby. He recalled that she had pressed a penthouse elevator button and it had whisked them without delay to a foyer that opened directly into her gorgeously appointed living room. Even in their hasty undressing he had been aware of the magnificent surroundings. There must be city and water views from every window he remembered thinking. It made his handsome Lincoln Park townhouse seem lifeless by comparison, which in fact it had become, since Clare's passing. What on earth was he thinking? He chided himself beneath his breath for the silliness of these idle thoughts. He had been with her for a few hours and a night and already he was making plans for a lifetime. Finally ready to lift himself from the bed, he now scanned the room for his clothes. When he eventually spotted them, his trousers were folded neatly over he back of a chair and his shirt and jacket were draped gently across the seat. How long had she been awake? Before he could rise, she returned to the room.

"Good morning," she said. "That dreadful habit again." She smiled and came to him, leaning in with an unapologetic kiss that smelled of tobacco and her delicious scent. "A fine mess you've gotten us into, Mr. Holiday," she offered playfully. With this comment she stroked his stubbled cheek gently with her soft palm and settled onto the edge of the bed beside him. "You know it will be positively scandalous," she added almost Hepburn-like.

"Scandalous doesn't begin to describe it, my dear," he replied. Hearing her voice, Steve was delighted that she seemed to be thinking the same way he was. At least she was referring to their new relationship in the present tense, so she clearly hadn't dismissed last night out of hand. That had been the worst of his fears as he watched her earlier—that she had sobered to the reality of their situation and was going to make the responsible decision that both of them knew was required.

"I have a pretty good idea how Ira is going to react," he said letting his other partner into the bedroom.

"Do we really care?"

"You know we have to."

"Of course we do. But can't we pretend just for today."

"I've already called and cancelled."

"Were they pissed?"

"Only Gordon. The New Yorkers are out of control."

"I should call, too."

"You better."

"Now?"

"Sooner the better."

"You're right."

"I know I'm right. I always am."

"Me too."

"Really? I think you exercised some pretty poor judgment last night."

He laughed.

"What do you want to do today?"

"You mean before or after breakfast? Right now I'm going to take a shower. Want to come?" As she offered this sassy invitation over her shoulder, Lane let her clinging satin robe spill to the floor. With a wink and a laugh she disappeared into the en suite. When they made love again a short while later, she was very nearly insatiable. In the throws of their desire she was driven by a hunger over which she knew she had absolutely no control.

"**W**ell Avery, what do you think? "Zig Cartwright coaxed from the deep leather wingback chair in which he sat. "Brilliant?"

Unfortunately, Cartwright used the word far too frequently for it to be taken at full value and he knew that the first comment Avery ventured would undoubtedly be much more measured. This was confirmed when he caught the quick interplay between his boss and Spence Playfair, who was seated in a matching chair an arm's length to his left.

As he waited for the verdict, he drank in the expensive trappings of Avery Booth's library and what he could glimpse of the magnificent home through the crack in the doors beyond Playfair's shoulder. It was nothing like the Spartan loft that he occupied down on the South Shore. And while he would he never aspire to such a place himself, he had to concede that it was decorated impeccably in the rich, classic style that appealed to folks who chose to live this way. No doubt this was the contribution of Mrs. Booth, the attractive woman who had met him at the door, taken his motorcycle helmet with quiet disdain, and shown him into her husband's cozy den where Avery and Spence had been waiting.

"Well Zig, all things considered there's some pretty damned good pictures. The girl ... the dancer ... she's absolutely breathtaking. But I have to tell you ..." Avery hesitated as he searched to shape his next remark more carefully. "I mean I'd be lying if I didn't say I'm more than a little bit concerned."

Before he could elaborate further, Spence Playfair cut in. Though he was dressed in weekend clothes, his manner was all business. The straining veins in his neck bulged from beneath the collar of his soft pink polo and he lurched forward in his chair as he spoke.

"What the hell is going with the her, Zig?" he challenged. "Is she some sort of goddamned lesbian? I mean, where the fuck did that come from?" he hissed trying to keep his voice hushed out of respect for Mrs. Booth and the family he imagined to be within earshot on the other side of the pocketed study doors.

Playfair had been steaming ever since he had screened the rough cut that was waiting on his laptop earlier. Seeing the images again on Avery's large flat screen television only magnified his irritation. "It's nothing like we talked about. Couldn't you just do what we'd asked, instead of having to find some prurient little angle that appeals to no one but yourself."

"Oh fuck yourself, Spence," was the Creative Director's

reflexive response. "It's exactly what we were after. Why don't you just show some fucking imagination for once," he answered throwing back a taunt of his own.

Before the argument could degenerate further, Avery Booth stepped in. "Now that's not exactly truthful, Zig," he countered more gently. "The way I understood it, the girl was going to take the diet pills, lose the weight and get the guy. This is ... how shall I put it ... a little more complicated."

"But it's the same bloody idea Avery," Zig protested. "All I did was try and rescue it from becoming just another cliché." As he offered this defense he focused all of his persuasiveness on the agency president and ignored the purpling Spence Playfair who seemed about ready to come out of the wing chair opposite. "If old Spencer here could lighten up for a minute, he would see that I'm just trying to push the edges of the envelope a little."

Hearing himself referred to so patronizingly fueled Spence Playfair's outrage even more and he narrowed his eyes in readiness for another attack. Though he sensed that he had Avery on his side, he knew this argument could be lost if he allowed Cartwright to tickle his boss's intellectual vanity. Too often the two ad snobs had overruled him on what were obviously matters of simple common sense. But he had to be careful he didn't alienate his ally by coming down too hard on the side of predictability. It would be just like Avery to waffle on such a critical decision and, if he did, it would be two against one. Worse, he was certain, the pitch would be lost.

"Come on Zig," he implored. "Just like Avery said. We all agreed that we are taking enough risk just by going with this 'Losing It' idea. I don't think we have to give the client a lesson in ..." he searched for the words, "ambiguous sexuality." He imagined the soundness of this logic would easily prevail. But, of course, it was seldom that easy.

"How do you know, Spence? I mean, how do you fucking well know that by breaking the mold of your precious stereotypes, we won't be bloody famous? Why don't you just leave the creative to me?" Zig countered.

With this last comment he invoked the oldest defense in the business—that the creatives should be the ultimate arbiters of taste and style and that they alone knew the path to glory. It was the Damoclean sword that every Creative Director lived beneath, yet at least for now, Zig seemed willing to take his chances. "When are you going to learn to trust me, mate?"

"All I know is that Carlton & Paxton is a pretty goddamned conservative company and the likelihood that they're going to let your little post pubescent sexual fantasy drive their most important product advance in decades is slim and none. Pardon the pun." Playfair argued. "Surely you agree, don't you Avery? Going with this couldn't possibly be worth the risk, could it?"

Now it was Cartwright's turn to launch a counter attack. Somewhat surprisingly, if he could manage to keep his profanity in check, he was actually quite good at it. Certainly he was used to the back and forth of the boardroom and, after working with Avery for the past few years, he most definitely understood the necessity of being able to rationalize his creative decisions with an appropriate amount of pseudo intellectualism.

"Listen gentlemen," he now responded, measuring his tone a little more carefully and striving to be at least a little bit inclusive of the opposing point of view. "I just need you to understand what I am trying to accomplish here. Contrary to your opinion Spence, it isn't to lose the pitch." Acknowledging this attempt at conciliation, Playfair leaned back into his chair and crossed his arms. He let out an impatient sigh, but at least with his body language, he seemed to be conceding to listen.

"The truth of the matter is we all know this business is

about nothing more than grabbing people's attention. As much as we pretend that we can accomplish it with reach and frequency numbers the way we always did in the past, the fact is, these days if we don't take hold of viewers by the throat, we're lost. We need a reason to make them say 'Holy shit! Did I just see what I think I saw?' A pretty girl dancing with her date? Well, that just isn't going to cut it. But maybe a bird hooking up with another bird, now that's something else entirely." As he said this he leered a devil's grin.

As much as either man hated to admit it, the soundness of the argument was undeniable. In the twenty-seven years that Avery Booth had been in the business he had seen a continuous erosion of the power of the media proposals he continued to sell to clients at enormous expense. Cable had cut network viewership in half. TIVO made it possible to skip through every message. And the Internet was kicking everyone's ass. All three of the men in the room knew that in order to extract value from the hundred million dollars they were going to push C&P to invest in electronic media, how much they bought wouldn't matter one bit if the message didn't succeed in cutting through the clutter of sounds and images that currently competed for their customers' attention.

"You said it yourself, Avery. The girl is drop dead gorgeous. I don't think I've ever shot anyone—and you know I've got a pretty good eye for the ladies—that the camera loved so much. But I'm telling you, that just isn't enough," he coaxed. "This isn't beer we're selling here. We can't count on the lads' testosterone to win the day. We need the ladies to get a whiff of it, too. We don't just want the fatties to *be* her. We want them to be *with* her." As he said this, he added deliberate emphasis to the verb.

What Zig Cartwright had neglected to mention to the both of them was the vision that he had been treated to just a few short hours ago at Wriggly Field's All Girl Cabaret. In fact, he himself was still having difficulty separating the wild images of the night before from the vivid imaginings he had taken with him to his bed. What he couldn't dare tell his colleagues, especially given Spence Playfair's pressing desire to put a spike in the spot, was that he had discovered the heroine of their mock Endrophat commercial in the throes a simulated lesbian sex act on the main stage of the popular gentlemen's club in one of the most erotic performances he had ever witnessed. Her pretended lovemaking had roused the crowd to a nearly uncontrollable frenzy and their model, Stella Starr nee Ellen Starnowski, had been quite a leading lady. He had seen her writhing in a rapture that was definitely outside the range she had demonstrated as an actress in front of his camera earlier. And she had even stolen the seductive Donna Summer song they had worked with all day. As far as Zig Cartwright was concerned, this was just something that they didn't need to know at this moment in time.

"You make some good points, Zig." Avery Booth now conceded. "What do you think, Spence? Do you think we can make it work if we pull it back a bit?" he offered conciliatorily to the man he had entrusted with winning the biggest potential assignment that any of them would likely ever see in their careers. But Playfair wasn't convinced and he allowed his tightened posture to continue to say, 'no'.

"Avery, I just don't understand why we need to take this risk," he beseeched. "I think we've already given the creatives enough rope. If it was up to me, and I believe you said I was in charge of this pitch, didn't you? I would prefer it if we played it safer. I just don't think this one's worth staking your career on, do you Zig?" he added quietly, elevating the stakes of a wrong decision with this fairly obvious threat.

His change of tone wasn't lost on the Creative Director who already knew he was taking quite a chance that no one else would ever draw the lines between their faux commercial and the pretty girl featured in it. He himself had felt more than a little betrayed by Ellen Starnowski when he'd recognized her on stage. He had told her as much when he had angrily confronted her following her performance. Though his memory of the precise words he'd used was still cloudy, he did remember that he'd somehow managed to put the fear of God into her with the threat that she would never work as a professional model again. That was, of course, before he'd forced her into the darkest corner of the VIP room and closed down the club with her writhing between his knees. Before leaving he had also extracted a commitment to see him again this afternoon.

"I'll tell you what, gentlemen," Zig now retreated thinking the better of getting into it further with Playfair on this potentially dangerous issue. "It's just the first goddamned cut anyways. I was anxious to see how far I could push it. Why don't we just agree that we've got some wonderful images, and that we'll all take a day or two to figure out what to do with them? In the meantime, I'll have Jamie put together another cut and then we can decide."

It was a compromise that Avery was delighted to have achieved. "Excellent," he concluded happily. "What about that, Spence?" he asked of the pitch manager. He was clearly poaching for ascent and Playfair offered it grudgingly.

"Fine," Spence gave up gracelessly. "I'll have Leslie come by with my notes. Is anyone else planning on going by the office this afternoon?" he inquired by way of punishment. By their expressions it was quite clear that neither of the other two had the slightest desire to commit another second of their weekend to the pitch.

ॐ

Allan Corbett hated Sundays. It was the only day of the

week that he was trapped at home with very little opportunity for escape. He had already used his hangover to beg off from church even though Helen reminded him that he hadn't put in an appearance there in more than a month. There were at least a half dozen Carlton & Paxton families in the congregation and his regular absences were becoming more and more conspicuous. Even among those colleagues that knew of his involvement with the top secret Endrophat launch and its importance to the organization, there was a general consensus that the company's culture seldom rewarded neglecting one's family and community obligations entirely.

But with Helen gone, Corbett was at least free to ease into this day on his own terms. This morning this meant adding a stiff shot of Absolute to his glass of orange juice and fixing himself a messy plate of bacon and eggs. That was where he sat now, staring vacantly into the unkempt garden that he had avoided cleaning up in the fall and that now begged for his attention with the pending arrival of spring, slowly eating breakfast. He would get to it within the hour and be out in the yard with rake in hand when Helen arrived home. At least this might earn him a reprieve from another day full of disapproval, or if he was lucky, perhaps even grudging permission to enjoy a glass of wine with lunch. Until then he continued his lazy perusal of the Sunday paper and quietly sipped at his surreptitious cocktail.

It hadn't always been this way in the Corbett household. When the kids were still around Sunday's had been a hectic scrum of church and dinner preparations and, of course, sports with the boys. They had all loved the Bears together— through both the good years and the bad. But Michael was long gone now and Daniel was away at Purdue. Even his daughter Erin seldom seemed to be around on weekends. Yesterday she had spent the night at a girlfriend's and that had allowed he and Helen to treat themselves to a second bottle of wine with dinner. This had been a godsend as it had sent his wife to bed early and he was able to settle in for a few more delicious drinks on his own. It was this nightcap that he was paying for now.

He stretched wide, yawned and then scratched at his bristled cheek. Sifting through the final few pages of the paper he allowed himself one last shameful indulgence. Ever since he had become acquainted with Stella Starr he now regularly sought out the tacky little ads in which she was featured that appeared along side the box scores and statistics in the deepest corners of the sports page. Sure enough, there she was in all of her glossy lipped glory, smiling beckoningly from beneath a headline that offered Wriggly's famous $4.95 businessmen's buffet and matinee performances by the most beautiful girls in the Windy City. Even in the two square inches that the sloppily designed little banner occupied, her appeal was undeniable and caused a stir in his penis. He closed the paper with a brief flicker of self-disgust while at the same time trying to visualize his day planner. It had been nearly a week since he had been with her.

In truth, she had been stuck in his mind since their rather intimate exchange on his last visit to the seedy club. After furnishing her with another week's worth of the pills that she now relied upon, she had seemed quite receptive to his suggestion that perhaps they could get together for dinner or a drink. It was the first time she had appeared willing to entertain this notion, though in all honesty, it had been the first time he had been drunk and brave enough to suggest it. All week long he had been struggling with whether or not to read anything more into the generousness of her dance that afternoon or the intensity of the way she had pressed herself into him. Did she actually care for him or was it just his pathetic middle-aged imagination? At one point during their heated interlude, the fervent whispers that she spilled into his ear and that excited him so much had sounded almost as genuine as his own desires. More calculatingly, he also knew that in just a few months time the magic pills that he fed to her, and to which she owed so much, would be available practically everywhere. If he were to be with her and have as much of her as he longed for, he would have to do something about this sooner than later.

What would he do? How could he manage through this? He didn't want an affair, but he definitely needed more than the near sex that he regularly bought from her with the Endrophat samples -- even though he was fairly sure there couldn't be much more to her than she had given up already. Yet as he remembered the warmth of her as she squirmed in his lap and the nearly frantic way in which she gave and searched for pleasure, he wanted her more than he had ever wanted any woman. He longed for her with equal parts depravity and desire. At the same time he was jealous of her beauty and the lust that she inspired every time she took the stage. At night, when he thought of her dancing for other men, he despised every one of them who wanted her as much as he did. Somehow he knew he had to steal this power from her and keep all of her splendors greedily to himself. In the helpless way of a man rendered impotent by his over imagined desires, he realized he had begun to hate her as well. He suddenly understood all of the lurid crimes that are committed against girls like Stella Starr. Am I really that close to the edge, he allowed himself to wonder?

In this respect Allan Corbett had quietly come to loathe who he was and what he did. While his chosen career was a nearly digestible failure, he also knew that it was fast slipping from his control and he felt helpless to stop it. At least it wasn't apparent to anyone else, he imagined to himself. He would be fine. He always had been before and he always would be, he denied. But in the darkest corners of his heart, where these kinds of questions are most honestly answered, he felt the lingering shadow of doubt. In fact, the only thing of which he was certain at this juncture in his pathetic middle-aged existence was that he was in a very dangerous place and that any chance of escape was quickly disappearing.

He knew his marriage was in shambles and that his job was at risk. His terrible lapses in both personal and professional judgment would catch up with him soon enough. He had begun an endless downward spiral and the depth of his depression was without bottom. Currently the only sign that he had not yet surrendered entirely was a selfish desire to take others with him to this same black place. The Endrophat review project had been born here. He knew that much. It was clearly just a byproduct of his deep antipathy toward himself. With the recognition that he could admit this to no one, the charade he had constructed had to go forward. While he now despised the process that had been set in motion, he clung to the power it provided. He would play out this travesty, but he already cared very little about the actual result. All that mattered for the next few weeks, at least until the final decision was rendered, was that he was the cause of the misery of a thousand other people. For now, despite the utter unfairness of it all, he was content to be that god.

What had that worrisome email on Friday said? The anonymous sender had suggested that Carlton & Paxton offered completely confidential employee assistance and substance abuse counseling twenty-four hours a day. Even after spending most of the afternoon trying to trace the source of the unwelcome message, he had come up empty. Maybe it had just been a prank by one his junior staffers—they were always pulling those kinds of stunts ahead of the weekend happy hour. Or perhaps it was just a routine fishing expedition that the assholes in HR were always experimenting with to justify their existence. In any event, it had caught him somewhat off guard and put him immediately on the defensive. With the pressures and scrutiny of the Endrophat review increasing, the last thing he needed to worry about was somebody noticing his discreet side trips and occasional unexcused absences. Passing by the family room wet bar, he topped up the plastic tumbler that he would take to the garden with another heavy slosh of vodka. Perhaps it wouldn't be such a miserable day after all.

Day 17

"Where the hell were you yesterday?" Ira asked breathlessly, his voice echoing around the rubber streaked walls of the squash court. As he spoke, he bent low to hold his bad knee while awaiting service. Fortunately, Ira was focused on the forecourt and didn't notice how this inquiry landed on the face of Steve Holiday. Detecting his longtime opponent cheating to his right, Steve delivered a hard drop shot tight to the corner that Ira didn't even bother to try and return. It finished the match.

"Just couldn't do it," he panted back. "Needed a day to clear my head," he added hoping that his partner's questioning would end there.

"You should have come out to the house for dinner then. Sarah was disappointed. I'd said I was going to try and drag you home for a decent meal." This was Ira's way of saying he had gone by the office. Normally, the President reserved weekends exclusively for his young family. Ira's second wife was a devoted mother and a wonderful cook -- much better with these kinds of responsibilities than she had been as a young account executive. But with three kids under the age of seven, there was just too much chaos in the Lowenstein household for Steve's taste. Sometimes he didn't know how Ira managed it at his age.

"Thanks anyways. Maybe next weekend."

"Not likely. Next weekend we'll be there 24-7."

"You're probably right," Steve agreed, knowing that crunch time was fast approaching. The next weekend would be absolutely critical to their pitch efforts. According to his assistant, Marsha, the sky hadn't fallen in yesterday, but he was definitely conspicuous in his absence. There'd been a lot of chatter—especially once everyone remembered the late phone call he'd received. "'Gave everybody a chance to do some thinking without me hovering," he added, laying a hand across his friend's soaking shoulder.

The two partners still tried to play a couple of times a week as they had for years. But their Monday morning 'wake up' match as they liked to call it, was virtually mandatory— even if it did necessitate hitting the court at 6:30 a.m. Steve had very nearly been late.

"Somebody said there was a girl?" Ira tried again.

"Nah, don't know what would have given them that idea," Steve lied.

The comical aspect of this gentle inquisition was that he had put Ira through it a hundred times himself. His partner had been married just twice, but over the years he'd had more affairs and illicit liaisons than Steve could count. The give away had always been a succession of missed appointments, mysterious business trips and other unexplained disappearances. He couldn't blame his partner for being suspicious based on his own performance yesterday. That was the way advertising people did it—in the afternoons, out of town, and on the sly. Indeed, this was practically the language of love at Lowenstein Holiday. Among the three hundred and sixty eight people on staff, Steve had once reckoned that there were at least thirty-five discreet and not so secret relationships going on in the office. And that didn't include the emotional affairs and various other entanglements that wed the people who worked side by side night and day so closely together. Lane and he had laughed about it over lunch yesterday when Steve lamented that it appeared they were just another sorry agency statistic.

"Be a real shitty time to start something," Ira continued to pry. Before the C&P pitch he had been busily trying to nudge Steve into a relationship with anything that had a pulse. Sarah had, too.

"Wouldn't it though," Steve responded dismissively.

He hated having to be so evasive with his good friend, but on the most obvious level, there was just no way he could come clean. The day with Lane had been fantastic. They had walked the path along the Oak Street beach and basked in the first really glorious day of spring. Clear and bright, the temperature had nudged its way to a surprising sixty and the park had come alive. After lingering over breakfast, he had scurried home and gathered up Sox. Together with Lane he had run the dog along the water's edge until the weary hound had collapsed soaking wet and smelling like the Lake. Later, they had oysters at Hugo's and washed them down with an over chilled but nonetheless delicious bottle of sauvignon blanc. They had made love twice more. It was the single best day that he'd had in a very long while. Unfortunately, now it was time to pay for this stolen time away. As they settled onto the bench in the locker room to undress, fortunately it was Ira who took the conversation in another direction.

"I saw some of the stuff yesterday. It's coming along pretty good." This was typically about as much praise as he would ever offer about work in progress. In this regard, he was a saint—preferring to trust the instincts of his partner rather than meddle in the executional side of the business. In the ad biz, a senior executive who didn't have to have his fingerprints all over the work was a truly remarkable exception.

"Thanks," Steve replied, grateful to have moved on. "I think you're really going to like the viral strategy we've been working through as well."

This was an allusion to the plan that was unfolding for using the Web to disseminate several of the key communications components. Ira was an integration freak and these days demanded that virtually everything they produced utilize the multi-dimensional resources of the agency. Too often work was siloed between the advertising, public relations, and web design arms of their company. Even though they all knew that the campaign had to speak with one voice, there was still tremendous competition among them in terms of who would steer the message. As far as Steve Holiday was concerned, advertising still drove the bus. But as the Internet emerged as the medium of consumer choice, this was becoming a tougher and tougher sell. This was especially true for a pharmaceutical product that required considerable information to be provided to the end user and for him to make this concession was definitely a first.

"My gawd that Darvoski kid is sharp," he said, complimenting the gifted code cruncher they had imported from Eastern Europe to work in their interactive division. "He's just an absolute bull for getting the work done. We fed him rough concepts for the ethnic messaging and he had the templates done in two days. I'm dying to see where he got over the weekend."

After studying the problem, a key thrust of Lowenstein Holiday's recommendations for the launch would be both inbound and outbound e-mail with Twittered enhancements. There would be no wall of spam, just well targeted, invited interaction that would be driven by a fairly wide reaching medical database and that could be linked into via Facebook.

As much as it grieved him to throw away a lot of magazine concepts, the necessity to burden every positioning ad with two corresponding pages of caveats and legalese had convinced the Creative Director to abandon a lot of their conventional media recommendations. The trick now was to find a way to make it pay—though Jack Blenheim had been pretty sure they could charge back a significant portion of the data management work in straight fees.

"I assume we're going hourly on that stuff?" Ira countered as if reading his partner's mind. This was the aspect of their relationship that made them such a potent force. Not only were they incredibly like-minded on most key business decisions, often they could virtually telegraph their thinking between each other. "How is Eberhardt behaving?" Ira now inquired after the head of their Public Relations group knowing that he likely wouldn't enjoy the answer. Dick Eberhardt had come into the firm via a shotgun marriage that a client had arranged when they'd won the state lottery business. He was an old fashioned PR hack with all of their worst habits. He drank heavily, entertained too often, and seldom brought more to a meeting than the same vacuous ideas every other public relations *expert* ever did. Three years later there were still serious issues with fit.

"Not bad, he's just such a fucking asshole," Steve confirmed. The previous Friday they'd had a rather heated exchange when a freelancer the PR group was using had decided he didn't like the '*Your Life Is Waiting*' theme and had introduced a series of slogans of his own. "I had to beat the shit out of him, last week. 'Went off in his own direction. I don't know Ira, we're going to have to revisit him when this thing is done," he added, bending over and pulling off his athletic shoe.

"Fine," Ira conceded. He, too, had just about reached the end of his string. "Let's be sure to keep him in the backseat on this one."

That was the nature of their easy rapport. Both men could be brutally honest with each other when they needed to be. In the twenty-two years that they'd been involved, they'd probably had only a half dozen serious falling outs, and even then, it was invariably other people that had wedged them apart. That was why Steve was so anxious about his new relationship with Lane McCarthy. As best as he could tell, there was just no way forward with Ira on this one. If he mentioned it ahead of the pitch, all hell would break loose. If he waited until after, and McCarthy & McCauley was the successful bidder, then the difficult turnover on the C&P business would make things every bit as impossible. Best to say nothing and let the pieces fall where they may. At least for now, he decided.

Zig Cartwright was spent. Even the second tall latte that he'd asked for was having little effect as he yawned and stretched and tried to focus on the status meeting that he was required to attend first thing Monday mornings. Slumping in a cool leather swivel chair in the dimly lit boardroom, he listened disinterestedly as Leslie Stride conducted a review of the projects that would require his attention in the upcoming week. Though she was dressed in his favorite black mini and a misplaced button offered occasional glimpses of her lacey little bra, for the first time in a long time, he couldn't be bothered trying to imagine her naked.

Right now all he could think of was the deliciousness of his encounter with the girl in the hours that had followed his meeting at Avery's yesterday. Ellen Starnowski was an

incredibly athletic lover and had approached the task of his
satisfaction with the same unwavering sense of purpose that
she appeared to take to work with her each night at the club.
She had even made her own climax seem real, though Zig
was not entirely certain that this wasn't just another trick she
had perfected as a performer dedicated to the art of gratifying
strangers. Still, there had been an urgency in the way she met
his thrusts and a gasping delight in her moments of rapture
that suggested the pleasure she was experiencing was every
bit as genuine as his own.

In the time they had spent together, before and after,
their conversation had been surprisingly pleasant. Zig had
expected Ellen to be somewhat more resentful of him. She
was after all, a professional, and he was extracting his favors
from her for free. But instead, she possessed a lively wit and
a curiosity that belied her current vocation. She seemed especially interested in Zig's take on what had been accomplished
during the previous day's shooting. And while she hadn't
exactly come out and asked, she had seemed expectant in the
same way as many of the other models who had slept with
him, that there might be the possibility of more work in the
future. At the same time, she had revealed an innocence that
was difficult to reconcile with her aggressive sexual behavior
and nearly insatiable appetite for making love.

Her apartment looked like it had been decorated from the
pages of a mail order catalogue. Zig knew this for certain, as
they had once come close to landing the business of the popular furniture and notions seller. The walls were dotted with
pictures of family—pure Midwest—prominent among them
several photos of an overweight young girl that he could only
imagine must be a sister based on the strong resemblance she
bore to Ellen. He had spent the afternoon and the early part

of the evening with her and they had ordered in Chinese. In between there had been several exhausting sessions of the most incredibly wanton sex.

Now sitting here, barely a half day later, the only thought that preoccupied the busy Creative Director was how he would be able to be with her again. It was doubtful that she would be as easily coerced into bed as she had been previously. And, of course, he couldn't hire her again too soon—especially given Spence and Avery's reaction to her performance in the demo spot. But once the damned Endrophat pitch was done, regardless of the outcome, he would be free to pursue her as he chose. The trouble was, though he had just been with her less than eight hours before and she had totally satisfied all of his whims and desires, his hunger to have her again was practically overwhelming.

"Did you get that, Zig?" Leslie Stride now inquired, hurtling him back to reality. She asked the question sharply suggesting that she had taken notice of his inattention. "I spoke to Spence and he has given me some notes regarding the re-edit you agreed to." The annoying request hit him like a splash of cold water.

"He doesn't waste any time, does he Les?" Zig shot back defensively.

"Who's got time for anything else these days, darling," was her smart-aleck reply.

Zig had little choice but to let her cheeky barb slide.

Lane McCarthy had begun to hate Mondays lately, though today she could do so with good reason. The team from New York not unexpectedly, had precipitated the argument that had caused Gordon Turnbull to resign. According to those who watched it go down, it had seemed to start innocently enough. It was definitely no worse than any of the other wrangles that had been going on since the disruptive group from the east coast office had arrived. As far as Lane could piece together, for once it was they who had appeared the more reasonable, but no doubt it had been a case of the straw and the camel's back.

Whoever was at fault, the simple fact remained that she now had a very delicate problem on her hands. How could she manage the optics of a high-level management resignation less than two short weeks from the critical presentation that everyone in the industry was watching so intently? No doubt this was the card that Gordon had been counting on when he forced this final angry showdown with his disrespectful counterparts. He probably never expected his bluff would be called. Sitting in a tiny cubicle with Lane tucked into the small side chair that was afforded to junior writers, Vince Pinsent a young protégé of Turbull's who at least had the ability to see things reasonably objectively, was recounting the story of what had happened.

"One of the guys from New York … you know that Terry Lassiter fellow. Well, he apparently had been surfing the web and had come across a porn site that was devoted to … what did he call them … plumpers? It was pure filth … you know … grossly fat women performing all sorts of hard core sex acts and stuff."

In truth, Lane had visited the site on her own an hour before, following her meetings with Turnbull and Rabinowitz. She, too, had been aghast. While, like everybody else, she had known that these kinds of fetish sites existed, she had never before had the need nor desire to visit one. Even a woman as generous to the spectrum of human behaviors as she was had not been prepared for the gross exploitation that these overweight women endured and that she had now witnessed. But this had been the nexus of the angry debate that had resulted in her longtime Creative Director's departure and she had to try and understand. How was this site and its troubling images relevant to a meeting that had ended in a fight?

"Well, Lassiter raised the point that not everybody was going to be as thrilled with the introduction of Endrophat as we all imagined," Pinsent explained. "He said this was probably an extreme example, but the fact remained, there is a segment of the population for whom obesity is attractive ... in some people's eyes of course. He also thought we should expand the competitive frame we were addressing."

If it hadn't had such disastrous consequences, Lane might have enjoyed the intellectual aspects of this argument more. It was a point she had pondered herself as she tried to imagine the assumptions around body image that motivated the likes of Carlton & Paxton. From the beginning, even during the agency briefing, she had struggled with the motivations of their prospective client. Did the health and medical aspects of their new drug's performance motivate them as Corbett had suggested? Or were they simply hoping to prey on the vulnerabilities and weaknesses of a group that society had already seemed to go to such great lengths to isolate? While she was fairly certain that the squabble that Turnbull had presided over had little of this integrity, however crudely it had been expressed, at least the curious copywriter from their sister office had had the temerity to ask.

"So what did Gordon say?" Lane now continued her line of inquiry.

"First off, he wondered about its relevance. Then he went after Lassiter to think of another example. Well I guess he didn't like it when the kid shot back Slim Shake ... and then Nutri-Meals ... and then even Oprah."

"Oprah?" questioned Lane. Nobody in their town would

ever dare cross the reigning queen of American media. She had been so good to everyone in Chicago—so good for Chicago.

"Yeah, but the way Lassiter painted it, even she was part of some great big conspiracy machine. You know … gain weight, lose weight, shed some tears. Then point to another wonder product or diet plan and send it through the roof. I'd never thought about it that way, but even for her it's big business."

"Hmm. And he called it a conspiracy?"

"Yeah, the way he described it, it was like he was accusing the food processors and the drug companies and groups like Weight Monitors of like getting together to perpetuate the problem rather than actually solving it.

"And Gordon didn't agree?"

"Actually, what he said was that he thought it was ridiculous. He might have even said he thought it was stupid. But none of the rest of the group saw it that way. They … I mean we all … just wanted to kick it around for a little while longer. You know, see if maybe there was some sort of angle we needed to anticipate in managing the message. Well, instead Gordon just decides we're going to move on."

"And that's where he and Rabinowitz got into it?

"I'll say," Pinsent said wide-eyed. Young Vince Pinsent was just twenty-five years old and had only been in the business for a couple of years. The easy-going Creative Department captained by Gordon Turnbull was his only context for how the process was supposed to work. "First Rabinowitz says, 'Wait just a fuckin' minute, did you call one of my guys stupid?' Well, you know how Gordon can get? First he gets defensive and then he just says that the discussion is pointless and that we have to move on."

"But Barry didn't agree?" Even though using his first name was uncomfortable for Lane, she found herself intuitively more sympathetic to his side of the story now that the actual details were coming out.

"Well Rabinowitz comes back with 'If you want to talk about something pointless and irrelevant, why don't we revisit all the work that was done last week before we arrived?'"

"He actually said that?" Lane asked incredulously.

"Damn straight, Ma'am. Actually, he might have called the work shit, I think," the naïve young creative added. "It wasn't that bad was it, Ms. McCarthy?" he questioned as an aside. The way he addressed her made Lane feel ancient.

"The answer to your first question is, no, it wasn't terrible. But it certainly wouldn't have given us a chance in this competition," she explained maternally. "Now what did Gordon do next?" she asked, anxious to get on with her inquiry.

She knew she would have to be able to give a precise recounting of the details if she were going to survive the phone call she knew would soon be arriving from Stuttgart. No doubt the lines had already been burning from Chicago to New York to Corporate in Germany with this latest development. Both Jeremy Whithers and Reiner Adolph would soon be on her like wolves. Lane knew she didn't have enough of a track record with these guys to maintain control much longer—especially given the stakes of the game.

"That's when he lost it. First he flung the marker he was writing with at Rabinowitz. Then he grabbed the flip chart and the easel he'd been standing in front of and tried to throw it, too."

"The chart *and* the easel?"

"The whole thing. It goes crashing into the table and nearly kills Ellie Wentzel ... you know ... that new girl in account planning. After that, it all started to go to hell real fast. Sorry, Ms. McCarthy. One second Rabinowitz is jumping out of the way and the next thing he's standing on the boardroom table. I think he might have kicked Gordon in the ribs."

"My gawd." Just when she thought she had heard and seen everything in the business, she never imagined her shop would host a street brawl—literally. Maybe it could happen at Boom where this sort of stuff was legend, but not in her notoriously civil and well-mannered enterprise. "Did Gordon fight back?"

"Well, the shot in the chest kind of slowed him down. He doubled over, but then he made a lunge and got hold of Rabinowitz's ankle. Barry came down hard and that's when the table gave out. And, of course, that's when the broken water glass cut his ear."

Lane's investigation had already taken her to the crime scene—a smaller meeting room that was occasionally used for client presentations when the main Boardroom was in use. It looked like the aftermath of a bar fight. In addition to the shattered table, several chairs were upended and, as the young writer had illuminated, there was blood everywhere.

"Thanks, Vince. "I'm sorry it came to this," she concluded. "How's everyone else?" Of course, she already knew the answer. The entire office was in an uproar. Most were calling on her to send the New Yorkers packing. Certainly that had been her first impulse. She had organized an all agency meeting for one o'clock to discuss what had happened and to announce Turnbull's resignation. She would see all of her department heads over lunch to organize damage control. After that, with just a week and a half until the pitch, who knew what might happen. At least, she acknowledged with a rueful smile that she was trying her best to hide, her former Creative Director had not gone down without a fight.

Day 18

For the second time in as many weeks, Allan Corbett now found himself in the dark but altogether too familiar surroundings of Wriggly Field's All Girl Cabaret. Navigating his way among the little tables that crowded the sticky floor of the lounge, he staked out a spot that afforded him a clear view of the curtained passageway through which all of the girls who were working eventually appeared. That was the irony of his current relationship with Stella. He didn't even know her real name or her cell number, nor any other way he could contact this girl short of sitting in the audience and waiting until she was called to the stage. He checked his watch impatiently, wishing on this particular Tuesday afternoon, that he could light up a smoke. Much to his chagrin, a sign announcing the club's new non-smoking policy had been posted last week.

He had arrived today resolved that he would press his relationship with the young dancer to another, far more intimate level. Enough of the pills and pretending, he'd decided. After thinking of little else since the weekend, he had determined that he would have her—must have her. He had done it several times before. But it had been more than a decade since he'd last been involved in a protracted affair and he had been very much more in control back then. Though he knew he was acting on a selfish and misguided impulse, his current state precluded the intervention of reason. He would seduce the girl. She would love him back. And he would deal with the consequences as they unfolded. It was the simple plan of a terribly confused man.

In preparation for this much-anticipated rendezvous, he had donned his most flattering business suit and paired it with a stylish shirt and tie that Helen and his daughter had once picked out for him. He had even buzzed his chin with the electric razor he kept in his desk drawer and dabbed his temples with styling gel in an attempt to disguise some of the emerging grey. To steel his nerve, he had ordered an icy vodka martini straight up and downed it in a single swallow. Now he signaled to the waitress, who had barely made her round of the adjacent tables, that he was ready for another.

Sitting in the swiveling club chair he nervously fingered the prescription bottle that he'd stowed in his pants pocket. The plastic cylinder bulged against the fabric and rattled as he shifted in his seat. Last week Stella had asked him if he might be able to get some more pills to share with a few of her dancer friends. As nervous as it made him to consider such a reckless maneuver, he now at least had another bargaining chip in his upcoming negotiation with the girl. Besides, the testing of the assembly lines had started and it would be much easier to get a steady supply. With Woodruff taking part in the marketing review, all he had to do was ask.

Three quarters of an hour later, Allan Corbett still found himself waiting. Not only that, the dancer who had been per-forming when he first arrived, had been called to the stage again. This was a pretty good sign that Stella would not be appearing, even though when he'd asked his waitress, she'd said that she was pretty certain she had seen her around ear-lier. With nothing to show for his lonely vigil but a collection of olive skewers and a numbing buzz, he was about to give up. He drained his cocktail glass angrily and pushed back from his table.

Only then did he see her standing outside the dimly lit entry to the Bullpen. She had her head bent over and was holding her hair to one side in a bunch. A tall man, whose features were lost in the dark, was helping tie a bow in the halter that cradled her substantial bosom. When he was done, she flashed the stranger a playful smile and rose on the toes of her high-heeled shoes to reward him with a tender kiss on the lips. It plunged like a dagger into Corbett's instantly jealous heart.

"I've been waiting for you," he said a few minutes later when Stella had finally recognized him sitting alone at his table and joined him.

"I'm afraid I didn't see you," she apologized. She crossed her long legs and leaned into him such that Allan Corbett could feel the heat that was still radiating from her and breathe in her intoxicating perfume. It only served to stoke his anger.

"I don't imagine you could from where you were," he responded coldly. Though the liquor had dulled his wits, it had sharpened the pain of his injury. "Did you get him off?"

"What?"

"Did you get him off? The guy you were with in the leather jacket?" It had been the only distinguishing aspect of the man that she'd been with that he had noticed. That and the single gold hoop that hung from his ear that had flashed in the light as he turned to depart. "Is *he* the kind you like?"

"Come on, Allan. He was just a customer." She dropped her hand to his thigh and tried to stroke it, but he pushed it away.

"Is that why you kissed him, you little slut," he now accused.

"Listen, I don't have to take this kind shit from you," She moved to get up, but he grabbed her wrist and squeezed it tightly, forcing her invisibly back into the chair. She scanned the room, but Mario was nowhere in sight.

"Oh, but I'm afraid you do if you want these." Reaching into his pocket he pulled out the small amber container and shook its contents. "Or maybe you don't need them anymore?"

None of this was in the script that he had been composing just a short while ago, but now he was committed to it. "Why don't we go back into that little room over there and you can earn them the hard way," Corbett hissed.

"Fuck off, you bastard," Stella spat back while standing up. This time she was quicker and managed to avoid the swipe of his hand.

The second time he grabbed for her was a huge mistake. Instead of her soft arm, suddenly he felt an iron bicep lock tight around his throat. A moment later he was being dragged forcefully across the room. As he fought against the vice like grip of the strapping bouncer, the little bottle that Corbett was holding tightly in his palm slipped from his hand. Seeing it spill to the carpet, Stella was on it in a flash. The only one quicker was the ever-watchful Max Weller, nearly bumping heads with the dancer as he plucked it from the floor a half second before she could reach it.

"They're mine … they're just diet pills," Stella pleaded. That was everything Weller needed to know.

Day 19

'Gordon Turnbull Gone. M&M Interworld Out!' Spence Playfair couldn't help but smile to himself as he read the bold headline in Marketing Week. Lacing his hands together behind his head, he raised his shiny handmade Kitons onto his desk and tilted back in his chair enjoying a moment of shameless self-congratulation. If you knew how to play the game, it was easy to get the rumor-hungry trade press to do your dirty work for you, he imagined to himself as he savored a sip from his coffee mug. He scanned the first couple of paragraphs of the front-page article again, allowing himself a delighted little chuckle when he got to the part where he was quoted directly as an unnamed industry source.

They were practically the same words he had fed to the lazy stringer for the popular industry rag a couple of days before. The only change from what he'd supplied was that he had punctuated the first half of the headline with a question mark. With word now filtering to the street about the melee that had taken place at M&M and confirmation of the resignation of their longtime Creative Director, the balance of the article he had penned about tensions in the rival shop had almost been picked up verbatim. The piece had plainly been rushed to press and any requirement to confirm its veracity had obviously been ignored.

While his intention had simply been to start the rumor mill churning, actual events had turned out even better than Playfair could have dreamed. Now all he had to do was dispose of the nuisance that Turnbull was already proving himself to be. He swung his feet off his desk, grabbed the phone and punched in his password. He listened again to the first of seven increasingly desperate sounding voice mails and jotted down the number given at its conclusion. Shaking his head with amused disbelief, he placed the call that would finish the job.

"Hello, Gordon?" Spence inquired. "It's me. Sorry I haven't been able to get back to you. I've been having trouble picking up my messages," he lied waiting for the man on the other end to calm down. "That was quite a stir you caused, but I guess congratulations are in order." After five full minutes of Turnbull's angry fulminations, during which time he could barely fit in a word, Playfair finally got the opening he wanted to close his trap.

"Gordon, you have to appreciate how sensitive this is from our point of view. You're just too hot for us to handle right now. Perhaps we can talk again when the pitch is over?" He delivered this last line with just the right amount of hesitation knowing that the implied uncertainty would cause the anxious man at the other end to unravel completely. "Give me a call in a couple of weeks, if I don't get back to you." While he wasn't completely certain, he thought he heard the man on the other end of the line let out a sob. The day was off to an exceptional start.

৵

"Lane, can you come down to the meeting room on sixteen?" It was Barry Rabinowitz, the self-appointed interim Creative Director. Even though he said it with that irritating New York edge that made it seem like more of a command than a request, she could sense the excitement in his voice. It was the kind of call she had been praying for nearly every day for the past two weeks. Coming as it had, within hours of digesting the ugly smear that Gordon's departure had received in the press, it couldn't have happened at a better time. Dropping the receiver to its cradle, she blew past Brenda barely pausing to let her know to hold all calls for an hour. "Or whatever it takes," she called over her shoulder.

Bypassing the elevator in favor of the fire escape, she covered the two levels that separated her office from the Creative Department in moments. Her impractical heels clattered noisily in the echo filled stairwell and again on the buffed concrete of the floor on which the writers and art directors were located. When the stakes were high enough, Lane could still muster a young account executive's eagerness for the unveiling of a big campaign idea. She rapped twice before slipping her head through a crack in the door that had been sealed just moments before. "Are you ready for me?" she asked brightly as all heads turned.

The scene that greeted her in the crowded little room was the last place one would expect to find a sense triumph. Yet that was the mood that infected the place and was being worn quietly by all who were gathered. On the gaunt, unshaven faces with dark circled eyes she could detect the self-satisfied smiles of a team too tired to hide the pride they were feeling in their accomplishment. This was as good as it was going to get. Though the room reeked with the sweet smelling astringent of their felt markers and the coffee that had fueled their efforts late into the previous night, for the first time since the C&P challenge had been issued, she sensed a renewed energy.

Beyond the waste strewn table and the overflowing trash bin, separated on the long wall plastered from at least a hundred other considered but rejected concepts, there they were. The monumental effort of this exhausted group added up to four little words, each one an unpolished gemstone. To the first of them, the name, someone had already presumptuously attached a registration mark.

Newera®
Your New Beginning

With an encouraging smile and much anticipation, Lane waited as the weary creatives mustered the energy to explain why these were the chosen words on which they would stake their agency's chances.

"Lane, I'm not going to bother with much foreplay. I know we don't need to set you up with the usual bullshit." Barry Rabinowitz began indelicately. It appeared that he would be the spokesperson for the group, but it was obvious that any one of the half dozen writers and art directors who surrounded him would eagerly help with the pitch if he faltered. "The first thing we came up with was the product name. Actually, it was your writer here, Kelly, working with Peter Klem. " With this remark he acknowledged the ad hoc team that had come together over the past couple of days. They beamed proudly at the recognition that Barry had so generously bestowed. At the same time Lane was delighted that there had been some bona fide cooperation between her people and the crew from New York. It would help her incredibly going forward.

"The name *Newera* is obviously a put together of 'new' and 'era'. It's almost a homonym. I don't know, maybe its a little Indian or African sounding. But the thing is," he continued. "What it does is frame what we think is the central proposition of this product which is the chance to start over." He labored the final two words of this sentence for additional emphasis.

"The longer we worked on the problem, the more we began to appreciate the power this product could have. It's all about renewal and getting a second chance," he pleaded to Lane who was nodding her head in emphatic agreement. To seal the point, one of the copywriters from New York hollered out 'Hallelujah, I am reborn!' and everyone in the group laughed and relaxed a little. Barry shot the young man an eye roll and carried on with a smile nonetheless.

"We've done a Google search and a basic registration check, and so far it appears clean. There's a bunch of companies using the words 'New' and 'Era' separately, but nobody is putting them together the way we are. And if we added a second 'w' we could guarantee copyright by making up a unique word if we applied it exclusively to the pharmaceutical category." Though it interrupted his flow, Rabinowitz seemed to want to make this point early on lest someone shoot down the approach on a technicality. "I used my own credit card to purchase the domain name last night."

"Fine. We'll reimburse you later," Lane winked. "Maybe there'll even be enough for a dinner and drinks for everybody at Gibson's if this is as good as I think its going to be." Rabinowitz blinked at the early compliment and took it as his cue to carry on.

"The next thing we came up with was the tag line." With that he pointed at the three words beneath the proposed new product name. We think '*Your New Beginning*' is just the right way to position the benefit. It captures the promise in simple but powerful language."

"Help me, here," Lane now asked. "Explain the

relationship again between New ... era and starting over?" This time one of her own people stepped in. It was the account planner Ellie Wetzel, the one who had nearly been injured in Monday's brawl.

"I think the mistake we were making with Gordon," she started but then corrected herself. "I mean, I think the break-through that happened last night is we now have a chance to meaningfully link the performance of the drug to the actual benefits that the users are looking for. Before we seemed to be getting hung up on just the weight loss ... as if the actual number of pounds lost was a destination unto itself. It isn't ... or at least we don't think so," she argued emphatically. "You take this stuff for what it lets you do after." This point seemed to be agreed unanimously by the group.

"I see," Lane answered sounding a little skeptical. She was already sold, but she needed to see them work for it. The price had been so high. "Can you show me how it plays out in an actual execution?" As she asked this question Lane could feel her own sense of excitement rising. Sometimes the subtle distinctions creative people recognized were a little arcane. Others, like the point they were making now, were pure genius. She wondered how it had eluded them all for so long, especially now that they had the answer in front of them. Again Rabinowitz cut in.

"Look at this," he said drawing Lane's attention to the screen of a small laptop. She had been expecting to be dragged through some crudely drawn marker roughs. Instead, some-one had already sourced a piece of stock footage and doctored it with music, graphics and a crude self-recorded voice over. The art director expanded the WMV player on the desktop and suddenly they were all watching three enormous bolts of vividly colored silk billowing against a pure white back-ground. There was an exotic new age music track unfolding underneath that they had goosed all the way to full volume.

Even on the tiny computer screen the effect was nearly hypnotic as the magnificent banners were swirled by a powerful fan that was located off camera. "At this point what we see is like ... like a beautiful woman dissolving into the scene draped in a fabulous haute couture gown ... almost as if she had been dressed by the wind. With a crude dissolve, a paper cutout from a fashion magazine appeared. On cue, the flat, unprofessional voice over of a young copywriter said simply, "Every dress you've ever wanted ... on the body you've never dared to dream of ...yours." As the colors flowed a title emerged reading: "*Newera. Your New Beginning.*

Even in this roughly assembled form, no one could misunderstand the meaning. What these disheveled geniuses had nailed was the absolutely incredible reach and impact of the product. They had correctly surmised that this was no longer just about weight control. This magic pill had the power to transform everything from how people looked to how they ate to whom they loved. It could reshape industry and even the economy by enabling a sea change of human behavior. Understanding as she did its remarkable effects, Lane already suspected this. Now she had goose bumps.

"Imagine the same thing with spectacular foods, for example?" injected Rabinowitz.

"Or ... like... we see people doing all sorts of active sports and stuff," another excited creative layered on.

"We could even do a spot with nothing but really good looking guys," a cute young writer whose name Lane couldn't remember chimed in. "You know ... the guy you always wanted, but never dreamed you'd get."

After pushing so many ideas forward they barely gave Lane a chance to respond. When the clamor of voices eventually did subside, she finally had a chance to feed them the reaction they'd been begging to hear.

"I love it. I absolutely fucking love it," she declared

without reservation. "I don't know how the hell you did it, but its absolutely goddamned amazing!" Lane's use of their favorite four-letter word at first startled and then delighted the team from New York. There was even a fist bump exchanged between Rabinowitz and young Vince Pinsent. "Where do we go from here?" she asked, feeling for the first time a rush of adrenaline that came from knowing they were finally in the hunt.

"I need the pills back," whispered the anxious voice on the other end of Corbett's cell phone. It was very difficult to hear against the din of the busy barroom, so he ducked into a hallway that led to the restrooms.

"What pills?" the advertising manager now replied, feigning ignorance. The fact that the caller was Harold Woodruff left little doubt as to which ones he was referring to.

"The Endrophat samples that I gave you last week. I need them all back. I'm afraid there may be a bit of a problem," the scientist asked. Even in his hushed voice he could barely disguise his anxiousness.

"What kind of problem, Woody?" Up until now Corbett's biggest fear was that a security audit might be conducted. This kind of spot check was standard procedure with the big drug company that handled so many controlled substances and it was a distinct possibility as they started to gear up for production. If this were the case, virtually every pill would have to be accounted for. "Not an audit?"

"No ... no..." the scientist answered agitatedly. "With the formulation. You know I've been wrestling with it for the past couple of weeks." Ever since he had been invited onto the marketing review team, and perhaps because he was so sorely in need of an ally, Woodruff had increasingly taken Corbett into his confidence.

"And?" Corbett anticipated.

" ... And I think we had some sort of malfunction with some of the test batches."

"A malfunction?"

"One of the compaction presses failed. When we checked the supply of active ingredient against the run, it was way out of whack."

"What exactly does that mean, Woody?" There was a pause at the other end. "Woody?"

"Well, I'm not sure until I can examine the actual pills, but ... well ... um ..." he trailed off nervously.

"But what?" Corbett now asked more insistently, encouraging the stalling man to hurry up and get to the point.

"Well, it appears that we might have accidentally doubled or even tripled the amount of dopamine that some of the pills received. I'm not sure, but others might have gotten none at all."

"And that's a bad thing?" Asking the question, Corbett had immediately assumed that what they were now talking about was just another production set back. "It just means some girl is gonna get skinny twice as fast right?" he joked, trying to calm his associate down. And then it hit him why the scientist had insisted on tracking him down after work. "It's not harmful, is it Woody?"

The long pause from Woodruff confirmed this guess.

"While I can't say exactly, I did run some more tests last week. You know, after Manufacturing kept pressing for final numbers ..." Again the scientist hesitated. "To answer to your question," he now finally confessed, "Probably ... yes."

Corbett's mind immediately raced to some of the major crises that the company had endured in the past. Over the

years they had dealt with a myriad of issues management situations involving everything from unintended complications
to product tampering. It was a pharmaceutical company's
worst nightmare. All of these problems had massive public
relations and communications implications. "What are we
dealing with here? I mean medically speaking?"

"Over stimulation of several glands and organs ... not
all of it bad ... but some potentially severe respiratory and
cardio complications. A lot of the stuff that I highlighted in the
registration application on misdosage."

"Oh shit!" Now it was Corbett's turn to respond in a
panic. "Have they gone anywhere?"

"That's the good news, I guess. I think I've been able
to intercept most of the follow up samples for the clinical
patients before they shipped." Having finally confessed his
problem to someone else, Woodruff was starting to regain
his composure. "Other than that, there are just the ones that I
gave to you and a couple of other special orders that I filled."

The truth was Harold Woodruff had been asked for samples from throughout the organization as the buzz about the
drug spread. Last week the Vice President of International
Finance, who every one knew had a fairly heavy wife, had
made a request. 'Just a month's worth to get my team familiar-
ized,' he had said with a wink. Yesterday it had been the pleasant but fairly chubby director of HR. To his credit, Woodruff
had done a remarkably good job of fending off most of these
kinds of special favors.

"Does anybody else know, yet?"

"Not yet. That's why I need your pills back," Woodruff
now explained. "I've got to run a couple of tests, then I'll
alert Bristow." Art Bristow was the Vice President in charge
of Research & Development and the guy that Woodruff ultimately reported to. Unfortunately, getting the top executive
involved would trigger a whole lot of further investigation.

"At least we found this out now. The last thing I need is a whole lot of noise about another fuck up. Allan, if you can just get me those pills back by first thing tomorrow morning, I'd really appreciate it."

"I'll see what I can do, Woody. You know I'm heading up to that sales meeting in Kohler tomorrow, " he said evasively. "I'll definitely get back to you by the end of the week," he dodged.

Before the doctor could protest, he quickly snapped his phone shut. Spence Playfair had just come into the bar and was making his way towards him.

"I probably shouldn't ask, but how did you manage that?" Playfair asked in reference to the bandage that knit together the cut above Corbett's eye.

"Damnedest thing," Corbett responded, a little embarrassed. "Jumping into a cab. Ducked my head in too quick and clipped it on the door frame." Actually, he was quite relieved that this was the only visible evidence of his scuffle at Wriggly's yesterday. While his neck hurt like hell from being wrenched from his seat and his knees and palms were scraped from where he'd hit the sidewalk, at least none of these additional scars were in plain sight. He'd actually gotten more grief from Helen for his torn trouser leg than for his collection of wounds. She seemed quite curious what he was doing wearing his best suit on a Tuesday.

"You're gonna look like one of the players," Playfair kidded. Their dinner reservation was early because the faceoff was at eight. "Go Hawks!" He raised his fist and cheered aloud. It was answered by a couple of echoes sharing the same sentiment from around the busy bar. Though he had plenty of time for the question he'd been itching to ask all day long, suddenly he decided he couldn't wait any longer.

"So, what did you think about that terrible news coming out of M&M? About that Turnbull fellow? " He pressed.

"I'm sorry?" Corbett now asked dully. Between the couple of hasty scotches he had already thrown back and his anxiousness about how to deal with Harry Woodruff, he was a little slow on the uptake. "What about M&M?"

"The article in Marketing Week … haven't you seen it? I don't want to tell tales out of school, but apparently their Creative Director quit after some sort of fight with one of the people they airlifted in from New York."

"No kidding," Corbett rallied. The advertising manager had never been particularly well connected to the gossip mill that the agency people seemed to set so much store by. Most of what he heard about the Chicago ad scene came to him second hand and this revelation was no different. All of the subscriptions to periodicals like the one that carried the article Playfair was describing were mailed to Andrew Sullivan who seldom bothered to distribute them. "What happened?" he now asked.

"Apparently he smashed a glass and went after him," Playfair now exaggerated the story that was flying around town. But instead of incredulity, Corbett again seemed lost in other thoughts.

A tired "Really?" was the best his guest could muster. "I guess that's going to be a bit of a problem for them," he added because the look of disappointment on Playfair's face was too obvious for him to ignore completely. In truth, the only question on his mind now was how he was going to retrieve the suspect pills from Stella Starr. Or worse, what would happen if he didn't.

❧

"I really thought you'd be having a shitty day ... what with the article and all. Did he really cut the New York guy's ear off?" It was Steve Holiday and, as had become their custom since becoming secret lovers, he had called Lane to say good night.

"Don't go there, Holiday."

"Where?"

"It was just a little disagreement."

"Bad manners?"

"Something like that? Look who's calling after nine?"

"Is it that late?"

"11:18."

"Sorry. I'm at the office."

"Still?"

"In my car, actually."

"Been trying to save a piece of business?"

"Maybe."

"Don't count on it."

"On what?"

"Winning, stupid."

From the moment she'd answered the phone, Lane had surprised him by being remarkably upbeat. In fact, she had been so animated that he was regretting his decision to work late and he was about to suggest that he hurry across town to see her as he had tried the two prior evenings.

"Not a chance, Holiday," Lane responded as if reading his mind. "Just because you're about to lose the biggest account at your agency doesn't mean you're gonna get any sympathy sex out of me."

"Actually I was hoping you would invite Gordon over and we could enjoy a little rough stuff. Just the three of us," he jabbed back playfully.

The fact that she had dealt with this crisis and not said

a single word was testimony to her strength. Resilience was the key to surviving in the business and she most definitely seemed to have a gift for bouncing back.

"It was horrible."

"I can't imagine."

"Seventeen years."

"Definitely over?"

"No way back."

"I'm so sorry."

It was becoming the familiar pattern of their conversations. First they would flirt. Then tease. Finally, there would be an intimate confession like this last one. Their relationship was only four days old, but already it had become a harbor.

"What are we going to do about this, Holiday?" Lane now sighed stretching out on her large, empty bed. Even talking to him caused that now familiar tingle.

"About what?" he dumbed.

"You know I'd give up everything for you," she confessed with a sincerity that frightened her. "Any chance you can take me away from all this?" she added like Garbo.

Day 20

W hen we came to understand the extent of the problem, our first concern was for Allan," said Ira to the
two men who were listening impatiently. Both were dressed
impeccably in expensive business suits and held themselves
with the stern posture common to old school executives. They
were attentive but anxious that he get to the point. "That's
why we thought it best to involve HR. "

John Carver was the former CEO of a national drug store
chain. Dr. Joseph Brandt had founded the genetic research
institute that carried his name and whose IPO had been introduced with assistance from Lowenstein Holiday's Investor
Relations group. Each of these successful businessmen had
been an independent Carlton & Paxton board member for a
number of years. Recently, John Carver had been appointed
to the Global Marketing Oversight committee.

"Allan Corbett has been a friend of the agency for a
very long time. We just hope he takes advantage of all of the
resources that the Employee Assistance program has to offer,"
he continued.

"Cut the shit, Ira," Carver cautioned. He, too, had been
a client of Lowenstein Holiday and the agency had been
instrumental in the rapid expansion that had made the former

retailer an extremely wealthy man. While he greatly respected L&H's contributions to his company's growth, the battles he'd fought with Ira over excessive billings and measuring the effectiveness of advertising were legendary. "What are you getting at?" he now demanded.

"Okay, fine…" Ira stopped. Sensing Carver's impatience, he changed gears and the tone of his voice simultaneously. "If you want it straight up, the guy's an asshole and I think what he's doing to us is grossly unfair. You already know he's an alcoholic, but I swear that's just the half of it."

As much as he hated to hear what was coming next, Joe Brandt signaled for him to continue. As a trained physician he was naturally more sympathetic of Corbett's condition than either of the other two men. But he was also among the most conservative of the pharmaceutical company's directors and, as such, he was extremely sensitive to any possibility of scandal or other impropriety. Selfishly, he also had fairly significant holdings and a bundle of vested options with the big drug company that he was hoping to cash following the successful introduction of Endrophat.

"I've also got pretty solid evidence that this guy is some sort of pervert and he might be trading company secrets for sex." Ira knew this bombshell would have its desired impact.

Indeed, he immediately had their full and undivided attention. Brandt bowed his head to avert eye contact. Upon hearing the *sex* word, he scratched hard at the silver bristles on the back of his head and in so doing betrayed his growing agitation. Carver leaned forward on the plump sofa of the grand suite that Ira had booked for the meeting and braced himself for the worst. Ira, who didn't get to New York often, had been appalled at the cost of the reservation. But now he was glad, at least at that this juncture in their difficult discussion, that it was being held within the discreet confines of a hotel room.

"I don't think there's any delicate way to say this. I've got a private investigator's sworn statement that on two occasions he witnessed Allan Corbett reward an exotic dancer at a strip club in Chicago with drugs in exchange for personal favors, if you know what I mean." Ira raised his palms in askance. "In the most recent incident the girl confirmed that he was providing her with diet pills." Now that it was said, he took a deep breath. The ball was squarely in the court of the other men.

The mention of the diet pills immediately caused the two board members an exchange of worried looks. The company's directors had been sworn to secrecy on the highly confidential Endrophat project and to hear that Corbett had allegedly committed such a gross breach of security took this issue to a whole other level. To risk compromising the multi-billion dollar potential of this product so foolishly was unpardonable to these two former senior executives.

"Can you prove this Ira?" John Carver was the first to speak. He knew his old business associate well enough that he couldn't imagine him making such an accusation without it. Nonetheless, he felt compelled to ask. With his fiduciary obligations to the company and its stockholders, ignoring what he now knew would be impossible.

"There are pictures," Ira confirmed. "I'm ashamed to say."

"What do you intend to do with them?" Joe Brandt now asked. The well-intentioned doctor, who initially didn't want to believe the accusation, was even more shocked. Uncertain of the ethics of Ira Lowenstein, he had immediately leapt to the assumption they were being set up for some form of blackmail.

"Relax, Dr. Brandt," Ira responded anticipating this concern. "I've got far too much invested and have far too much respect for Carlton & Paxton to let something like this go beyond this room." He stood up and began to pace.

The two experienced businessmen now waited in anticipation for the request they were sure was coming. Indeed, it was at this point where Ira had to be most careful. To overplay his hand might result in not just Corbett, but Lowenstein Holiday, being disqualified from any further involvement with the Endrophat project—especially if these powerful gentlemen felt they had been pushed into a corner.

"In a week's time Allan Corbett will be presiding over presentations on the introduction of the most important product C&P has launched in a decade ... if not the history of the organization." The two men confirmed their knowledge of this process with a nod to the affirmative. "He will be making decisions that involve hundreds of millions of dollars. Frankly, gentlemen, I don't think it is in the best interest of any of us to allow this to continue." Ira studied the faces of the board members carefully. "Do we agree?" he asked before carrying on.

While it was a given that Corbett needed to be marginalized, it was another thing entirely to expect that these two independent directors would be willing to risk their comfortable roles and generous board stipends by taking decisive action in the matter. As well, all three men knew that ousting the rogue ad manager might be difficult to accomplish in the glaring spotlight that the review had attracted—especially in the short time remaining. However, to his relief, Carver and Brandt both indicated agreement.

"I must tell you, I believe my agency's work on this account always has and always will stand on its own merits," Ira began again. With this reminder he forced the two men who had worked so successfully with his company in the past to concede this point as well.

"All I'm going to ask is that you do whatever you can

to ensure that this review be conducted on a fair and level playing field. That's all." Ira used another pause to allow the simplicity of his request to sink in. "In seven days Carlton & Paxton is going to see three remarkable advertising campaigns that will make or break this product. All I want is to be absolutely certain that the best solution goes forward and the right agency wins," Ira concluded.

It was a huge gamble, but the maneuver immediately won him the high ground. Carver and Brandt seemed visibly relieved that this honorable request appeared to be everything that Ira would ask of them. Carver was again first to speak. His gratitude took the form of an apology.

"Thank you for your candor, Ira. I can't thank you enough for bringing this matter to our attention ..." he dropped his voice, "...and for the professional manner in which you have handled it to date. On behalf of Carlton & Paxton ... I think I can speak for the company, even as an outside member... I am so terribly sorry for the untenable position this has put you in and for the shameful way this has all been handled."

"I agree entirely," Joe Brandt added effusively. As he said this he stood up and pumped Ira's hand. His response was a mixture of surprise and relief. The older man seemed pleased that his trust and belief in honor among men of business had been so artfully validated. "We can't thank you enough."

It was precisely the reaction Ira had been hoping for.

"I can also assure you we will take this to the very highest levels of the organization. As much as two old men on the Board of Directors can make a difference, you have our word that we will do whatever we can on your behalf."

"It's nothing short of remarkable," Angelica, the seamstress from Fuchsia, wondered aloud as she slid the tape around

Lane's hips again to check the measurement that had startled her so much the first time. "Ms. McCarthy, there are nearly twelve inches missing since you were in here in early March. They've just vanished!" She snapped her fingers like a magician while crouching at her client's hemline.

"My, oh my. Where could they have gone?" Lane responded playfully, putting her hands to her cheeks in mock disbelief. She then pretended to search around the fitting room, her eyes darting in all directions, as the other women laughed warmly.

"Three on top ... four around here ... and nearly five off your backside," Diane, the sales assistant confirmed, as she checked her notes and dutifully recorded Lane's new measurements.

"Amazing," Angelica marveled again as she stood up and checked her work in the fitting room's three-sided mirror. "How'd you do it?" she continued chattily.

It was precisely the question Lane had been hoping to avoid, especially since she would not be able to tell them the truth. But with a week to go before the most important presentation of her career, her best suits and dresses were hanging loosely everywhere, thereby making this trip to her favorite store a truly delightful inconvenience. Besides, she was quietly beaming inside—thrilled that the results of her recent weight loss had translated so beautifully to her figure. As the astonished dressmaker's reaction testified, she seemed to have shrunk in exactly the right places.

"I'm not exactly sure," Lane answered less than honestly to her tailor and the helpful sales associate of the chique little boutique where she preferred to shop for her business suits and special occasion wear. They were all ears. They had assisted Lane countless times before and kept her precise measurements on file. Until today, during most of those visits, they had been making discreet adjustments to help their client avoid moving up to a size twelve. "Maybe I've just been working my butt off," Lane now chose to joke.

The stylish salesperson smiled encouragingly and the seamstress, with a half dozen pins held tight between her lips as she fussed with the final adjustments of the fitting, chortled again in response. The undeniable fact was that Lane hadn't worn an eight in years, but somehow she had melted through two dress sizes in as many weeks. The prospect of sliding into the tidy little Doris Ruth A-line sheath that they were nudging her towards pleased her to no end. She had been an ardent admirer of Allie Adams ever since the talented young designer had arrived on the Chicago scene, but Lane had never had the courage to actually try one of her beautiful creations on until today. Such beautiful clothes belonged to girls half her age whose figures were reliably measured in single digits—even if she knew she would have to disguise this one beneath a much more serious jacket.

"I don't know ma'am," Angelica now added as she smoothed the pinned back dress over Lane's tapering hips "If we have to take it in any more, maybe we should be looking at the six."

"Thanks, but I do have to breathe in this meeting," Lane replied. She was enjoying the flattery, but dismissed the notion immediately. While she was truly pleased with her reflection in the mirror for the first time in a very long time, the success of her little experiment was definitely starting to make her nervous. Despite her anxiety and the curious side effect she seemed to be experiencing, she was in awe of the spectacular results of the drug. Part of her wanted to tell these ladies to put everything above a size ten on sale—starting now.

"I haven't seen any of our clients drop three sizes so quickly without, well you know, getting sick," Angelica prattled. "You're not are you?" she added with an anxious look. The much more appropriate Diane frowned at the directness of the question, but was just as curious about the answer as her assistant.

"Heavens no," Lane replied with a laugh. "Maybe its love."

"Really?" Diane brightened. "Are you seeing someone new?" Presented with this prospect, the shop girl forgot her own rules about discretion. The fact that there might be a man involved seemed a better explanation of Lane's phenomenal transformation than any other solution she could imagine.

Why was it so many young women want to tie their weight issues to the men in their lives, thought Lane as she watched Diane try to knit these two unrelated issues together. Then she realized that she had done the same thing herself for as long as she could remember—imagining her own attractiveness through the eyes of who she was with at the time and never feeling wholly pleased with this unsatisfying assessment. It had never been a truly healthy measure of her self worth. Why did physical appearance matter so much? Who caused this? Surely she shouldn't hold herself to blame, even if it was her work that helped define what others saw as beautiful.

Part of Lane very much wanted to attribute the extraordinary excitement she was experiencing to the disappearing weight and the newness of her relationship. But the truth was that while Steve was a generous and patient lover, his performance was by no means exceptional. Even he had remarked, early on, that he had never succeeded in exciting and pleasing a woman as much as he appeared to be able to achieve with Lane. Jokingly he had wanted to attribute his success to the thrill of cheating on their respective organizations.

But the evidence of the drug's effect was undeniable. In the twelve days since she had been using the pills that Carlton

& Paxton had invented, nineteen pounds had disappeared. Just as startling was how natural the effects of the drug had been. Rather than simply going slack with the absence of fat, her body had responded magically to the effects of the drug. It wasn't simply a weight control product, it seemed to almost be reversing her age.

Even Tahur was coaching her more enthusiastically these days. While he wanted to take more credit than he was due, he had been extremely complimentary. He'd even had to step up her reps to keep her toning at an even pace with her suddenly slimming figure. During their last session he had actually seemed more interested in her than a covey of young women barely half her age who were doing floor work nearby. Where once he had suggested that maybe the only way to reduce the growing bulk of her upper arms was brachioplasty, last week he had increased the weight on her dumbbells by a couple of pounds and playfully attempted to stretch the thumb and forefinger of his large hands around her tightening bicep. There were, indeed, amazing changes taking place. And, of course, that was just the half of it.

"I love it," Lane said as she did an approving half turn in the mirror. "I'll tell you what ladies. I'll take the black cocktail dress and the two summer business suits as well." She felt absolutely marvelous.

Avery Booth pushed his bi-focals down low on his nose and began a slow walk around the meeting room where the completed comps for the presentation were being marshaled as they emerged from the art department. The splendid array of mock advertisements, each laser printed in glossy full color and mounted against a field of black matte foam board, had a gallery like quality about them. Already there were nearly twenty or so layouts assembled on the ledge and there appeared to be room for twenty more. Stepping from one to the next, the agency president would pause and admire the clever headline, the stunning photography, and the tastefully arranged typography that comprised each offering. It was simply amazing, he thought to himself, as he studied the ample intellect and artistry of the work that Zig's people had managed to craft in such a short time.

It was after hours and Avery had his sleeves rolled up and his tie loosened at the collar. In his hand he held a bulky document, the sheaf of white papers bound in the unyielding jaws of an oversized bulldog clip. He appeared to be about half way through the neatly printed manuscript. What he'd already read was rolled over the metal fastener and the first page of what remained was a mash of colored scribbles and notes. He let the entire heavy handful settle to his side as he moved gradually along the display wall, seeming to weigh the contents of the ads he was studying against the words that he had been carefully digesting. When he paused to study one of the layouts more closely, he could feel the heat of the tiny halogen spot light that illuminated the wall warm the back of his neck.

Sitting at the big table that occupied the center of the room, Leslie Stride held her breath as the President performed this dawdling appraisal. Spread out on the wide surface in front of her was the same document that Avery had in his possession; only hers had been unfastened and arranged into a series of orderly piles. In each of the stacks, dozens of yellow stickers flagged the revisions and changes that had been suggested by everyone who had reviewed the strategy deck to date. Beside her, Zig Cartwright lolled in one of the tilting ergonomic chairs that had been rolled in from an adjacent office. His work was done for the day, but he had chosen to sit in on Avery's review since the last thing he wanted was for his boss to start doubting the approach that had been agreed and executed. It wouldn't be the first time that the President had changed his mind.

"Zig, what is the font you've chosen for all of the headlines?" Avery inquired without looking away from the comp that he was examining.

"Century Gothic," Zig replied directly. "With a European cut." It was best to answer such questions with unwavering authority. "We wanted something simple and elegant. But not so much that it lost its sense of didactism. Why do you ask?"

"No reason. Just admiring the cleanness of it," Avery complimented. The senior executive who was so good with words and strategy was still startled by how much the power of language could be improved by the skillful selection of the right typeface. Zig tipped a look in Leslie's direction, hoping to have impressed her with his big word and delighted that he appeared to have dodged a bullet. They both knew that the next inquiry in Avery's meandering line of questioning would be directed towards her. He didn't let them down.

"Leslie?" Avery now turned toward the young lady who was busily pecking away at the master document that she had loaded into her laptop. Seeing her sitting primly, wearing a pair of serious glasses not too dissimilar from his, he was suddenly struck by how youthful she appeared. He wracked his brain to remember how Spence had managed to convince him to bring someone her age with so little experience into the heart of the agency's management team. "I'm reading this headline: *'Why count calories, when you can count on this?'* Do you really think we can get away with saying 'this' instead of 'Endrophat'?"

It was obvious that while Avery was asking one thing, in reality he was circling back to another. The naming issue had been dogging everyone's efforts for weeks and Avery was now making it clear that his doubts had not yet gone away.

The brief had most definitely asked the agency to recommend an alternative name for the product but so far they hadn't come up with one. Initially, the team had promised that they would only use Endrophat as a placeholder until they found a better option. But after drilling several dry holes, Zig had one his writers craft a fairly well articulated rationale for retaining the awkward sounding name and hoped the debate would end there. Unfortunately, it appeared, Avery was not content with this kind of expediency.

"Oh, come on Avery," Zig was now forced to wade in. "I thought we'd given up on that. The category is full of odd and clunky sounding chemical names," he argued for the tenth time. The trouble was, the President of the agency was just as stubborn as his Creative Director.

"I thought I've always made my position on this quite clear. I think we're taking too big a risk ignoring the client request in this area," Avery responded.

"But you weren't there at the briefing Avery. I swear, the way it was discussed then, it was a throw away. The way those wankers at Carlton & Paxton were tossing it around, they knew they were going to use it. They are just hoping for one of us to validate them."

"But how can you be so sure?" Avery countered. This was typical of the kind of debates the ineffectual agency head often waged. While by title and right he had the authority to override Zig on anything, he lacked the strength of personality to force his views on anyone. Instead, just like many of the clients they served, he attacked the position he objected to with a million little nibbles of dissent. "You were there too, weren't you Leslie?"

It was the kind of question the ambitious young account director hated. Instinctively she knew the right answer was to side with Avery. But she also knew that by doing so she might put their schedule back by days. Before responding she conducted a mental inventory of all of the work that needed to be completed and how many times the word Endrophat occurred in their required presentation materials. She wished Spence were here instead of out of the office.

"Yes I was Avery and I agree with Zig's take." It was about as brave a stance as Leslie had ever taken without the approval of her boss. "I know Spence has used the name throughout the portions of the deck that he's been working on," she said invoking the authority of the absent pitch leader.

"You're absolutely sure you've got nothing that would work better?" Avery asked Zig one more time.

"I'll tell you what Avery." Zig was always prepared to make a deal where the top boss was concerned. "I promise that we'll prepare a list of our best attempts and have them mounted on display boards and we'll hold them in reserve. If we get questioned, it will be a simple matter of us taking them through our thinking. But mark my words, I think the likelihood of that is quite slim."

Avery seemed doubtful, but he decided to forego further discussion of the matter with the duo of Zig and Leslie Stride. He had done quite a hatchet job on the preliminary draft of the leave-behind document and, while he felt little remorse, he knew that his extensive changes were more substantial than anyone expected. Even the agency president had to be respectful of the give and take required to get the work completed on time. He would gladly barter his consent on the approach to the name for additional editing time on the document. Besides, if he had to, he could always pull rank later.

"Ziggy ..." By using his pet nickname for his Creative Director, Avery signaled that he would let the matter pass. "Have you figured out how you're going to present the television concepts?"

"Well, there's the mock spot of course," Zig reminded. "I trust you've seen the revised cut that Spence signed off on yesterday, haven't you Avery?" He said this as much to Leslie at the same time. She and Spence had also developed the habit of keeping work out the reach of the meddlesome President. It was also quite possible that they had withheld screening this new version to Avery pending further requests for changes from themselves.

"Yes, I did manage a peek at it this morning. I must say, that line ... *"up to a half pound a day until the weight goes away,"* really seals it for me. Did you write that?"

"I meant about the ending," Zig asked. He was still prickly about the compromise and the secondary selling line that had been included at Playfair's insistence, too.

"I'm afraid I'm much happier with the more traditional version. I know it's more expected, but the girl carries it off brilliantly." Avery's compliment was genuine, but it did little to assuage the resentment Zig still felt about being overruled. He took some consolation in knowing that he would be seeing Ellen in just a few hours time.

"The rest of the TV will be shown as boards or animatics, depending on how quickly the illustrations come back." If they had time they would scan the finished pictures and bring them to life in a series of computerized simulations. Zig hated these. He said they always reminded him of Japanese porn. If it were up to him, he would rather explain what was happening in a commercial by acting out a script and painting pictures with his own words and actions. But it had been decided that Carlton & Paxton was likely far too buttoned down for such a casual approach.

As a result, the storyboards for the television creative would be among the last exhibits to be assembled. Because hand drawn illustrations were required for each of the scenes of the proposed commercials and Boom was recommending six executions in all, the studio manager had farmed these renderings to an outside supplier. The punch line was that the same artists who were drawing their frames, could very easily be doing work for their competitors. All they could do was wait and hope that what arrived would be correct.

"I really wish we had been able to go to China with them," Zig now complained. Recently, he had been sending a lot of this kind of work to talented illustrators overseas and reviewing progress over the Internet. "But Spence wanted to be more hands on."

This last comment amounted to little more than exchanging tit for tat. New business was one of the areas in which the decision of the Creative Director was not always law. And indeed, Playfair had insisted the work be directed to a local vendor with whom he had a long-standing relationship. This was a source of ongoing annoyance to Zig, so he made sure Avery was aware of who was responsible. He wanted absolution in case there were any problems with the work or the bill, when it eventually arrived.

"I see," said Avery. But it was clear he didn't really grasp why Zig was lodging such a complaint. "Otherwise, I think the advertising components look great. Another couple of days for the rest of the print and collateral elements?"

"I've got a couple of point of sale and rack displays coming that I think you're really going to like. We're going to actually Photoshop them into some real in-store situations." Zig carried on courting favor in the absence of Playfair. "And I think both the electronic and print brochures are bloody marvelous."

"I look forward to seeing them," Avery fed back. "But I'm afraid I've now got to turn my attention to the deck." As he said this, he lifted up the draft document he had been hard at work editing and dropped it on the table. Leslie Stride, who had been busily typing, looked up startled. "I'm afraid it's going to take a whole lot more work, young lady." With that, the agency president grabbed hold of the back of the chair next to her and wheeled himself in beside her. Avery liked to do revisions the old fashioned way—over the shoulder.

Day 21

The visit from Harry Woodruff caught Lane completely off guard. When Brenda called through to let her know that the Carlton & Paxton scientist was at reception, she was both unprepared and nervous. It had been her plan to avoid any further contact with the review committee until the actual presentation—thereby magnifying the results that she had achieved with her unauthorized use of the drug that the good doctor had provided. Now he was seated in a chair across from her desk and she was struggling to make conversation with the socially clumsy visitor.

The tall, graying man with the large glasses looked curiously out of place in the relentlessly chique office that Lane occupied. He was wearing a tweedy suit the exact style of which Lane couldn't place. She was fairly sure it belonged to a period almost two decades prior. It hadn't been a particularly glorious time in the history of men's fashion and his wide lapelled safari jacket most definitely had not made a comeback. Sitting with his stork-like legs crossed at the knee, one of his hairy shins was exposed. The sock on the foot that he wiggled nervously, its elastic tired, was bunched at the ankle of one of his scuffed brown brogues. While Lane was always leery of stereotyping, it was hard not to think of him as anything other than the nerdish professor he appeared to be.

"Thank you for seeing me, Ms. McCarthy," he began formally in his fading English accent. "I can only imagine you're quite busy with all this pitch business going on."

"Not at all Dr. Woodruff. But would you please call me Lane. I've been half expecting the entire review team to visit, but the only one whose been by so far is Allan. As you can imagine, we've been quite anxious to show off our facilities." Saying this, she spread her arms to suggest the breadth of M&M's offices.

"Yes, I'm sure there's lots of people on our side who would like to see this. It's quite impressive," he said taking in the splendor of Lane's office as if noticing it for the first time. Until then he had been more or less staring at his host, studying her features carefully. "But I'm afraid that's not the actual purpose of this visit."

"Then what can I do for you?" Lane questioned brightly. "Thinking of joining the agency business?" she offered playfully, trying to put her anxious visitor at ease.

Her disarming smile melted him as it had at the very first briefing meeting. Today she looked even more attractive than she had three weeks ago. Over the past year Woodruff had become surprisingly good at noticing changes in a woman's appearance. Lane McCarthy had obviously lost weight and was exhibiting several of the other signs of Endrophat use that he recognized immediately. Not only was she thinner, she had lost much of the bulk that seemed to settle high on a mature woman's hips. Her face was less full and her jaw line was taut in the way of someone who might recently have undergone cosmetic surgery. The differences were unignorable.

"Ms. McCarthy, those samples of Endrophat that I sent over a couple of weeks ago ... I'm afraid I'm going to have to ask for them back," Woodruff now said quietly, getting the purpose of his visit out in the open.

Lane felt herself flushing at the request. The visible signs of this reaction were not lost on the observant scientist. In fact, since first seeing her, he would have been willing to bet that this would be her response to his request.

"There's been a bit of a foul up," he continued.

"Nothing too serious I hope," Lane gulped, suddenly attentive and more than just a little bit anxious.

"Heavens, no. Just a little manufacturing problem," Woodruff replied calmly, watching her closely. "Unfortunately, we somehow managed to get the mix wrong in some of the initial samples. Some have gotten too much of the active ingredient, you know that brain tickler I mentioned, and some have too little," he added trying to sound matter of fact. "It might even prove to be a blessing."

"In what way?" Lane questioned. She was desperately trying her best to sound concerned for her prospective client's problem, but inside her heart was racing.

"It would give us some more test data, sort of. You know we've been pushing hard to get this to market. The clinical trials notwithstanding, the more we can learn about its potential side effects, the better."

"I see." Lane had a pretty good idea about one side effect that she could report on, but for obvious reasons, chose to remain silent as Woodruff continued. He actually seemed to be a very nice and thoughtful man.

"As far as this situation goes, my guess is that unless there was prolonged use at the higher dosage rate, the negative impact would be quite minimal. On the other side, we might learn something more about the placebo effect."

"Placebo effect?" She had a pretty good idea what this meant, but was eager to hear of its relevance to this circumstance.

"With drugs like Endrophat, that work in concert with the brain, its always a possibility. Sometimes the results we achieve are as much a result of mind over matter," the scientist now explained patiently. "More frequently than you'd imagine we see evidence of people achieving the same outcomes with a placebo as they might by taking the actual drug. Its astounding really." As he said this, Lane could almost sense his mind wandering off. Clearly, the irrational nature of this phenomenon was difficult for the always-analytical scientist to comprehend.

"So what you're saying is ..." Lane let her words linger, forcing Woodruff to return from his mental meanderings and fill in the blank she'd left dangling.

"Well, because of this manufacturing problem, we've probably got a whole lot of pills that have no active ingredient in them whatsoever. Yet if someone were to use them, it's quite likely they might lose weight simply because that's what they imagined was supposed to happen. There's no scientific reason for it, of course." He made this last comment as if he had to apologize. "Just the mind playing tricks on the body."

"But what if they got too much? It wouldn't be harmful, would it? " She now had some genuine worry in her voice.

"Lane, there's always a risk where dosage is concerned," he answered. "At an elevated rate, which is what we think might have happened to some of the other pills, we expect we'll see increases in heart rate and blood flow. Some women might even experience curious sensations of ..." Now it was the doctor's turn to feel a little embarrassed. "... increased pleasure during sexual activity."

"Uh huh," Lane nodded. As she listened to what was very likely the scientific explanation of what had been occurring during her brief experimentation with the drug, she began to relax.

"Again, one or two pills wouldn't likely do any serious

harm. When we heard about this during the secondary trials, we chose to interpret it as something of a … what is the best way to say this … bonus," he smiled.

"Like discovering Viagra," Lane joined in, alluding to the vascular medication that ultimately turned into a treatment for erectile dysfunction.

"Very good, Ms. McCarthy," he praised her for her quick grasp of the problem. "But of course, like everything else, where we invariably get into trouble is when we get too much of a good thing. In such a case I would be quite concerned if someone were receiving a sustained heavy dose without proper medical supervision." His tone got much more serious as he said this. "Which is, of course, why I'm rounding up all the samples."

In her mind Lane was quickly counting off the number of pills she had consumed and was subtracting that number from the nearly full bottle that had arrived at her office. As best she could tell, she had used roughly half of them. Surely, she hoped, that wouldn't count as prolonged heavy use.

"I don't even remember precisely how many pills I sent over here," Woodruff added. Reading minds seemed to be another of the uncanny abilities of the brilliant scientist. "To be honest, I'm not even sure if they were from the affected batch. But you can't be too careful."

Hearing these words, Lane brightened considerably. "Well, I think I can pretty much round up everything you provided to us," she said feeling very relieved. "One or two might have disappeared in the Art Department, but the rest of what you sent over is right here." With that she opened her desk drawer and turned over the half full bottle of samples.

"Excellent," concluded Woodruff. "I would greatly appreciate it if you didn't mention this little problem to anyone else. It's really quite embarrassing actually … especially this close to the introduction."

"You can be sure of that," Lane reassured. "I'll also check down the hall. But you never know with those guys. They've probably cut a few in two, crushed them up or covered them with glue. Do you really need those ones back?"

"No, I'm sure these will be fine, Ms. McCarthy. The important thing is that nobody has used the bloody things." As he said this, he tilted his head to one side, studying her pretty face and newly trim features from another perspective. "By the way, you are certainly looking very nice to day." He matched this compliment with just a hint of a smile and then excused himself from her office. Reflecting on the developments of the past twenty minutes, Lane was both relieved and bewildered.

The cell phone that Ira had been asked to turn off moments after boarding chirped for the second time and earned him another disapproving look from the cabin steward who was working at the entrance to the plane. But the flight was still a few minutes from pushing back and the moment he recognized the name on the Caller ID, he was quick to flip it open.

"Hello, Ira?" said the voice on the other end. "It's John Carver. I tried you at the hotel but they said you'd already left for the airport."

"Thank you, John. I'm just about to push back. What's up?" Hearing from the older man so soon after their meeting had caught him somewhat by surprise.

"I'll try and make it quick. I've got some good news and bad. First, I spoke to Andy Sullivan directly. I don't know how to put this any other way, but it seems like he was already quite aware of some of the problems with our friend." Carver was obviously using the term facetiously, but also for reasons of confidentiality. "My guess is that the Employee Assistance group you spoke so highly of isn't all that discreet."

"Did he say what they were going to do about it?" Ira interrupted. The flight attendants were now patrolling the aisles, slamming the doors of the overhead bins and making final preparations for departure. Even the more sympathetic stewardess assigned to the First Class cabin was now urgently signaling him to wrap up his call.

"I'm afraid they've decided that train has already left the station. With the review, I mean. They intend to take pretty swift action as soon as it's wrapped up. Don't ask me why. I guess some of the people from Legal got involved and they're nervous about cause for dismissal—especially since he's a career guy. They want everything airtight before they move on it."

"Can't they just fucking whack him?" Ira hissed. The older couple across the aisle looked aghast at his use of profanity and Ira slid over to the vacant seat closer to the window to shield his conversation from further eavesdropping.

"But that's not the real problem for you, Ira." Carver continued. "I'm afraid that now that Sullivan is involved, this thing has taken on a life of its own." Carver seemed to sense that their time was extremely limited so he spoke quickly and succinctly. "He's done a helluva job convincing the rest of the executive that an agency with strong international credentials is absolutely a must."

"Shit!" was all Ira could respond. He had suspected this was a possibility as the scope of the launch had become apparent. "Sorry, John," he apologized.

"I don't know what the strength of your network is ... if you even have one. But its likely going to be the deciding factor," Carver now counseled. He had been away from the game for a few years now, but he was still a deft player. "You might want to do something about that and fast." For a few moments, he heard nothing but silence. "Ira?"

Upon hearing these last words Ira unfastened his seatbelt

and stood up. With the phone still at his ear he leapt into the aisle, popped the lid and grabbed his garment bag from the storage compartment above his head. Ignoring the angry admonishments of the flight crew, he slung it over his shoulder and bolted across the threshold of the jet way moments before the exit was sealed. Safely off the flight, he stood in the corridor and half yelled a final urgent request. "John, I can't thank you enough, but can I ask you for one more favor?"

"Go ahead," the old board member allowed. "I guess I'm in deep enough already." Part of him had actually enjoyed rolling up his sleeves and getting involved in this mess. It was a lot more fun than sitting through the reporting of quarterly results.

"Do you think you can get me a little time offline with Sullivan or somebody higher up when I get back?" Ira now pleaded.

"I'll see what I can do, but I can't promise anything. You know you've pissed a few people off over there the last little while."

"I hear you," Ira conceded. He knew that Carver was right about his behavior. "I just hope it isn't too late."

With his worst fears confirmed, he signed off from the call. Storming hastily up the fuel-scented passageway as the engines of the departing jet whined to a crescendo, he searched his pocket for the piece of hotel stationery onto which he had hastily scribbled the number. Suddenly there was another important meeting he would have to arrange while in New York.

Who knew what constituted the right way to begin a relationship these days? Between work and the bar scene and online introduction services, Zig Cartwright had used a hundred ways to meet women and never found anyone or anything that lasted more than a few months. Was there really anything wrong with falling hard for a girl who worked in a strip club? You certainly knew what you were getting into—no surprises. Besides, he reminded himself, he had first decided he liked her when he thought she was just a model. Cradling a bag of groceries in one arm and carrying a bottle of wine by the neck in the other, Zig eagerly climbed the stairs to the apartment he had been sharing with Ellen for the past couple of days. With things going so well on the pitch, he had actually been able to sneak away from the agency early and now he was hoping to beat his new girlfriend home. Amazingly, she had already entrusted him with a key.

They seemed to have settled on her place, at least for now, since it was only a short train ride from Zig's office and just around the corner from the Club. It had been quite some time since Zig had played house with a woman and he was thoroughly enjoying the novelty of it. Or at least he had, for the past three nights in a row. Historically, he was more of a slip away in the darkest hour of the night kind of guy. But his infatuation with Ellen Starnowski was total and her desire for him seemed every bit as intense. They had even found a way to laugh about the way they met and the discovery that Zig had made afterwards. Though, for the past ninety-six hours, most of the time they had spent together had been in bed. Before, during and after their lovemaking, Zig had explored nearly every part of Ellen's magnificent body and he had not been disappointed by a single inch.

"Hello? El ... anybody home?" he called out as he pushed his way through the stiff, paint-swollen entry door. His arrival was immediately greeted with a full wet nose to the crotch from Clancy, Ellen's enormous but exceptionally friendly Rottweiler. Despite its menacing appearance, the hundred and fifty pound beast offered no resistance to the intruder

R. Bruce Walker

who seemed to have settled in so comfortably with his mistress over the past few days. Instead, he slathered Zig's hand with his foot long tongue, even if it soon became apparent that it was the meaty juices that had seeped from the steaks in the grocery bag and not Zig's mere presence that was being rewarded with such affection. Kicking the door closed behind him, Zig deposited the damp paper sack on the island that divided the living room and kitchen and turned to give the dog a loving maul. He had already become quite attached to the portly hound. Poor Clancy had seen and smelled more of Cartwright's most intimate parts in a few days than any loyal pet should ever have to. As far as the dog was concerned, they had bonded for life.

After rough housing with the dopey animal for a few more moments, Zig peeled off his leather jacket and tossed it toward the hook by the entry to the cozy little apartment. It was then that he remembered the other small surprise that he had packed along for Ellen this evening. Picking his coat up from the floor, he reached into the inside breast pocket and extracted a clear plastic clamshell containing a disk marked 'Party Girl'. It was the newly completed cut of the commercial that featured his beautiful lover in her first leading role. Actually, it was an extended play version of the finished spot that ran nearly a minute and a half. In addition, there were nearly all of the other outtakes from the production. He had asked his editor to put it together and he was certain she would be delighted. She looked fabulous in nearly every single frame. Zig had promised her that he would help assemble a compilation of the very best of these images that she could use in her portfolio as soon as the pitch was complete.

A half hour later, with the groceries put away and dinner started, Zig located the spool of pretty red ribbon that he had bought for this occasion and tied a neat little bow around the plastic box. Then he signed the gooey card he'd been almost too embarrassed to purchase and leaned it, with the DVD inside, against the stem of the wine glass at the romantic little place setting he had arranged for Ellen. He uncorked his reasonably well-considered Australian cabernet, struck a match to the candles and waited, in a thrall, for the young woman who had so completely and utterly won his heart, to appear. As unlikely and obnoxious as it seemed, for the first time in his entire selfish and shallow life, Zig Cartwright was in love.

Where the hell is Ira? That was the question bothering Steve Holiday as he gathered up the roughs he had laid out on the coffee table for the meeting that his partner had insisted on but for which he'd failed to appear. His assistant, Karen, had been reluctant to leave Steve alone in the office that she guarded so ferociously and she continued to hover nearby. Apparently, she hadn't spoken to Ira since first thing that morning and his flight had been scheduled to touch down at one. It was now after five.

"So you've heard nothing?" Steve asked again impatiently. The trouble with Karen was that she was such a sneaky little bitch that Steve was having a hard time deciding whether or not she was lying. He was quietly infuriated and vowed to take this up with Ira later. "Not a word?"

"Nothing. It's really not like him Mr. Holiday," Ira's assistant apologized.

"When he does surface, let him know that I was here and waited half an hour. I'll be here until around seven if he still wants to get together." Steve hated it when someone wasted his time, Ira included. The session they had planned was ostensibly a review of the direct marketing components, but in reality it was just another opportunity for his kinetic partner to fuss some more details and exorcise his nervous energy. Perhaps it was a blessing that he was nowhere to be found.

As far as Steve Holiday was concerned, the DM elements they were recommending were among some of the strongest work that they had developed. This in itself was highly ironic given how passionately the Creative Director had once resisted the merging of advertising and direct response communications. Or how strenuously he had fought to make sure that image advertising was always the primary driver of positioning. But in a late arriving conversion, Steve had recently become an ardent disciple of the three hundred and sixty degree brand.

Treading back down the hall towards his office, Steve stuck his head inside the art studio where they were putting the finishing touches on several of the magazine concept comps. If he had any doubts about the campaign they were recommending, this was where he felt they had a problem. He couldn't quite put his finger on it. And everyone else had reassured him that the work was great. But the instinctive part of the experienced Creative Director wished he had another week or two to fuss this work further. Eighty twenty he reminded himself. It wasn't going to be the work that sunk Lowenstein Holiday, he reminded himself. There were a whole lot of obstacles that would have to be overcome before anyone looked even remotely seriously at the advertising that they were about to recommend.

Day 22

The U.S. headquarters of Interworld Advertising had a distinctly European feel, its übercool interior design making a statement as bold as the agency's stylish advertising. At least this was Ira's impression as he paced the reception area in anticipation of his meeting with its top executive. He knew that he was being kept waiting on purpose. In truth, it's what he would have done if the situation were reversed, but right now his host was dangerously close to crossing the line of being downright rude. Never one to waste a moment though, the idle time provided Ira with an opportunity to study the distinctive décor more closely. Somewhere he hoped to find a sign that this organization and his much more modest Midwestern company might possibly share something in common.

The floor of the waiting room was overlaid in gleaming onyx tiles and the walls were constructed of translucent glass that glowed a luminescent white from within. Around the perimeter a dozen poster-sized sheets of transparent acrylic hung by chains from the ceiling. They held examples of the company's best work sandwiched between invisible layers that gave them the effect of floating magically in air. Beyond these displays was a solid concrete slab, also suspended from chains, which constituted the main reception desk. Behind it was seated a statuesque Aryan beauty dressed in a cruelly short skirt whose lipstick and nail polished matched perfectly the red lacquered letters of the company logo that appeared above her left shoulder. In almost every aspect the space was a faithful homage to the minimalist architect Walter Gropius, though taken in its entirety, the already agitated Ira Lowenstein couldn't help but feel it imparted a peculiar zeitgeist several years beyond the founding of the Bauhaus. As time ticked away and a bit of annoyance began to set in, he briefly contemplated greeting his host with a sharp click of his heels.

"Ira Lowenstein?" Reiner Adolph inquired, arriving suddenly. He was breathless and his manner hurried. "I'm so sorry to have kept you waiting," he said extending his hand to receive this most unlikely visitor. "Let's go right into my office."

He was dressed smartly in a severely cut Hugo Boss suit that was as black as the smartly tailored shirt he wore beneath. There was no tie, but he kept his collar buttoned tight at the neck. He wore a pair of flawlessly polished dress shoes, their blunt toe cut in the latest continental style. He glowed with the healthy tan of a man who had recently spent time on the ski slopes or at the beach.

"It was fortunate you were in town," Ira commented, falling into step beside the taller man. As was his way, he had decided in a split second that he could like the big German— his earlier reservations notwithstanding.

"I have to confess, I was headed your way … to Chicago," Adolph said in his precise, slightly accented English. "I just had some brief business to attend to here first."

"I was hoping to get there sometime soon myself," Ira answered, though Adolph seemed to miss the irony of the remark as they arrived at entry to the office that was reserved for occasional visits by the CEO. It was huge and offered a commanding view across the East River.

"I'm afraid it's a bit excessive, isn't it?" Adolph correctly read Ira's first reaction to the imposing space. "That's the trouble with having to impress the bankers," he added trying to beg a little sympathy.

"They're always eager to lend you money, but they get angry as hell when you spend it," Ira commiserated and both of the tough businessmen laughed. He settled into the chair that Adolph gestured him towards and waited as his host also took a seat.

"So Ira Lowenstein, we finally meet." As he said this, he flexed his fingertips against each other and leaned toward his guest smiling. " You said on the phone that you had a proposition. I can only imagine that this has something to do with the Carlton & Paxton review?"

Ira was pleased his host had chosen to get to the point so quickly. If he'd had to wait another minute or another day to discuss the outrageous idea that had been percolating in his mind since he jumped off the plane, he would probably have managed to talk himself out of it.

"I'll cut right to the chase, Reiner," Ira began. "If you asked me right now who is going to win this Endrophat thing, I would say neither of us." He paused a moment to let this critical assumption sink in before carrying on. "If you wanted to bet a million bucks, I'd say one week from now, Carlton & Paxton will be awarding this work to Boom and you and I will be left out in the cold."

"I see," said Adolph as he weighed this possible outcome. "Boom ... really?" Even he couldn't help but wince when he repeated the silly sounding name of their competitor. "May I ask why you think that we don't stand a chance?"

"A couple of reasons," Ira continued quickly. "In the first

place, I think *we're* truly fucked," he said bluntly in reference to his own agency. "This fellow who is conducting the review, Allan Corbett, is a real piece of work. But more importantly, I've been told from a very reliable source that what Carlton & Paxton is ultimately after is a really strong international network."

Adolph smiled broadly at this suggestion. Clients seeking global marketing continuity were the corner stone of his costly expansion strategy. He had understood that this was Lowenstein Holiday's biggest vulnerability from the beginning and he was pleased to hear this honestly acknowledged by his competitor. "So how does this not favor my company, Ira?" he asked. It was hard for him not to feel smug.

"Because you're in a shambles on the ground in Chicago and you're not likely going to get your shit together in a week," Ira countered directly. The incisiveness of this observation caused Adolph's smile to disappear immediately. "Reiner, with all due respect, I've worked with this client for a decade and a half. You may have all of the right stuff on paper, but you're not going to carry the day with a couple of guys you've airlifted in from New York, however strong you may be around the world."

"Fine," countered Adolph respecting the point. "But Boom has no network either, do they? What are they going to do?"

"I have it from my guys that Spence Playfair over at Boom is so far up Allan Corbett's ass we'd have to go in via the tonsils to get him out," Ira shot back. He was fairly sure that Playfair's reputation would have traveled all the way to Germany and Lane McCarthy definitely would not have missed mentioning this important point in providing her assessment of the competition in the review. His own particularly vivid visual image had left the big German somewhat bewildered. "My guess is that Corbett will try and move the cheese ... downplay the international stuff until Boom can get up to speed and go shopping for a partner. That and they'll probably be brilliant creatively."

As he listened to this, Adolph tried to conceal his reaction. However, the reality was that his stopover in New York had been directly tied to this very pressing issue. Jeremy Whithers had filled him on the messy departure of Gordon Turnbull and, at the same time, presented him with a list of candidates who might be willing to parachute into the Chicago office on short notice. It had been quite unimpressive. Worse, both senior executives knew that any decision they made would have to be negotiated with Lane McCarthy. If she walked away unhappy with their choice, they would have no chance at all to win the pitch. His spies on the ground had already reported the impression Lane appeared to have made on Corbett.

"So what are you thinking, Mr. Lowenstein?" He had a pretty good idea where the conversation was leading, but he hadn't yet lit on the solution that had occurred to Ira Lowenstein. He knew, from his own circumstance, that acquisition was out of the question since he was already seriously strapped for cash. There was no way he could raise enough capital to purchase a company of the size and stature of Lowenstein Holiday—most certainly not overnight.

"A joint venture," Ira said simply and then paused for moment. "A strategic partnership that brings the best resources of the Interworld network together with Lowenstein Holiday to serve the global needs of Carlton & Paxton with a strong and knowledgeable local service provider." He delivered the second part of his explanation as if he were reading from a script or the inevitable press release that would announce the formation of such a partnership. "We promise them the best of both worlds!" he now exclaimed enthusiastically.

The simplicity of the proposition startled the quick

thinking German. While such a thing was practically unheard of in the cat and dog world of advertising, as soon as the two words were out of Ira's mouth, Adolph was already leaping ahead to the practicality of the audacious solution that had just been put on the table. Divide the revenue. Share the risk. Build a relationship with Carlton & Paxton even if the project-based partnership didn't work out. It was practically a no lose proposition. "Would they ever buy such a thing?" he wondered out loud. There was both incredulity and excitement in his voice.

"I'll tell you what my friend," Ira now began selling in earnest. "What have we got to lose?" It was an outlandish approach, but he could tell immediately that the shrewd businessman Reiner Adolph was intrigued.

"Do you think we could pull it off in time? Of course, we could," he asked and then answered himself rhetorically. "We have to … if what you say is true." The gears of his nimble mind were now fully engaged and he was quickly churning the concept.

"I have to tell you, I haven't even discussed this with my partner, Steve Holiday," Ira now volunteered, sensing Adolph's rising enthusiasm." He had decided he could not risk distracting his Creative Director from what was going on back in Chicago.

"But he will agree, of course?" Both men were used to bartering with their creative people, but neither trusted them when it came to the really hard decisions that were required to run a business.

"I'm fairly certain he will see that it's our only chance. Although I think we're going to have to promise him complete creative control," Ira began negotiating. This was the immediate value that Lowenstein Holiday brought to the party and he was confident Adolph would yield to this important condition.

"Fine. As long as my people take the lead on Account Management," the astute Adolph countered, demonstrating his equally quick reflexes. Ira had expected this would be the first and most logical concession he would have to make. It was a no brainer. Besides, they definitely couldn't do any worse than his own team had done over the past few months, he had already decided.

"Of course. And we can split the media down the middle. Billings and service. We'll take domestic and you can take international," Ira quickly suggested. They were horse-trading now and both men were immediately in their element.

"As long as its reconciled quarterly. We'll also have to come up with a formula for cost sharing." Adolph was lit with excitement and obviously enjoying the exchange as much as Ira.

"What about Lane McCarthy?" Ira now asked. He had speculated enough about the nature of her arrangement with Interworld to know that she, too, might be a potentially significant stumbling block. "Will she be willing to play?"

"I wouldn't worry too much about her Ira," Adolph said, addressing his new friend with growing familiarly. "I think we will find her most cooperative. Between you and me, she's got less than a year and a half left on her contract and the price has already been negotiated," he confided.

"Excellent. It's only money," Ira smiled and the big German nodded. He hadn't had as much fun in years. "Now, can I tell you something else in absolute confidence?" As Ira prepared to play his final and most valuable card, he studied Adolph closely. It was a daring revelation, but one that was necessary to seal the deal.

"Go ahead," Adolph encouraged. He knew that there was a necessary honor amongst thieves since, after all, he nearly was one.

"We have two more things going for us, Reiner, " Ira nearly whispered.

"And what are those, my friend?"

"When it's done, Allan Corbett is definitely out," Ira revealed. "I've seen to that. And more importantly, I have a meeting with Andrew Sullivan on Tuesday morning."

Now it was Reiner Adolph's turn to make a bold gesture. He offered his strong right hand to the man he had met for the first time barely fifteen minutes before.

"Mr. Lowenstein, I believe we have a deal," he said squeezing Ira's hand firmly. "Of course, we'll have to talk to the lawyers."

Allan Corbett had decided that the safest strategy for reaching out to Stella Starr was to wait in the coffee shop opposite the well-illuminated front entrance to Wriggly's Cabaret and watch until she appeared. From his place across the street he would likely be able to spot her as she exited the club. With any luck, he could intercept her without an intervention from the burly doorman who flagged down cabs for the girls and seemed to bid a watchful goodnight to the ones who headed away on foot. Hopefully, she would be among these and he would be able to catch up with her a block or two away, thereby avoiding any trouble. At least that was his plan. However, after an hour or more of observing the comings and goings of a dozen dancers in their inconspicuous clothing and without the heavy make up and piled hair that they wore inside, he prayed he would be able to recognize her. It was going to be harder still as the afternoon faded into twilight.

He had already rehearsed what he would say. It wouldn't be at all desperate or pleading. After a couple of days of reflection, he had decided that further pursuit of the beautiful young woman was both pointless and risky. Instead, he would keep his composure and pertain himself strictly to the warning he had decided that he owed her. Having performed a rough calculation of the quantity of the drug that she had likely used, and wracking his brain to remember the precise dates on which he had delivered pills, he was fairly sure that she would have received some of the defective samples that Woodruff had alerted him to. In fact, based on the voice message the scientist had left him yesterday, he was now virtually certain that the last batch he had intended to give her was among the most potentially dangerous of any that had been produced.

Perched on an uncomfortable stool, his coffee cold and stale in his cup, Corbett stared into the gathering gloom of the early evening. The sidewalks were busy with people rushing about their business and foot traffic beneath the club's illuminated portico was brisk. Peering over two parked cars that shielded him from sight, he couldn't help but notice how many of the pedestrians stole a peek at the provocative posters that advertised the illicit entertainment going on inside or whose heads turned curiously in the direction of the music that blared whenever the door to the club swung open. There appeared to be a shift change taking place and a steady stream of young women now arrived and departed with regularity.

He tried to imagine the scene inside the club. The air would be warm and moist with the exertions of the attractive dancers working the happy hour trade. The bar would be bustling and alive with boisterous businessmen eager to watch the ladies take their clothes off. He longed for a drink and the numbing comfort it would provide, but knew he would have to wait. He touched his torn brow and remembered his last visit to Wriggly's. Piecing together the booze-clouded sequence of events from that afternoon, his only clear memory was from before the scuffle started. At one point he recalled that he had been holding a full bottle of pills in his hand. But that was prior to big Mario hooking his arm around his throat and nearly causing him to blackout. His best hope now was that the bottle had spilled or simply disappeared into one of the dark places on the filthy bar room floor that a broom seldom found. Only a fool would pick up something that they found down there.

This was what was on Corbett's mind as he watched and waited. But everything changed in a moment. Suddenly, the wild wail of a siren and the flashing lights of an approaching ambulance interrupted his thoughts. Dodging left and right, bullying its way up the car clogged avenue, the circling beams of its red and white warning signals slashed across the storefronts and darkened buildings further down the street. There was little doubt about its intended destination. Moments later, the big box shaped vehicle jerked to a halt in front of the garishly lit marquee and two attendants tumbled out. As a crowd gathered and people were restrained from blocking the double doors that had been flung wide for the gurney that was being hastily assembled to enter, Allan Corbett slid off the seat from where he had been observing. Stepping into the cool of the night, he shot one more glance in the direction of all the excitement and disappeared unnoticed from the scene. He didn't need to see the ash colored skin of the girl wrapped in a blanket and hidden beneath a pinching oxygen mask that emerged a few minutes later, to guess what had happened.

"Do I look fat to you?"

Steve Holiday thought she had to be kidding. It was the most famous trap door in the history of relations between men and women. To agree was suicide and to not notice suggested indifference. Of course, he was anything but.

"Perfect. Better than the first time I ever saw you."

Lane was standing naked in front of a long wardrobe mirror in the corner of her bedroom still glowing from their recently completed lovemaking. As she considered this response, she peered over her shoulder and attempted to check out the reflection of her trim backside.

"Good answer, Holiday."

"It's what I do."

"Even my legs?"

"Some of the finest getaway sticks I've ever seen."

"Not too thin?" the inquisition continued.

"Absolutely perfect." At forty-three, she was still one of the most beautiful woman he had ever been with, yet it was not this aspect of Lane McCarthy that he realized he had fallen in love with.

"It makes you wonder, doesn't it?"

"What's that?"

"What Endrophat will do?"

It was the first time Lane had actually introduced the subject of the prize they were both so diligently pursuing. Steve Holiday lifted himself on one elbow in the bed and, despite his fatigue, decided to find out what was on her mind.

"In what way?" he asked, his interest now piqued.

"I don't know, relationships maybe? Sometimes I think that it's a woman's doubts about herself that keep some couples together."

"I always imagined it was the sex."

His response was a little too glib and Lane frowned. She reached for the robe that hung from the carved finial of the mirror frame and tied it tight around her narrow waist.

"Funny. But seriously, what if the drug did more than just take weight off?"

"Like what?"

"I don't know. What if it freed a woman to make better choices?"

"In men?"

"It's always all about you, isn't it?" Much to Lane's relief, the sex they had just enjoyed had been every bit as pleasurable as it had been two days before when she was still using the drug. "No. I mean in terms of how couples interact." She sat down on the end of the bed and made it clear to Steve she expected a more serious response than what he'd contributed thus far.

"I'm not sure I get what you mean?"

"I mean in terms of everything. I'm no anthropologist, or whatever, but it seems to me that allowing every woman to have a nearly perfect figure certainly changes the rules of the game."

"And what game would that be?"

"The one that has allowed you to take advantage of women's insecurities for as long as we've existed."

"You mean men?"

"Of course."

"Then it's going to be a pretty dark day for us, isn't it." Steve didn't enjoy being held to account for the behavior of his gender throughout history. Annoyed, he decided to weigh in with a few philosophical observations of his own.

"Look at me," he now explained. "I'm tall, skinny and insecure. My partner Ira is short, fat and balding and he thinks he looks like Brad Pitt. I'm just saying that women don't have the market cornered on self-doubt. "

"Do you really believe that?"

"Sure."

"But you don't think men would use Endrophat if it were possible?"

"Some might. Most wouldn't?"

"And you? "

"The latter." He could feel himself getting frustrated. Much like Lane's first question, there was no satisfactory answer.

"But you'd disapprove of someone who did?

"I'm just saying that this drug is no different than liposuction or cosmetic surgery. Apart from people who are at risk from the health effects of obesity, frankly, it's just another procedure that preys on the vulnerable and indulges the Narcissistic.

"That's very cynical."

"It's a very cynical fucking world."

It was the first time that the two of them had ever strongly disagreed about anything. While the last thing that either one of them had the energy to do this evening was fight, it was inevitable that the pressures that had been building over the last few weeks would boil over.

"So you're telling me that you think this is just another vanity product?" Lane now countered.

"Well, isn't it?" Steve pushed back a little too aggressively. "I mean, what kind of bloody idiot would expose them self to the risks of using a drug that does God only knows what, in the name of squeezing into another dress size?"

He knew better, but he couldn't stop himself from delivering this particularly harsh indictment. In response, Lane went silent. She had swung her legs up on the bed and now drew them tight to her chest. Wrapping her arms around her shins, she drew herself into a tight little ball and began rocking slowly back and forth.

After a long pause, Lane finally asked, "What if I told you there is a potentially serious problem with the drug?" Turning towards him, she now studied Steve's face closely to get his honest reaction.

"Are you kidding me?" Steve asked incredulously.

"What if I told you Harold Woodruff came to see me the other day?" Lane continued. "And he said some pretty disturbing things about potential side effects."

"I'd say, please don't tell me anything you may regret in the morning." Steve now backed off. He knew she was about to say more, but for the first time since in their long dance around this most delicate subject, it was he who was counseling discretion.

"But what if ..." She paused again letting the pregnant question dangle in the air unanswered as she carefully weighed the virtues of the confession she was about to make.

"What if what?" Steve asked in spite of himself. But watching her eyes and brow, he now really didn't expect an answer.

"What if I told you I tried it," Lane admitted.

"What?"

"Endrophat."

"Not really?" Her words took his breath away.

"I think you better go," Lane now requested.

Though the last thing he wanted was to leave her, he had little choice but to respect her wishes. Her confession had left him stunned. This entire affair was getting just a little too complicated. And both of them knew it.

Day 23

"**A**re you out of your mind?" To Steve Holiday it seemed like a perfectly reasonable response to the subject Ira had just introduced. "A joint fucking venture?"

His angry hiss of profanity caused several heads to swivel in their direction and even the busboy topping up their orange juice glasses did a nervous double take. Ira had thought he might be able to keep his partner calmer by meeting him for breakfast in the bustling dining room of the hotel around the corner from the office. But now it didn't seem like such a brilliant strategy. It was becoming clear that Steve would require a lot more coaching to get on side with the deal that he had struck the day before.

"Keep your voice down," Ira cautioned sternly. "It was our only goddamned chance."

"Was ... what do mean was? You've already done something?" Holiday struggled to contain himself. Still raw from his conversation with Lane and tired from a night of wrestling with the secret she had revealed, he was totally unprepared for Ira's bombshell. "How could you?" he questioned with immediate indignation.

"I was in New York. I met with two members of the C&P board. We were going to be shut out." Ira encapsulated. "There was no other way."

"Really? And you were going to ask me ... when? In case

you forgot, it's my name on the other half of the goddamned door."

"Don't be such a child," Ira shot back.

"You think this is about ego?" Steve said acidly. "This is about respect."

"Fine. I respect that you're angry. But that doesn't change anything. According to Carver and Brandt, we'd been on the endangered species list for quite some time."

"How do you mean?"

"We needed an international connection. Not the usual trumped up bullshit, but an honest to goodness network ... with real offices and real people. Otherwise it was over. This thing has gone way above Corbett's head ... apparently it had been on the agenda at the top of the house for a couple of years," Ira laid out his case.

This frank explanation blunted Holiday's assault somewhat. He had always known the international issue was their Achilles heel. In fact, the businessman in him had been fairly sure this would become a problem once he'd digested the Endrophat brief and thought about the rollout plan. He and Ira had long debated the need to form a tangible global alliance to protect them against this precise situation. The trouble with what was now being proposed was that they had exactly five days to make it work.

"I hope you don't mind me asking," Holiday now queried, still reluctant to acknowledge the fact that Ira might have actually gone ahead without involving him. "But just who the fuck have you found for us to partner with that's gonna be worth a shit? You know there's less than a week to go."

"Interworld," Ira responded succinctly. The ingeniousness of his brilliantly constructed coup was immediately self-evident.

"McCarthy McCauley Interworld?" Steve now asked

weakly. For the second time in the past eight hours he was stunned like he'd been whacked with a plank. "Partners?" he mumbled in a daze.

"Just a joint venture. Not a merger," Ira now began to explain less defensively. "We're still waiting on the papers, but we put the lawyers to work last night and they thought they would have something for us to look at by lunchtime."

"With Lane McCarthy?" Holiday responded dumbly. It was as if he hadn't heard the balance of Ira's words.

"Why? Do you know her? Rumor has it she's pretty hot." It was a fairly adolescent comment coming from a man who was over fifty, but it was so typically Ira. He had dropped the confrontational edge that had guarded their exchange for the past few moments. It was now time to ease his partner along more gently. "I really am sorry Steve," he apologized. "One thing led to another yesterday afternoon. Before I knew it, we had a deal. It truly is the only way," he rationalized.

Emerging from the numbness that followed what had just been revealed, Holiday realized he now had to react to what minutes before had been just an abstract notion. Suddenly it was an unignorable reality.

"Fine," he said. This ambiguous little word was his first signal of assent. "But who … what … how are we going to pull this off?" He was still reeling, but at least he was regaining consciousness.

Ira watched somewhat bemused as his partner picked himself up off the canvas. He was relieved. He knew that he had crossed a boundary in their relationship, but for now at least, it appeared as if the friend he had floored only moments before would be willing to play along.

"We've only got five fucking days."

"Fifteen," countered Ira. It was a joke that had sustained them in the early days of their partnership when the two of them would often toil night and day to beat impossible deadlines. "There are fifteen working days between now and showtime."

"How the hell?" Steve asked of himself out loud. "Which campaign?"

"Relax, buddy. We've got a meeting over there at eleven. We'll figure that out on the way over," Ira smiled. The hardest part of his morning's mission was now complete.

The last person Lane McCarthy needed to see with less than five days to go before the presentation was Reiner Adolph. Yet there was his garment bag tagged with a dozen international baggage tickets draped over the arm of her elegant chaise and the end of his laptop charger dangling loosely from the antique side table where a handsome lamp normally stood. The priceless cloche jardinière had been unceremoniously relegated to a corner in favor of the chunky black transformer. Where he was now, she hated to imagine? She summoned Brenda and the search for the rogue executive currently loose in their offices began in earnest. It started with a page that went unheeded and ended in the war room in the Creative Department where the bulk of the exhibits for the Carlton & Paxton presentation had been assembled. It hadn't taken much detective work on Lane's part to deduce that this was where she would find him.

"Ah, there you are Lane," Reiner said calmly as if it were she, and not himself, who was the visitor. "Why don't you come in and close the door? I've got something very important to discuss with you."

Steve studied Lane closely for any signal as to how she was reacting to everything that had happened since this morning's surprise announcement. Despite overtures with his eyebrows, she remained sphinx-like on the sofa letting the two brokers of this hastily arranged marriage do all the talking. Reiner Adolph had commandeered her favorite chair at the head of the gilded coffee table and was holding forth like the Pontiff. Ira, who was seated to his right, hadn't taken his eyes off Lane's shapely legs since the four of them had sat down. She was keeping her knees locked and her eyes averted. She had been even more chaste when she was introduced to Steve, almost acting as if they'd never met. But then Ira remembered that the two of them had shared the stage together at the Ad Council forum and they had permission to assume at least a little familiarity. To this point neither of them had contributed more than a few polite words to the discussion.

"I think what we first have to do is figure out how we position the positive benefits of our..." Reiner searched for the correct words in English, "... little arrangement."

"Exactly," Ira smiled. He had been greatly enjoying the company of Adolph since the time they'd shared together on the private charter that his extravagant new partner had arranged to fly them back to Chicago yesterday evening. He didn't even seem to mind yielding the floor on issues he had already worked out in his own head. Quite atypically, he waited patiently for Reiner and the group to catch up. "We need to be able to present an air tight case to Sullivan when I meet with him tomorrow."

"Are you sure you can trust him?" Lane now asked of the linchpin from Carlton & Paxton. But in truth she was more curious about Ira. She knew little of him other than industry chatter and, of course, the things Steve had shared over the past week and a half. Self-conscious from his leering gaze, her first impression of her new partner wasn't at all favorable.

"I think we have to trust him Lane," Ira answered a little too sharply. Ira was deftly playing a power game. While he had been willing to yield the lead role on this initiative to Adolph, he wasn't about to cede his penultimate position to anyone else, let alone a woman. "I have assurances from my Board contacts that he will be discreet."

"If he blows our cover on this, we're screwed before we even get into the room" Lane pushed back. Steve smiled to himself. She was as tough as either of the other two executives and he was glad he wouldn't have to fight her on creative issues. At least, not yet.

"She's right," Steve now ventured. "If Corbett gets wind of this early, he'll find a way to undermine it." With this show of allegiance, he expected Lane to offer at least some sign of approval, but her face remained as neutral as it had been when he'd attempted to overstate their previous collaboration at the luncheon presentation. She clearly didn't need him in her corner for this fight.

"Why don't we just assume for now that my meeting with Sullivan will play out as we hope," Ira moved on. He wasn't use to being second-guessed on account management issues and he didn't like it one bit.

Reiner Adolph sensed trouble brewing and injected himself into the potentially hostile exchange before it could escalate. "Then the next thing we have to figure out is who's going to deliver the pitch."

Lane backed off as she had been instructed to do earlier. But it didn't stop her from hinting her disapproval. Steve was pretty sure she doubted Ira's ability to pull off what he'd promised in terms of paving the way for them to enter the presentation room as one agency. But there was something else in play, as well.

" … And how we're going to get all the bloody work

done," Steve added in what was becoming an increasingly annoying refrain. He had decided to keep reminding the group of the enormous unanswered questions about their creative presentation until it received appropriate acknowledgement from the other three.

"So what are you thinking, Ira?" Lane asked coyly. For the first time since the meeting began she turned herself to face directly towards him. "You're better at this than the rest of us."

It was a clever move on Lane's part and the little man couldn't help but puff with the compliment. In fact, he was so taken with her apparent acquiescence that he uncharacteristically dropped his guard.

"My gut tells me to keep it simple. After Reiner and I deliver assurances about our ability to deliver seamlessly, I think its pretty much over to you two," Ira now responded amicably. Knowing that he was such a control freak, Steve was quite surprised that Ira would concede this point so easily. It was also generous enough to fool Adolph, who seemed delighted to get past this most ticklish issue. Sill, Lane didn't seem quite as convinced and pressed for confirmation.

"Everything?" she asked batting her eyes and closing her trap. "Just Steve and I?"

"If that's what you'd like." Ira yielded. "Just let us sign off on the money."

"You see, Lane," Adolph coaxed. "I told you Ira would be most cooperative." It was clear they had engaged in the same kind of suspicion-filled debate that Steve and Ira had sparred over earlier. "So what do you think?"

"I think we've got a deal," said Lane immediately offering a handshake to Ira. It was the first time in a long time that he realized he'd been had.

Now that the matter of who was going to decide what would be presented had been successfully negotiated, Lane finally seemed to relax. She beamed a smile in Steve's direction. Her performance was pure genius. Without raising the issue or her voice once, it appeared she had gotten exactly what she was after.

"I think you'll find that Mr. Holiday and I will be able to work quite well together," she promised to the relief of the other two men. When they turned to congratulate each other, she slipped her new colleague a nearly imperceptible wink. "Don't you think so, Steve?"

"Absolutely," he agreed.

"We'll leave the two of you with the lawyers," Lane now took control. "Mr. Holiday and I have got some real work to do."

'What? No honeymoon?" the Creative Director kidded. He was quietly in awe of the skillful negotiation he had just witnessed.

"Oh, and Reiner, would you mind meeting in the main boardroom? You're in my chair," Lane added.

She said this with a wounded smile and hurt look that caused Reiner to apologize profusely and both he and Ira to immediately excuse themselves from her office. She was quite something, this woman to whom he'd just been married, thought Holiday.

Spence Playfair studied the list of names that Allan Corbett's assistant, Tiffany, had forwarded by e-mail the afternoon before. It was the team from Carlton & Paxton who would be evaluating the presentations and the group who would ultimately render the decision on which agency would be awarded the project. It was the last piece of the puzzle that Playfair had been waiting for as he made his final preparations for the pitch. Now he could determine who from his own side would make it into the room. So far, the only person he had shared this information with was Leslie Stride. He was anxious to hear her opinion.

"Clearly, it's gotten bigger over there." Her first reaction had been the same as his. "I really didn't expect we'd see this kind of weight so early on." She said this in reference to Alex Spearman, the North American CEO of Carlton & Paxton, whose name had appeared at the top of the list."

"I told you," Playfair gloated. "I knew this thing was the key to the entire bloody kingdom."

"I knew we'd likely see Andrew Sullivan. But who is Art Bristow?" Stride puzzled.

"He's Harold Woodruff's boss. He's in charge of R&D and global manufacturing." Spence had done his homework. As always, he was anxious to show this off.

"The other surprise is Marlene Horcoff. She's President of the Family Health Division. I guess they thought they needed a woman's perspective?"

"It sort of makes Allan and Woody look pretty light doesn't it?" Leslie ignored the patronizing tone of the previous comment. "What do you make of that?"

"Like I said. I think we're pitching for the whole account," Playfair answered with rising excitement. "Otherwise there's no way they would pack the room with these kinds of heavy hitters," he added with certainty.

"So I guess this means ..." Before she could finish, Playfair anticipated.

"We're going to need Avery. And we're going to need him to really be on his game," he concluded. "How was he with the document the other day?

"Like an old lady," Leslie moaned. "He's managed to get himself all wound up in the name thing again. I think he might even be working on a list of his own."

"As long as he's seeing the big picture," Playfair remarked

snidely. Both of them laughed, but the truth was they were becoming increasingly doubtful of Avery's ability to carry the day when the stakes were so high. He had such a tendency to go egghead. Plus they were fairly certain that the top team from Carlton & Paxton would be razor sharp and all about the numbers.

"What about Zig?" Leslie now asked about their other potential liability.

"Can you get him to get a haircut?" Playfair hated Cartwright's black presentation suit and loathed it even more when Zig's straggly mane flowed over the collar. He'd seen him the other night slipping out the door and had added a note about personal hygiene to his list of to dos.

"Seriously?" Leslie knew she was the one who would be asked to broach this difficult subject. It would be nearly as difficult as the conversation she'd had to have prior to the Christmas party about having his rather pungent smelling wardrobe sent out to the drycleaners. "Can't somebody else do it this time?"

"I'm afraid that's why they pay you the big bucks, my dear," Playfair teased. In truth, young Miss Stride had had more salary increases and bonuses lavished on her in the past three years than any other employee in the company. But, like the demands for favors that accompanied them, she definitely paid a price.

"I'll do it if you'll let me into the room this time," Leslie now attempted to barter. In most presentations, her boss preferred to keep his bright young protégé invisible—unless, of course, the prospective client seemed to be shopping for more than the agency's usual services.

"We'll see," Spence responded without committing. Actually, as soon as he had seen the list he had been busily carving out a meaningful role for Leslie in the show. Based on what he'd learned about Andy Sullivan's vanity and now, the appearance of a senior woman on the review team, he was fairly certain her attractive appearance and quick mind would play well with both. He was holding out for other considerations. "By the way," he now asked. "Have you seen Zig yet today?"

"I can't say that I have. Somebody said something about him walking a dog," Leslie replied. Both looked at each other puzzled. Their meeting was coming to a close and she was quite frustrated at not having sewn up an invitation to the big presentation for herself. "I've sent him a note about the rehearsal. I'm sure he'll be along then."

"In the meantime, why don't you shoot along the list to Avery. Attach my bio notes," he instructed.

"Zig, too?" she questioned.

"I guess. Though its not like he's going to read them." Playfair gathered up his yellow pad full of lists. "Just don't forget about the hair, darling. It'd sure be nice if it had a couple of days to grow back in." He gave her a playful wink and hurried off.

"Asshole," she mouthed as he disappeared around the corner. She refastened the second button of her blouse that she always undid for their meetings and collected her own notes. "Should I book a manicure for you while I'm at it?"

Playfair was a nail biter when tensions mounted. It had not escaped her notice that his chubby little fingers were presently a mess.

"I think she likes you." Ira said it with the mischievous grin of a twelve year-old. "I really do," he taunted some more.

It was nearly seven and both senior partners were exhausted. Ira had been locked away with Reiner all day. And, of course, Steve had been sequestered with Lane. It was the first time the two partners had a chance to talk after their whirlwind of a day.

"What makes you think so?" asked Steve. He was listening, but he pretended to be more interested in the carton of takeout Chinese that he was poking at.

"I don't know. Just the way she looks at you. If it were any hungrier, I'd swear she thinks you're a steak." Ira could be such an adolescent when it came to discussing grown up relationships. His own poor choices certainly provided ample evidence of that.

"It could be worse." Steve and Lane had already decided that there was no prize for revealing what they had been up to. In fact, they had nearly laughed themselves to tears as they recounted for each other the way their respective partners had approached them about the joint venture. "I mean she's not bad looking. Don't you think so?"

"Sure," Ira concurred. "But a ball buster. Her kind always is." Suddenly, he was the experienced older brother. That, and he had figured out that she had most definitely taken advantage of him earlier. He wasn't so sure he liked being so easily manipulated. Steve, on the other hand, was delighted. He couldn't believe their good fortune at the way things had worked out. Serendipity?

"Do you really think so?" Steve now asked. "I mean, she was great once we ditched you guys," he teased. If Ira had even the slightest inkling of what had been going on for the previous two weeks, he would have gone crazy. But he was none the wiser and Steve intended to keep it that way.

"Man eater," Ira observed succinctly. As he said this, he seized a piece of mushu pork with his chopsticks, dangled it dangerously over his gaping mouth and expensive silk tie and then made it disappear. "She'd chew you up and spit you out," he said as he chewed.

"Really?" Steve had no choice but to continue to play out the charade. "I didn't get that from her at all."

Lane had also decided Reiner would be better off if he were kept in the dark. According to her, prior to the meeting, her boss had behaved more like a protective father. "Don't let him bully you," he had warned and she had struggled to keep a straight face. "And don't let him misunderstand your intentions. I'm not sure a guy like Holiday knows how to work with a woman." That was the wisdom he had imparted yesterday. It was as if the German were projecting his own desires onto Lane and she sensed that he was already a little jealous of the amount of time Steve would get to spend with her in the days ahead.

"Reiner and I talked about it," Ira now confessed. He said he's found her to be cold as ice." He was absolutely unselfconscious of the total inappropriateness of his remarks. "You want to be awfully careful with a bitch like that."

As Steve thought about it, this advice was not inconsistent with the insight that Ira had offered before their meeting at Interworld. We absolutely have to be the ones in control of the creative bus, Ira had insisted during the walk over. They had to be sure to get the majority of face time with the C&P executive team and make sure that the international connection was seen as entirely their idea. At one point during his slightly paranoid briefing, the little man who had conceived the joint venture concept had even referred to Reiner Adolph as 'a fat Kraut'. Lane had howled when this was recounted.

"We didn't have much trouble this afternoon," Steve said in reference to the time he and Lane had spent together. In truth, it had been absolutely delightful.

They had enjoyed a terrific first working session and he had been pleasantly surprised by the progress her team had made. After everything in the press, he'd been expecting that the disruption of Gordon Turnbull's departure would have resulted in total dysfunction. Instead, he had been impressed by the quality of the strategy document Lane had shared. Not only was the thinking tight, but most of the rollout and media recommendations were also remarkably in synch with L&H's thinking. He was quite looking forward to the meeting they had scheduled for early tomorrow morning to review the concepts that both shops had developed. While he suspected that it would very likely become contentious, he was extremely excited about the prospect of seeing another full-blown creative presentation.

"Steve old buddy," Ira now said as he burped back his Chinese. Pausing to let the gas escape and to add importance to the verdict he was about to render on Lane McCarthy, he finally concluded, "We've been together for nearly twenty years and you know I love you like a brother. But I've got just one more favor that I'm going to ask of you."

"And what exactly might that be, Ira?" Unfortunately, Steve had made the mistake of responding a little too earnestly. He fully expected it to be another serious directive on the pitch.

"Well, given that we've agreed to share that one hundred and fifty million with Reiner Adolph," Ira said solemnly. "I don't want you starting any more joint ventures."

"What do you mean?"

"Well, just don't jump her until after the pitch." With that, Ira snorted out a merry little pig laugh. He had absolutely no idea.

"Thanks, partner. I'll keep that in mind," Steve yawned wearily. He was due to spend the night at Lane's and he couldn't wait to get there. It had been quite a day.

Day 24

"The girl ... she's dead," Max Weller announced.

"What girl?" Ira answered befuddled. "Who is this?" he asked uncomprehendingly as he collected himself from a sound sleep that had been interrupted by the persistent chime of his cell phone.

The digital alarm read an ungodly three a.m. He shushed his drowsy wife back to sleep, then slipped from the room and padded down a darkened hallway, the phone never leaving his ear.

"It's me, Max, Mr. Lowenstein," the private investigator now explained. "Max Weller." He finally began to appreciate that his client was not fully awake. "Sorry to call so late. I tried to reach you yesterday, when she went into the coma, but they said you were in meetings."

"What girl?" Ira asked again, still not understanding. He had managed his way quietly down the night lit staircase and settled into the discreet little alcove below.

"The stripper ... Stella Starnowski ... the one Allan Corbett was doing," Weller explained mixing Ellen's two names together.

"She's dead?" Ira's sleep clouded mind was finally beginning to focus.

"Yeah. They brought her in the day before yesterday." Weller spoke quickly, telegraphing his news in concise bites. "I spoke to the floor manager at the club and he says she collapsed right in the middle of her act. They rushed her to St. Anthony's. That's where I am right now."

"But she died ... tonight?" Ira questioned.

"Yeah. Initially, they were talking about a heart defect. She wore a Medic Alert," Weller elaborated. He was eager to demonstrate the thoroughness of his investigation. "But .... And this is the part that's really interesting ... now they're thinking overdose?"

"Drugs?"

"Not just any drugs, Mr. Lowenstein." He paused dramatically before delivering the payoff. "According to my nurse friend who overheard the pathologist, this poor kid's system was so full of some kind of crazy hormone, they didn't know what to think. They were talking about notifying the cops."

"Holy shit," Ira now connected the dots. "Do you think Corbett is aware?"

"What? About the pills?" Weller misread what he presumed Ira would be most interested in. "Yeah, sure. Remember? I saw it go down with my own eyes," Weller confirmed. "I actually had the goddamned bottle in my hand for a split second. Like I told you before, she said they were diet pills." He had spoken to Ira prior to his New York trip.

"Not that. I mean does he know about the girl ... what's her name again?" Ira's voice dropped to a near whisper now that it appeared the police might become involved.

"Ellen? Nah. The only one whose been here is some guy ... a boyfriend maybe?" Weller had not done much by way of investigation into the mystery man who had appeared on the scene a week or so ago. "He was pretty torn up when he got the word," the PI added. By his tone he dismissed any relevance to their agenda.

"But Corbett hasn't been by the hospital?" Ira wasn't sure why he needed to know this, but intuitively he knew it might be useful.

"Don't think so. I've been here pretty much round the clock and I haven't seen him," Weller said. One man's tragedy was another's billable time.

"Thanks, Max," Ira concluded. "I don't need to remind you to keep this quiet."

"Sure thing. I'll keep you posted, boss." Weller signed off.

Now fully awake, Ira slipped into his den to ponder this latest development. What did it all mean? Was there potentially a problem with Endrophat or was this just purely coincidence? There had to be a way to exploit his newly acquired knowledge such that he could finish off Corbett, but not compromise the project. The last thing anyone needed was a story linking a mysterious drug-related death to an executive at Carlton & Paxton. He was managing the spin already and he hadn't even been awarded the job.

"I'll show you mine, if you show me yours," Lane flirted in the general direction of Steve Holiday who was seated in an uncomfortable narrow-backed stacking chair with a large black art bag guarding his knees.

Having already assumed the role of cheerleader, his vivacious counterpart was on her feet and pacing back and forth across the ugly broadloom of the windowless meeting room. They had requested an out of the way location and the hotel had more than obliged by sequestering them deep in the bowels of the building. The airless room was nearly toxic and they had already been interrupted twice by the clatter of the freight elevator that was situated right outside the door.

"Come on Stevie," she coaxed playfully. "It won't be so bad." Lane loved an audience and even the small, confused one that was assembled for this highly confidential meeting was forced to smile. It consisted of Steve, Bryan Raider, Barry Rabinowitz, Jack Blenheim and another guy from Lowenstein Holiday whose name Lane couldn't remember. She suspected that it might be Toby Meyer. They were all hanging on her every word.

"Very funny," Steve shot back as he started to unzip the oversized portfolio case that was bulging at its seams. He tried to appear calm and by so doing attempted to impart his ease to the other anxious attendees. "Before we pull our pants down, why don't you take a minute to explain to everyone why we're here and what we're hoping to accomplish?"

Judging by the expressions on their faces, it was obvious that the other four were still in a state of shock. As it became clear that his boss was about to share the creative work they had been toiling at for the past three weeks with one of their closest rivals, Toby's jaw dropped and his eyes bulged with disbelief.

"Relax ... Toby is it?" Lane stepped in noticing the man's visible discomfort. "We're all friends here," she smiled as the nervous man looked toward Steve for confirmation that this was indeed the case. He nodded his agreement.

"Perhaps you can take a moment to explain the JV concept, Lane?" Steve coached. He had chosen not to brief his team in advance for fear of a leak or some other unproductive protests.

"Fine," said Lane, realizing that things were moving too quickly for this group to grasp. "As Steve indicated, we have agreed to form a joint venture for the Carlton & Paxton project. For reasons I'm not going to get into today, but you'll no doubt figure out on your own, we ... the senior partners that is ... have decided that our only chance to win this thing is to pitch it together." This news was greeted with puzzled looks and silence.

So much so that Steve felt he had to step in again.

"It's not a merger and nobody is buying anybody else. We've just decided that in order to have a chance and to provide the client with the best possible solution, two agencies are better than one."

While both of the senior people in the room had already moved to a position of comfort with this proposition, the larger group remained unconvinced. The opposing teams eyed their counterparts suspiciously. Years of frequent battles and the very competitive nature of the business made such a notion quite counterintuitive.

"Think Apple and Microsoft getting together to bring you Windows for Mac," Steve tried to explain, using an easily remembered but not quite precise analogy. "We don't have to love each other. And we intend to continue to compete in the future. But for this project, right now, our only way forward is to collaborate."

"Didn't that take a law suit?" Blenheim interjected, his dim intellect lagging. He could be such an oaf.

"Only because of Bill Gates," tagged Rabinowitz. Like every creative, he was a Macintosh devotee and rushed immediately to his sacred computer maker's defense.

"You know what I'm getting at," Steve bickered back.

Before it could deteriorate further, Lane coughed aloud and brought the discussion back on course. She even gave an eye roll of rebuke to Steve for allowing himself to be drawn into such a petty little aside. He bowed his head sheepishly in return.

"While Reiner and Ira hammer out the business details, our challenge is to merge our best thinking and creative work,"

Lane now said firmly. "We've got to turn the two campaigns we've developed into a single set of recommendations."

"Can't we just deliver both plans?" Barry Rabinowitz asked immediately. It was a practical notion and one that made a lot of sense. "I mean, we've all made pitches where we've presented more than one concept before."

"Not a bad idea Barry," Lane answered quickly, fielding the question ahead of Steve. "But something tells me Carlton & Paxton won't buy it if they think this partnership isn't real. You know how it would play out. Pick our campaign not theirs. But we're really one company. No, we're definitely not going to go that route. "

Gratefully, Rabinowitz seemed satisfied with the answer, as did the rest of the group. Reiner, Ira and Lane and Steve had anticipated this potentially contentious issue during their earlier discussions. They had agreed that a single approach was the only way to go.

"I think that's part of the reason we decided to keep the team so small. We only wanted people who could look at the work we've done to date and evaluate it objectively," Steve flattered the assembled group.

With that Holiday took a thick handful of art boards, perhaps twenty in all, and loaded them onto the easel that had been set up at the front of the room. Steve had thought about loading the exhibits into PowerPoint. Projecting them would make them seem more permanent and less negotiable. But fairness dictated that he use show cards instead. Another display stand, its aluminum legs bare and ledge empty, stood waiting for the Interworld presentation that would soon follow. He took a deep breath and prepared to do the unthinkable. Fifteen minutes later he had revealed his agency's entire hand.

❧

Allan Corbett was terrified to look at the computer screen again. Even after attempting to steady himself with a throaty pull from the nearly empty bottle that he had been working on all morning, he had barely been able to summon the nerve. Yet there it was for the entire world to see. Sitting alone in the dark in the little home office that he kept for himself in the basement, the PDF attachment that had arrived with the anonymous e-mail caused his bowels to churn uncomfortably. Barely four inches long and a single column wide, the scan of the article described in a few short paragraphs the mysterious death of a young adult entertainer and the potential homicide investigation that was being contemplated by Chicago police. It had arrived along with the batch of other urgent messages that he had downloaded from the office earlier. Like the other phantom e-mails that had haunted him recently, it wasn't clear exactly where it had come from. That made it all the more unnerving.

He hadn't left the house in nearly seventy-two hours. Ever since Helen and his daughter had departed for their spring college swing, he had been holed up with a bottle and his rising anxiety about what had happened since the ambulance had taken Stella away. Now he knew. Having not met a razor for three days, he cradled his unshaven face in his hands, a prickle of new whiskers stabbing angrily at his tender palms. With a silent prayer, he pinched his eyes shut and opened them again quickly hoping against reality that the troublesome image that glowed back at him from the screen might somehow magically disappear. But even through the thick veil of vodka that clouded his ability to think rationally this morning, he knew that this wouldn't happen. It couldn't happen. His worst fears were now an indisputable truth that he could no longer deny. He tried to image how quickly the investigation might find its way to him. Could it? Would it?

What evidence would there be? Was anyone at the club able to connect him directly with the unfortunate tragedy that had befallen Ellen Starnowski? He was glad at least, in an abstract sense, to finally know her real name.

He had stopped answering his cell phone. His electronic mailbox was overflowing with unanswered messages from Woodruff and he thought he had even seen the scientist's name on the caller ID of his home phone yesterday evening. He knew what his colleague wanted. But he also knew that he could do nothing about it. In the time since Woody had given him the word about the defective drug samples, he hadn't been able to concoct anything close to a passable lie. Instead, he had spent these last three days on a binge of the worst type. He hadn't even pretended to be sober when Helen called through to check on him. Rather than speak, he had left her begging questions from an unattended phone and wandered into another room. Only an annoying hang up signal had caused him to return the receiver to its stand once she'd given up. She hadn't bothered to try again.

Normally, he was a cunning drunk as most of the good ones usually are. He had been able to hide the tracks of his first two days absence by pretending to attend an out-of-town conference. Tiffany was great at covering for him, but even she was nervous that things were starting to unravel. Andrew Sullivan had been stalking him at the end of yesterday afternoon and, according to his loyal assistant, she had spoken to four of her counterparts who worked for the other members of the review committee. They were all anxiously chasing an agenda and a briefing about what would be required of them. As he instructed, she had released their names to the competing agencies.

Now, with the most important meetings of his entire career barely seventy-two hours away, he found himself drunk and alone in his shabby basement den with the threat of a police investigation hanging over his head. He was practically paralyzed with fear. He looked to the corner where the fantastic weapon that Spence Playfair had sent to him stood along side its handsome carrying case. Perhaps the man was psychic. Thank goodness he was so inept with the extraordinary instrument to even begin to know where to source the ammunition it still required. Otherwise, especially in light of the circumstances in which he now found himself, the generous gift that Playfair had provided might prove more useful than the man from Boom had ever imagined. He took another swig from the bottle and deleted the terrifying e-mail.

The tragedy of the stalemate was that the room was now littered with nearly a hundred perfectly executed print and television exhibits and all of them had been rendered useless. The magnificent comps, that just a day before were going to be revealed as each agency's best thinking, had fallen victim to the sneers of a far tougher jury than they ever would have faced at Carlton & Paxton. Both sides knew that there was thousands of dollars worth of artwork on the floor and no one could have cared less. Right now it was all about the work. Unfortunately, both sides seem to have decided that neither of them had nailed the perfect solution.

"As I said before, I don't mind the line. I just hate the product name. Achieva is just ... I don't know ... it's just a little too strident. It feels like some sort of sports supplement or something." The critic was Barry Rabinowitz. The debate had been going round and round like this since both sides had finished presenting their work well over an hour before. His point was valid.

As much as he would have liked to feel otherwise, Steve Holiday was now having a hard time disagreeing. It was the same way he regarded the Interworld campaign. There was some stuff that he loved and some executions that he truly hated.

"We've heard from Barry. Does anyone else have an opinion?" Since it had become apparent that neither camp was going to enthusiastically embrace the other agency's efforts, Lane had taken it on herself to facilitate the awkward session. While this responsibility ordinarily would have fallen to Steve, he was far too personally vested to render judgment objectively.

"Like I said before, I like both campaigns," Jack Blenheim waded in. Regardless of their agency stripe, the creatives dismissed this fatuous response with an even angrier jeer than the first time he had offered it. At least they had that much in common. With so much talent in the room, the criticisms were definitely incisive. No one waited for the account guy to elaborate further. Even Bryan Raider had decided that his account management counterpart from L&H was a fool.

"I kind of feel the same way about 'Your New Beginning'." It was Toby Meyer's turn to speak again and, not surprisingly, he was breaking along party lines. "It's just too bland. I have to admit, I do have a bit of a hard on for *Newera*. It kind of gives off … I don't know … a far eastern holistic kind of a vibe and I don't think that's all bad."

"What if we put the name and the line we like together," Lane jumped in. But the idea of sandwiching the two disconnected thoughts into one approach yielded an audible moan from everyone in the room except Blenheim.

"Let's not make a fucking camel," Barry Rabinowitz now chided profanely. It was a similar concern to one that he had expressed early on. In the democracy of this free flowing debate, being able to articulate your objections clearly was a powerful asset. The young punk, Rabinowitz, was proving this point repeatedly.

Despite having control of the conch, Steve had decided to let the decision of the tribe rule. There was no way this alliance would hold if one group or the other felt they had been screwed over. Besides, enough damage had been done that no one felt good about any of the work that was being debated.

"What are you saying, Barry?" Steve now hurled in the face of the petulant New Yorker. "That we should throw it all away and start again?"

He studied the determined look of the scruffy young man and knew that this was exactly what he had in mind. After the last round of squabbling, he'd become convinced that the combative young creative was using his bandaged ear to pretend not to hear the arguments of the others. Where do they come from, these passionate ones, he puzzled to himself. But he already knew the answer.

"Maybe?" the defiant young man now confirmed. He didn't say it with disrespect, just the arrogance that comes with supreme self-confidence. "We're definitely not going to win with what we've got here now. I think we've all agreed that much."

He can't be much more than thirty years old, thought Steve. But, dammit, the annoying little prick was right. Even though the group had agreed from the outset that they wouldn't dare go there, Rabinowitz had fought them all to a standstill. Searching the faces of the others in the room, Steve could tell that there was, indeed, a consensus building. Though it was an irresponsible conclusion to draw, it was now the only one that seemed possible.

"Do you really think so?" Steve probed one last time to be sure that Rabinowitz's bluster wasn't just a ploy to get Interworld's stuff back on the table. But he already knew it wasn't. If the kid knew the meaning of the word compromise, he certainly didn't let on. He was already scribbling away at a new idea.

"Lane? Do you think we can keep our powder dry for another twenty-four hours?"

The other grown up in the room winced, but didn't say 'no'. Instead, she just shook her head as she surveyed the carnage that littered the floor and tried to imagine how she would break the news to Reiner and Ira. Steve was taking a hell of a gamble.

"Okay then, if we want it to look like a collaboration, then I guess it should be a bloody collaboration," Steve conceded. "We're going to start again from scratch.

Day 25

"I don't fucking believe it," called out Pete Zwicki. "I think I've got it," he exclaimed breathlessly as he scratched away with the thick black marker as quickly as he could write. "It's been here all along."

The exhausted little group around the table looked up hopefully, but at the same time steeled themselves for further disappointment. There had been so many false alarms as the session had dragged on through the night that no one was really expecting to find a perfect solution any more. Maybe there wasn't a good one out there? Maybe there just wasn't a better name to accompany the clever positioning line they had hammered out late yesterday evening? All they knew was that the absolute deadline for delivering their recommended solution was only hours away.

"Look at this," Zwicki begged excitedly as he tore a page from his pad and pushed it toward the front of the room where the more senior players were sprawled. Even the energetic kid was too tired to stand up.

"Goddamnit, he's right," said Toby Meyer who intercepted the sheet as it floated across the table and was the first to make sense of the words that the young writer had scribbled out.

"In ...fucking ... credible," Rabinowitz marveled once he'd had a chance to look. This was high praise indeed coming from the difficult New Yorker. "Right in front of our eyes the whole bloody time."

"Holy shit," Steve concurred. He shook his head in disbelief, pushed his hand through his tangled hair and his face broke into a weary but beaming grin. He rose to his feet and laid an awkward high five on the young writer who was slumping in his chair exhausted. Then he pulled him up into a hug. "I think you've nailed it."

For the second time in a dozen hours, the desperate little coterie of creatives who had committed to finding a miracle by morning, had struck paydirt. When Rabinowitz had nailed the new slogan just ahead of midnight, Steve imagined that was as lucky as they were going to get. He had already been working on the rationale in the back of his mind for why they had decided to recommend hanging onto Endrophat. Or weld the tag line to one of the other two names that they had been working with. But now here it was. Staring back at them from an ink-smeared piece of yellow foolscap was the answer that had danced above their heads for the last three weeks. It was startlingly simple.

ENDORTHIN®
Live the promise of you.

Every one of them in the room had played with the Endrophat name for countless hours and had not seen it. It had been typed out a thousand times in the various briefs and documents that had circulated throughout their offices. On the walls around the room there were lists of literally hundreds of alternatives. But with the stroke of a pen in one barely lucid moment, a young copywriter had plucked this most obvious of solutions out of the air and turned a month's worth of thinking by a hundred people entirely upside down. In doing so, he answered the problem more elegantly than anyone had dared to imagine was still possible. Where did it come from? How did it happen? Maybe there had only been this single answer all along?

Steve checked his watch. It was not quite six. He could hardly wait for the troops to arrive. He'd sent them home so they'd be fresh for the wild thirty-six hour ride ahead. They would all be in the office in an hour. Now that they had an idea, he would crank things up to ramming speed. Their only enemy now was the clock.

"I'm going to take it upstairs," Steve announced. Reiner and Ira wouldn't be anywhere to be found, but he knew that Lane had spent the night grinding out the revised presentation document. He could hardly wait to see the look on her face. She would get it immediately and she would love it. Maybe even the senior executives at Carlton & Paxton would, too.

Zig Cartwright stared at the blank screen that just moments before had been alive with the dazzling smile of the beautiful young girl. It seemed incredible to him that someone with so much vitality could now be gone and, more improbably still, that it should cause him such pain. Yet twenty-four hours and a thousand unanswered questions later, his heart still ached with the knowledge that he would never be with Ellen Starnowski again. Nor would he probably ever understand exactly how she had been taken from him.

"Do you want me to run it again?" a voice squawked over the intercom to the man sitting alone in the darkened screening room.

"No, that will be fine," Zig said, forgetting to press the

button that would transmit this message to the technician in the control booth. After the question was repeated, he shook his head and waved his hand in the direction of the two-way mirror to signal that he had seen enough. In fact, the last three days had been among the darkest of his entire selfish life.

First there had been the urgent text message he'd received from Mario, the big bouncer he had befriended, advising him that Ellen had been rushed to hospital. Prior to being admitted there had been some questions about who would handle the young dancer's medical expenses and he had been the only one they could think of. Then there was the impossibly awkward call he had fielded while taking care of Clancy. In the end, it had been Zig who had confirmed the news of Ellen's death to her disbelieving mother. Throughout the entire painful conversation the woman had never understood who he was or how it was that he should be the one that was telling her such terrible news. The hours and days since had been a blur.

"Then can I burn it onto the disk?" the same disembodied voice persisted over the small hollow speaker. All of Boom's presentation materials were being transferred to a single master CD. The completed commercial that featured Ellen Starnowski would be embedded into it to run on the appropriate cue. At least that had been the plan until her untimely demise.

"No ... most definitely not!" Zig made no mistake with the intercom control this time. "It's out, Ronnie. Don't you dare consider putting it on ... even as back up. I don't care who asks," he added emphatically. He couldn't believe that he would be presenting in just a couple of days. The work was nearly complete, but he was nowhere near ready.

❧

"Long time, no see, my friend." Andy Sullivan's overlapping handshake and congenial greeting immediately made Ira suspicious. Especially given how little time this client had ever invested in their relationship. "I'm so sorry we haven't had a chance to talk since this whole review business got started." It was a bald lie, but both men let it stand.

"Yes, I appreciate you taking the time to see me," said Ira. Settling into the seat he'd been offered at the small table in Sullivan's office, he studied the boyish face of the senior marketing executive. If he's thirty-five, the agency president thought to himself, I'd be amazed. "I'll try and make this brief."

"Thank you. I do have a lunch," Sullivan said without apology and in so doing, thoughtlessly placed an unreasonable time limit on their meeting.

"Excellent, then we've got fifteen minutes," Ira said looking down to hide the anger that this unintended insult deserved. "That should be plenty of time," he rejoined with barely concealed sarcasm.

"I won't ask you how things have been going," Sullivan began. "I know you've all been under a lot of pressure."

Ira shook his head at the understatement. Then he remembered how Sullivan had rocketed his way through the organization. Every now and then, even staid companies like Carlton & Paxton surprised you and promoted a bright young financial guy straight to the top without regard for tenure or experience. The Wharton MBA diploma hanging proudly on the wall opposite was Sullivan's only obvious qualification for the role he currently occupied. He had never made an important or meaningful decision about advertising in his life.

"But you have to try and see things from our point of view Ira," Sullivan now continued. "There's just a tremendous amount of money at stake. And you know that we've certainly had our differences about costs over the years."

Preparing for the meeting Ira had had to remind himself that Sullivan always looked at advertising from the expense side and had never really seemed particularly interested in the magic. Since taking the position, he'd made it clear that he viewed the agency as just another vendor—and an expensive one at that.

"I didn't realize this was a compensation negotiation," Ira countered doing his best to conceal his resentment. He was now glad that their conversation would be brief. He and Sullivan had locked horns annually over the fees that Lowenstein Holiday charged. For the past two years, the young accountant had been winning this fight.

"When is it ever not about the money?" Sullivan sparred. "But you're right. John Carver told me how well you've been handling the Corbett situation and I really appreciate your discretion. Having someone like that on your team can be, as you know, quite embarrassing."

Finally, the young executive was beginning to speak the kind of language Ira had been expecting and he decided to press this advantage quickly. "Well, it is what it is," he agreed. "But you're right. You certainly don't want to find yourself tarred with it," he concluded making doubly sure that the less experienced man understood his meaning.

"Nevertheless," Sullivan countered a bit uncomfortably. "I'm afraid this whole review thing has taken on a momentum all its own. I've got people calling me from all over the world."

"I'll bet." Ira nodded. Sullivan was creating precisely the entrée to the subject of the joint venture that he had been hoping for and he decided to let Sullivan run off a little more line before setting the hook.

"No, seriously Ira. Ever since this thing started, I've had approaches from country managers and their agencies from all around the globe. You'd be surprised how many believe they've got the qualifications to handle our entire business."

"And do they?" Ira asked. He was at least confident he knew the answer to this question.

"Well, that's what this review business has really become, hasn't it?" Sullivan concluded a little too quickly. "I mean you've done some truly outstanding work for us over the years. But this is really about your company's inability to help us create a truly global brand, isn't it Ira?"

"So its not about the work?" Ira repeated dumbly.

"It never has been, Ira. At least not at the top of the house," Sullivan labored to explain. "Even Allan has said there is no one better than … what's your partner's name … Steve Holiday."

"Thank you," said Ira pretending to absorb the compliment. "I'll be sure to pass that along to him."

"But don't you see, that's exactly why Interworld is on the list?" Sullivan continued. What was now apparent was the international angle had become the back rationale that the VP of Marketing had concocted to explain the irresponsible actions of Corbett to his superiors. It was exactly as Ira had anticipated.

"I see," he said feigning puzzlement.

"If we could just put your brilliant creative people together with an international resource like they have to offer, we could probably call this whole thing off right now." Sullivan concluded.

Maybe he would enjoy his own lunch after all, the agency president now thought to himself. He couldn't wait to replay this conversation to Reiner.

"You can't imagine how glad I am to hear you say that,"

Ira smiled. "We've only got a couple of minutes left, Andrew. I wonder if I could use them to fill you in on how we intend to approach the pitch."

Now it was Ira's turn to play.

అ

"I don't care if she was his own fucking mother," Spence Playfair raged at Leslie Stride. "Have you ever heard of anything so bloody unprofessional in your entire goddamned life?"

"Calm down, Spence," the young woman at the opposite end of the long table tried to counsel her angry boss, her eyes not leaving the screen of her laptop. "We've got too much else to worry about."

"And what about fucking Avery?" Playfair swore again. "I can't believe that he would side with that pathetic little piece of shit. When on earth did this agency become so goddamned sentimental? I could have fucking choked him."

"It's only one exhibit," Stride said, trying to soothe her agitated mentor. "We've got plenty of others." Fully interrupted by his tirade, she pushed back in her chair and crossed her legs high at the knee hoping to reveal enough of her thigh to distract him. He was having none of it.

"But it's the only finished fucking commercial we've got," he seethed. "Don't you see? If we pull it, the only thing we've got to sell the entire TV campaign will be that stupid bloody monkey trying to walk them through some lousy goddamned pictures." Spence was up and pacing.

"That's not true. You said yourself the illustrations look good," she added calmly. "Besides, Zig has sold through some great creative reading from scripts. He'll be just fine with what he's got." After failing to capture his attention, she returned to editing the speaking notes that Avery had insisted be prepared for everyone on the team.

"Are we talking about the same Zig Cartwright? Didn't you see him? He looks like a goddamned zombie ... or worse. I don't even think we should be taking him into the room in the shape he's in."

Both he and Stride had remarked earlier on how badly Zig seemed to be reacting to the news of their young model's demise. Neither had bothered to find out precisely why.

"You're not serious are you?" Stride now questioned. One of the cornerstones of their carefully choreographed meeting plan was the nearly seventy-five minutes that had been dedicated to the presentation of the creative work. What had happened to the Spence Playfair who had earlier believed that the work wasn't going to be all that important, she thought to herself. He's coming undone. "Who would you suggest does it then?"

"I don't care. Anyone but him. Imagine him going behind my back to Avery like that. I just won't stand for it," Spence raved. "I'll do it, goddamn it." With that Playfair went to the large whiteboard where they had been blocking out the final presentation order and began erasing Zig's name from various slots on the agenda.

"Come on Spence, be realistic. There's no way we can go into that room without Zig," she reminded him. "You know it and I know it," she added with an impatient sigh.

"Maybe ... maybe not?" Playfair answered stubbornly. "I'll bet that if I can convince Avery that we're doing this out of sympathy for Zig, he will let me present at least half of it. Or at least run the spot."

"But I thought Avery was fairly adamant about dropping it?" Leslie reminded.

"I believe what he actually said was that, under the

circumstances, we can't ask Zig to present it," replied Playfair, parsing the truth. "Besides, all will be forgiven when we win this thing. You'll see."

Nearly seven-hundred-and-forty employees in two Chicago offices. An active roster of fifty-nine clients—most of them respected national advertisers. Collectively, nearly three-quarters of a billion dollars in annual media billings. And not one of them was going to have a single scrap of work done on their business for the next twenty-four hours.

That was Steve Holiday's simple directive and it was the only way that they stood a chance of meeting the impossible deadline that his decision to run with a whole new campaign now required. Even though they had a great idea, they would have to accomplish in less than two days what they had been working on for nearly two months between them. Less, actually, since it was already nearly six o'clock. Ira was furious. Reiner Adolph was dumbstruck. But both of them had the presence of mind to say absolutely nothing and get the hell out of the way.

The good news was that the creative teams had been cranking out new ads and approaches like bullets. With their backs to the wall, the time consuming process of review and discussion had been replaced with reflexes and intuition. Barry Rabinowitz and Toby would give initial thumbs up to loose marker squibs and headlines. When they were sufficiently tight, the work was then passed to Steve for final approval.

So far there had been very little disagreement and Steve had already signed off on more concepts than he could count. While he was used to the productivity curve of his people spiking in the days and hours ahead of presentations, he had never seen anything like this. The output of the combined resources of the two shops was simply incredible.

Despite his nearly overwhelming fatigue and the vast volume of work that had been laid to waste when they changed directions, he was now pleased that he'd listened to Rabinowitz. So was everyone else. Even Pete and Evie had split and joined up with new partners from the New York office of Interworld. It was scary to see how easily these young people adapted to the switch and how much energy they could still summon. Steve, himself, was very nearly spent. He'd been running on adrenaline since they nailed the new name and tag line. For the past three hours a steady of queue had been lined up outside his door. He couldn't remember when he'd signed off on so much work so quickly—and had so much fun doing it.

In fact, there was a smile on the face of practically every-one in the place. This, despite the fact, that they were facing another full night of work. Music blared, people scurried from task to task and the entire floor reeked of rubber cement. Running on a diet of takeout food and high-test coffee, the place had found another gear. Even the fussy old veterans in the assembly studio seemed to have gotten a jolt of the juice that was flowing through the place. It took a lot to excite these talented craftsmen who now leant their considerable tech-nical skills to the mundane chores of trimming boards and mounting work—especially when so much of their previous work had been discarded.

Somewhere along the line, everyone on the team seemed to sense that they were now a part of something truly special. That the campaign they were working on was a winner.

He hadn't seen Lane for a couple of hours now, but he got a report that a similar scurry was going on in the account service area two floors above. She had sequestered herself and Raider and Blenheim in a meeting room and they were grinding out a comprehensive set of documents and slides that would support the new direction. Fortunately for them, much of the media and tactical strategies had remained the same so they could dedicate the bulk of their time to massaging out mentions of the previous concepts. Working off the core of the Interworld presentation, the lion's share of the task had already been completed. Thinking about how this would have been accomplished in the old days, Steve shuddered. They would have been dead in the water.

Day 26

Harry Woodruff had a big problem. Actually, he had three of them, but they were really all related to the same thing. The first of these was the memo that he had just finished reading from his chief production engineer that summarized his findings on the suspected equipment failure on the Endrophat line. Having just digested its contents, he was relieved to be confined to the relative security of a toilet stall in the laboratory's executive men's room. Boiled down to its essence, his fellow scientist had concluded that Woodruff's previous theory about a failed injector was probably erroneous. Certainly, in his opinion there had been some sloppy recording of input levels and some room for additional human error as the production line was brought up to speed, but by and large the report explained, the likelihood that the problems Woodruff was encountering with the weight control pill were, for the most part, not the result of mechanical failure.

Unfortunately, this conclusion dovetailed neatly with Woodruff's own recent experiments on the samples he had retrieved from various beta test subjects and, most recently, from the wife of the head of international marketing, the girl from human resources, and that woman from the advertising agency. What had occurred with Lane McCarthy, and indeed, with several women's data he'd since retrieved was remarkably consistent. While there had been tremendous early success with the weight loss side of the equation, the pleasurable side effect of the drug had a much more pronounced impact as the subject got lighter.

It was for this miscalculation that Woodruff was now kicking himself. He had wrongly concluded that the excessive hormonal stimulation must be a direct result of misdosage. That was, of course, what had led him to theorize that the problem must have originated in the manufacturing process. But now, based on the data that he had been pouring over since yesterday evening, he was forced to conclude that there might be an issue with the isolation of the neurons that created the satiation effect. Or worse, the area that was being stimulated was being altered or mutated over time with regular use of the drug. If this were, in fact, the answer, it would have grave repercussions for the underlying chemistry of the entire program. It was this possibility that had dragged Woodruff into the lab this morning to audit a late arriving set of beta subject diaries. If they yielded what he feared they would, there was going to be hell to pay.

The second problem Harry had been wrestling with was an extremely disturbing piece of news that a nearly wild-eyed Allan Corbett had shared with him when he had finally caught up with the advertising manager after he returned to the office yesterday. Not only had Corbett failed to deliver the pill samples he had been evasively promising for nearly a week. But with a look of absolute terror on his face, he admitted that he been providing these test samples to a young woman for nearly a half a year and recently that woman had turned up dead. That a member of the development team could be so irresponsible caused the scientist to shudder in horror.

Not only had Corbett violated the strict confidentiality

code of the organization, he had allowed this woman to consume the drug without prior medical testing or any clinical follow up. He shook his head imagining the potential problems. Just last week he had been reviewing the side effects declaration that would have to accompany the drug when, or if, it ever went to market. At the top of the list had been potentially severe consequences for patients with minor heart and respiratory ailments. And that was before this issue of the potentially mutated neuron had surfaced.

Compounding the alarm that Corbett had sounded was his mention that the police and the county medical investigator were likely becoming involved. While he said he thought that they would have a hard time tracing any of the details of the young woman's cause of death to Carlton & Paxton, the scientist was nowhere near as confident. In the first case, any reasonably capable pathologist would easily identify irregular levels of the specific hormones that had been manipulated. Based on the volume of quiet buzz that had been stirred in the local medical community around Endrophat, it was possible someone might imagine a link—especially if the results the woman had enjoyed had been as spectacular as Corbett described. Second, there was the matter of the missing pills themselves. He recalled that he had been particularly generous with the last batch from the test run that he had provided to Corbett and there was no telling how many of these might still be around. He hated to think of the consequences if either of these connections were made.

And that brought Woodruff to the third of the onerous issues that he was facing this morning. Sitting on the worktable adjacent to his desk was the final approval declaration from the FDA that was awaiting his signature. The document that had been so elusive for the past two months had finally been delivered to his office late yesterday afternoon. All that was required for the drug to be blessed into distribution was for him to sign off on the densely worded document that they had been laboring at for what seemed like forever.

Unfortunately, it was also this declaration that would send Dr. Harold Woodruff and any number of Carlton & Paxton executives to jail if they knowingly or willfully attached their names to any falsehood or other misstatement. Suddenly, with a fatality potentially associated with Endrophat and some grave doubts about the drug's underlying chemistry, he could not in good conscience render the signature that was required. Suffice to say, the scientist had some very serious issues to confront. He unspooled some tissue and prepared to wipe himself.

The only question that remained was, what he was prepared to do about them. As was typical of the fearful scientist who was already in far over his head, he would choose to do as he had done since assuming responsibility for the project. He would keep all of this to himself and try and buy a little more time. The declaration document was his for final vetting for at least a week. Maybe something would happen that would make his course clearer. Considering this after a sleepless night, Woodruff's roiled bowel shifted violently. In response, the unsettled scientist folded the print out of the engineering memo under his arm and sat back down.

To Steve Holiday it was always like Christmas; the joyful surprise of waking up and discovering a roomful of treasures that had magically arrived in the night. And that was definitely the feeling he had upon his arrival at the office this morning. When Toby had insisted he go home and get some sleep after working through the previous night, the first few finished exhibits had been dribbling in from the art studio. But now, miraculously, the elves had completed much of their work and the scope and scale of what had been accomplished was apparent to all. It was quite overwhelming. So much so that Steve felt compelled to sit down and drink in the impressive sight by swiveling slowly across the panorama in one of the big boardroom chairs.

It was quite a view. And it had been accomplished in less than half the time he had estimated. Every inch of ledge space and at least a dozen easels were covered with tightly rendered mockups of every type and description, each one double mounted and encased in a sleeve of Mylar. There were full color magazine layouts in single and double pages, newspaper spreads and various pieces of collateral literature and direct mail. In the middle of the table, a laptop glowed with a fully functional website, and this was supported by a sprawling printed exhibit of its navigation functions and overall content platform.

But more important than the sheer quantity of what had been accomplished in the thirty-six hours since the idea was first conceived, was the unquestionable quality of the thinking represented. It was unabashedly brilliant, thought Steve. It was definitely among the most intelligent, thought provoking and exceptionally well-rendered campaigns he and his people had ever developed. Regardless of the outcome of the pitch tomorrow and the unfairness of the entire process, he beamed with pride at the dedication and professionalism that this hastily thrown together team had exhibited. It was a compliment to his leadership that they had lent themselves so unselfishly. It was a fitting elegy—a remarkable campaign that Steve had pretty much decided would be his last.

"It's a hell of a show," said a voice from behind him. It belonged to Ira. Nursing tentative sips from a steaming coffee cup, like Steve before him, he too paced slowly around the room stopping and admiring the ads that caught his eye or piqued his interest. "I don't know how the hell you did it."

"Actually, it's how *they* did it," Steve corrected. For one of the few times in his career he owned neither the winning slogan nor the very best of the ads. The most compelling work had come from Rabinowitz and the rest of the team that had been put together quickly and had worked together so well. Ironically, Steve felt absolutely comfortable with this. There was no wounded pride and no bruises to his ego. "It's all theirs and it's fantastic."

"Toby said you let that kid from Interworld talk you into throwing practically everything out the other day." Ira circled towards him and settled into a seat near where Steve was slumped.

"He was right." Steve's intuition told him where Ira was starting to go and he wasn't about to suffer any of it this morning. He was too tired and too raw. And there was still much to be accomplished.

"Lot of waste," Ira now complained. "I've had clients screaming bloody murder for nearly two days."

"Better work though," Steve replied matter-of-factly. He really didn't want to get into it.

"But it's not what we talked about, is it? I told you we absolutely needed to drive this thing." Ira waded in.

"We did. Sort of." Steve knew this unsatisfactory answer would not sit well with his partner, but he was well past caring about the politics that Ira managed to layer into everything they did. "Our guys did enough."

"When Adolph figures out his guy nailed it, there'll be problems," said Ira, showing the side of himself that Steve had always despised.

"Your issue not mine." As he said this he watched the

color rise in Ira's cheeks. Problems were what Ira lived for, but he hated being called out on it.

"Our issue, my friend." The irritation in his voice was obvious now. Ira only used inclusive expressions like the one he just had when he was extremely annoyed. "A seventy-five million dollar fucking issue if you think about it."

"It's not an issue if we don't win this thing." Steve countered, admitting aloud for the first time that he expected defeat. For nearly a month he had been approaching this pitch like losing was a forgone conclusion and, despite the great work, he remained confident that this would be the case. When he threw this back at Ira he was surprised by his partner's response.

"You think I haven't already taken care of that, " Ira now shot back aggressively.

"What? Taken care of winning? Taken care of Corbett?"

"Of course," said Ira with his usual impatience. "Do think I would have dared to try this whole joint venture business if I hadn't taken care of Corbett, first?"

"How do you mean ... taken care of?" Steve asked with disbelief. After years of playing this kind of chess with his cagey partner he had learned to expect the unexpected. But this was definitely beyond his reach. Or was it, he began to doubt. "What have you done?

"Do you really want to know? Or do you just want to continue to pretend that this thing is really just all about the work?" Now it was Ira's turn to go on offense.

"What have you done, Ira?" Steve repeated. Sometimes his partner genuinely frightened him. It wouldn't be the first time he had underestimated what Ira was capable of doing in the name of winning.

"Let's just say there was a little bit of investigation work done," Ira continued. "And a few of Mr. Corbett's personal failings came to light."

"What? Like you hired a private investigator or something?" The look on Ira's face confirmed this without the necessary confession. "My gawd, you're not blackmailing him are you?"

"Of course not, Stevie," Ira said a little too patronizingly. "I just made sure that some of the people who should know about such things were kept informed."

"So we've got the fix in, then?" Steve now inquired. He was thoroughly appalled.

"Not exactly," Ira conceded. "All I've been able to do is level the playing field."

"Leveled the playing field?" Steve was incredulous at what he had just heard. This was a new low. Even for Ira.

"Just a fair chance is all we've been given. Nothing more and nothing less." Ira showed his palms signaling he had nothing further up his sleeves.

"Does Adolph know?" It was important for Steve to understand whether or not he was the only fool in the room. The worst part of him was suspicious that Ira had kept him in the dark so as not to get in the way of getting the work done. He hated being used in this way.

"Not much. Only in the little I told him?" Ira confessed. "I might have mentioned that I had managed to take control of the situation," he continued quite satisfied with himself. It was this conceit that Steve found most offensive—that only the suits could play these kinds of games. It also violated everything he held true about the proper way to conduct business.

"What about Lane?" On this question Steve was desperate to know if she, too, had been in on the secret. He had many obvious reasons for this.

"Nah." Again Ira shook his head. "Couldn't trust the bitch with a secret like that. No telling what she would have done with it." Satisfied that he had made his point and that he was once again in total control, Ira got up from the table to signal the end of their conversation. As always, he remained oblivious to the damage he had wrought.

"Rehearsal starting at ten?" he questioned, though he already knew the answer.

"Ira…" Steve now called out to his partner's back as he reached the boardroom door. "When this is done, so am I." It was a resignation that was long overdue.

The police investigation that was underway was more or less routine. Guided by the pathology report and the anguish of a distraught mother who had not seen her daughter in over a year, the two detectives assigned to the case were still inclined to treat it like just another unfortunate overdose. Whether it was an excessive amount of hormones or some other abnormality associated with excessive drug use, the callous policemen weren't inclined to make huge distinctions.

If Ellen Starnowski hadn't had such a blemish-free background and her mother hadn't been so insistent, they would probably be doing even less than they had since the case was assigned two days prior. Given her recent profession and the reputation Ellen enjoyed with her employers and the patrons of Wriggly's, their first instinct was to dismiss the case as little more than another pretty young girl coming to the big city and getting caught up in the always questionable exotic entertainment business. Not surprisingly it had ended badly, as it so often did. But at least they had secured a key to the young woman's apartment and conducted a cursory search of its contents. Apart from the big dog, who seemed to be being taken care of, very little seemed out of the ordinary.

In fact, as investigations into the private lives of exotic entertainers went, young Ms. Starnowski seemed to be leading a fairly normal existence. However, what they had uncovered without much effort were three potentially interesting pieces of evidence—though they, of course, still remained quite reluctant to assume foul play. The first of these was a DVD that was still located inside her computer's disk drive that contained some very professional looking footage of Ellen Starnowski appearing in what seemed to be some sort of television commercial. The second was a business card for the commercial production studio where the disk had been burned. And the final thing they acquired was an unmarked bottle of what looked like a prescription drug. It was located, quite appropriately, along side the other contents of the young woman's bathroom medicine chest. Inside were fourteen small pills marked with a 20 mg dosage measurement and a thinly etched corporate symbol.

It was barely enough to begin asking some more questions. But they would send the pills in for analysis at the lab even though the fact that they were marked with a logo likely meant they were just a prescription that had been left unconsumed. While they waited for the results they would chase down the engineer and the production company and see if that led anywhere. More likely, based on the small portfolio of modeling photos they had come across, the commercial and accompanying out takes, were probably exactly what they appeared to be. If it hadn't been for a neighbor's comment that there had been a suspicious looking young man in a motorcycle jacket around in the last week or so and a lot of noise coming from the apartment, the report would have been filed and the case would have been closed. Instead, they decided to follow their instincts for a few more days and see where things might lead.

Day 27

The private elevator that would whisk them to the executive floors of the Carlton & Paxton tower was much smaller than Steve remembered. He had only ridden in it a few times over the years, having made most of his presentations in the meeting rooms on the lower levels of the impressive corporate offices that the big drug company occupied downtown. Initially, he'd felt uneasy as he stepped into the cramped compartment. But now, with his back to the mirrored wall and Lane standing in front of him, he was able to inhale the delicious smell of her hair and felt himself beginning to relax. She looked absolutely fabulous in her immaculately tailored suit, the skirt hemmed at precisely the right length to compliment her well-chosen heels and model taut calves. A double string of pearls filled the bare opening of her wide flared shirt collar and her makeup was perfect. The presentation materials having been delivered earlier, Steve's hands were free. He let one hang awkwardly at his side and with the other cupped Lane's soft padded shoulder. He stroked it nervously until she turned at the neck and gave him a reassuring smile in return.

To his left, Ira and Reiner Adolph made a decidedly less

natural looking couple. The big German loomed over Ira by at least a foot. His grey eyes and dye streaked yellow blonde hair were a marked contrast to his counterpart's closely shaved dome and dark features. Both men had decided on powers suits, though of the two, Adolph's more muted tone on tone showed best. Ira had chosen a chalk stripe that looked far more like a banker's than an adman's, thought Steve. It made him feel slightly uncomfortable with his own choice of a black cashmere blazer, crisp white oxford shirt and faded blue jeans. But, then again, he was a creative guy and such impudent attire was practically expected from the jesters.

In the end, it had been agreed that just the four of them would deliver the pitch. Ignoring the whining protest of Jack Blenheim, it was decided there was no need to demonstrate bench strength this afternoon. That would be self-evident. Instead, this was going to be a serious presentation made by the agency's most senior people. They were playing an all or nothing game and there wasn't room for even the slightest misstep. This pressure, of course, had been further magnified by the addition of the CEO, Alex Spearman, to the head of the table. Even Ira had only met him a dozen times in the agency's long tenure on the account. Clearly, his board allies had been true to their word and had taken this matter all the way to the top.

A sickening half-minute later, the high-speed capsule's doors parted to reveal the opulent inner sanctum of the global pharmaceutical giant. They had arrived at precisely one o'clock, exactly an hour prior to their scheduled beginning. Yet even at the height of the business day, the richly appointed executive suite functioned in a somnambulant hush. Very few people resided on the sixty-eighth floor. The handful that did, occupied it silently. Those who dared to speak did so in subdued whispers and even the ringing phones seemed muted by the invisible weight of importance. It was a stark contrast to the noisy rush of the street and the relentless energy of the bustling agency they had departed barely twenty minutes before.

As part of the element of surprise, the newly formed joint venture company had elected to utilize the first presentation slot that was available to them. It was the one that had been designated for Lowenstein Holiday. Despite assurances that the order had been determined randomly, this position violated the long observed custom of allowing the incumbent agency to make its case for retaining their client's business in the final presentation of the review. Instead of batting clean up, they would go to the plate first. Allan Corbett had tried his best to screw them in every way he knew how. Hopefully, they could now turn this to their advantage.

Much to their relief, a handsomely dressed middle-aged executive assistant was awaiting the elevator's arrival and she escorted them immediately into the sprawling boardroom. One of their worst fears had been that Allan Corbett might be there to greet them. Fortunately, it appeared that Andrew Sullivan had honored his end of the bargain as well. The cordial hostess had been most helpful. She introduced them to a very capable technician who was assigned to assist them with connecting their laptops and other supporting equipment to the facility's sophisticated audiovisual system and offered them refreshments that they politely declined.

As soon as the woman exited the room, the gentlemen from Lowenstein Holiday removed their jackets and set to work unwrapping the carefully packaged art boards and exhibits that had been couriered ahead. This risk had been necessitated by the unrelenting vanity of Reiner and Ira. The two senior executives had been unwilling to arrive with their hands full imagining somehow that this might be perceived as demeaning. Fortunately, none of the parcels looked like they had been tampered with and Steve breathed a sigh of relief. In a fit of paranoia he had secretly marked the tape that bound the packages closed. One of the worst scenarios he could imagine was Allan Corbett and his people inspecting the work prior to its presentation and using this knowledge to sabotage their efforts. As they peeled back the craft paper to get at the art boards, the glue from freshly mounted exhibits burned at his eyes and nostrils. His fears had proved unfounded.

At the same time, the much more mechanically minded Reiner Adolph busied himself with the technician setting up the complex PowerPoint that would support their individual speaking parts. In a good sign from the gods, this sometimes-tricky process appeared to be going smoothly. Only Lane seemed to be comporting herself with the dignity befitting the titles on their business cards. As each stack of boards was loaded onto the horseshoe of easels they had arranged at the front of the room, she perused their contents thoughtfully. With the ruby red nails of a flawlessly manicured hand, she delicately flipped through one after another, carefully checking the order in which they appeared against a mental checklist of how things were intended to unfold. If she was nervous, she gave no sign. Though he had presented with the senior women at Lowenstein Holiday thousands of times over the years, Steve had seldom seen anyone who seemed so cool and composed prior to delivering such an important pitch. Thirty minutes later, with everyone's work complete, there was nothing to do but wait for the appointed hour.

The afternoon's first rehearsal was like nails on a chalkboard. Even though it had been going on for nearly two hours, the projector was still stuck on the very first slide. As expected, Avery had arrived with an onslaught of opinions and objections and it was taking everything in his power for Spence not to snap. Worse still was his boss's stumbling delivery of the little bit of foreplay that had been assigned to him. At this rate, they would be here until midnight. Plus, based on some of Avery's other nitpicking, there would have to be at least three finished exhibits rebuilt along with corresponding revisions to the binders that were still being assembled next door.

"Avery, why don't we just move on and try it again later once you've had a chance to revise your notes?" Spence asked with fraying patience. So far he had managed to hold his temper in check and he intended to keep it that way. With less than eighteen hours to go, he was wrestling with his own nervousness. Why did it always have to be this way, he wondered with annoyance, smearing his hand across his brow in exasperation?

"I'm just not sure I can get through all of the set up in fifteen minutes," Avery complained to the room at large when it became obvious that Spence's question was rhetorical and he had already moved on. When no else answered, Leslie Stride looked up from her laptop and offered a little coaching.

"You just have to, Avery. We've got so much ground to cover," she encouraged without betraying her own irritation. "By taking out the live spot, Zig and Spence are going to need every second they can find to set up the TV executions. We just can't take the chance that they won't get them."

"But that's my point," Avery complained in the direction of Spence and Zig. He was definitely uncomfortable taking presentation advice from the young AE. But Spence had assigned her to the PowerPoint and with that responsibility came control of the pace of the show. "If they don't buy into the strategy first, the creative won't matter."

"But Avery," she disagreed, "We've already been through this a half dozen times. As Spence said, these people will have sat through two presentations before we take the floor. If we labor the strategy, we'll put them to sleep."

Hearing his name mentioned, Playfair broke off the sidebar conversation he was having with the desktopper who was amending the document to reflect some last minute changes to the creative rationale.

"Truthfully, Avery, I know we'd all like a little more time. But it just isn't there. You know yourself how quickly two hours will pass. And there's bound to be a thousand questions," the skilled impresario argued.

"They'll let us run over for that." Avery countered.

"Maybe or maybe not. What do you think, Zig?" Playfair dodged. But his question was wasted on the haggard looking Creative Director. He had not said more than ten words since the session started and he now seemed hopelessly lost.

"What?" Zig asked vacantly. The crush of the last minute work and the events of the past few days had taken a visible toll.

"The Q & A?" Spence prompted to no avail. "Do you think we can count on it being exclusive of the allotted presentation time?" He repeated the question more loudly and, in doing so, allowed some of his exasperation to show.

"Does it really matter?" the desolate Creative Director responded. "Either we're going to have hooked them or not. We're the last fucking group up. If they want us, they're going to let us go as long as we want."

It was a fairly practical and accurate observation, but Spence Playfair could not abide the insolence in Cartwright's tone. In his current state, Zig was becoming even more of a concern than Avery.

"Don't try that fucking act with me," the new business maven finally snapped, his face turning crimson as he began his rant. "The sooner you get your head out of your ass, the better our chances of pulling this thing off. For the past three goddamned days, we've all been busting our humps, while you've walked around here in a daze. If it was up to me, you'd be getting nowhere near that goddamned presentation room."

As inspirational speeches went, it was hardly Knute Rockney. But instead of reacting angrily, Zig simply pushed back from the table and quietly left the room. To a person, everyone watching was stunned.

The first slide of the Power Point presentation was the newly devised Lowenstein McCarthy Interworld logo. It comprised the backdrop for the two senior executives who would be making the opening remarks of the pitch. Already boiled down to the initials LMI, the new corporate symbol of the joint venture company borrowed artfully from the well-established pedigrees of its parents. The 'L' and the 'I' in the cleverly kerned type design utilized the brilliant red that was so prominent in Interworld's identity. The navy blue 'M' was a clever inversion of the serious color long associated with the Lowenstein Holiday brand. All in all, the hastily concocted badge that had been applied to all of the slides and exhibits was holding up pretty well, thought Steve Holiday as he sat awaiting his turn to speak.

At this exact moment Ira and Reiner were presenting the concept of the new joint venture company. Standing on opposite sides of the large projection screen, they took turns describing the concept. Their contrived interplay was designed to demonstrate how well the two most senior people of the agency were already working together. They had been swapping explanations of the features of their proposed service arrangement to Carlton & Paxton non-stop for nearly ten minutes now and they were scoring points heavily.

Up and down the row of stern adjudicators from the big pharmaceutical company, heads were nodding enthusiastically at the endless stream of promises and benefits that the two presidents were offering. The only exception, of course, was the stony expression on the bloated face of Allan Corbett. He had been nearly purple with rage since he'd arrived and, even in the dim light necessitated by the projector, Steve could tell that his demeanor had clouded further as the details of what was being proposed began to unfold.

To that extent, their surprise had been complete. The first person to arrive from Carlton & Paxton had been Marlene Horcoff. The head of the Family Health division was an enormous woman who had huffed into the room apparently winded from her walk down the hall. She looked vaguely familiar, but Steve couldn't place her from among the hundreds of C&P executives he had met over the years. Next to appear was Harold Woodruff. But the normally affable scientist seemed quite distracted and failed to notice that anything was amiss. Finally, moments ahead of two o'clock, Allan Corbett had escorted the remainder of the review team into the boardroom. After holding the door for the president and the rest of the executive entourage, his jaw had dropped and he blinked uncomprehendingly when he realized who was present. The shock did not appear to have worn off yet and that had been nearly fifteen minutes ago.

Studying Allan Corbett more closely now, Steve decided that he looked absolutely ghastly. Not only was his disposition sour, but his face was flush and blotched with a rash of razor burn. A small lesion seemed to have broken open high on the right side of his cheek and earlier, before the lights had dimmed, Steve had noticed a spider of Rosaria he had never seen before creeping across Corbett's swollen red nose. During their awkward reintroduction to Spearman, he had caught a whiff of booze and body odor that could only have belonged to the man with the glistening brow and the yellow sweat stains at his collar. Normally a bit of a dandy, especially when rubbing elbows with his superiors, he also thought his client's attire also seemed uncharacteristically disheveled. He tried to remember the last time Corbett had eschewed a suit for the over worn navy blazer that he had donned for this important meeting day. Something was most definitely amiss with Allan Corbett and it didn't seem to have anything to do with the business at hand.

Before he could give any further thought to the matter, he felt an anxious tap on his wrist. It was Lane. She had noticed his distraction and was now pointing to his watch. The floor would be turned over to them in less than five minutes. Steve took a dry swallow, wiped his moist palms across his thighs and closed his eyes. He shifted his focus to the first line he would deliver in the most important presentation of his life.

While the team from Lowenstein Holiday was busily engaged in delivering the pitch of their lives, Max Weller was happily completing the final request that had been made of him by his most generous client. One last anonymous e-mail message and he could close the book on this whole sordid Corbett business. The sooner they were rid of this slime ball, Weller concluded, the better for all concerned. While he was not normally one to judge the subjects of his investigations too harshly, what had happened to the pretty young girl had been tragic and the fact that this creep might walk away from it made Ira Lowenstein's simple plan seem far too lenient. Indeed, if the police got nowhere with their inquiry into the matter, he had quietly resolved that he might just send them along a couple of additional clues of his own.

But he had already received his payment in cash and Ira

Lowenstein had thoughtfully included a handsome bonus. He was, after all, the boss and he seemed to know exactly what he was doing. It wasn't blackmail. Not the kind that could earn him jail time. It was just a warning, really. And while it was not exactly the way the private detective would have handled the matter himself, he was fairly sure that it would probably be enough to put that dickhead Corbett over the edge in his current fragile state.

As the laser scanner hummed to life, he pecked out the message Mr. Lowenstein had wanted. "Remember Me?" was all it said. To this he added his own iconic happy face and a moment later both messages were affixed to the glossy publicity photo of Stella Starr that he had snagged from Wriggly Field's. A second later it was embedded in an e-mail and was on its way. His final chore complete, Max Weller smiled, closed the lid to his laptop, and reminded himself that he never wanted to find himself on Ira Lowenstein's bad side.

There is a magical moment in some business presentations when everything has gone so exceptionally well that winning is virtually assured. Steve Holiday had become quite familiar with this sensation having experienced it many times over the years and he was most definitely feeling it right now. There were exhibits propped on every ledge and several more strewn across the big boardroom table. Never in his career had the dance seemed so natural with each show card flowing so seamlessly into the next. Seldom had he ever made a presentation where each layout that had been rendered so elegantly anticipated a client's question or deftly allayed a concern. Their allotted time had long since expired and both he and Lane were still basking in the adulation that had greeted their stunning presentation.

Sprawled in one of the big leather swivel chairs with his jacket off, Steve was still enjoying the adrenaline rush. Even as the soft whirring fan of the now darkened projector echoed his exhaustion, he couldn't help but smile as Lane easily fielded another inquiry about their recommended umbrella strategy and proposed media plan. She had been absolutely magnificent. They were into overtime at the insistence of the executive group and Lane was responding to questions left and right without missing a beat. If Steve had been impressive, then she had been even more so. If the sum of everyone's efforts over the past forty-eight hours had shone brightly, then she had singularly been even more brilliant.

"I think the beauty of our situation is that we still retain the element of surprise," Lane now said. She was standing at the far end of the table, taking weight off one leg by resting herself against the edge of the enormous mahogany slab. She was barely ten feet from the North American Chairman of Carlton & Paxton and he was absolutely mesmerized. He loved it every time she referred to the agency and themselves in a collective pronoun. "I think we can dictate the terms to the market and we can control the timing," she added, intuitively knowing that each inclusive offer was earning valuable points with her captivated executive.

All of this was being enjoyed immensely by everyone in the room, with the obvious exception of Allan Corbett, of course. From the moment she stood up to speak, Lane had held the other men in the room in the palm of her hand. "Outstanding," Alex Spearman had once volunteered out loud when she had completed her assessment of the competitive framework into which Endrophat would be introduced. "Right on the money," Andy Sullivan had heartily concurred when she revealed the plan that allocated supporting funds equally to above and below the line media. The young Vice President of Marketing had even playfully teased Ira and

Reiner about how he wished they could have put the joint venture together sooner. But this high praise was really intended for Lane alone.

With each generous compliment, Allan Corbett's mood darkened. In the absence of any dissenting opinions, the senior advertising manager was absolutely powerless.

It had been this way since Lane presented the *Endorthin* name and the recommendation had been embraced so enthusiastically. Even before Steve could offer up a rationale, the group had leapt ahead and apparently seized on it without reservations. From the moment discussion began afterwards, the typically restrained executives had begun to venture the new word tentatively into their questions and now, after half an hour, it was practically a part of their common parlance. It truly was an elegant solution and everyone recognized this immediately. There had been similar enthusiasm for the positioning, the slogan and several of the specific executions as well.

Sitting back watching, just about the only thing that concerned Steve now, other than the tortured expression on Allan Corbett's face every time another accolade was issued, was the unnatural silence of Marlene Horcoff. While Corbett's reaction was totally expected, the longer the President of the Family Health Division remained quiet, the more expectations seemed to be growing for the verdict that would come from the large woman. While none of the senior men in the room had come out and said so, it was becoming more and more clear that they intended to yield to her personal experience with the problem and, more importantly, her opinion with regard to the advertising. Even Alex Spearman seemed willing to defer.

Throughout the presentation the overweight executive had sat sphinx-like. It was not that she wasn't engaged. On the contrary, she had been extremely attentive. It was just that she had not yet in any way betrayed her reactions and had waited an unusually long time to wade into the fray. This, in Steve's experience, was seldom a good sign. Watching her closely now, he wondered briefly whether she might choose to abstain from speaking while they were still in the room and offer her assessment behind closed doors. But a moment later this impression was quickly dispelled. Waiting respectfully for Lane to finish and for Ira to layer on another of his gushing embellishments, the big woman finally cleared her throat and prepared to speak.

"Mr. Adolph and Mr. Lowenstein," she now enjoined. "First, I would like to thank you both for the extremely interesting proposition you have made to us today. Your proposed joint venture is, how shall I put it, quite intriguing." Perhaps because of the strength of the presentation, everyone else on the executive team had forgotten to remark on this critical consideration. This adroit observation earned her an approving nod from Alex Spearman and his encouragement to continue.

"But turning my attention to the strategic plan and the proposed creative, there's just so much here to talk about. Congratulations on an absolutely terrific solution to the name question. I can't imagine a more important first consideration." She bestowed credit for this on Lane, who had presented the bulk of the naming recommendation.

"Thank you very much, " Lane responded to the unearned compliment. "I wish I could say that I had thought of it," she added modestly.

"As for the creative work itself, I don't know where to begin," Horcoff started slowly. "I can't remember for the life of me when I've seen such a ranging exploration. I must say, I find myself asking why the Family Health Division insists on keeping its own agency." This fact had long been a sore point with Ira and for the head of the division to acknowledge his team's creative efforts in this way was very generous on her part.

"You must also be commended, Mr. Holiday, for avoiding many of the traps that have made the advertising in the weight control products category seem so banal," she observed. "It takes more than a little courage to pin your hopes on an emotive rather than a rational benefit."

Steve acknowledged this second compliment with a smile and a nod. However, at the same time, his trained ear could almost already hear the word 'but' taking shape in Horcoff's thoughtfully considered remarks. So too, it seemed, could just about everyone else in the room. In anticipation, Allan Corbett had practically risen from the edge of his chair so hopeful was he that someone might finally attempt to poison this nearly perfect presentation. Unfortunately, he would be sadly disappointed.

"But I have to say ... and I say this emphatically ... I am absolutely delighted that you did. Ever since this product was announced I have been coaching my colleagues here to avoid jumping to the, you know, tried and true *"Use this and lose this"* approach that we are so famous for here at Carlton & Paxton. Personally, I'm absolutely thrilled with the intelligence and sensitivity you have exhibited."

As the depth and strength of her endorsement began to register, Allan Corbett shrank in his seat. Not only had the big woman failed to deliver the bullet he was praying for, she was making things extremely difficult for Boom to follow. He wondered if he should try and contact Spence Playfair, though his political instincts told him that this might prove fatal given the strength of the endorsement LMI was receiving and the likely outcome.

"When I saw that one, I practically wept." As she said this, Horcoff pointed her thick index finger at a double page spread that was recommended for Wedding Day magazine. *"No little girl ever dreams in size sixteen,"* she read aloud and smiled wide. "Where did you ever come up with a headline like that?"

Though the question was rhetorical, Steve could not resist responding. The ad that she was commenting on was one of the most challenging his team had developed and, as recently as last night, both Reiner and Ira had been lobbying for it to be removed from the presentation. "Actually, that one practically wrote itself," he said as he prepared to recount the genesis of that particular idea. And it was then, in that precise moment, that Steve Holiday realized why this woman now seemed so familiar. He had, indeed, seen her once before. Marlene Horcoff was the very same woman he had witnessed trying on the outfit at Suite Sixteen and who had caused him to author his single most important contribution to the campaign. This coincidence now rendered him silent. Perhaps remembering the same encounter, she met his puzzled look with a broad smile and a wink. Her specific evaluation of the creative, more or less complete, the big woman returned to rank and addressed the larger audience along with her counterparts on the review team.

"I don't know if it's something I've read. Or maybe something that's been mentioned here this afternoon," she said with an enormous grin. "But for whatever reason, I feel like I'm going to have to give this *Endorthin* stuff a try," she concluded with a booming laugh.

It was a sentiment shared by every person in the room save one.

Day 28

By Zig Cartwright's calculation, he had exactly enough time to swing by the apartment and let big dog out before getting to the office by seven as had been agreed. And that was where he found himself now, shivering in the pre-dawn darkness waiting on the enormous Rottweiler who seemed far more interested in the previous visitors to his favorite fire plug than the important business at hand. Zig tugged at the leash impatiently urging him to hurry up. But his efforts were met with little response on Clancy's part and another chill shook through his scrawny frame. His best black presentation suit most definitely wasn't up to the early morning cold.

Zig still hadn't figured out what to do about dog—or very little else in his life for that matter. For nearly four days now he had been lost in the confusion of his despair and the surprisingly strong feelings that had accompanied the death of young woman he had known so briefly but whom he had so quickly learned to love. If he'd had a moment to think about it, he might have found a kennel or some other way to ensure that the abandoned pup was being properly taken care of in the helter skelter that followed Ellen's demise. The big brute was most definitely unwelcome at his place. So instead he had taken on the chore himself. Once the pitch was over, he imagined, he would have the time to get this situation and his other most unlikely mixture of feelings sorted out. Clancy was just one more messy leftover from this entire sad state of affairs.

Unfortunately for Zig, the two detectives responsible for the Starnowski case successfully anticipated the reluctant dog sitter's likely schedule and had staked out the apartment overnight. No sooner had he delivered the animal back inside and returned to the curb to wait for the taxi he'd summoned, than they were at his side. Startling him in the vacant street, Zig initially fought them back as assailants. But moments later, after identifying themselves as police, he found himself being forcibly folded into the rear seat of their unmarked patrol car. Unable to convince them neither of his innocence nor of his urgent requirement to get to work, he was strongly encouraged to remain silent and accompany them for further questioning.

Seven-thirty and still no Zig. Leslie Stride tried his cell phone again and then dialed his home number as she had at least a half dozen times in the past half hour. Almost unimaginably the Creative Director remained unaccounted for. The limo that had been hired to shuttle the pitch team downtown was loaded up and idling outside and she paced impatiently at the curb in anticipation of his tardy arrival. Even Avery had cursed Zig's lateness and seemed to be about ready to give up on the no-show as he climbed into the waiting Town Car. At best they could only give him another couple of minutes before setting out into the gathering morning traffic.

Sitting in the front seat next to the driver, Spence Playfair remained unexpectedly calm. With the seatbelt drawn across the shoulder of his handsome cashmere topcoat, he checked his enormous gold Rolex one more time before reaching toward the button that would lower the side window. Maybe it wasn't all that bad that Zig has gone MIA, he thought to himself. There's no way that he was ready to put on the kind of show that would be required if his performance at last night's final rehearsal was any indication. Maybe it was, in fact, a blessing Playfair decided. He would deliver the entire creative portion of the presentation on his own. At least that way, he felt, he would have no one to blame but himself if things didn't come off as planned. He held up his watch for Avery to see. He quickly depressed the silver switch with his calfskin glove and the frosty window slid open. "Get in Les," he now said decisively. "We've got to go."

The mood of the hastily arranged meeting was grim. Perhaps it was the excitement that followed the LMI presentation the day before. Or more likely it was the terrible weight of the secret Allan Corbett had just shared about the young woman and the potential police investigation. But late yesterday evening, Harold Woodruff had requested an emergency audience with the company's executive committee. And that was where he found himself first thing this morning, seated most uncomfortably at a small table in the anteroom that connected the CEO's office to the main boardroom. Gathered opposite were his boss Art Bristow, Andrew Sullivan and Alex Spearman. All of them were understandably furious at the confession they had just heard. An urgent call had been placed to Carlton & Paxton's head of legal, Carter Winchell, but thus far, the attorney hadn't yet appeared.

For nearly an hour, a dry-mouthed corporate scientist had admitted all of the details that he had been withholding for the past several weeks. He had started with his current theory about a potentially lethal side effect of the new drug and carried on to recount what appeared to be evidence of an accidental fatality—along with Allan Corbett's ill-considered efforts to conceal this very damaging development. Additionally, he came clean about several other errors in judgment including his distribution of the drug to several senior level managers and to an individual outside of the organization. All of this was in direct contravention of the strict confidentiality rules that corporate security had attempted to put in place. In a startlingly candid, career-ending confession, Woodruff owned up to the entire toxic mess. Since then, the group had been busily weighing their difficult and limited options.

"What we certainly can't afford, at this point, is a leak," said Alex Spearman grimly. "If word gets out now, we'll get hammered in the markets and God only knows what this police investigation could lead to in terms of potential liability."

The chief executive's grave opinion immediately gained currency among his fellow officers, all of whom were keenly aware of the financial impact that such a dramatic public failure would have on Carlton & Paxton's balance sheet. It could add up to billions. In this respect they were grateful that the company's lawyer had not yet arrived. At least until he appeared, they could talk through a damage control strategy without having to suffer the opinions of their overly cautious in-house counsel.

"It seems to me we've got three things to worry about," Spearman continued. "Our own people, Ira Lowenstein and that woman ... what was her name ... Lane McCarthy?" As he mentioned Lane's name it was obvious from the furrow in his brow that he was extremely troubled by this aspect of

Woodruff's revelations. He had been genuinely fond of her and was greatly taken aback when the scientist suggested he was virtually certain she had experimented with the drug.

"I think dealing with our people should be fairly easy," volunteered Art Bristow who had been quiet since being so shamefully compromised by Woodruff. "I'll need a list for security, Harry. Then I think we have to come down hard. Get them to sign off on something and then whack 'em immediately."

The clear implication was that this same fate awaited Harry Woodruff. But, of course, he already knew this. If they hadn't needed him to fill in the details as they talked, he would have been dismissed on the spot. Now the best he could hope for was some sort of stay of execution in exchange for his cooperation.

"And you know we've already got a plan for Corbett," Andrew Sullivan jumped in defensively. "As we agreed before this whole review business got out of hand, we're probably best to handle this through Employee Assistance. Maybe we'll just have to accelerate it somewhat with … an intervention of sorts."

"I want it done by the end of the day," Spearman instructed icily. "I want that little fucker put away where they'll never find him." He was still deciding who was more at fault, Woodruff or Corbett? Whichever way he went, both of their bosses were going to pay.

"So what about Lowenstein and McCarthy then?" he probed. "Can they be taken care of?"

"I think based on how he's behaved thus far, we have to be quite grateful for the discretion of Mr. Lowenstein." Though he'd had less frequent dealings over the past few years, Art Bristow remained a longtime friend of the agency.

"Frankly, I think we all know how to take care of Ira," Sullivan answered quickly. He could feel Spearman's heat and knew the only way to save himself was to take responsibility for the mess immediately in front of them. "We'll award him the business, celebrate it with a big public make up, then boost the budgets on a couple of our other consumer brands and he'll go away."

"You're certain?" Spearman second-guessed. After the enormous screw up by his subordinates, he wanted this slippery young overachiever on record with his response.

"Leave it with me." Sullivan said with his head bowed. "I've already had a discussion with Lowenstein. I think he'll be more than satisfied with what I intend to offer."

"Okay. Now what about her?" Spearman pressed. "I mean, I wouldn't be at all disappointed to keep her on our business, especially if it would help keep her quiet."

"Maybe the same thing?" Sullivan thought out loud. "Why don't we jam this whole joint venture idea right back down their throats? We'll make the international thing a condition of doing business in the future and insist that Lane McCarthy and Steve Holiday are tied to the contract."

He didn't like playing defense and at least this maneuver allowed him to salvage some pride. He hadn't particularly enjoyed the box Ira had put him in during their previous conversation, but at least now he could regain a measure of control by forcing his hand with Interworld.

Alex Spearman grunted his agreement. Before he could continue working over the Marketing VP, Art Bristow, perhaps sensing that his own turn was next, waded in with a question.

"What do you think the possibility this other firm ... Boom ... knows anything?" the Ops head asked uncertainly. As he said this, he glanced at his watch and in doing so reminded everyone that the team of presenters from the other company was due at any moment.

For the first time since he'd completed his confession,

Harry Woodruff ventured an unsolicited opinion. "I wouldn't be at all surprised if they know something. Corbett has spoken rather highly of a fellow over there named Playfair."

"Dammit, that's right," agreed Sullivan. "He spent a lot of time talking up Boom with me last week, even though I told them I didn't think they were a fit. It felt like he might have made some promises."

"Shit. Then I guess we'll have to see this little charade through … at least for today," instructed Alex Spearman. He stood up quickly and pulled on his suit jacket making sure that everyone understood that they would be picking up where they left off immediately following the untimely interruption caused by the arrival of Boom. "Let's get this thing over with. Send in the damn clowns."

The whistling sound of the descending bomb that marked the beginning of every presentation made by Boom seemed oddly out of place in the distinguished boardroom of Carlton & Paxton. But it may have also been an apt harbinger. When the roiling cloud of the nuclear explosion unfolded in slow motion and the company's logo emerged from the inferno, most clients tended to smile at the fairly obvious connection. But if Alex Spearman got it, he didn't let on. And he most certainly didn't signal that he enjoyed it. Avery Booth gave a nervous laugh and tried to fill the empty void created by the awkward beginning to this most important presentation. He had always quietly despised the silly video primer that Zig had created to brand their agency. Suddenly he felt like the unwelcome warm up act in a particularly hostile comedy club.

"Thank you very much for the tremendous opportunity you have granted us today," the President of Boom began enthusiastically. Unfortunately a quick inventory of the expressions on the faces of everyone present quickly fed back that his excitement wasn't shared. "I hope we will prove worthy of your expectations."

Having peeled off his jacket during the playing of the introductory video, Avery Booth now stood before the C&P executive team with his shirtsleeves rolled at the cuff. It was a well-worn shtick that he used to suggest he was energetic, hardworking and eager to get down to business. But with Zig missing and Spence Playfair already chaffing to jump in, even his own voice quivered with an uncharacteristic uncertainty. Trying to shake it, he reached for a water glass and nervously nodded to Leslie Stride, who was in charge of the computer that controlled the PowerPoint, to move to the first slide. Confronted with the stony demeanor of the review panel, all of his initial fears about the legitimacy of this review came rushing back. With these doubts in mind, he pressed on without confidence.

"This morning we have exactly two hours to convince you that not only do we have the best and most effective creative ideas to introduce your amazing new weight control product, but that we also have the resources to ensure that your service requirements can be most efficiently met here in the U.S.A. and around the globe by Boom. "

It was a gaudy, overstated beginning that was more befitting a lawyer framing a defense before a jury than an ad man setting the stage for a dynamic presentation and none of the impatient C&P executives seemed particularly impressed. Even Allan Corbett, who moments ahead of the presentation had been busily retrieving e-mails on his Blackberry, was not offering the encouragement that Spence had promised Avery to expect. In fact, instead of appearing enthusiastically engaged, their biggest ally in the room had at first appeared quite agitated and now, ever since the actual presentation had gotten underway, his expression seemed progressively more ashen. It was going to be a long morning.

"So what you're saying, Mr. Booth is that you didn't respond to the specific request that your agency come up with some alternative name recommendations."

The inquisitor was Marlene Horcoff and she pressed this point with very little effort at hiding her irritation. Overnight she had consolidated her view that the joint venture was the only viable choice to represent them and she had been correspondingly aggressive with her questioning since the Boom presentation had begun. The challenge caught Avery Booth off balance again.

"What I said, Ms. Horcoff," he corrected while trying without success not to betray his own doubts, "is that Endrophat is a potentially very useful name that, with extensive repetition, could be easily adopted into the consumer vernacular. For that reason we are quite comfortable working with it."

"But it's not particularly memorable?" she queried again quickly. She wanted a confession that they had not invested sufficient effort on this important task and she wasn't prepared to rest until she got it.

"No. I didn't say that," Avery countered defensively.

"But you didn't come up with any others?" Andy Sullivan joined in.

In the half hour since the president of Boom had taken the floor to present the strategic assumptions that would justify his company's creative approach, the game had been deteriorating rapidly as one executive after another took runs at Boom's strategy. Certainly, this was the easiest way of achieving their pre-desired outcome and Sullivan, Bristow and Horcoff, even without having to be invited, had been eagerly piling on.

"Actually, we did," Avery was now forced to confess, "But none of them had the traction that Endrophat seemed to provide."

"Traction?" Alex Spearman now interjected pretending to be somewhat puzzled. He had a strong personal dislike of buzzwords even though his organization and business was rife with them. He decided, he too, would have a go at making his agency counterpart feel extremely uncomfortable.

"The ability to take hold," Avery explained before he realized the question was rhetorical.

The relentless peppering was beginning to take its toll on Avery. Part of him was irritated and the remainder was confused. He looked first to Spence and then to Allan Corbett for relief. But from the former all he got was quiet urging to hurry along, and from the latter, even less. Their friend, Allan Corbett, seemed lost in another world.

"But as far as you're concerned, Endrophat is the best name?" Marlene Horcoff summed things up. Her prosecution was complete and the verdict was obvious.

"Up to this point," Avery conceded weakly. Clearly, the first real stumble of the morning now belonged entirely to him.

Boom's second blunder of the day was not so much a specific error as it was the anxious performance that was offered up by young Leslie Stride. Despite the admiring looks that were awarded by the men in the room when she stood up in a skirt that was cut nearly a foot above her knees, it was immediately obvious that the young woman was well out of her depth with such a senior audience. If the much more experienced Avery Booth had been reduced to a blather by the withering barrage of questions that greeted his introduction and remarks, by the time Ms. Stride attempted to provide a quick overview of their media recommendations, some serious self-doubt had set in and she never really stood a chance.

Again it was Marlene Horcoff who wielded the bludgeon. Her dislike of the slender young account executive was immediate and she decided she would suffer very little of what the young bantamweight had to offer—especially now that the feeding frenzy had been enjoined by all of her executive counterparts. Nothing that the shallow little coquette, who seemed to pander shamelessly toward the men in the room, said was worthy of her approval. And she made this abundantly clear very early on.

"I'm not sure if you're aware, Ms. Stride," Horcoff asked at her first opportunity, "but the page rates that you quoted for your media planning are substantially higher than the direct rates C&P already has with many publications."

It was a piercing arrow. A money issue that went straight to the heart of the credibility of the entire Boom media plan would be devastating. On any other day, Allan Corbett might easily have deflected this or taken blame for providing inadequate background, but today he seemed incapable of coming to anyone's defense. Instead, asked antagonistically as it was, Horcoff's question had the effect of suggesting that somehow Boom was attempting something underhanded or lacked the necessary muscle to achieve the media discounts a company the size of C&P invariably commanded. Leslie Stride, who was in well over her head in the nuanced area of media negotiation, fumbled briefly and the battle was lost. With her brief presentation complete and its veracity in serious doubt, she was quickly relegated to the subordinate's role that she had occupied since she first switched on the projector.

Spence Playfair needed to make the save. That was the only thought in his mind as the new business maven prepared to take his turn on the floor. Trying his best to ignore the hostility that had greeted the performances of his predecessors, he responded instead with a broad grin and a twinkle in his eye that was direct from Dale Carnegie. Indeed, through the labors of both previous speakers, Spence Playfair had remained undaunted. Puzzled as he was by Allan Corbett's inexplicable behavior, or more accurately, by the review organizer's nearly invisible presence, he was convinced that as soon as he managed to get control of the room he could carry the day with their mind-blowing creative. And today, they would be even stronger. Not only were they armed with a bold and daring campaign, finally it would be he, Spence Playfair, who got to make the big reveal.

Having watched Zig Cartwright in action for many similar presentations, he was fully confident that he could do an effective job of explaining the solutions that Boom had developed with none of the little stumbles and gaffes that his rough spoken Creative Director typically brought to the boardroom. In fact, for years he had quietly attempted to dissuade Avery from ever including creative people in presentations, having convinced himself that the socially awkward and often over-invested people who actually produced the work were incapable of sharing their solutions objectively. Certainly, none of them had any of his professional salesman's polish.

And that was the approach he took as he strode boldly to a place directly in front of Alex Spearman and took control of the show.

"Endrophat. Use it. Lose it," he declared immediately upon summoning up his first slide. Without pause for the review team to digest that this was Boom's proposed slogan, he plunged directly into his well-rehearsed spiel. "For four weeks we puzzled for twenty-four hours a day to find the four words that say everything we need to say about your amazing new product. And if I may be so bold as to say, I believe we've nailed it."

His supremely confident style was a marked contrast to the cerebral meanderings of Avery Booth and the self-conscious stutter that had marked Leslie Stride's performance. Unfortunately, despite this daring declaration, the hostile group of executives seemed nowhere near as convinced of Boom's genius. Sensing their skepticism, Spence Playfair moved from the screen that bore the slogan to the first of the easels that were arranged at either side of the screen. Deftly flipping the show card from back to front, he revealed the first of the agency's proposed magazine advertisements with a flourish that resembled a pretty hostess presenting prizes in a television game show.

Stepping to one side smartly, what confronted the review team was a double page spread with a full color photo of a slender bikini-clad beauty unfastening the halter of her swimsuit in order to tan herself more completely. The amount of skin on display was nearly pornographic. Sitting closer and able to see it more easily than the rest, Marlene Horcoff twisted her face into an expression of disgust. Soon after, Alex Spearman and Andy Sullivan swapped similar looks of concern and displeasure. Only after studying the picture more carefully had they noticed the presence of a man's hand filled with creamy white sunscreen that appeared to be destined for the young woman's inner thigh rather than her back. The extremely provocative image was punctuated by a headline smeared in red lipstick that read: *Losing it can be much more fun than you think.*

"What do you think?" shone Playfair in the direction of Allan Corbett hoping to elicit the encouragement he needed to carry on. There were at least a half dozen other similar sized exhibits that were waiting to be unveiled and he wanted tacit permission that he at least scored a hit with the only professional advertising critic in the room. Instead, what he was met with was a look of slack jawed disbelief. "Don't you see how it works? It's a visual double entendre," he explained a little bit over eagerly, nervous for the first time that the campaign may not enjoy the reception he imagined it would. He even wished, briefly, that Zig were now here beside him.

The only person who seemed to be enjoying the spectacle was Art Bristow. And this was most likely because he had never been invited to attend an advertising presentation before and he somehow imagined that a positive reaction to the proposed work was part of the protocol. The remainder of the group starred silently—too dumbstruck to interrupt. Choosing to interpret this as rapt interest, Playfair then turned over the remainder of this series of concepts—each one more shocking than the one that preceded it. Only after they were all on display did any of the members of the executive team choose to speak up.

"You're not worried it's a little too … sexual?" Andy Sullivan asked. "I mean we have a fairly conservative brand image," he said looking to his colleagues for validation.

"But that's entirely the point." Playfair countered. "To be provocative and to get noticed. That's what you asked us for wasn't it Allan?" With this question he tried to bring his most sympathetic supporter to his defense. But again, there was little help forthcoming from Corbett. Instead what Playfair and the rest of the group noticed when their attention shifted his way, was that the senior advertising manager was looking decidedly uncomfortable. A sweat had broken out on his forehead and much of the color had drained from his face.

"Are you alright, Allan?" Marlene Horcoff asked with some concern, unaware of the fate that awaited him following the meeting. The question seemed to bring Corbett back to life briefly.

"I'm fine, thank you." He responded rallying. " Just a touch of something going around the office I imagine."

"Are we okay to proceed?" Spence Playfair asked with exaggerated concern. Perhaps this explained the tepid reaction the work was receiving and Corbett's non-committal expression.

"Of course. Carry on. I think we should reserve judgment until we've seen the whole campaign," the advertising manager now counseled the group. "Perhaps you could show us where you're going with the television, Mr. Playfair? Then maybe we'll have a better sense of the overall tone and manner you're striving for."

That's more like it, thought Spence as Corbett fed him the straight line he needed to transition to the most important component of their proposed campaign. While things weren't playing out according to plan, once they saw how the TV worked, the rest of the pieces would fall neatly into place, he allowed himself to imagine. In that respect he was delighted with himself that he remembered to pack along the disk that contained the completed commercial. There would be no problem with showing it now that Zig was no longer in the room. He swelled at this stroke of good fortune and smiled inwardly at the deftness with which he'd been able to think on his feet. "An excellent idea, Allan."

So instead of heading for the easel at the front of the room that held their thick bundle of oversized storyboards, in a few quick steps he was suddenly in front of the computer where Leslie Stride was sitting flustered by this unexpected turn of events. Ignoring her puzzled expression and the surprised look of Avery Booth, who seemed to want to remind him that he should be using the exhibits at the other end of the table, Spence Playfair reached into the breast pocket of his suit jacket and withdrew a plastic jewel case. Without hesitation, he popped it open and thrust the shiny silver disk into the young woman's nervous hand.

"If you don't mind Leslie," he instructed with a great deal of flourish. "I'm sure this will make everything that we're trying to accomplish absolutely clear." As his assistant fumbled to open the disk drive that was hidden on the side of the machine, Playfair reached for the remote control and slowly dimmed the lights. A moment later the big projection screen flickered to life, Boom's logo appeared briefly, and then a black and white synchronization code began its steady backward count down from the number ten.

The first splutter from Allan Corbett was lost against the angry cadence of the rap singer who pounded out his lyrics against a throbbing wall of percussion. The volume of the boardroom speakers had not been adjusted since Boom's noisy introductory clip and the audio levels on the rough cut DVD were considerably hotter. His second moan, which coincided with the first full close up of Ellen Starnowski smiling rapturously as she moved to the driving music, caught the attention of Art Bristow who was seated immediately to his right. Startled by the sound in the darkness and illuminated only by the glow of the flashing colors on screen, he thought he caught a glimpse of Corbett's eyes spinning wildly and his jaw flapping uncontrollably as if gasping for air.

Only when the music came to its abrupt end and a deep baritone-voiced announcer had emphatically intoned the name Endrophat and an urgent request to use it and lose it, did the group fully appreciate what had been going on while their eyes had been glued to the screen. Allan Corbett, had indeed, lost it. As the lights came up slowly, it was immediately apparent that the senior advertising manager was in a state of severe medical distress. With his teeth chattering spastically, Corbett collapsed into his chair in an apparent seizure. With Art Bristow now ministering to him urgently—desperately trying to loosen the tie that had turned his face the color of death -- Corbett's bowels emptied involuntarily. An instant later he blacked out only to regain consciousness a moment later sobbing and weeping uncontrollably. With his eyes bulging and his voice shrieking in terror, Corbett then pointed repeatedly to the place where just moments before the apparition of the vivacious young model had appeared and his crime had revisited him with such shocking effect.

Not unexpectedly, the assembled group reacted to the horrific scene with revulsion. Leslie Stride, who was seated nearby, caught an unfortunate whiff of the stench that emanated from Corbett's pants and gagged involuntarily. Desperate to avoid further discomfort, she held her nose and ducked her head beneath the edge of the boardroom table. With her free hand she covered her nearest ear hoping to block out his wails and moans. Standing closer to the scene, Avery Booth and Spence Playfair were both wide eyed at the effect that the screening of the commercial had apparently caused. Though neither entirely grasped the significance of Corbett's frantic raving, they instinctively knew that it most definitely had been precipitated by the appearance of the spectacularly beautiful young woman who was the star of their little movie.

As each agonizing moment unfolded, Avery Booth found himself becoming increasingly incensed with Playfair for the situation he had caused with his insolence. Before any explanation could be offered, he had immediately mouthed the words, "You're fired."

On the Carlton & Paxton side of the table things were every bit as chaotic. Thinking first about his two thousand dollar suit jacket draped over a nearby chair, Andrew Sullivan whisked the handsome garment out of harm's way lest it be pressed into service giving relief to the struggling ad manager. Selfishly unfamiliar with even the most basic first aid, instead of joining Bristow at Corbett's side, he starred with obvious disgust at the unpleasantness unfolding on the rich broadloom of their boardroom floor. At one point he drew a fine linen handkerchief from his pocket and held it over his nose and mouth, so overcome was he by the unpleasant odor of Corbett's untimely evacuation. At the same time, Marlene Horcoff managed to locate Avery Booth's expensive blazer and ball it beneath the fallen man's head while making repeated pleas for medical assistance. Joining Bristow on her knees at Corbett's side, as the distraught man briefly regained consciousness, she mopped his brow and soothed him with quiet words of comfort.

Only Alex Spearman seemed in control as he calmly picked up a telephone and reported the medical emergency. Fascinated by the sudden onset and ghastly nature of Corbett's condition he then turned and studied the distressed man on the floor more closely. In his own mind he was going over the sequence of events that had precipitated Corbett's collapse and how it might relate to the details of all that had already unfolded this morning. Perhaps because of this dispassionate view, it was he who was the first to figure out the link between what Harry Woodruff had confessed and Corbett's apparent breakdown. It was Alex Spearman who spotted the

Blackberry that had dropped from Corbett's hand and that still had the picture of the deceased young woman showing on its LCD display. It didn't take much imagination to knit together the connection between that image and the girl who had recently appeared on the big boardroom screen. Before anyone else noticed, he discreetly deleted the photo from the phone and slipped the incriminating device into his jacket pocket. He would perform his own investigation later.

Finally, in the last confused moments before the room was cleared and the paramedics arrived, a nearly incoherent confession spilled from Allan Corbett's bloodied lips. "I did it. I did it. It was all my fault," he wept aloud. However, this last desperate act of atonement did little other than further underscore the depths of the debauched advertising manager's spiraling descent. He had definitely lost his mind. Though little sense could be made of his last rambling admission, there was no mistaking that he had repeatedly declared that he had killed the girl. As they wheeled the stretcher carrying the moaning man from the room, his unquestioned guilt was apparent to all who were present—even if no one knew the precise nature of the crime that had been committed.

If there was any doubt as to the future of the Endrophat project, it was decided in the uncertain moments that followed Corbett's breakdown. If there was any question about who was to be the winner of the entire ill-considered competition, it had been answered in the self-incriminating confession of Harold Woodruff and the glaring misjudgments of Allan Corbett and Spence Playfair that followed. There would be no prize and no glory for anyone involved in the entire obscene debacle. That much became immediately clear. In the tragic death of a beautiful young woman and the humiliating demise of the senior advertising manager, any hope that the wonder drug would ever see the light of day was all but extinguished. Any dream that its miraculous effects would be enjoyed by a world in need was lost in the ignominy wrought by his foolish actions. There are no requiems for scoundrels and, most certainly, none was heard nor deserved on this day. Apparently an authority far higher than the officers of Carlton & Paxton had chosen to decide the fate of Allan Corbett and that final judgment proved a crude but worthy jest.

After

The criminal investigation and subsequent FDA inquiry into the development and testing of Endrophat caused no end of damage and embarrassment to the executives of Carlton & Paxton. Both the police and the federal authorities took an extremely dim view of the apparent willingness of the company's top managers to race an unsafe product to market and their subsequent attempts to walk away from their culpability in the wrongful death of Ellen Starnowski. Their stern rebuke included substantial restitution to the family of the young woman and additional awards to those subjects that had participated in the initial clinical trials. Though no one would reveal the actual price tag of these reparations, it was rumored to be in the hundreds of millions.

Throughout this period, the corporation was lashed by the media and pilloried by an extremely disappointed investment community that at one point shaved nearly forty percent from the big company's share price. The apparent lack of management oversight and suspect internal security procedures sent a shudder through the entire organization and cast a long dark shadow over the leadership of entire enterprise. Alex Spearman somehow managed to survive, as did Andrew

Sullivan. But Art Bristow was an unexpected and undeserving casualty. He was thrown under the bus early on to save the chief executive and to staunch the bleeding on the beleaguered company's balance sheet. Failure to closely monitor the actions of his lead scientist was the publicly cited reason.

Finally, after promising to suspended development of the new diet drug indefinitely, the media maelstrom subsided. In the aftermath, the matter was quietly turned over to the company's lawyers and a hastily appointed internal team from Regulatory & Governmental Affairs. But the truth was that everyone associated with the debacle wanted the entire unfortunate affair to disappear as quickly and quietly as possible.

Spence Playfair and Leslie Stride were fired on the day of the pitch before their elevator even reached the ground. Playfair was expelled for his deceitfulness and she for her blind obedience. Though Avery Booth wasn't exactly sure what it was about the woman in the commercial that had caused Allan Corbett's breakdown, he did know that his new business officer had deliberately ignored his specific request that the inappropriate commercial should not be shown. In light of what happened, his instincts had proved absolutely correct. Never before in his career had he seen anything so frightening as Corbett levitating in his chair and then collapsing in violent convulsions before his very eyes. That Playfair was somehow responsible for this obscene spectacle was absolutely unforgivable. Later, after learning the reasons why, he was doubly ashamed. As Booth unraveled the entire unseemly story of his new business officer's inappropriate relationship with Corbett and the unscrupulous tactics he had employed in pursuit of the Carlton & Paxton prize, he was almost relieved when it was announced that the Endrophat project had been suspended indefinitely.

Then the bills for the pitch started coming in. The most inappropriate among these was a particularly troublesome invoice for nearly twenty-two thousand dollars from a gun dealer in St. Louis that had been authorized by Playfair. Not only was the acquisition of such an expensive weapon inexplicable to the agency president, any trace of its existence had vanished with the man responsible for its purchase. This rude surprise was followed closely by an equally unanticipated lawsuit initiated by a Mr. Gordon Turnbull alleging employment tampering and breach of promise. As details of these and other stories began to filter to the street, several of Boom's largest clients quickly departed. The rest began trickling out the door in a steady stream after the announcement of a major reorganization following the resignation of the agency's brilliant Creative Director. There are few things more spectacular in the advertising business than the flame out of a creative hot shop. The demise of Boom was like a supernova. Six months after the failed Carlton & Paxton pitch, the company Avery Booth founded thirteen years prior stopped paying its media bills. By Christmas it was gone completely.

Zig Cartwright rolled the proposed layout into a tight wad and flung it angrily toward the terrified pair of young creatives seated on the handsome sofa across from his expansive desk. The recently appointed Creative Director of Interworld Chicago was eager to impress his new bosses and the work that his people were turning out these days just wasn't going to accomplish this goal. The department was still in chaos following the merger and the subsequent departure of Steve Holiday. Even though the headhunter had intimated that he was selected only after a leading internal candidate had declined to relocate from New York, Zig had leapt at the job when it was offered. Fresh back from an extended holiday, he had somehow managed to put his grief behind him. Now if he could just sit down with Ira, he was certain he could convince him that a violent purge of Holiday's complacent underachievers was an urgent necessity.

But Ira Lowenstein was a hard man to pin down in the days that followed the Endrophat pitch. Offering his usual sage counsel and billing nearly a thousand hours in crisis management fees, Ira had successfully salvaged the careers of Alex Spearman and Andrew Sullivan. True to their word, his reward for this remarkable accomplishment and for the mistreatment his people had endured at the hands of Allan Corbett, the agency was awarded several substantial new advertising contracts. With all of this new business predicated on the assumption of a merger with Interworld and with the salvaging of their global reputation required by his largest client, the marriage of the two advertising companies was swiftly consummated.

Ira had finally found his soul mate in Reiner Adolph and the opportunistic German entrepreneur had immediately appointed his clever friend as his President of Worldwide Brands. At the same time he was extended an invitation to sit on the company's board of directors. Ira's first major assignment would be the consolidation of Carlton & Paxton's advertising agencies into the Interworld family. Though he would be based in Chicago, Ira Lowenstein would now spend his life on a plane and living from a suitcase. While the latter was an inconvenience, the former suited him perfectly. He began his discreet affair with the attractive Managing Director of the London office barely two months after stepping into his new role.

❧

The door closed and his wife was gone. Just as quickly as she'd appeared, she was nearly forgotten and Allan Corbett was alone with the package that she had delivered to his dingy den. Like he did with so many things lately, the former senior manager fumbled with the box absently, not remembering exactly where it had come from or why it was addressed to him. Ever since returning from hospital he'd retained very little ability to focus. Between the ample medications and the exhaustive rounds psychotherapy he had undergone, many days he actually had trouble remembering his own name, let alone accomplishing anything in the hours he chose to spend in his cramped hideaway.

There was nothing to be done, of course, other than tidying up the insurance claims and perhaps, one day, updating his résumé. However, his generous medical allowance and the settlement of his Carlton & Paxton employment contract did not necessitate a hasty return to work. In fact, it was distinctly possible that he never would work again. As his exit counselor had explained, he was probably set for life. Between the long-term disability pension that he would receive following his stroke and the diagnosis of a deep clinical depression plus the other proceeds he'd accrued within his defined benefits plan, he was in better financial shape than he had been in years. Ironically, he had also been prescribed a twice-daily dose of Contentra, Carlton & Paxton's recently registered anti-depressant. The company had agreed to supply it, free of charge, for the rest of his days.

Compared to the many others who had been rounded up during the witch-hunt that followed the detailed investigation conducted by internal security, Allan Corbett had fared far better than most. Certainly he had done better than Harold Woodruff who had been the public scapegoat for the failed Endrophat initiative. Not only had Woody been immediately dismissed, there had been persistent rumors in the weeks following of an unprecedented legal action that would seek further redress for the code of corporate confidentiality that he had so egregiously violated. Pursuing the aggressive crisis management strategy recommended to them by the Interworld PR team that Carlton & Paxton had recently placed on retainer, Woodruff's name had even been linked to allegations of sabotage during calls to several influential analysts. In doing so, the company attempted to portray itself as the innocent victim of a deceitful corporate rogue.

However, Allan Corbett's improved circumstance offered little comfort as he sat alone in the dark retreat where he took daily refuge from the barely concealed resentment of his angry wife. Even after the diagnosis of his depression, there was no sympathy or escape from the deep disdain that Helen projected onto him. She had forgone an offer of treatment for herself and the continued presence of alcohol in their household was proving troublesome for both of them. Helen drank heavily and Allan desperately wanted to. Yet for six hellish weeks since returning from the rehab facility, he had somehow managed to maintain his sobriety. This morning he wasn't at all certain how much longer his willpower would sustain him. He still yearned desperately for the balm that only a bottle could provide, but mostly he longed to forget.

Unfortunately, it was to the same dark place that Allan Corbett returned again and again. There was very little he could imagine from the last few months that he had not confessed to in therapy that did not continue to cause him deep regret. With the recognition of all that was lost still torturing his mind and the image of the beautiful young woman, Stella Starr, still dancing in his troubled head, Corbett reached for the package that would finally grant him his freedom. The carton from Federal Munitions contained twenty-five cartridges of Storm Cloud steel birdshot. Allan Corbett smiled as he read the package insert. *"A deadly combination of controlled scatter, increased take out strength and longer range means surefire results. When there's Storm Cloud on the horizon, birds 'll be ducking for cover. "* That's a fine piece of copywriting he thought to himself and laughed aloud. A short while later, Helen was startled by the angry report that shook the floor beneath her feet. Boom!

Leaning into the arm of the chair beside him, trying to catch a first glimpse of the tiny island below, Steve Holiday was certain that he and his attractive companion had made absolutely the right decision. From the seat on his side of the small plane he craned his neck like a tourist as the Beechcraft banked into its final approach across the crystal clear depths of the Caribbean. They would be on the ground in Alice Town in just a few more minutes to be picked up by the architect who'd hopped over from Miami a couple of days before. They had been pouring over the sketches for much of their journey and now were eager to see how these initial renderings translated to the remote beachfront property where they would soon begin construction of their private retreat.

The newly formed partnership of McCarthy & Holiday had decided that their first order of business was to take a vacation. Or, more likely, once their remaining contractual obligations were fulfilled, a permanent departure from the business that had consumed them both for so long. Their extrication from their respective agencies had been messy, especially given the terms that Carlton & Paxton had demanded in exchange for their support of the merger between Lowenstein Holiday and Interworld. C&P's insistence that both Steve and

Lane remain actively involved on the company's account had taken several months to work out.

As was typical of Ira, he had immediately assumed that Steve's desire to quit was simply a negotiating tactic and he managed to insult his longtime partner further with repeated offers of more generous compensation and a host of extravagant perks. But Steve had resisted these overtures without blinking. And Lane had been just as firm with Reiner Adolph. In the end, it was the sudden increase in the value of their stock with C&P that gave them the leverage they needed to finally get away. After much back and forth a compromise was struck and the two of them agreed to sell their services directly to the big pharmaceutical company. As the designated troubleshooters for Carlton & Paxton's worldwide advertising consolidation, their independent consultancy would evaluate the work of Interworld in the more than one hundred countries where the agency had just recently been awarded the business. It was an ironic twist that proved irresistible to the newlyweds and caused both Ira and Reiner to swallow hard. McCarthy & Holiday's responsibilities would, of course, be overseen from a soon to be erected global headquarters in Bimini.

Gripping Lane's hand tightly as the small aircraft bounced onto the narrow landing strip, it was hard for Steve not to smile. Somehow he had managed to successfully slip away from the dance floor before the music stopped and the chairs were filled once more. After nearly three long decades in the advertising world, remarkably, he had somehow been allowed to waltz away free with the woman he loved.

Immediately, the temperature in the cabin rose with the heat of the bleaching equatorial sun. Popping the hatch door, he heard the last powerful roar of the plane's engine before shutdown and felt the warm breath of a sweet scented tropical breeze. He unfastened his seat belt and turned towards the beautiful woman perched expectantly beside him. Leaning across the armrest he offered a tender kiss and signed the contract that would bind them together forever. Maybe later, he decided with a playful grin, he would ask his new wife if she thought she had put on a little weight.

Acknowledgements

I am indebted to many people for their contributions to this book. Mostly, I owe thanks to the extraordinary people in the advertising and commercial production industries with whom I had the privilege of sharing twenty-three long years in the trenches.

Also, my undying gratitude to the most unbelievably supportive group of clients a Creative Director could ever hope to have. Your trust and investment in my ideas truly made working for you all a genuine pleasure.

Thank you Terry, George and Egon.

Thank you Wilf, Henry, Jennifer, Peter, Paul, the Ricks, Richard, Strathie and the rest of the extremely talented people at Ogilvy including, of course, the indomitable Tro, the mad genius Art, and most unforgettably, Mark.

Thank you Arlene, Rusty, Randall, Lily, Janay and everyone at Venture.

I remain in awe of you always, Trevor.

Thank you Derrick for your friendship and support at work and play, and for your encouragement to write it all down one day.

Thank you Steve and Terri and everyone at Telemachus Press.

Finally, thank you to Lynne, Lauren and Mary for your unfaltering belief that Dad could write a book that someone might want to read.

About the Author

R. Bruce Walker is a twenty-three year veteran of the advertising industry. As a copywriter, Creative Director and senior executive with a leading global agency, he has earned numerous accolades and awards for his work. Having fled the business for a different life, he currently resides near Savannah, Georgia with his wife, Lynne, and two irrepressible Labrador Retrievers. JESTERS' DANCE is his debut novel.

To find out more about R. Bruce Walker and his writing, please visit:

http://www.rbrucewalker.com

CPSIA information can be obtained at www.ICGtesting.com
Printed in the USA
242101LV00001B/61/P